IT MUST BE NOW THE KINGDOM COMING

Books by Perry Lentz

THE FALLING HILLS
IT MUST BE NOW THE KINGDOM COMING

IT MUST BE NOW THE KINGDOM COMING

An Historical Romance

BY PERRY LENTZ

Crown Publishers, Inc., New York

Inquiries should be addressed to Crown Publishers, Inc., 419 Park Avenue South, New York, N.Y. 10016.

Library of Congress Catalog Card Number: 72-96656
ISBN: 0-517-504219

Printed in the United States of America

Published simultaneously in Canada by General Publishing Company Limited

Designed by Shari de Miskey

To Jane

Contents

THURSDAY
1
DECEMBER
1864

Chapter 1

IN DARKNESS DUSTY WITH CANDLELIGHT, BEHIND THE COLUMNED AND moon-ivied housefront, behind valance and brocaded heavy curtains, Thomas Jefferson Malory, one-eyed ex-captain of Confederate artillery, swayed toward climax above his nineteen-year-old wife.

Straining recollections carried him toward release, images of lace slipping from rose-brown nipples, ribboned pantalettes pulling free from the thighs of a Savannah dancing girl he had once seen in the fifties. His wife, Celia, lay inertly, looking at the dim light upon the ceiling. Her brown eyes were relaxed in mild resignation, her lips in a weary, patient smile.

Celia's ivory soft face was innocently sensual and large-eyed. Her body was rich in hourglass Victorian shapeliness, small, smooth and large-bosomed with a porcelain tiny waist, all hidden from her husband beneath a coarse nightdress. His eye was squeezed in imagining, and he held himself rigidly above her on straining forearms. In the cemetery beside the house was one stillborn infant boy, and she had had two more late miscarriages. In her husband's mind, the Sycamore plantation house and the old divided garden and walks—the "family's" grounds—were reprovingly sterile.

His plunging member was lost in her flesh, sentient only at the entrance. He cajoled up specific images of the known rich breasts of black women, then their thighs and buttocks. Malory grunted, lost his frenetic recollections in modest, blue brown pleasure, spurted. Celia sighed.

He lifted himself back and out and she closed her eyes modestly. Malory rose, half turning so that she would not have to see his private parts. He wiped himself and pulled his old officer's trousers over his hips, the red striping faded to pink. Malory was thirty-eight, spare and compactly ribbed. His long black hair was combed back over his ears in sharp wings, and truncated by the strap of his eye patch. With the moustache and spade beard, his face was fever sharp.

Celia Coates Malory, wife of four years, sat sleepily and unguardedly on the edge of the bed. As Malory reclothed himself, she brushed absently at a lock of raven hair which belled down over her cheek, the movement of her forefingers just touching away a bead of sweat upon her temple. Malory noticed the innocence of the gesture, as he pressed his shirt down into his trouser band: it moved him greatly. Their wedding, above polished cool floors, had been the fete of Coffin County in 1860—florid hot men had drunk their health in acid-sweet toddies and talk about Lincoln and the advisability no sir the *necessity* of reopening the slave trade.

That time seemed particularly remote.

But this evening, her face was soft, with affection and the muted sheen of recent sleep.

"Did that relieve you some, Mr. Malory?"

"Oh, my sweetness." The pleasured smile was oddly shaped upon his sharp face.

Incited by that innocent single gesture and her guileless bemused smile, he pressed ahead into the softness of the moment, he could not restrain himself. "Were you lonely today, honey? Tobe and I got back as fast as we could make it without taxing the mounts. And I *swear* it is the last time both of us will go to Coffinville again until these times are past." He knew he was speaking unguardedly. At *these times*, her eyes suddenly fell from his face to study her clasping thumbs. Damn it! He plunged on. "A fool's errand, just as you predicted. Fool's errand on both scores, Dr. Gazzo and the Home Guard, both. This is the last time we will leave, until these . . . until *you* are more easy."

But the sweet, weary tenderness had left her face. Her eyes flared maskedly, as his last sentence fumbled. She put on self-consciousness, and pressed the dark strand back so that it held.

"Did you have a good day, my dearest?" Malory asked, trying to deflect her away from Coffinville and Sherman and *the times*. But even as he asked, he patted his clasped belt smooth against his lean belly and straightened his shoulders, and his lips became pursed and pompous.

The corner of her small mouth drew in with distant, formal irony.

"Yes, Mr. Malory. Except of course for trying to deal with the people, now that they know the Yankees are on the loose. Otherly, just a *fine day*. . . . Is there any word, then, about the Yankees? You must have spent nearly the whole day at headquarters, to have been gone so long." Her eyes were no longer upon him, but focused upon the darkened window.

He sighed. "They on all the roads to the south, we hear tell. The damned Home Guard expects them any minute, but I talked to Ed Guice and the Porter boy, and we figured they passed on off toward the coast. Guice says they left Louisville for good going east."

Malory watched her as he said this. Staring out of that window: she wanted both of them to refugee to her father's house in Columbia, he knew. Her mouth compacted. Staring out of the window she was, formally and self-pityingly, the unheeded seeress, the Cassandra.

"All of the roads to the south?"

"Ah, like I said, it is just the word of the Home Guard. Ain't worth a damn. I expect they have gone on to the east."

"The Louisville road, too?"

"A day ago. But I expect they are gone on off."

She raised her round eyes tragically, and held her polished small hands against her bosom. "The Louisville road? So close?"

"But from all reports, including Ed Guice and you know where his place is, and the Porter boy who is from outside Louisville, from all reports they are going off east."

"But you cannot be sure. You cannot be sure, and they may be coming this way, too! Why, they are only ten miles south, if they are on the Louisville road." Her voice cried softly. "*Listen*, Mr. Malory, let us be off before they come! We could get to Augusta and then to Columbia without any trouble at all. We could be in Columbia in three days."

Malory was hereditarily nearsighted. He reacted to things when he saw them closely, and his reflections were composed of clear images of seen people and things. He saw Columbia as an amalgam:

spires across the Pee Dee, blockaded cotton rotting beside the railroads, and her father's beaked, liver-splotched face, his damnfool way of handling servants, his habit of drumming on the floor with his cane for attention in his own house. Malory despised being dependent on another man's whims, in another man's different world.

Her pleading suggested she did not think he could protect her. With Tobe, he could protect her and the house both.

"Celia," he said, "Celia, we are not leaving this house, and running off before some confounded damn rumor."

"But you cannot be *certain* they won't come. What if they do?"

He clasped his hands rhetorically behind him. "Well, they ain't coming. But if they do, I don't expect their regular soldiers would touch a thing, anyhow. And I ain't going to leave this house to their stragglers and bummers, I promise you that."

"But what can we *do*," she asked, her voice fluting on the word, "if a great *many* of them come?"

"This has been the Malory house too long to abandon it at a hint of trouble, dear." The house seemed as solid and permanent as his feel of himself. He felt its weight cluster about him in the dim light, fabric of pegged floors and columns, fragrant dim odors, the standing jest about the unfinished garden to the south side, the jovial family story of Uncle Walter's drunken confusion about bedrooms, the unique curve of the stairs at the upstairs hall.

"But, Mr. Malory. If you knew how worried I was here, day by day, with you off at your labors, how I start at every noise!" She was shaking her head sorrowfully, hands still clasped between her breasts, which showed roundly through the pressed cloth. "If . . . there was some *purpose*, or something which we could *do* if they came. . . ." She stared despairingly off into the blackness.

Malory's attention was still cloyed by their lovemaking, but a stale, familiar irritation was growing.

"No, honey. This has been the Malory house too long to abandon it at the first hint of trouble. We are safe enough here, I reckon, between Tobe and me, and we are not leaving this house."

He knew, as he said this, of a forgotten tightly mortised window looking out over the south, over a lemon-green willow tree on a spring day. His father was framed by that window, while he watched from it. It suggested all that was unabandonable, all that was advantageous. He even sensed, with his repeated "been the Malory house too long," high-breeched men in velvet collars from before his birth.

Celia sighed again. "This house is not worth your life to me."

He smiled, and took her hands in his traditionally. "I will be all right. They ain't going to fool with an exchanged one-eyed prisoner, I expect. And Tobe and I, well armed, can deal with any stragglers."

"Let us leave this place." He looked at the smooth precise part in her black hair.

"No, my dear. I am not going to abandon it."

There was an all but ritualistic pause. Malory could tell she had one more argument to make. He was aware of his growing anger. In the last three weeks, since the Yankees had marched from Atlanta into a fog of suspense which made the blue, pine-smooth western horizon quiver, he had feared desperately for the house. His reaction had been to count the steps, to try to memorize the patterns of wallpaper and plaster, to look with possessional, permanent memory at shapes of varnished wood, while he assessed Home Guard and newspaper reports and built up his own frenzy of determination. He just had little energy to expend with her.

"But, Mr. Malory, it is *you*, not this house, that . . ."

Her hands became an embarrassing weight. He turned away from her, and she stopped talking.

"I will not discuss it further, honey."

Malory looked out of the window, into the liquid mirror of the room they were in: small beads of fire in the grate, curve of rocking chair, massive black furniture brought here by his grandfather. His own image was spectral before him. She was gathering herself, he knew.

"If you truly loved me," she said in a weak, moist tone, "you would take me away from here."

He turned back to face her, his expression arched. She was looking at him with misty eyes, hands in her lap. Her recent sexual compliance was suggested: Malory squared his shoulders, in an overpowering awareness of time and place and propriety. "What does that have to do with, I would like to know?" She subsided meekly, dropped her glance, raised her hands again to her bosom.

They were both aware that she had exposed an embarrassing, almost lascivious weakness. She swallowed. "Mr. Malory, I think . . ." Her eyes flicked over his face, and fell again. "I think I saw the ghost again, this evening."

He accepted the change of subject. "Did you?"

"It was before you came back."

"Oh?" The ghost was a legend of the place, gathered out of the house's antiquity. Before the War, he had amused guests by showing off the recessed cellar door in the downstairs hall at which supposedly it had been seen. The legend threaded perfectly into the fabric of romance all planters tried to secure for their lives, above the routines of cotton planting.

(She complains of it damned near every day, by God.)

On a spring evening in the late fifties, with the trees and bushes just pressing into first darkness, he had half convinced himself that he had seen the ghost: a figure standing on the lip of the porch, half behind a column, face in shadow, swell of muscle beneath the shoulder of a fawn-colored coat. Malory had walked toward it expecting to find a visitor. His feet had sounded curiously on the gravel, he could remember, and a strange sense of having seen this man, face-shadowed, body out-thrust, exactly like this, had come over him. There was the feathery sense of a pattern curving to completion. He had cleared his throat for his greeting, and the legs and chest had drawn back against the opposite side of the column. Malory had stepped for him, and there was nothing at the spot.

Since then, there had been other glimpses, forms seen out of the corner of the eye. Possibly they were more distinct now. In the autumn of '62, at home after his first wounds, he had sensed the ghost in lax moments. But he still had no concern; he applied familiar equations to the thing. There was something African about it, and with a half-dozen runaway slaves since the War began, who was there to blame a man for feeling edgy at dusk?

But Celia said she had seen it often—not the face, just the twisted form and muscular shoulders, on the verandah, at the head of the stairs, sometimes in the hall near the rear entrance. She was terrified of it. Malory suspected her vision of the ghost was too much like his own. Damn that I ever told her of it that evening, I believe she really thinks she sees something, after all this time. I swear I do. But she wants me to run away with her to Columbia, and her father.

"Where did you see the damned thing this time?"

"Twice, Mr. Malory . . . it is why I want to leave so much, it is . . ."

"Where?"

"Both times, down by the cellar wall."

"What were you doing down in the cellar?"

"Burying the last of the silver. Those two Highland goblets that you only remembered to bring down from your bureau Tuesday night. And s-some other things." She breathed deeply. "Well, Zeenie and I were near the wall, when I saw it. Zeenie said she did not see anything. Then later I went down alone and saw it again . . ." She shivered. "This time, I th-think it moved."

Malory stepped over to her with dubious solicitude. Her face was bright with pleading. "It . . . it is an omen, I fear, Mr. Malory."

"If you see it in the cellar, don't go down there. Let Tobe do the burying."

She still looked at him, her eyes round, darker than the shadows in the room. She was testing the moment, waiting to ask something. She breathed very deeply, drawing in her chin.

Malory felt his patience would break if she asked him to leave the house one more time. His recollection of her willingness to make love thinned against a rising anger. She reminded him of his little four-year-old sister when he had been ten, wanting an impossibly broken doll whole again, immune to all facts. (He saw his sister's stone in the walled little graveyard across the garden.) He knew that he was losing his temper and he cut off her question. "I must go and see to Juno. She is in a bad way, Tobe tells me. She is another reason we cannot leave soon." He was curt: his blank refusal, his family duty should have been reason enough for her. "I must go. If you are afraid, you can come with me,"—he knew she detested the slave cabins—"or wait out in the kitchen with Phrony."

She looked blankly at him. He shifted from one foot to the other, wishing to be outside in the night air. All of her breath seemed to leave her at once. "All right, Mr. Malory, I will wait here."

"Wait in the kitchen." Guiltily, he thought how pleasant its warmth and light would be to her.

"No. I will wait here."

"Wait in the kitchen, why don't you?"

She pressed her lips together, drew a sob-entwined breath, and shook her head.

"Why not?"

She shook her head.

"Why the hell not!"

He shook his head wearily. "All right. All right. Suit yourself. But do not . . ." He chewed down on the words. Do not come crying to me about ghosts, then, he had started to say. But he controlled himself. He was divided by a usual frustration. The rectitude of his position overwhelmed him in familiar images—house and columns and graveyard, riding beside his father on his first pony, that December armchair satisfaction of 1856 when they made the finest crop in the county, almost nine bales a hand—all images bathed in the clearest yellow light. But his recollection of his sister, in the weak, stubborn petulance of Celia's voice, moved from image to image, too—from the pale curve of his dead sister's forehead to the upraised round chin of the girl before him, her desperation glistening upon her flesh, the anciently exposed soft curves of women's faces. Her chin quivered in purposeless defiance: six months ago she had tried to hold her face up bravely through her last late miscarriage (what was to have been Francis Marion Malory). His anger was blunted. He was wavering between the conflicting, solid images. His single weak eye batted above her. His hands twisted slightly in gestures of helplessness, even as his mouth pursed to say Do not come crying to me over ghosts, woman.

Malory left the room abruptly. He walked along the second floor of the high central hall, bootheels clattering over the carpetless old pine floors, the wood pale where the carpets had been and wax-dark along the edges. The hall ran the length of the house, with angular banisters and the abrupt plaster-splitting angle at the head of the stairs where the banisters curved, and the sweeping central stairway. He unconsciously counted the strides—*twelve* to the urnlike vase in the rear window—then pivoted back down the stairs toward the front door.

He went down briskly, heels striking the front edge of each stair. The worn carpets had been removed last winter. They had found no replacements. The large central hall was two stories high and divided each floor, and in Malory's intense familiarity it had always been a vast, ancient, uplifting chamber, a rectangular expenditure of gallantry and size. He descended amid echoes of high endeavor. Beside the stairway hung four paintings of Malorys, lean aquiline faces emerging from thick-slathered green backgrounds and black frock coats.

The hall was stiff with wainscoting and wallpaper of green false velvet with cream-colored stripes, but it was cluttered with furniture: vases, a long old couch of curved wood and frayed upholstery, an antlered hat rack. It would have been shorter for Malory to have gone back through the lower hall, past the cellar door set beneath the staircase, and out past the kitchen. But Malory gathered up his cloak from the antlers and went out the front door, striding down the wide steps between the fiercely white old columns.

Fatly curved black wood and faded upholstery, column and plaster and paint, vases foaming with ferns at the angles, these caught his attention. They masked the simple utility of the big hall and the foresquare rooms, they suggested marble, instead of pine and oak and slave-baked brick. In the winter darkness above the house were the massive central chimneys and the delicate brick tubes of the side chimneys. Malory's vision of Sycamore mansion was of a house elegant in its line and its upflung dimension, rich in furnished curves and the rolling patterns of ferns, above all antique, classical, elegant.

He circled the house back toward the people's rows. He found himself counting the steps along the north side of the house, with its shuttered twelve-foot windows. Boxwood grew between them. To his imagination, even in this December night the bushes proffered the collected, speckled warmth and the sandy timelessness of a boy's summer afternoon.

Without Celia before him, Malory abandoned himself to the unimpeded flow of his rectitude. Well, she is with them, I expect. They are all trying to force me off my land, and she might as well throw in with 'em. Yes sir, they are all trying to force me off.

"Force me off," he said aloud, striding past the kitchen and toward the slave quarters. That chuckleheaded Goddamned moron we have up at the statehouse. Up at Milledgeville. That chuckleheaded Joe Brown. To think I voted for him! Well it is like Father said, never trust a man who shaves his face clean but lets his beard grow under his chin. Brown's face, framed by the white beard, came clearly to his imagination. At Louisville two weeks earlier and again at Coffinville this morning he had become incensed by newspaper clippings posted outside the Home Guard headquarters, exhortations to fell trees across the roads and burn crops "so that the Invader finds the wilderness ahead of him he expected to leave behind." The exhortations were of public tenor: he instinctively associated them with the governor, whom he knew personally. (He had heard for certain only that Beauregard had issued one of the proclamations. But he had never met Beauregard, and George Husband had told him that Beauregard had fought very well on the second day at Pittsburg Landing, where Malory had taken his first wound. So against his conscious knowledge he associated Brown with the orders.)

Two days before, the rains had cleared off, and he and his slaves had spent twelve hours a day at work, building stock pens in the swamp, burying a barrel of salt in the barn and a barrel of molasses in the floor of the smokehouse, gathering corn and potatoes, clearing brush for the spring planting in the fields to the northwest. Recollection of the pleasure of those days was as strong as the smell of the winter-thick land itself. Burn our crops! I never heard of such a thing. And what the hell are we fighting for, then? The right to burn ourselves out? Brown's face, recalled in all its hot joviality during a reception in the octagonal hall at the Governor's Mansion three years before, suggested either duplicity or sheer stupidity. Thought at the time, yes sir, that he was a little man for the job. But I admit I voted for him. I have to admit that, and I will freely admit I was wrong, by God. Brown's wilted, limp greeting stood against the fierce pleasure Malory took in his own self-sufficiency. And then I expect Joe Brown will feed us in the winter? Joe Brown? I'd as soon ask Abe Lincoln to feed us!

Time I can't feed my own from my own land is the time I will seek my eternal reward, by God. He rehearsed the rest of the discussion he and his friends had had about the exhortations as he walked through the darkness toward the slave quarters. Ed Guice had said that *Wheeler's cavalry* had orders to burn the crops ahead of Sherman. Porter said it was so, when Malory couldn't believe it, and said that they had burned out the richest man in Louisville the day before. Time I can't do with my land what I intend to, is the time I will *know* I am through. Ain't that what the war is about? Who the hell is Wheeler, to burn my crops? Who gave him those orders? Hampton I'll wager, that (Goddamned South Carolinian! I expect he's willing to burn every plantation in Georgia to keep them out of South Car'lina, by God. But I'll bet my bottom dollar Joe Brown had a hand in those orders. Just like him.

I expect I will have something to say about it, time somebody, government or Yankee, lights afire my crops. 'Y God, if there's burning to do, let the Yankees do it, if they can. Let every man look out for his own.

House and land—the Malory land sloping southeast to the river bottoms, ravines and hillocks and ponds and pine trees, acreage sloping eternally down to the primal swamp itself, the Malory house upreared above it—in image of house and land and his own ability to control his family's land and the people upon it, in these images did Thomas Jefferson Malory have all individual identity, all political identity, all cause.

Chapter 2

PAST THE KITCHEN AND THE OUTBUILDINGS, SMOKEHOUSE AND PRIVies and garden shed, Malory could see the dim outlines of the slave cabins through the winter night. They were shielded from the house by old entangled trellises and arbors which were matted now with the last clustering leaves of late autumn and the ropelike vines.

The air was water-chill. Human breath hung in frosty sparkling clusters. He was aware now of curtains of stars. Two nights ago, toward the southwest, fires had stained the horizon at ten o'clock. Now there were no fires. Curfew was fifteen minutes away, and Tobe would be out to enforce it.

Moving down the path between the arbors, Malory consciously shrugged off Joe Brown and his political anxiety. Doubts about the governing of public affairs had squinted his eyebrows in concern. Now he loosened. A trace of the bedroom lingered in his imagination, perfume of sex, thin reedy discontent. He fastened his cloak down the front.

He began forming himself, out of lifetime habit, into the arching self-confidence of slave owning—head back and brow raised, mouth enfolded with public, friendly suspiciousness that could become successively more stiff. Past the trellises, the cabins were before him, whitewashed against the clear blue black night, windows and doors black. Two small fires burned before the rows. Their embers were orange and red, the logs now like bones cupping the mild colors against the surrounding dark.

Half-composed, just emerging from the arbors, Malory suddenly intersected the delighted flight of two boys. They thumped and fluttered against him mothlike, breathless, surprised. Their polled heads were dimly outlined by the light from the cooking fires.

Malory genially and paternally clutched them both by their upper arms. They rolled their eyes up at him, blue liquid pools in the dim light. The one in his right hand squirmed twice, quickly, while the other froze.

"Where are you boys goin'?"

"Ain't goin' nowhere, Marse Tom," the one who had squirmed said.

"Ain't, eh? Are you sure you're not goin' to run off to the Yankees?"

"Naw suh! Marse Tom. What for we do that?"

"Who are you, boy?"

"I be Zeenie's Bob, Marse Tom."

"And who are you?"

The other boy was more angular, his flesh lighter even in the half darkness, more a silky sheen, not reflecting the firelight so bluely. He drew himself up straight. Even before he had answered, Malory knew who he was.

"I be Covey."

Malory opened that hand quickly, still squeezing Bob's shoulder with his other. As his vision slowly acquired the slave boy, Malory could see his own aquiline narrow face in caricature: arrowhead sharp, high cheekbones descending from skullcap of kinky hair. He remembered instantly the twelve-year-gone night he and Lu-Belle had made love twice, once on his way over to the Husbands' for poker with George Husband and the two Guice boys, and then again when he had come back, Lu-Belle's wide hips and her pendulous breasts hanging before his drunken attention all the hour's ride in the spring evening.

"Well," he said, wiping his hand on his trousers, "you boys know what the Yankees do if they catch black boys?"

"No suh, Marse Tom." Bob was giggling and now twisting again in his grip. Covey, named Alcovey, stood silent.

"They carry you off, and put you in the front lines with a gun, and let the white folks shoot you instead of them. That is what they do."

"Sho now! I don't wants that, Marse Tom."

He watched the two boys leave, Bob sprinting whooping through the freedom of a mild winter night before curfew, Covey walking now with self-conscious rigidity. I should have recognized Covey, by damn! I could almost tell him by the smell of him, time was. I expect that boy knows.

He would have to be a fool not to. And he is sharp.

Down in the slave rows a few blacks stood about, men leaning back against the cabins, hands in their pockets, women shapeless in headcloths. Not as many as before the war, by a damned sight. But these are the good ones. We could not feed many more. He walked down the path between them, feeling the confidence of his authority purging him more completely of his earlier divisions and anguishes. He felt there was something eternal in his easy striding among the Negroes.

He stopped before a small black man with a round skull. "Shorty?"

"Yes suh?" Shorty shifted, grinning emptily. Malory comfortably cloaked himself with authority.

"Shorty, what the hell you been up to?"

"Ain't doing nothing, Marse Tom."

"Well what in the hell you doing outside Lu-Belle's cabin?"

"Nothing, Marse Tom. Hee hee hee. Nothing, no suh."

"Nothing, my ass." Shorty twisted his head in masculine pride. "You keep yourself at home, evenings. What Juno going to think?"

"Why she ain't no wife of mine, Marse Tom. Ain't you know that?"

"Son of a bitch," Malory said, "you ol' rascal." Shorty grinned again, while Malory walked on toward Juno's cabin, shaking his head in vast public disavowal.

What would you expect, he thought. His woman sick, and he out tomcatting. He felt a rich superior delight. Them niggah bucks, 'y God . . . he must be damned near to sixty.

There were two dozen whitewashed slave cabins, but now there were Negroes in only six. There had been thirty-eight slaves when the war began. His younger brother had let the labor drafts claim eight of the strongest hands for work at Fort Pulaski, and they had died of disease or run off—they had not come back. Under his younger brother and then under the overseer, when he had been at the war, there had been steady attrition. Now there were fifteen slaves all told, enough for self-sufficiency. Malory was delighted to be in control of them again. None had died or run off in the six months since he had returned, even half blind as he was. The cabins were arranged in rows of eight, with the corner cabin in the first row double-sized for the overseer. Malory on his return from parole had dismissed the overseer and made Tobe the driver, and it was now Tobe's house. As Malory, still chuckling to himself about Shorty—of course she's not his wife, they only been married forty years—as he came to the front of Tobe's cabin, Tobe stepped down from the door and joined him.

"Tobe, how you?"

"How you, Marse Tom?"

Tobe was tall, muscular, jut-jawed. The two men went on a few steps past the cabin, to the edge of the quarters. Tobe walked with the swaying shoulders and arms of his power. In the dark, he looked immensely capable. In daylight, his yellow-ringed eyes were too cold and his rigid mouth never smiled comfortably, but beside Malory, in rough trousers and Malory's own cast-off green corduroy coat, he contained all capability. Tobe's power among the blacks was almost visible, expanding from the easy swing of his forearms and the stiffness of his back. His habit was of silence, self-composure, strength of will.

"Juno still laid up?"

"She worse off, Marse Tom."

"Say she is?"

"Yes suh. It hurts her pretty good."

"Well, I expect we better look in on her tonight."

"Yes suh."

Malory drew patterns in the sand with his boot toe. "Well, why don't we wait until curfew, and then go down and see."

"Yes suh. I expects that would be the best."

Malory reached into the inner pocket of the cloak and drew out two brownly redolent cigars. "Want a smoke while we wait, Tobe?"

Orange globes of light filled their cupped hands; their faces wondered over the curled cigars as they lit them, Malory's face sharp featured, the eye patch satanic, Tobe's face thick-lined.

Shaking out the match, Malory looked off into the night. The evening cool, the cigar smoke, the deferential presence of Tobe, the dim shadows among the dying cooking fires, these reminded him of their campaigns together. Standing with Tobe, Malory felt the black world around him gather into the shapeliness of personal command. He was reminded of the military, with the sense of personal responsibility and power curving in upon him.

Increasingly he dwelt upon one memory of the war, that of the road to Pittsburg Landing—he had had both eyes, then. He had been myopic, details at a distance refusing to coalesce into shape until he got up on them, but two-eyed, mounted, and potent. And Tobe had been behind him on the road through the sun-drunk spring meadow morning, the men behind and around him in flowing column, their hats plumed with feathers, bright homemade blankets slung over brown shoulders, rifles and canteens rattling. Bare feet had splayed with brave brightness along the red staining mud. Malory had felt chivalric, armorial, his squire and himself mounted above footmen on the road to Agincourt.

(He had been on that road only after a clan duel with his younger brother Francis Marion, who was left at home with their wives—of that duel he remembered the jocose seriousness, motes of dust in the shafted light on the barn floor, his brother pinned helpless and laughing against the worn boards).

And that morning on the road in Albert Sidney Johnston's army, he had gathered about him a richness beyond any he had ever received from woman or cotton harvest, beyond any he had ever anticipated from offspring. They heard the first speckled sounds of battle, and then he had looked down at the bony, freckled faces of all the boys from Coffin County, faces sharing the same cast of eye-squint and leanness from the soils and sunrises of the same land, faces sharing the same cheekbone and eye socket from the score of bloodlines the eighty men represented—from the few old county families, the Ingrams and Donalds and Husbands and Mannings. " 'Y God they can't stop us, can they, boys?" "Naw suh, Cap'n, we give 'em *hell!*" He could not conceive of their being checked once they got started, human will was never so intense as in the purposefulness of this minute. He remembered (in the crystal winter darkness) how the bright sun of Austerlitz had been at their right shoulders.

His heart had slammed into the top of his chest with his fulfillment: the brigade emerged and re-formed itself along the dogwood-bright rim of the woods, grass still wet with dew around the bare feet of the men and his own fine leather boots, the squirrel-shooting skirmishers weaving ahead. Ahead had been a ridge glittering in yellow and spring green, more vivid than possible in his eyes, where the Yankees were flecks beneath the smoke and muzzle flashes. The whole brigade formed with panting alertness beneath popping high shots from the Yankees, and then started forward with the commanded restraint against yelling like a hand across their throats, and the barefooted drummer boys beating out "The Southern Marseillaise" on primitively fierce red drums. They had gone toward the Yankees upright and measuredly, Malory holding himself drill-book straight, feeling the tubes and soft flutes of his body facing the Yankees. Their line bathed in transparent, then clotted, smoke and the popping over the brigade increased, spots of earth ahead (bright shadowed by the sun and smoke) flipped and jumped, Colonel Whitgift floridly controlled his stallion. And as Malory knew they could not be stopped by the spattering of the bullets—forming up every twenty strides when a man went down, schoolyard contemptuous of the Yankees' aim, hands beginning to shift the muskets for the final bayonet rush—the Yankee artillery had opened on them.

The bronze yellow batteries had formed along the ridge behind the blue infantry. The Yankee soldiers had been almost within reach: Malory had felt his men exultantly twitching their hands along their rifle barrels. Malory had almost stumbled himself, so close were his hatreds—once in a lifetime, once in a lifetime—to taking exposed human shape. Then, as he watched, blood-jarred vision clearing for once, penetrating the smoke depths, the artillery pieces blotted themselves into the smoke, and the air ahead above had bunched with arching head-sized iron menace, then downPLUNGED just over and behind him, and he had turned, hatless, eyes stinging, wetly showered. The man behind him was striding on without a head, and behind that one, in the second line (he was thinking Who was that, thinking of himself Who was that? as the headless man sank down in puppetlike loosenings) in the second line, Johnny Manning was split foamingly through the waist like a tree, and behind his flank-cheeked smiling agony Malory saw Corporal Thaddeus Gazzo somersault on one leg. The circus horror stopped him. Manning's shriek was knifelike. His own hair was violently upswept, and his thick sweat turned icy. Whitgift's horse pranced under the smoke shadow ahead as the regiment curled ponderously around this stung spot. Men stumbled and collided, Whitgift's sword slashed dramatically at green, black, and bright gold, they started forward, the rifle volley came like a spring shower, more solid shot blotted among them, they turned away moaning, the colors dropped, they ran.

Wesley's Georgia brigade had gone back four times that morning, each time adding men from the support lines behind them, and dazed men from the pelting, burning haze on both sides. They mingled their enthusiasms, screamed their determinations back and forth, sprinted whooping out of the covering ravines and woods. But the artillery flattened and scattered their cohesion and spirit, battering them into isolated, slobbering individuals blinded by smoke and sweat, without the support of shoulders and known faces. On the fourth and last charge, without his sword but with a bloodslick rifle, Malory had finally closed with the bluebelly infantry. He lunged at one stunned-eyed Yankee who was mechanically ramming a charge into his gun, flailed at the man with his musket butt as the Yankee's little blue cap dropped beneath the swipe, hammered down at shielding forearms, remembered that the rifle was loaded and aimed it toward the squirming man on the ground, and as he aimed saw the Napoleon's ringed mouth down the halls of smoke and light and blood exhaustion. A man in shirt-sleeves pulled the lanyard, which blotted out the man at his feet, the blue kepi, leather visor, all sight and sound, and hurled him face-stinging into the thorn thicket he had just dodged past.

Tobe had found him in the rain that night, after the Yankees had been beaten back. Malory was entangled in a net of human bodies, angled arms, legs, beardless open cheeks, boyish lank hair—all the Coffin County boys who had followed him on the fourth charge. His wounds were networked from his shoulder to his thigh, bitten long scratches from the scrap metal, a bleeding bright-stinging chunk gone from his side, a remaining single case-shot ball aching dully in his thigh amid the flaming pain of the scratches, his face and hands stung and shot through with powder. 'Y God that nigger stood by me all night, Malory cherishingly recalled. Tobe had brought him water while the Confederate boys around him thrashed, called for their mothers, babbled revival phrases, and died. He rested with his head in Tobe's lap, stinging in pain; drowsed fitfully, then bolted upright as the night grew luminously huge, whooped, and burst a hundred yards away. "Them big riverboat guns, Marse Tom. They firing." When the gunboat shells fell, the woods and brush ceased raindripping and the men, clothing the ground, scuttled and screamed.

He had left the service because of his wounds and had run Sycamore while his brother Frank took a turn in the army. On a smooth, flushed May morning he had gone down to the depot at Station No. 13 to collect his brother's body, slain at Chancellorsville. He and Celia and Agnes watched in the shade of the platform as the yellow cars creaked violently toward them at ten miles an hour over the crude roadbed. By God, he had told the veiled women, when I go back, I'm going back with artillery.

That spring day before Pittsburg Landing was still accessible, still so palpable to him—that morning with the brigade curving away into the dazzling new foliage, fog-smell and damp-brightness on the men, their innocent furious faces washed by the sun of Austerlitz—that it seemed choked back by some mere trick of time, almost rewillable. By God, to do it over, give me Johnston's army and what we know now, and just one thing, just don't let 'em stop in the center to loot, tell 'em to go until they see the water. Yes sir, go until they see the water. He had made up and honed the imagined order, he repeated it softly to himself, standing beside Tobe in the cool winter evening. Sometimes the memory curved even further along that day to the moment with the colonel in front of them and the brigade starting out of the woods. Give me that moment, he thought, his hands curling to grasp it, those men—he recalled how their faces glistened—those men, only put that Alabama brigade behind us on our right instead, and come in there right *under* those damned guns. His hands squeezed the reins of Whitgift's long-immolated horse, playing with and against his personal recollection of frenzied confusion, just go on right up to that line, and they'd follow, by God they'd follow.

That moment was still accessible with exhilaration. The service with the artillery was blotted by frustration, by the very inertness of a thirty-pounder Parrott with its blocky breech sunk hub-deep in chill, early spring rains. The rains had spattered them leadenly across their soaked shoulders as they all, knee-deep in the creek, pushed until their hands were claw-rigid and their jaws aching. Damned thing won't move, he remembered saying, as the rain glistened across its inert rough metal barrel. Won't move, God damn it! Carry a God-damned gun to hell and gone across this state and now the son of a bitch won't move! thrashing his legs through the creek, emerging greyly from the grey water upon the mauve bank, amid sodden woods and the burnt bridge pilings.

The human, familiar excitement of those Coffin County faces had become the savagely inert iron of the heavy siege gun.

He had been second in command of fifty men, two guns, two caissons, and a hundred slaves to do the work. They had inched the guns with epic, straining anguish all the way to the bank of the Tennessee River below Johnson City, with clouds of guerrillas supposedly sweeping the countryside all about them. They had planted the guns at waterline, slaving—Negro and white man all night—to wrench ramparts and gun embrasures out of the riverbank. With full midmorning upon them, they had sighted smoke coming downriver.

The river lay long and sour and shining after the rain, bright on a dull March day. The water's edge was slappingly imprecise where toothlike stumps and busheled grey reeds grew along the bank. Major Perry had been ill all morning. Malory had told the corporal hell yes we'll take the bastard on, as long as it floats and wears the Yankee flag. The sharpness of their white-hard faces now pinched, their beards bunched and tufted, the men cheered with a high tension that had none of the Shiloh throatiness. They were veteran Atlanta mechanics turned artillerymen. They picked up the long spongestaffs and handled the shot, looking to his vision unlike soldiers, looking oddly soft without crossbelts and buckles and cartridge boxes protecting their mid-flesh. The greasy, acid grey day, lacking sharpness, the sketchy trees and cold stench of the river and the gunners' defecations along its edge, all the morning gathered into the two downriver shapes making for them, rusty against grey.

"Tinclads, I expect. We will take them at two thousand yards."

The gun barrels had dipped and swayed as twenty men heaved each into position. Malory had mounted the four-foot earthen bank they had thrown up during the night. He had dressed in his new frock coat its sleeves so heavily rank-embroidered that they seemed to have weight, a red silk sash his wife had fashioned for him, a braided red kepi, and a letter from Celia and a watch from his grandfather's estate both buttoned into his breast pocket. He studied the coming gunboats with formal drama.

They opened first, columns of smoke jumping up and out from

the side of the lead boat, right from the muddy slick water. The air thrummed menacingly and his gunners flinched. The first Yankee shot skittered wetly through the woods behind them. "They have seen us. Well, we are ready for them, by God."

He told his men to hold their fire, while the boats worked up toward the battery with sloughing massiveness. Even with the brass field glasses his vision would not focus upon them; they swam into vague blurring on either side of precise focus. Angular metal and dull rustiness and billowing smoke. The first boat fired again. This time the shell burst in the water with hot mistiness. Again the men huddled, and he had still waited, arrogantly unsure—with his weak vision—of its distance.

Finally he gave his men a range of seventeen hundred yards and told them to load and fire. The gun captains cut the fuses with their knives, and passed the shells to the first loaders, who handled them deftly at the muzzles. Front to the gunboat, head cocked supervisingly down at the first sponger on the left-hand gun wielding his rammer head toward the muzzle, he heard the next shot. When he had partly turned his weeping limited vision back toward the river, again as at Pittsburg Landing he had that hurtling sense of some great arching iron THING which had burst right at the mouth of the left-hand gun, cartwheeling him in webs of sound and milking his left eye into white pain.

Tobe had stayed by him then, too. The two tinclads had taken only one hit from the dozen rounds the rebels got to fire. Then a shell burst one of the caissons and the surviving men crashed away ear-split into the wet spring forests. When the Yankee sailors had captured him, Tobe had been pouring river water into his flecked, cracked lips while Malory still asked blind questions of the long-fled ordnance sergeant. Maimed, fever-ridden, Malory had been casually paroled by the lieutenant commander of the gunboat. Tobe had brought him home through the lines at Dalton, Malory with wound still dripping, bewildered with fever, and the side of his face slick with swollen poisoned flesh.

So, twice ruined by their Goddamned metal, he was now paroled and, by God, through, worn down, wearied out. But here, this evening, the black quarters around him, walking with Tobe toward Juno's cabin, healed and freshened by Sycamore—here all potency returned.

Chapter 3

AS MALORY CLATTERED DOWN THE STAIRS, CELIA SAT ON THE BED IN the cream-dark light, bitterly still. She felt the stiffness of her cheeks. Her teeth clenched evenly. I nearly said it, then. I nearly said it.

Malory seemed standing before her again, so hard was she pushing her will and desire into the yellow grey light of the room. Before her with that flat hard impatience. As she was preparing her ultimate statement, nerving herself for it, the moment humming in her ears, he had said he had to go see about the servant woman and had left. It was to have been elegant and severe: Very well if you will not come away with me, I shall go alone. A major declaration: he would not permit it, but could not ignore.

She had practiced it all the morning, a fit climax first to the offering that she cared more for him than for the house, then to the pitiable mention of the ghost.

But he had come back late and she had been asleep and desire had been upon him. His eye had traced out the lines of her body beneath her robes, as she was curled dozing in the rocking chair. When he desired her (his pants tenting, his hands squeezing beside his thighs), yet was occupied and anguished with other thoughts, at these moments he seemed so pitiably helpless and worthy of love. She felt a simple, yearning affection for him, standing squeezing his hands, eye shadowed. She could see the struggling human being within the man.

So his reception had been warm, this evening. She blushed.

It seems that when I—open myself to him, it only aggravates his pride and determination and self-centeredness the more. She was embarrassed now that she had acceded to him, that she had taken his hand and that even at one moment her flesh had moved (slightly) with his. The way he stormed out! You open yourself only to exposure and worse, my dear, her mother had said. If this is his reply to my wholehearted love, well then, never again!

Her youthfulness was limitation enough. When Malory was away, her resentment was vast, and what passed between them seemed sharp-edged and brittle. But when he was with her he flattened her will. Then she fumbled weakly against the smell of his tobacco, the slight tangy male sweat, the warm brown smell of his bearded flesh; her voice became child-shrill in her ears. So she had prepared herself all during the lonely leafless bright winter day, and then she had surrendered to mere affection for him!

All he wants from me is to be a child, a doll, she thought. I can do his—lovemaking with him, but nothing else. She conceived of herself flourishing in Columbia, in the Ravenels' drawing room, in the little pale-silk dress with the white stippling. She had bought it before the War (the War! I have spent a lifetime in its shadow, it does seem like), and she could let out the sleeves and wear it again. I would be an ornament to him there—his wife fully, there.

The room was beadily still. She held her breath in the darkness. The edge of her anger was dissolving wetly.

I hate this damned house. Its odors were strong as colors in the half dark: the flat odor of well-worn wood, cedary closets, the thick purple smell of close-hanging draperies and overstuffed furniture. These reminded her of responsibilities toward cleanliness and polish.

Nooks and corners of the house seemed to trap dirt and dust, and Zeenie was untrainably lackadaisical in cleaning the room. Nap-worn furniture was gradually showing the network of coarse weaving beneath the original luxury. She would turn her back and the rooms would bustle soundlessly into dirt and decay. In the kitchen, grease mounted on the fireplace bricks and on the cabinets. Phrony's old blue shirt was violent with ancient sweat, as she served their dinner plates in the dining room. I *cannot* supervise every detail of this house. It was wearing her down merely to keep food on the table and a modicum of cleanliness about her person.

Malory's increasing desperation about the Yankees wore at her, especially over the last days. The horizon itself remained deceptively still. They were masked by helplessness and distance and ignorance. The shine of light on the pine needles, the glistening of sweet potatoes cooking in sugary juices, the mild blue shade of a distant ridge, all these things seemed the coating of disaster itself.

She was determined to return to Columbia, and was justified by the menace from Sherman. She was not so afraid of the Yankees: she had confidence in herself. But Columbia was permanent, was her father's household authority that permitted her her own power and large influence. Columbia suggested stone buildings instead of a wooden, flaking house, servants who could do the cleaning and mending she had to do here, a vast permanent gallery of society instead of this yawning haze of distance and loneliness. She saw Sycamore as unraveling and dust-channeled, and contrasted it to the cleanliness of line she felt standing beside the grey granite walls of the unfinished new capitol, and seeing the city spreading softly away in its precise squares, the trees of the summer twilight sugar-rich amid the sharp roof lines and all the brick.

In the glistening days of her girlhood this very house had seemed a visible, wonderfully solid, superior ornament, into which all her appreciation flowed. Then it had appeared in bright whiteness and blue shade, its clean lines elegantly shadowed by the feathery green of embowering sycamores and arbors on a sunlit day. Sycamore crowned a valley south of Coffinville, its dactylic name stood for claret cups and polished floors and the elegance of more niggersn you can shake a stick at, amid the whitewash and heat of the little town where her family visited in the summers.

Finely poised, Malory had ridden through Coffinville with his hair brushing the padded collar of a green corduroy jacket. Tiny in muslin, sunshine glistening on her sober forehead, she had watched from the dappled shade by her grandfather's iron fence.

Her power had come to her almost full-blown one summer, with cool-eyed beauty in a piquant rounded face, and puerile enthusiasms pursued with daringly mature energy. "But, Mr. Malory, I just must have a dressing room of my own, if I ever marry! You don't really think we ladies *always* look like this, now do you? Why, when I first get up in the morning"—canted eyes suggested wanton clothesless disorder, exposed plumpness—"I look such a fright my husband would divorce me on the spot!" Celia had strolled musingly through the shadows of a summer evening, shining in a lawn dress, while men including Thomas Jefferson Malory had smoked cigars in the honeysuckle-drifting dusk. Darkies were made for confirming her pride, scuttling about her as she arrayed herself in the first evenings of her new maturity. One spring evening, her dear father had beamed him into the room. Seely, my dear, Mr. Malory has asked for your hand. Ears thumping, hearted with accomplishment and the mild sense of control, she had dropped her eyes demurely and almost willed a blush.

But since then! She lay submissively, almost bored except for the embarrassment, while Malory dropped into the act of intercourse. One expected this, of course. But all shapes of anticipated control, all forms of anticipated new identity eluded her. They had married in the midst of political confusion and almost on the eve of the War. One morning soon after their return from their seacoast honeymoon, she had entered the drawing room where the men were still closeted, to inquire about refreshments. Old neighbors Husband and Nance and Whitgift had risen to their feet, but Mr. Malory had looked up irritably. *Hush!* while Colonel Whitgift is talking, Celia. The edges of things frayed in impatience and confusion and disorder.

Frank's wife, Agnes, a severe woman with hard round eyes and straight mouth, had run Sycamore even after Mr. Malory had come back after Pittsburg Landing. Celia should have taken over the full management of the house with her husband's return, but Agnes was six years older, and had a masculine, country brusqueness that was better in these times than her own cultured helplessness. (We used to laugh at her humorlessness: one thing about Agnes, she will never embarrass Frank by *laughing* at the wrong time!) During Mr. Malory's convalescence, Agnes had even negotiated and banked the money from the sale of three of Sycamore's most troublesome blacks, one of them a sixteen-year-old girl. Celia had been schooled that selling inherited slaves was the very sign of codeless white trash. She had been unable to hide her disapproval. There is a war on, Celia, Agnes had said. Then Frank had been killed in Virginia, and Agnes had gone back to Alabama, and all responsibility had descended upon her.

Celia had always foreseen a future in which she held firm, capable sway over some large estate (though her parents' holdings were mercantilely modest—four servants over the carriage house—in Columbia). Steel behind velvet, dear. Men were to be controlled like large children, blacks like smaller ones. Typically, though, controlled with patience, mild firmness, and charm. Her firmness and youthful charm, she had ever believed, would win them all over. Shambling fat mammies in aprons would beam when she laid out large dinner parties, trusted portly house darkies (cooks' husbands would be nice) would follow her about in striped waistcoats and fat cravats. She would borrow grinning young bucks from her husband to lift and shovel in the gardens, and would tend the pickaninnies through childhood fevers. Such things would come without unseemly exertion, because all she had ever known was that gentility and charm would empower. They always had.

The first day after Agnes's departure, she had put on a dress she had patriotically made herself—striped homespun flannel, disastrously inadequate for entertaining but what could be better for day-to-day managing? She had asked the first black whose name she recalled—one of two, lounging in the shade whittling at midmorning—"Shorty, please fetch a shovel to this side of the house." She put all the rich variety of tone into it she could, and then turned away in the May sunshine, heading back for a hog-ravaged corner of the old formal garden. Heart-sinkingly, he had not moved. She had turned back. The other was looking at her with opaque eyes. Shorty kept whistling. Celia had stamped her foot. "Shorty?!"

"Yessum."

"Shorty, come away with me. I need you in the garden."

"Where Marse Tom?"

"In town." She had a terrible sense of error, exposure, when she said that.

Shorty shook his head ruefully. The other continued to stare.

"I ain't no garden nigger, is I, Jade?"

"Well, I am sure Mr. Malory would tell you to do as I say."

"Nome. Marse Tom told me to wait here for the supply wagon. Told me . . ." He looked shrewdly at the splinter of wood. "Told me wait here, help unload it."

"Oh. Well, perhaps you could come just for a moment."

"Nome. I 'spect I better wait here."

"Oh, well. Oh . . ." She started aimlessly back toward the house, her ears burning, immersed in helplessness. Why Celia, that ol' buck! He no more had to wait, Malory had said. He just lazy. What did you want him for? What is wrong with the garden? But in his presence, in the odor of his tobacco and the day's muscular strain he was exuding about him in his office, the garden seemed vastly trivial. Nothing, she had said, chastened.

All of that prefancied world had been there, she knew. She had seen it, and even now she could see women like that Widow Whitgift running it. But the leisure of certainty they had had to assume such control was gone. The war had unraveled that, as it was unraveling everything. She recalled the gentility of the past in images always set in the lavender early evenings: men lounging on bricked walks or wisteria-tangled verandahs, cigars glowing, women luminescent, air weighty with yet undispossessed summer warmth, the white men's rich political talk coming from gathering darkness where features were indistinguishable and yet crisply marked by cuffs and collar. All insisting on the permanence of forms and traditions. I told Nance, I said we gone ahead and got out then, we would be better off. Calhoun, I said. Don't talk to me about Calhoun. What did he do—thank you, Bluespark—what did he do but sell us out? Blacks hovered on the perimeter of the talk, the talk itself not threatening, just filled with a hard, muscular purposefulness beneath the waistcoated ease, and a deliberate disdain for what the blacks might overhear. (Of course he saves money! He is bound to save money, but he is still a fool for letting a free nigger come among his people, good blacksmith or not—Thank you, Bluespark—good or not—Your health, Mrs. Coates—I never knew it but what it stirs them up.) And the women fanning themselves within the web of the talk, blooming inside it, whispering with forehead-close confidence about men's foolishness while the talk arched like the brick arches or the verandah beams around them. Mr. Husband gets so *warmed up* about Joe Nance. Why I must agree—we've had nothing but trouble from free darkies—but I wish he wouldn't get so *warmed up*. My dear, they all do. I ask my George, he says it is these times. And the black servants (on the less prosperous plantations smelling of field sweat through the handed-down frock coat) circled with the trays around the edges of the talk, handing down over the men the glasses fringed with mint leaves. Mrs. Husband snapped her fan angrily at Theophilus. Theo, I declare! Mrs. Whitgift's glass has been empty these two turns. Foolish uncertain smile, Yessum Mistess. Those damn Yankees! Celia's image of them was steel-engraving caricature, huge-headed and reedily dressed, hypocritically stirring the people up. The gentility of old times had made over everything into happy darkies and comfortable overarching patterns of timeless culture. Our people wouldn't *dare* have acted this way, before the War.

Celia had learned all the patterns of a mistress' power, the way it was wielded before the War. But back then, servants had moved about with alacrity and beamed at signs of attention or affection. Their mistresses had moved among them regally. Celia held valiantly to the patterns, tasting the soup decorously, listening with feigned attention to their interminable excuses, scolding them in terms of genial amazement that tasks had gone undone: I swear, Zeenie, these valances have not been dusted yet! But none of it worked, for her. The black men were touchy and ominous, leaner than in the prewar days, eyes yellower than she recalled. Loyalty among them, once Malory's back was turned, was a tenuous thing. They refused even Celia's direct orders with bland wooden lies. Nome I ain't goin' to do that until Marse Tom tells me to. Ain't my job. I'se carpenter. Phrony and Zeenie were the house women now. Phrony bulged with brute patient joviality and unteachable obtuseness. Zeenie was brisk-handed and impatient, a tall elegant coffee-colored woman with sharp features. She frequently argued with Celia, touching upon the way Miss Agnes had done things, and Mist' Malory's mother before that. Before the War, Zeenie had been one of four house women. Now she was relishing the power she had over all the domestic arrangements and her complete control over Phrony's mindless good nature. As soon as Celia left her daily instructions in the kitchen and started out toward the house, she could always hear the flutter of Zeenie's sarcastic, incomprehensible reinterpretations.

When Malory had gone back into the army last year, he had arranged an overseer for the plantation, up from Louisville, a vulpine man named Boozer who had moved into the overseer's house with his wife and three children. He had paid his respects to Celia two days after Malory had gone. She had met him, businesslike as possible, in the office across from the dining room. He spat tobacco massively. Them niggers high-handed, ain't they? I 'spect they been too much for a young lady like you. But I 'spect I knows who can change that, too. Donchee worry none about 'em, anymore.

On a beautiful, crisp winter day, Celia had gone out with a pleasant, melancholy loneliness. She liked the Gothic twistings of the arbors in such a mood, because they suggested the layered entwined lines of ladies' book engravings. Too late to turn back, she was discovered by Boozer's warty Irish wife. "Heigho, Miss Malory," the woman called, hanging out her wash. Celia waved back modestly. Then she heard a vicious whistling snap. She went to the trellis and peered through the vines. Boozer began bellowing at Jade, who was curling on the ground at his feet in the open space between trellis and quarters. "You lousy nigger bastard. You black bastard. Pick up that air hoe one more time like that, see what it git ye this time." Boozer circled him easily, running a three-foot whip through his hands. Celia could see the untanned hide curl and snap, while Jade himself shifted on his haunches, feeling behind him for a hoe. "Touch it one mo' time, sport. One mo' time, nigger." Jade's hands touched the handle of the hoe and Boozer raised and the jacket snapped on his shoulders as the whip descended. "HOT damn, boy, that is the game!" The whip had no cracker on the end. Jade knelt, then crouched, then huddled in the sandy earth, whip each time whistling down and licking at his flesh, curling around his ribs, pulling strips of flesh free. Brilliant blood spread over the man's sides and back so the tears looked liked the exposed threads of a shiny red shirt.

"Give it to him, Jerry." Celia heard the wife.

She looked over. "Some sport, eh Mrs. Malory?"

Aghast, she walked back to the house with feigned insouciance—a bright smile for Zeenie, who was peering from beside the kitchen. She could hear the popping of the whip even in the front room. It filled up the corridors of the house, pop then pop-snag, a wet sound. Mr. Malory always said, "A great deal of whipping ain't necessary. It is the sign of a poor owner, if you ask me. But *some* is." Her father had nodded agreement over the Christmas toddy. Mr. Malory's own whip had a soft snapper at the end. "Never whip in a passion." In the parlor, she shuddered violently, still hearing the screams. After that, she received Boozer's reports at her sewing desk in the living room—and quickly, offhandedly.

She could not tell whipping helped. Trump, one of the biggest blacks, told her to shut up, Linkum's coming. Her eyes widened while he watched her coolly, hands still clasped behind his head against the wood of the cabin. Ain't got to work. And don't call on that

Boozer, I 'spect I got his number. That they would think I would call on *Boozer*. Tears rimmed her eyes.

Four of the men ran off during December and January. The patrol brought Trump back one yellow afternoon in January, and she was almost too afraid to go see them, with the bleeding panting flesh splayed between their horses. They tried to be gentle in the late afternoon sun, but were only brusque. Don't ye worry none, ma'am. You don't want him, we take him down to Louisville and give ye receipt. The head of the patrol grinned gently, tobacco juice rimming the base of each tooth. She could not look clearly at him or the slave, and regally took the printed piece of paper.

The slaves shuffled. Zeenie, taller than Celia, said that Marse Tom wouldn't have let a patroller take one of his people off down yonder.

When Malory had come back, maimed, in the early summer, the few things, the small circles in which she had some control—house and garden and a few details of table setting, tentative suggestions about food in the kitchen—were already enormous to her. She did not go back to the trellis until the day after Malory dismissed Boozer.

Before the War, women had been treated as objects of romantic fascination, worthy of public, protective veneration. (Celia knew that there were scandalous relationships, but believed that these were detestable exceptions.) She knew it was proper for women to have been thus regarded, as the supreme adornments of their culture—women were the vessels of family honor and social tradition, after all. She admired the way in which women could test and exult in this treatment, with flirtatiousness, feigned easy affection, daring freedoms of wit and temper. She had most admired her plump and bombazined Coffinville grandmother, replying to charmed men, "Water, drat! Fill out the glass if the whiskey is any good." Now the florid, engraved, thick-calved circle of admiring men was gone, dispersed, and her own husband's attentions were fleeting and sporadic.

Two days before this evening, Malory had been in a towering rage, edged with desperation, about Sherman. "That damned fool Hood has lost Atlanta, but that is not enough for him. He has gone and left us, you know." Malory had speared another chop from the tray. The five thirty November light was mahogany and yellow in the fields after the rains had cleared. "Hood! I remember the time I saw him outside Dalton, I said if that man is ever made army commander, God help us all."

Celia listened sympathetically.

"What a hotheaded fool! Sherman's out yonder somewhere"—a fork-jerk showed it might be the north lawn of the house—"and all we are left with is the worthless Georgia militia, which ain't worth a . . ." He shook his head, blocked by the unsuitability of the metaphor. "The Georgia militia, and Joe Brown." As he chewed corn bread with despairing short shakes of his head, Celia helplessly and inevitably began talking.

"That reminds me, Mr. Malory. Do you know, I was trying to straighten up the parlor a little, and I could not move the settee by myself—I could have called Zeenie but she had her little three-year-old in the kitchen with her, and if I have told her once I have told her a dozen times not to bring the little thing into the house—well I saw Tobe passing the front of the house, and I opened the door and asked him if he would mind coming in and lending a hand, just for a minute. . . ."

Malory was chewing the meat, then buttering a piece of corn bread.

"Do you know what he said, Mr. Malory? Do you know?"

Malory bit into a corner of the bread and shook his head vaguely.

"He said, 'I ain't got time I'm too busy.' Can you imagine that? 'I ain't got time I'm too busy.' Even to pause for a moment! Of course I know how important what he is doing for you *is*, but still and all! To talk that way. Why I *never* heard a darky talk to a lady that way before, any lady, not to mention the mistress of the house."

Malory was looking absently at the fireplace across the table.

She continued with desperate assertion. "I don't see what you see in him, Mr. Malory. I do know he has been a staff for you when you were in the army, but . . ."

Malory ate slowly, imaginative rage spent, weary once again with things to be done. "I expect, dear, that he was on his way to build a stock pen in the swamp. And that reminds me . . ." tossing the napkin. He bowed sketchily and went out.

Stunned, she witnessed the futility of her own actions, her own identity. She had sat for minutes soaking in self-pity with her fork still holding a decorous tiny piece of meat. Her eyes (moist then as they were now in the bedroom) stared at pine and horizon in the fading mellow light until the colors bled together without linear distinction. She was not blindly willful, but the knowledge she had been a little fool to intrude on Malory's calculations only made his lack of recognition the more agonizing.

Nothing to do, she thought plaintively, over and over. She wrung her hands. Except this, she thought, her nose wrinkling in disgust at the tangled bedclothes around her. There was none of the promised leverage, power which she had assumed would come from this surrender (even her mother's efforts to tell her at age twelve what would come on her wedding night had promised plainly that it was through such surrender women had power over men: You know, my dear—she could remember the flaking wicker chairs in the arbor in Columbia—that we women must put up with these—things—and in return, we are cherished and respected). There were women who were slaves to their physical being, she knew. They were like grotesque puppets, strung not from the head and shoulders, but from the nether regions. A woman controlled herself and, through such control, the world of moral decorum. Sublimated, passion was the flower of culture. But now there were no men about to cherish or respect her. Her own husband was distracted with concern beyond all courtesy. One might as well be a . . . a black woman, and like the act itself—practice it in the nighttime f-fields, the way they do!

The War had worn away all of the softer courtesies, all of the softer patterns. She still found the Cause of the War an ennobling thing, but she had clenched her teeth in hatred for three straining years. So in her helplessness, her anger turned more and more (reasonlessly, she thought) against her husband.

Outside in the darkness a gate slammed shut. She flinched, her eyes wet with tears of frustration, gazing fixedly at the lions' feet of her armoire. He is going to his nigger whore, I bet.

No, that is unfair. He would not leave my bed for one of theirs. (Which one, she began to speculate. She could imagine her husband making love, since she had so often seen him, his straining up-arched neck in the second before his release—but she was unable to imagine anyone else making love. Embarrassment confused her. She only glimpsed dark black flesh beneath her husband.)

That boy they call Covey. . . . She shrugged on the bed, moving restlessly, abandoning rational thought in simple physical movement. The mattress filling scraped deep beneath the sheets, huskily, drily.

Perhaps . . . Mr. Malory has suggested that where a Negro lives gives his features their expression . . . perhaps it is that Covey and Mr. Malory both grew up in the same place (suggestions of sunlight and arrangements of windows so the faces received precisely the same quotients of atmosphere). She thought of this the same way she had speculated when her older sister had returned triumphantly from her two-month honeymoon with no outward sign of change. She had wondered intensely, and created circumstances whereby her sister was still virginal, and hence could share her confidences in the openness of complete chastity, the way she had before.

That train of speculation dissolved in the haziness of the place: the haziness of her authority, identity. She twisted on the bed.

I would be a good mother, she thought. A fine mother. She could almost envision the lost children. The first son would be three now, with his grandfather Coates's fine sturdy build. Alec. She could almost project him before her features, sailor-suited, soilless, soundless, hopelessly mature in her mind. And her daughters, both of them, a year apart but dressed in the same bright stripes. She arrayed them as dolls, then remembered she was clothing the dead with her imagination, and thought of ghosts.

In this lonely house, three times she had seen vivid ghosts of boys she had grown up with and flirted with. Tommy Malcolm had touched her wrists, his head bandaged and his eyes all dark, and the next week she had heard that Tommy had been killed at Sharpsburg that very day. Mr. Malory, recovering from his first wounds, had appreciated her anguish, and she had been enormously comforted. Twice more boys had appeared to her as the Malcolm boy had, though the third time she was not as certain (*something* she had seen, soldierlike in the room, and when George Husband was reported to have died of his wounds after Fleetwood Heights, she assumed it had been him, though the face had eluded her).

Her fingers twitched at the quilt. The other ghost, the Sycamore ghost, was quite another thing. It was legend, and the sweetly pleasing thrill of nighttime terror tales. Her pleasantly typical memory of those few early weeks of their marriage was of an evening between Sumter and her husband's departure, when just the two of them had sat on the moonlit verandah, and Malory had sent sprays of delighted fear across her shoulders with the legends of the mansion: the story from the last century of the slave named Acteon who had vanished from the work lists, claimed and carried off 'twas said by the Devil himself, and then the tale of the ghost who appeared upon each anniversary of the house's completion, seeking the body which had been slain in its construction. She had quivered and posed. Malory had gone on relentlessly, seemingly oblivious to her feigned horror, his two fingers illumined by the lucifer flame as he delayed lighting his cigar to explain about the mangled arm.

Yet lately, and unlike the ghosts of Confederate boys—dear boys—she had indeed seen It, that One, she knew. And no surface sudden pebbling of the flesh, half-promoted out of shadows or a darkened chair back, in memory of that long-ago evening of childish horrors and mature lovemaking. She had had the visceral, heart-stopping sense of a *presence*. And this morning it had seemed to stand against the blank long whitewashed cellar wall, just behind a pillar, its face again hidden, and for the first time she had seen it move. Zeenie, not seeing it in the gloom, bending over the wicker basket and furling the cloth over the silver goblets, had finally turned impatiently. What's the matter with you, Mistess?

He would not even heed *that*, tonight!

And as she looked out from the curtained bed, she felt a sudden fear twine itself through her vertebrae and the nightdress over her back. She wondered with horror—all self-sorrow evaporated—if the ghost was in this room. Behind her now? Had—seen them?

Celia turned about, the fine long line of her throat exposed, breasts moving beneath the cloth. Gaping at her were the panes of the windows, squared into large eyes above open mouth, mottled with liquid yellow shadows.

Chapter 4

MALORY WENT INTO JUNO'S CABIN WITH FAMILIAR DISDAIN TIGHTENING his lips. The fire, violently hot on this mild December night, drew out the stink of airless stale sweat and old grease, what he thought of as the nigger-smell. The smell was distinctive in this cabin only by the additional, beady, thin stench of cat piss. Cats, wantonly loved and wantonly destroyed, had from his earliest days been anticipated signs of Shorty and Juno's cabin—cats to be tormented, petted, to have lie heat-soakingly upon his lap in front of the fire.

He glimpsed the relaxed entwined cats right on the hearthstone, before he saw Juno on the bed. The front room was oppressively tiny. Time was in his youth, when the fields had been brilliant with heat and when brothers and sisters and little black children had all run down the clay-red roads of childhood, that this room had been enormous, rich with secret pleasures, filled with delights. Warm, delighted, he and Tobe had sat among the cats while Juno rocked back and forth telling tales full of horrifying animal justice and rabbit-clever cunning. Since then, his maturity had opened new proportions, the attractiveness of waxed floors and cool corridors kept clean and leisurely.

'Y God the Yankees tell us to give them wages! What the hell would they do with the money? Tell me that, Mr. Garrison. Look at what they do with what they got. He cynically demonstrated the unemptied chamber pot and the dirty grey bed linen. All they need is animal heat. But as well, he lovingly remembered how the room had embosomed his youth.

Tobe followed him into the cabin. Juno had been moved to the front room of the two-room cabin for more sociability in her illness. The room was lit garishly by the orange firelight. Tobe fumbled with a lantern, while Malory's eye made nothing of the tangle of quilt and darkness on her bed.

"Juno, where you?"

"Here, Marse Tom." Dry, pain-shrunk voice. He bent down toward the blankets, and saw her with abrupt clarity as the light in the room rearranged into patterns of red and lantern-yellow and shadow-brown.

Her bland, jovial, wide brown face had bathed him with good nature in the days of his youth. Now it was distorted in jagged edges of pain.

"Hit's my side, Marse Tom. Cain't hardly catch my breath . . ." Then her voice exploded in a violent bursting "Ahhh—Hcuhh! Cuhh!" Her tongue belled between her teeth like a bubble of blood, the coughing was splinteringly dry. Malory's own chest ached.

"Good God." He was stunned with the change. She was incalculably worse than last night.

"Marse Tom, it hurts."

"Whereabouts, Juno? Where does your side hurt?"

"Ohhhh, Marse Tom, it hurts. Give me some*thin'!*"

He peered down desperately. She coughed again, first a vomit prelude "Ahhh—" then the dry cushionless wracking that splintered air, room, the thick heat. As he looked, she coughed up pus, which drooled down into the old quilt.

"It hurts-ss . . ."

Malory's tight-lipped aloofness melted with the sight. He sank to his knees beside the bed.

"Where, Juno? Tell me how it hurts."

Her breathing rattled.

"Does it hurt when you breathe, Aunty?"

"Yes suh, Marse Tom. It hurts worse an' worse. Cain't hardly catch my breath. . . ."

Malory put his hand down on the quilt, realized that amid the old diamond shapes were patterns of pus, but still squeezed and squeezed her shoulder.

Tobe was right beside him. "She say this morning that it hurt her ribs when she took breath."

"Did?"

"And then she say, it hurt her pretty near all the time."

As Malory watched, Juno's eyes suddenly glowed with desperation, and the open, pleasant old face convulsed against a new spasm of the pain. She sucked in, her capable old hands threshed weakly beneath the quilt. Malory's face fell with pity. "She been sick these last two winters, hasn't she, Tobe?"

"Yes suh." They both spoke in conspiratorial whispers while Juno twisted beneath the new pain, then arched up as if hooked by the chest, then lapsed back, coughing away into soundless heaving.

"Boozer say it was the consumption."

"What the hell he know?" He reacted to his own helplessness before Juno's agony. "Why didn't anybody *tell* me, when I got home?"

"They say it's only bad on her in the cold, Marse Tom. Say that's when it's bad. But she had been pretty bad off each winter for some time, now."

Malory's hand rested on her brow. She moaned. He could feel her tense in anticipation of the next blow, her flesh grow rigid, fists squeezing beneath the quilt. Her eyes burned hot again and then closed.

He took his hand away. "She don't have much fever."

"Say she don't?"

"No." He put his hand back on her forehead. What the shit, he wanted to say. How the hell do I know. I ain't a doctor.

"But she is worse, Tobe. She bad off." On his knees, face pale, he looked at the woman who had nursed him and had amused him, whose cabin he had identified with pleasure and warmth—against the waxed coldness of the plantation house itself—in his childhood.

"We got to help her." He rubbed his hands on his thighs. "Fetch the medicine from my office, and bring down my medical books—they are on the rolltop desk. And bring me down my jackknife."

Malory was cold with helplessness. Disease undercut his self-sufficiency at Sycamore and exposed him and his people to the blisterings and purgations of the doctors. During the sickly seasons of late summer, he always ignored his personal fear in his pity for his people, but he could not be everywhere at once. He huddled his slaves inside against the menacing night air and the fogs which were custardy with disease, yet they still crossed the bottomlands and would not take care. (The Sycamore whites traditionally took enormous precautions, and his Uncle Walter even used to flee to the Tennessee mountains.) Niggers should be able to thrive where white men could not, but something belied their supposed hardiness, and every August and September there were funerals in the slave cemetery, Malory reading the funeral services against the violent mid-morning rasp of insects.

And disease was hydra-headed. In the winters, the slaves all coughed and choked; Malory could not get them to clean their fetid cabins. And black infants died in all seasons. (Malory did not believe, as George Husband did, that their mothers killed them out of spiteful defiance. It was malevolent disease.)

In between the doctor's quarterly visits, Malory fought against it as best he could. He fumbled with all the lotions and poultice layers and bubbling cauldrons of legendary remedies. He could remember a day in his adolescence when he had been sent to find swamp snakes, so their heads could be used for a cancerous old cook. Malory's father had had great success with three-inch metallic rods, purchased from Philadelphia, painless in the application. The rods were still in the rolltop desk, in a box minutely printed with patents. Malory regretted he had lost the knowledge of how to use them (though they had not kept his three sisters and his older brother alive past adolescence).

He knelt in the darkness while Juno panted and squeezed her eyes in anticipation of pain. His rage could find no focus in the room. Sickly season past, and now the good Lord strikes us with this!

"Would it help to turn on your side, Aunty?"

He buried his arm beneath the side of the woman, feeling the wetness and curdy stink. He pulled her over gently until she faced him and then patted the bedspread back. She arched against the pain again, but this time she relaxed with a gradual easing. He felt her breath across his face, vile with yellow stench.

Malory had gone to Coffinville that morning in part to find Dr.

John Gazzo and fetch him to tend Juno and look at Crisp's big blister. Gazzo was a cynical, self-indulgent, blear-eyed man with lank brown hair. His wit had seemed to promise a hidden fund of generosity, and Malory had always treated him to a round of stiff drinks after his semiannual visits.

On this bright December morning, he had found Gazzo in his office, his yellow brown face rising incredulously between brown paper bundles and the bottles plungered with worm-eaten corks. "Me?" He exploded with the same cynical hyperboles Malory had always assumed were farcical. "Me, come south? No sir! Why, I'm prepared to leave here at a moment's notice on the *north* road. That is my intention. To leave here on a moment's notice on the north road." He bent back over his account books, strapping them together. "If I wanted to get caught by the Yankees, I expect I would at least hunt out Kilpatrick himself, instead of risking the roads with their bummers all over 'em.

"I expect she will be in worse pain today. Here." He had handed Malory some white, pasty pills. "Calomel. Dose her with these, or bleed her, or both. You can't bleed a nigger too much. It might give her some rest."

Ed Guice had agreed, as they talked on the gallery of the Coffinville Hotel. "I expect ye might as well bleed her yourself. That's all the Goddamned doctor would do. You cain't bleed a nigger to death, hardly."

Now, he and Tobe looked closely. The calomel pills only whitened her lips, already greasy with pus.

The pains seemed sharper: the splintering cough again. "Marse Tom, it hurtsss."

"Son of a bitch, Tobe, we got to do something!" He rocked back on his hams, stroking his hands over along his thighs. "We got to do something." He looked helplessly at her. Dr. Richard Carter's *Valuable Vegetable Medical Prescriptions* was open to the second part: useless. Tobe had not found Ewell's book. I expect I lent it out during the last sickly season to Widow Whitgift. Carter's thick pages were divided by big black words *Receipts*. I expect a recipe ain't gonna do any good.

You cain't bleed a nigger to death. Bleeding is what I have seen them do, at the least. The metallic rods were useless to him without instructions. The medical book beside him was filled with elongated prescriptions for house-brewed remedies, but he had no time, and they sounded generally improbable anyhow. That left bleeding. He knew his slaves had sometimes rested better after bleeding, but he suspected that old Dr. Phelps had bled his sister Annie to death. He studied recollection after recollection. He had pulled teeth but he had never bled a person.

While his mind turned over and examined each possibility, old equations of past slave diseases came. The sickly season of '49 almost wiped Father out. (Lose a good hand you lost near about two thousand dollars.) We barely got through the sickly season of '52. Beneath these memories of loss lay his simple, aching pity for this old, now worthless woman. And a creeping sense of personal fear that by serving her he would become smeared with the stuff of death itself. He wiped that thought away, rubbing a thumb across his forehead.

"We got to bleed her, Tobe."

"Say we got to?"

"I expect so. That is all I know will give her some easement."

Tobe nodded.

"Hand me that jackknife."

It was the sharpest knife in the house. Tobe held a bowl and some towels. The bowl glistened with baked clarity in the thick welter of odor and fading light. Malory wiped the knife along the thigh of his pantleg, more for luck than cleanliness.

When he pulled her soft, thick arm from beneath the quilt and turned it upward, Juno began to plead in sudden panic. "Oh please don't, Marse Tom! Please don't cut me!"

"Which side is it, Aunty?"

She tried to thrash upward. The thought of the lunging of that old, pain-soaked chest made Malory ache and his eye blur. "You best hold her down, Tobe." Tobe put the bowl and towel on the floor, and held her down by the shoulders.

"Which side is the pain in?"

He and Tobe decided the left side hurt the worst. Malory only knew two things for certain about bleeding. You had to bleed on the same side as the pain, so it would not draw it across the heart, which would be fatal. And you must not bleed in the hot weather or it would thin the blood fatally. Or was it, in the cold weather? He laid the knife on the floor and wiped the sweat from his hands along his legs. One of the cats rubbed along his side with dirty softness and purred.

Her arm was laced with the slick scars of previous bleedings. She had been bled twice to arrest miscarriages, he remembered. He found a section of skin between two of the slick places, guessed, and steeling himself dug in the tip of the knife blade. The scream stunned him despite the preparational flex and stiffening. The blade wandered hideously, wrote in the flesh, cut sideways. The two men struggled against the thrashing, while the knife probed again and slipped in his palm.

He fumbled for it while Tobe held her with jaw-straining force. He found the knife, felt the sweat blister his vision, wiped his forehead. The whole lower arm was awash with dark blood. He noted the upcurling flow. Maybe I done it enough. I can't tell in this light.

He brought the old lantern closer while the steady noise thrummed through his head. There it is. I better cut a little more. "Hold on, Tobe. Aunty, I got to!" He said it again and again while the knife pricked and the blood drooled out in tiny lantern-bright flickings. It was regally purple in the lantern light, black when he put the lantern down.

How much, then?

The screaming became hoarse. Malory realized she had been screaming only when it hoarsened, and the sound that had for those seconds been as familiar as the cabin itself now subsided in wracking, helpless wheezes.

Let it flow more.

Tobe and Malory studied the accumulation of blood. The white bowl grew dark, and almost obscenely warm with the blood's vital heat. When it was filled, they decided to let the flow continue into the cracked cat dish Tobe found on the hearth.

They began bandaging the arm, but the bandages soaked up the blood too quickly and they had to throw them away. Then they used a towel Tobe found in the back room. It too filled and did not staunch the bleeding. Then they tore up some dirty linen from the bed in the back room, and now it finally blotted and then held: they held hands poised above the cloth. The bleeding had stopped.

Then they noticed Juno was placid. Her befouled mouth was half-closed, eyes shut amid now unsqueezing flesh. Her breathing was short but seemed more regular.

"She resting better, Marse Tom."

Malory was stunned with his expenditure of nerve and will. He sat back on his haunches, his eye blinded by sweat and tears.

"She better, ain't she?"

"Well . . ." he sighed. "She resting better, Tobe. I expect she is some better."

Tobe helped him up. The uncurling of his legs was cool with pleasure. Malory took two deep, measured breaths. His incautious foot kicked the bowls and blood spread over the wood floor, soaking into it in black deltas in the firelight, shining in drying paintlike puddles. The cats sniffed and wrinkled at the warm blood.

"Let us get some air, Tobe."

"Yes suh," Tobe said as the two men went out into the night air, looking back at the reclining woman whose breath whistled now in her unconsciousness. "Yes suh, I 'spect you helped her to rest better, Marse Tom. She resting better."

Outside of the cabin, the air smelled as fresh as water. His eye found blue and grey blue and deep purple colors beneath hanging huge winter stars. He breathed deeply, feeling the insucked air displace—like rain through smoke—the air of the hot blood-lined cabin. The sweat upon his flesh felt crystal cold.

Tobe behind him, Malory began walking down the street. It was deserted, blue, mild. He put his hands across the small of his back and stretched. His flesh eased, he turned to Tobe.

"Check on her tomorrow morning. Tell me before breakfast."

"Yes suh." Tobe stood cleanly in the middle of the moonlight and blueness. He had Malory's cloak and spread it capably. Malory turned his collarless neck and shoulders. Tobe patted the cloak smooth with a spreading soft flex. Malory could not remember Tobe ever doing that. Malory looked at him.

"You love that old woman, don't you, Tobe?"

"Yes suh, I 'spect I do."

Tobe now walked nearly beside him. They came to the end of the lane, and the cooking fires were rose and cool white in their waning. Malory paused before turning out of the lane, along the path up to the big house. The best sense of competence, that of competence spent in generosity, was upon him. His sweat felt warrantably cool beneath the thin collarless shirt and the cloak. He shrugged the cloak more comfortably, and wished he had a cigar. Send Tobe for one. Not after what we been through. Tobe stood too, not yet turning for his own driver's cabin at the far end of the lane.

"You love that old woman, Tobe. I expect I do too."

"Yes suh."

"She raised both of us, I expect."

"Yes suh, that's right."

"She could not have done a better job of it if she had been our own mother."

"That is the truth, Marse Tom."

"Well. We see what we can do for her tomorrow morning."

Neither man moved. Malory mused out over the night. Tobe shifted his head down a fraction. Malory prided himself on his ability to read niggers' thoughts, and he knew Tobe was about to say something of this shared moment. Among blacks who lurched out into verbal and emotional display, Tobe's reticence was part of his power. But now, by God, I believe he's going to say what he feels. Malory waited with vast patience.

Whatever Tobe said would surely reflect their shared hard labor of generosity. Malory awaited one of the rare rewards of slave owning: merited, unsycophantic respect, praise from a man separated by the most fundamental condition.

Tobe's head raised in rhetorical calculation.

But then in that mildly, cleanly, sweetly cool moment, waiting for Tobe to find the right word, Malory heard a woman's pliable, yielding, impenetrated "yess—ohhhhhhh," unembarrassed, flaccid with pleasure.

Malory turned toward the sound, so that he did not see Tobe's head come up, readied at last. Malory saw the third cabin on the left, where lantern light gleamed through a shutter like a wet hot net.

June, Malory thought. He saw the form of what he had heard, June's firm yellow flesh, breasts full and jiggling over some nigger, hair entwined, eyes closed with pleasure, her flesh shining in the light, itself liquidly yellow. June.

Again, he loosened in reaction to the flesh.

Malory's sense of certain, complete power hovered over his shoulders, swelled his genitals, hollowed his belly. The cloak swirled about his thighs, its feather touch trembled his flesh. June, bare-assed.

His hands squeezed the full air. Be slow and take time. Have spent once, slow this time. He felt his flesh stiffen, still wet-lined after love-making with his wife.

" 'Minute, Tobe."

The Georgia earth sprang beneath his feet. Malory's world once again pivoted upon immediate reaction. His vision blurred the cool shapes of the evening actually before him, but culled up recollections of her accessibility, of June's naked, hanging, malleable rich flesh. Yellow gold. As he had sunk to his knees helpless before Juno's pain, he now walked with liquid helplessness and a pounding in his chest toward June's cabin.

The best times with June and before her Lu-Belle were spontaneous, he thought, with cresting physical delight. Tobe behind him made some preparatory sound, blurred then into silence. "A minute, Tobe. Got some business first. Be right back with you, old hoss."

The bleeding, the exhaustion of self in service had earned him some pleasure, no? Sweat sprang anew, scalding beneath the cloak.

He put the flat of his hand on the door to the cabin, heard a thrashing resettlement of flesh within, and drew his hand back into a fist, battered it against the door of the hut and burst it open into the intense yellow light.

The yellow woman herself was raised on the bed, facing the door, hair swaying in thick braids, the brown gold nipples of her shining yellow breasts swaying too; eyes opening toward the door were divided animal-brightly between pleasure and surprise. The black man beneath was as dark as ebony beneath gold. His flesh and hers came together like the soft concussion of two hands, him finger-erect within her, in an unstoppable completing spasm.

Malory tingled against his rough army trousers, face taking a yellow cast from the light, his one eye roving.

The black man was Jade, hands clutching her shining suave hips, eyes yellow in his black flesh as his head raised back and up.

"Out, nigger."

Jade's eyes blinked. His flesh still stretched into her, his glistening body still arched up between her long, smoothly yellow thighs. He blinked as though awaking from a warm sleep. His body still shuddered—chest and neck—to complete the motion.

"Out, nigger," Malory said pleasantly.

"Marse Tom," June said. She giggled.

Jade said nothing. His face had lost its usual sullen opacity. It is the light, Malory thought. The black man moved from beneath June. He half rolled back against the wall beside the bed, shielding his flecked, helpless, throbbing flesh with the quilt. In his upraised face the yellow light pooled at his teeth and his eyes.

"Out, damn it!" Malory moved toward him.

Jade still watched, his expression unfamiliar to Malory's recollection of him. When Jade spoke, his lips moved over his motionless teeth.

"She mine."

"Hell she is."

"She my woman."

Malory's eye hardened, his initial, facile anger—like catching a neighbor's disliked child in your garden—now becoming hard-edged. "God damn you, Jade. You are mine, she is mine. Now get out."

Jade moved to the corner of the bed, hands squeezing the brown-patterned quilt. June squirmed off the bed.

Malory picked up a chunk of firewood in midstride with one sweeping motion, his cloak flaring. In the next stride he brought the chunk up with two-armed backswing and as his weight came down one third time brought the thick raw wood right against Jade's skull, so hard his fists swung by and down the branch-piece. The pop was as sharp as a percussion cap. Jade, hands tangled in the quilt, half rose into the blow, rocked back into the wall, and then fell dead-weight down across bed and floor. Malory swore at the greasy weight of the man as he dragged him off the bed and rolled him in lazy somersault over onto his back.

Then Malory squatted on the bed himself, turning to face June. She held her hands in giggling decorum above crotch and across the swaying bosom. He unbuttoned the face of his trousers, his upstarting flesh framed by pants and cloak.

June simpered over to him, flesh warmly yellow and jiggling in the light. He put both hands on her plump sweat-glistening hips. "Oh lawd," she said. He pulled her against the bed. "You quit fooling with me, Marse Tom. You being naughty." She got on her knees on the old stained feather mattress—not made of husks, as in the other cabins—and he pulled her against him, feeling his shaking heat cooled by the cool rubbery flesh and freedom of her thigh.

"Ohh lawd," laughing. "What you wants, Marse Tom? What you got there upside me, Marse Tom?" He had intended to mount her. But she closed with a slight heft of her thigh over his quivering flesh—coolness to furry warmth. On his back, his flesh rose into the yellow sheathing. She crooned over him, dispassionate once he was lost in his pleasure: "You quit fooling with this nigger gal, Marse Tom." Mouth frozen, neck cord straining, he moaned and released almost at once with a flooding wild concentration on her sweaty naked flesh, spending all that his wife had left in him, all now channeled and released as she settled down twice with hollow soothing peeling touch.

"You quit fooling with me, Marse Tom. You stop being naughty, Marse Tom." The words were like yellow honey, but her eyes were hard in her fine-boned, tightly molded golden mask.

Coming out of the hut, Malory looked for Tobe, expecting that he would still be lightly outlined by the moonlight. He had been inside no more than three minutes, he calculated. He looked about. The clear mildness of the evening was more stale than it had been. "Tobe? Tobe?"

Tobe had moved from the intersection of the lane and the path. Malory looked with irritation into the blue shadows beside the cabins. "Tobe?"

"Yes suh," Tobe said dully. He stepped half out of the neighboring shadow, his face above his nose in the clear light, the rest in darkness. "Yessuh, Marse Tom?"

"Where you go, ol'hoss?"

"I waiting here, suh."

"You black devil," Malory said, clapping him on the shoulder, geniality still on him, though faded. But the flesh was stone-opposing beneath the corduroy coat. Malory dropped his hand.

"What were you going to say, Tobe?"

"Nothing."

"Well. Tell you what." Malory lowered his voice in a sudden access of generosity. "That high yaller woman in there is fine, Tobe. You know what I mean? She is yours if you want; all primed for you." He was dimly conscious that his voice was huskier, more liquid, than when he talked to Tobe normally. But he leered with his generosity.

"Naw suh."

Malory straightened himself, aware that he had been exposed.

"I'spect I better see about Jade," Tobe said.

Malory cleared his throat.

He walked alone back to the house, through the white-bleached spots on the black night earth where the washing was done, then between the arbors. He sucked deeply at the night air but it was no longer clear to his lungs. His single eye made out the house ahead, rising abruptly, bleached bone in the light. The moon slid from pane to pane in the big windows as he crossed toward the house, the night and countryside all his, the lines of his land spreading away grey-dim then blue then blacker, finally all black, as he looked over his fields.

As he looked toward the north, he saw the monstrous belly-bulk of the cotton press. As a child it had stalked him on moonlit nights. Tonight the big headless skeleton seemed to stalk him anew. He thrilled.

Turning the corner into the splay of light from the front windows, he saw the hung hairy flowerpots, a squat barrel-half chair tucked into one of the angles of the columned front. Give it up to the Yankees?

Giving Sycamore to them was tantamount to surrendering completely. They plan to put the niggers over us. I do not like slavery, but I will not live with them any other way.

Striding up the front steps, Malory thought of what a Yankee victory would mean. He could not imagine that they would not obliterate and abolish, would not remain to strip the whites of their power, administer the niggers' wishes. A kind of subconscious image of this doomed future came to him as a colorless engraving, all grey black intricacy of line wherein the clarity of the white—the white of flesh on forehead or bosom—was achieved by minute dozens of lines accreting about a clear, clean island of white. In the engraving glimpse, a man in a frock coat and a woman delicately bosomed and bare shouldered were in a garden of spidery pines and moss, beneath a brilliant, empty-white southern moon. While the man and woman strolled, Negroid arms and teeth, thick lips and thighs were sheltered sheathed in the hairy southern plants (sheathed as in children's puzzles with boats or faces in cloud and tree limb). All was formal, decorous, and ominous.

Even Tobe, he thought, as the image of reaching, menacing

African flesh was couched in the spidery bushes of his inward vision, even the best of them like Tobe have got their dangerous side. They are unstable. Jade, of course (it is a good thing I stopped him before he struck me. I saved a fair field hand worth a clear two thousands of dollars)—but Tobe, too. Their problem is that they cannot cling to one thought for a length of time. Ten minutes at the most for some, but not more than a half an hour for any of 'em. As Tobe could not recall what he planned to say for ten minutes, himself.

And Tobe is the best of them. And the image in his mind, as he blew out the lamp on the mantel, was of his own bedside with Celia benignly giving her dead husband's prized repeater watch to a grieving, no longer impassive Tobe.

FRIDAY
2
DECEMBER
1864

Chapter 5

THE MORNING SUN WAS PROMISE PURE, SEVEN O'CLOCK BRIGHT. Under an ice-blue sky, the sun flooded the winter fields and the pine-woods with yellow and cream and purest white. The light was honey soft along the sandstone square of the farm's cemetery wall, and in the yellow grass and the small fir trees. Sunlight spread across the focuslessly mild lambs and the flat stone slabs and softened the letters on the slabs into the very butter color of the stone:

Eliza Anne
Sept. 8 1843
died
Nove ber 1844
Suffer the little
ones to co e nto me

Ellen Adair
July 1862
d.
January 1863

The wet earth was blood red under the sunlit grass, and with the color of caking fresh blood it stained the heavy nailed brogans of the soldier, his thick wool socks and his blue trouser legs.

The soldier was turning from his waist, his torso buttoned into the government dark blue and strapped with breastplated leather, his freckled young face violently exuberant, Springfield model 1861 rifle upthrust by the right hand, wood and brass and bright lock-metal glinting in the sunlight, arms held back bat-winged from shoulders, then shaking while the whooped "GawDAMN!" and the volley itself still telescoped away with hard flat blue cracks into the distant pine trees.

The soldier next to him was also half rising from his crouch within the stone walls of the cemetery, his rifle held jubilantly horizontal in both arms, shaking with his joy. Both were young, both wore heavy-shouldered blue coats and wide-brimmed blue hats. "GawDAMN, Teddy! I got me a rebel!"

Four other Union private soldiers rose from cemetery and fence, their breath frosty on the clear morning, smoke from their volley sparkling and uncurling in the bell-clear day. Their sergeant still stood half-crouched, rifle swinging from its shoulder strap, smoke-heavy revolver cocked back upright in his hand, his blue eyes focusing with icy distance after the fleeing rebels.

"God damn, we did it. I knew we could do it," the first soldier said. "Didn't I tell ya, Teddy? Didn't I tell you?"

"Johnny? Hey Johnny?" Ted said to the sergeant. "Hownhell you know they was only six of 'em?"

All six looked across the spangled air at the sergeant. The rebels had burst violently out of the woods sixty yards away, just when Sergeant Deall said, and they had been along the little cemetery wall and behind the wooden fences where Deall had posted them. When the rebels bunched between the house and barn or swung wide, whooping and firing, three had shot at the first one to come into the space between the house and barn, and the other three had fired at the first one to come around the barn, and Deall had covered with rifle and revolver any who came around the house on the right.

The one rebel in the shadowed space between the buildings had rocked into spewing wood and chips and they heard the whack of bullets and the man and the horse had sprawled violently motionless. One on the left had been unhorsed, and the Union soldiers' fear exploded into bright pleasure as the caped blundering man dodged out of their sight and the others wheeled their horses after him.

"There were only five," Deall said, almost to himself. "Three clear shots at the one on this side, and I believe I only hit him with the one." He shook his head.

The soldiers clustered around him. They were all uniformed in the same thick blue wool. Philip Sullivan had a close-trimmed black beard and Hostetler was blond, but all six of them looked youthfully the same in the thick uniforms, youthfully competent. On their caps and hat crowns they wore small white acorn badges. The flesh was browned and compact under their jaws, jackets close about their lean sturdy trunks; Ohio farm boys capable of girth and furniture-heavy stolidity but now restrained by youth.

"I thought there was a regiment of 'em, Johnny, they yell so. How did you know they was six?"

"Five. I saw them back in the woods."

The soldiers looked into the pinewoods, fifty yards off across yellow sedge fields, tightly thatched and glistening jaeger green in the cold morning. Johnny Deall had the best eyes in the Army of the Cumberland, by God. They turned back. Deall was reloading the fired chambers of the pistol.

Sergeant John Winthrop Deall was clean shaven, his light brown hair cut nape-even by bayonet. His flesh was tight and pure over big facial bones, his chin was clenched, his lips brown and thin, and his eyes were cold blue and farsighted, with a sailor's web-surrounded strength. Deall was twenty-eight years old. As his fingers loaded the revolver, threading among cylinders and rods, he studied the woods and fields. The six men around him became deferentially silent. He had come from New England and had been a photographer in Mount Union, Ohio, on the eve of the War. He had served on the river gunboats, then had transferred to the 112th Ohio Volunteer Infantry, refusing an officer's commission. He snapped the revolver closed.

"Let us see what we have got for ourselves, boys."

Trailing their rifles, they filed after him across the back lot toward the house and barn. The house was a big paintless frame building set on brick pillars. The farm boys sniffed their contempt.

"Why'n hell don't they paint their places."

"Too lazy."

"They could make the niggers."

"Niggers probably too dumb."

"You can't make a nigger work worth a damn."

Deall said nothing.

The house was abandoned, but there was the feel of recent life. "I ought to get to search this one, Johnny," the freckled boy said.

"Me too, Johnny."

"Keller got a watch at that first one, and Hostetler got some spoons. Our time, huh, Johnny?"

Deall looked at the near woods, then back across the fields, calculatingly. "Those must be the Negro cabins," he said, jerking his chin up toward two squat cabins in the shadow of the barn.

"I reckon, Johnny. Can me and Ted search this house?"

"All right," Deall said absently, looking deeply at the two cabins. "Bring out any guns you find and share any food."

The two boys gleefully hammered down the door with their rifle butts, the whacking noise echoing up the pine aisles after the rebel cavalry. The other four stood around uneasily, listening to the two boys clatter through the house, pause in the front room, then burst toward one corner simultaneously. "We can go in after them, Johnny, can't we?"

"You want to burn this one, Johnny?"

Deall looked around quickly. "They come at us here, John," Sullivan said. "We ought to burn the place."

"I guess," Deall said. The boys inside were still scuffling over something they had seen in the first room. "Phil, take Saul and Joe and see what is in the smokehouse and barn. Carl and I will look in those cabins."

"Then we get our chance at the house, John?"

"All right."

The Ohio boys bounced with a holiday zest: the two in the house were banging at some lock, still in the front room. But Deall walked toward the two cabins with sober rigidity, staring intently at them. Carl Winters looked at him with bright anticipation. "What you think we'll find, Johnny?"

Deall did not know. The two houses were as stonily quiet as the main house itself. The yellow fields stretched around them to the surrounding pinewoods. Ridges declined into blueness in the winter sun.

They tried one of the small cabins, Winters shoving the door open while Deall kept his hand on his pistol hilt. The cabins were two-room boxes with glassless shuttered windows and sandstone fireplaces. The first they tried had the grey acrid smell of disuse.

Deall stood looking about vacantly as Winters prodded the earth floor and stirred up the dry flat smell of old wood.

"Nothing buried here I don't believe, Johnny." Winters pulled the bayonet out of the floor and moved toward the door. "Johnny?" Deall seemed to look for something instinct within the walls. "Let's go, John. Those bastards will get done with the big house before we get there."

Deall nodded without focusing his gaze, and they went to the next house. This door was locked, and Winters brusquely drew his rifle butt as high as his cheek and hammered the metal stock against it near the knob, then kicked it open.

This house had been lived in as recently as the main house. Winters ducked into the odored darkness, and Deall followed him this time with intensity.

John Deall gave up the pure winter sunlight, the clean feel of the sun across his shoulders, as he stepped into the house. To his right, Winters fumbled with the latch of a shutter. Deall struggled to make out shapes amid blackness and stench and sudden flakes of dust. The smell was of unwashed bunched clothing and grease. To Deall, it was strangling. When Winters finally beat the shutter open with his rifle butt, the burst of sunlight fell on yellow, bruised flesh: the flesh became a stained buff quilt wadded over a bedstead and trailing on the floor.

The air would not penetrate far into the room, and the smell of quilt and old food and wet dead ashes was thick on Deall's tongue. He raised the slick quilt onto the bed, and moved a plate swirled with white grease off the straw mattress.

"Nobody here neither, Johnny." That did not seem possible.

Clothes hung from wall hooks like cut meat. There were two beds in the front room, both wadded with heavy quilts, and a chair with its back broken like a shoulder blade. A table, and a chest. Winters began to pry at the chest lock with his bayonet while Deall went into the second room.

There was a bed in this one from which a black man stared at him with hollow huge eyes.

Deall froze, mouth open.

"Nigger trash in this trunk is all, Johnny. . . . Hey, what have we here?" Winters made chinking noises.

Deall stared at the man. His head alone was visible, the face fragilely carved, his body so thin and frail it barely mounded the rabid diamonds on the quilt. There was a jug of water beside the bed and a plate half full of yellow crusted food; the thick smell from the next room was paled whitely by age and fever in this. There were the ashes of a small fire still in the fireplace, though the stones were chill.

Winters filled the door behind him. "Look here, Johnny. Three old gold pieces. Eighteen and. . . . Hey!" Winters shouldered past.

"Look at that old nigger! Like to scared me to death."

Deall took a deep breath and stepped toward the man. The black deep eyes followed him. "They leave the old ones, who can't work." Deall put his rifle carefully in the corner beyond the bed, while the huge eyes followed him. "God damn them. They leave them to die."

Winters looked at the Negro man with bright interest. "This ol' nigger's damn near dead, at that."

Deall knelt beside the clean spread. The black man's face was dry. There was the thin dry flavor of fever above his head, and the flesh of his neck was as clean and dry as old leather. Deall folded the quilt back, pulled back the clean frayed sheet and rolled it over the quilt. The man's chest and arms were as dry and light as bone itself, visible at the wrist and throat of the grey nightshirt.

"You're free, old Uncle. You're free at last."

The black man swallowed with almost wooden dryness, throat clacking. "Do you want some water, Uncle? Some food? I've got some . . ." Deall fumbled in his knapsack beside his hip, looked down, then back at the deep hollow eyes ". . . some bully beef and hardtack . . ."

The man closed his eyes heavily and reopened them, his breath now rasping. Deall looked at him with patience which softened his eyes and even the tight surfaces of his face. "Free, Uncle, free at last."

The black man's breathing rasped against the back of his throat so dryly that Deall felt his own throat ache. Mouth slightly open with his helplessness, Deall looked about the room for a moment. It was constrictingly tiny and steeped with confinement and false heat. There was a print of a pudgy white baby with a sheaf of flowers by the door, and over the man's head a mezzotint of a white Christ at prayer, forehead yellow green with light. "Let's get him out into the light."

Winters moved uncertainly to the head of the bed, eyes on Deall instead of the black man. The Negro's eyes switched, warily it seemed, to Winters. "We won't hurt you, Uncle. We are going to take you outside, into God's light." Deall continued to talk softly as he shoved his arms palm up under the quilt to cradle the old man's half-exposed trunk. "God's light of freedom at last, Uncle. We'll set you up in the big house. Not in this hellhole another day. Not another day." Deall almost could feel the warm clean light upon this man's flesh.

He half rose, the old man's body clasped to him like a bundle of fragile reeds, Winters holding the old man's head. As he rose, a sharp vivid stench stung his eyes: deep into his nose. His hands and arms felt queasy chunks. From beneath the man, his yellow last feces were coating Deall's arms. The old faded mattress, exposed as they lifted the man, was blotted through its ticking with yellow and bloodstained green. Will-lessly Deall rolled him out against wall and cot edge, while his stomach squeezed his chest against his chin and opened his tongue-swollen throat and he vomited blindly against bed and wall and pale brown flesh.

When they got the old man outside his eyes were still hollow with vision, but he was dead.

Chapter 6

THE FLAMES ROARED BILLOWINGLY, CONTAINED BY SPECTRAL, CHARRING timbers. Deall himself had splashed the coal oil between the children's beds on the second floor. The heat pressed upon their faces. Deall stood closer than any, so close Phil Sullivan didn't see how he could take it, and told him so.

"Bring up the mounts, Phil."

While they waited for Sullivan to bring the horses and mules, the boys stood by their piles of loot and compared their finds, hat brims touching as they tried to assess silverware and brooches. "That there knife, Saul, that'd be worth ten dollars when you get back to th' regiment."

"Maybe I'll take it to Mary."

"I don't see how I missed the knife . . ." Billy said petulantly. And he obviously was sorry not to have thought of the hall closet; Saul had a beaver hat, and even Phil Sullivan, arriving far later than the rest after searching the smokehouse, had found an old green frock coat. "Fact is, that knife ought to be mine. You got eve'thing the first two times."

"Finders keepers, Billy boy," Saul said. "Ask Johnny. That's what he said, he said . . ."

"Ah, shet up." Billy had not taken his eyes away from his one best treasure, a small gold locket engraved "Ellen." He twisted his fingernails trying to open it.

"Johnny, didn't ye say . . ." Saul looked around for Deall. He saw him across the yard.

"What you doin', Johnny?"

With the rebel soldier's sword, Deall was cutting at the hind quarters of the dead man's dead horse. He was sweating, for the horse had fallen very near the kitchen of the burning house. He sawed, scrubbed his forearm across his face, then swung the sword down twice into the dark hairy warm flank. "Johnny?"

He pulled a knife out of his haversack, and bending beneath the billowing heat, prying with the sword and cutting with the knife, ripped off two chunks of blue dripping meat. He straightened up, face a mask of sweat which glistered above his tight flesh like bronze, and then turned and walked with the meat back past the barn.

"What the hell is he doing?"

The soldiers edged slightly away from their separate piles of treasure—clothing, a birdcage, tin cups, edges of metal and glass which glistened under the winter sun—to watch him. They eyed each other, Sullivan and Johnny being away, with the school-yard nervousness of muscle-assertive equality.

Deall walked to the trellised well and tossed the chunks of meat in it. Then he hoisted the bucket, and looping the rope over the sword edge, cut it with one certain jerk and pitched the bucket down the well.

He came back over to them, his face still masked by the sweat over the tight skin. "You boys got to piss, piss in that."

"In their *well?*"

"Damned right."

"Sure, Johnny."

Billy finally got the locket opened, and only a child's lock of hair fell out. "I be Goddamned," Billy said, near tears. The others all laughed.

Deall could hear Sullivan swearing at the mules, back toward the road. He wiped at his face again, using the sleeve of his right arm. The sword in the hand swung in glittering short arcs. He looked distantly at the men.

"Tell ye what, Billy," Keller was saying. "Give me that there locket, I give you the shawl. What say?"

Confronted, Billy stared doubtfully at the locket.

"Know somebody name Ellen, Saul?"

"Yeah—hey Saul, what your wife say about that? Thought her name was Mary Phelps."

"Make him throw in the drawers too, Billy Boy."

Left him to welter in his own excrement. Left him . . . Deall's mouth set viciously, and he clenched his teeth. The skeleton of the house collapsed into a fresh roaring burst, and cinders flew like flecks of light. As he abandoned himself to his anger, he could still tell from twenty yards that the locket was worthless. His eyes assessed.

These Ohio boys—he compared their boisterousness, their featureless, plow-handle ease, with New England reticence. They seemed infinitely more the democrats, but they violated his sense of the need to earn contacts of affection, to achieve personal identities.

The day's brisk chill overlaid by sunlight-yellow warmth reminded Deall of a New England day in the early fall. He had been born and had grown to maturity in North Liberty, Connecticut. The smell of smoke against crisp coolness heightened his memories: that yellow light of October which was almost reflected in the white houses across the Common, the red purple orange autumnal burst of nature which was morally reprieved by varnish-white houses and the chocking of axes, the coming winter cold as potent in the air as the cool blue smoke of the burning leaves. But here, the lateness of the season made the warmth a fetid softness, a moral reproach.

"Hey Saul, I don't know if Billy knows what women do with these things."

"Tell him to put 'em on."

Billy Gass was blushing furiously, studying the locket with desperate intensity. Joe Hostetler snatched the woman's cotton drawers from his pile, drawers trimmed with ribbon as light as the sky, and held them across his own waist, swaying.

"Only you got to imagine I'm a Southron belle, Billy."

Deall's wife Lucy had been a small, clear-fleshed, fine-boned girl, the miraculous product of severely rawboned parents. Her face had been shyly determined, with a pure round chin and straight nose—blue and white, all fair, pretty determination and slightness. They had grown up together in adjacent, square, clean-shuttered houses between big spruce trees reminiscent of time itself. He had stood outside a bay window, appreciating the fall of light upon Lucy through the three sides of glass panes, the sense of warmth within against the autumn chill. They had heard Theodore Parker speak at the Lyceum one October afternoon, and had taken a long "ramble," youthfully sober, scuffing at fallen leaves and probing Parker's statements about human perfection and purity.

In the months of their marriage, happiness and the indwelling of Eternity had seemed as palpable to him as porcelain (but dangerously so, so fragile was the vessel!). Deall's intensity was the inherited habit of applying spiritual questions to the world of experience. He still had the mental habit, a reflex of mind after Puritan generations and his own Transcendentalist adolescence and young manhood, of seeking to wring utmost truths out of physical perceptions. But the old Puritan sense of natural doom was absent: autumn trees were flaming symbols of life, the decomposition of dead plowhorses demonstrated nature's inexhaustibility and thus the promise of Eternity. The landscape was symbolic, ideal, and could become glazed by Intuition—downreaching granted moments of insight—which would carry a man far beyond mere reason, to the cataracts of all potential. During his marriage, there was amazing, eternal joy in squares of sunlight on the clean yellow floor of the kitchen, the image of virtue and completeness in clean wisps of hair upon china-white flesh. He was amazed by the soothing calmness of his rapture, and the future seemed open before them in blue and white shapes.

But all had been contained, had been vesseled so fragilely! At her temples her fair skin had always been darkly shaded with blue. When she spoke, it had always been with a determined, slight fold at the corner of her mouth.

Lucy died in childbirth. All her cleanliness, all the soft perspirationless joining of limbs, all gone in two days of mud on the staircase and the crablike trackings of ice upon carpets, and pain-filled, terrified screams. And the familiar, absolute patterns of consolation, stiff in sobriety, clothed in the eternal black odor of crepe.

Deall had given up his schoolteaching after six more months and had gone west.

Sullivan brought their mounts up. While the other six made shift to strap on their finds along with a brace of slaughtered chickens, Deall decided to wash his hands. They itched beneath the drying blood. The well, he remembered, was ruined. He thought of the water jug in the slave cabin, the only building (including the backhouse) he had not had them burn. He went to get the water, passing again beside the heat of the now flattened house from which mothlike cinders flew in spiraling droves.

When the War came, Deall owned a dying photographic studio, inherited from its dead previous owner, in Mount Union, Ohio. Waste, perhaps, of a Harvard degree. Perhaps continuing schoolteaching would have been better. But he was drained of intellectual enthusiasm. At visionary moments before Lucy's death, Deall would lower the volume of natural philosophy, breath-taken with visions of evolutionary progress. In them, he had seen spires of promise, rising amid golden shafts of sunlight and dim green shadows of life. But the world no longer coalesced in structures of hope. In daguerreotypes even scarlet maples beyond slate-green lakes lost their color, as the acid emulsion worked upon the wet plate, and became blurred motion and wintry grey, each line of the bark precisely visible. Life was filled with such reductive horror. To see the thing, he kept thinking, though it was more a habit of tone than a thought, to see the thing.

(She *ever* spoke with such affecting, such . . . virginal gravity. But do you not think there is real, physical evil in the world, Mr. Deall —I mean, John? Her hand swiftly, shyly upon his elbow, he had burned with fulfillment and pride, and their feet had scuffed up and turned over the fallen leaves, turning each leaf from dull autumnal buff to gold. Her death burst in the midst of recollection. He still felt it in his throat, the childbed become deathbed, his own hand-groping lies about their future family.)

He did both daguerreotypes and photographs. Collodion process was cheaper and easier, the "coming thing," his rival down in Newark kept telling him. But Deall still took daguerreotypic studies despite the cumbersome, unreproducible plates and the lost money, because he admired their flawless, infinite clarity of detail—lines in bark, myriad wrinkles beneath bright bonnets, eyeballs hard as stones.

And the news of the War had come early one spring afternoon. He had been in his own worn old sitting chair, alone amid the cidery light of his studio. He heard the first fretwork of untoward noise from the newspaper office at the end of the street, the thumping of feet, the first hollow jerks of rope before the bell began to ring, and he knew that it meant war. *It has come.* The fire bell began to clang in bone-splitting reverberation, but Deall sat as if frozen to the chair furze, his wrists tendonless along the cool wood. Thank you . . . Lord.

He treasured the moment. *If the world is ever to be a symbol, man must purge it.* His vision lost itself amid feathery tree branches. Where he had tried over and over to rebuild Lucy's image, he now saw slavery, in echoes of the old Hutchinson song: "Steeped in infamous corruption, sold to sugar-cane and cotton"—the stiff false sweetness of the cane, the fibrous seed-entangling cotton—"lo a nation's heart is rotten, and the vampires suck her blood." Other public evils, the degradation of the Irish, the loom villages, were defined by compromise and came from the wearying effort of men to live with one another. But *slavery,* the plunging depravity of human bondage, *slavery* was so unnatural and massive a corruption that it subsumed all others. There is no compromise, surely, about the owning of a man! And *They* have fired, it is said, *They* have fired! Be it upon *Them.* It had become instantly visible in the unleafed bright light of spring that this had all the shape of a granted test. At last, evil and all horror was wrapped up into one ball, one demonic apparition. (*All horror* included the blood which so slickly stained the hands of the doctor as he came down the carpeted, muddied front stairs—bright red on the surfaces, black in the foldings of his flesh.) Deall knew he had been singled out for horrific disappointment. But now this test had been offered for him in repayment.

With sudden knowledge of this immense symmetry of the event —all for him!—Deall had plunged out of the chair to the windows of the studio. Below him firemen sprinted through the clear light with copies of the *Mt Union Evening Patriot,* and the words *Fire* and then *Union* again, struck his eyes from the crenellated huge headlines of the sheet.

In the old man's cabin, Deall scrubbed at the itching with stale water. He looked about briefly, indecisive, for a towel.

—To this very morning, Deall had not found what he had expected, whatever action, whatever purging transcendent moment, whatever demonic apparition. As he dried his hands upon the old man's quilt, he was quietly chagrined at the memory of his heedless, mindless purity of enthusiasm. He had not lost himself in any single, cataclysmic moment of union. Rather, he thought as he walked out to his waiting men, he had dissipated himself in fragments—in enervatingly mundane responsibilities toward stamped papers and boxes of hardtack, in months of simple boredom and physical discomfort, in a few brief seconds of violent, formless, incoherent action.

Deall had believed that he should seek out the very crux, the key, of the coming war for the Union. With his shrewd assessment of strategic significance, he had enlisted at St. Louis, in Foote's river fleet. But even the June day above Memphis, with the rebel ram creaking and swaying toward them wreathed in fire and smoke and gap-jawed like a slaver's hell itself, even that had not culled from within him his personal climax. A gunner's mate, he had watched it coolly, his wrist on the lanyard of the thirty-two pounder, watched until he could measure brass stanchion and see the old flecking red paint and the webbed bagging on the cotton bales the rebels used for armor, all shifting and swaying in one fabric. Then one swift precisely measured jerk of the lanyard and his shot had penetrated jaws and cotton bales and old woodwork and steam drum within, blowing it up and shadowing the city bluffs with the steam cloud. It had been too sterile. At too long a range. He had itched to close with his human opponent, not stand a quarter mile away behind three inches of iron holding a lanyard dispossessed of potency, with afternoon light-bars shifting across the naked shoulders of his gun crew, and watch scalded men swirl amid the sinking remnants of treason.

Twelve-month naval enlistment expired, Deall had reenlisted in one of the three-year volunteer regiments recruiting in the early autumn of 1862. Colonel Price, who had owned a printshop in Mount Union, welcomed him into the 112th Ohio Volunteer Infantry, pleased at his modest refusal to take a commission. They had garrisoned Louisville against Kirby Smith, and heard of Gettysburg and Vicksburg while struggling through briered coves in East Tennessee.

The 112th had spilled out into their initiation down the slopes of Snodgrass Hill at Chickamauga, where concatenating rebel volleys—flame-burst sheets and vicious grey sleet—hammered them back upon themselves, gasping, words beaten back into their mouths. For twenty seconds every man Sergeant Deall looked at fell, gutted like flopping cod, faces blotted jawless, hands smashed. They were brigaded with two raw regiments and another Ohio regiment that had broken badly at Perryville. Moaning, whimpering, they blundered forward again with the regiment on their left screaming, "Wipe out Perryville!" Rebel yells curved through the smoke. Deall quickly discovered that lithographed promises of posturings and sword duels were lies: team desperation and comradely concern alone shaped his thoughts. He shepherded and cajoled his men into a sheltering tree line and got them firing. These things took the place of any personal quest. The brigade's own rifles blotted individuality out of the enemy.

At Chattanooga they had struggled fruitlessly over against Tunnel Hill—even breaking once when Pat Cleburne's men came sprinting around their right flank in a counterattack—while the rest of the Army of the Cumberland had hurtled up Missionary Ridge in the center. At Kenesaw Mountain, Deall's skirmishers huddled for five hours behind limestone outcroppings and wrist-thin pine trees, forty yards beneath the rebel rifle pits. Rebel volleys showered them with pine needles and burning paper. They could hear the rebel officers preen themselves and exchange elaborate requests instead of giving orders, but could do nothing about it, not even squirm about to reload.

During the last of the battles for Atlanta, their division finally left the rifle pits along Peachtree Creek and moved toward the sound of the guns. But they had been in column all day, jostling forward for a half mile, resting in the shade of blackjack oaks and brewing never-quite-ready coffee, then jostling forward again. They finally came to the battlefield far too late, in the evening after Hood had been thrown back for the last time. The rebel dead lay in splayed, entangled bunches in the slash pine and along the breastworks. Lice crawled along their open collars; they were boys in homespun shirts with rusting blood over their cheeks. They seemed half-starved. One dead, tall boy in a river pilot's cap was surrounded by a packet of letters from home which had burst open. Deall's men jeered at the semiliterate spellings and the lack of punctuation. Rebel wounded whimpered and crawled toward the light. They were not the vampires he had sought.

He had been at all of these victories, but he had not seen them —had not seen the moment at hand when his own exertions would help push the rebels into flight.

At last, at Jonesboro, they had vengefully whipped Cleburne's own division. Deall had been in the first line to cross the breastworks, eyes watering from the last discharge of a Confederate fieldpiece. The man he had bayoneted lay at his feet, blood trailing from his mouth. Deall had cheered with the regiment and shaken his rifle in victory. Five yards away, a wounded rebel major was holding his bandaged arm, frock coat casually open against the heat, sharing a canteen of bourbon with one of General Davis's staff officers. They had known each other before the war. "Blood is up in your boys, I reckon." The mildness decayed his personal lust. Ranked again, the 112th Ohio had pelted down the railroad after the rebels, his own footsteps jarring him into rude identity with his regiment, jarring him out of individuality.

He discovered he had a ferocious, purposeful identity only as a part of the regiment (he did not think the other men fully appreciated what their training and their superb system of supply did to them); he bellowed only with the others. Gass, the youngest man in his company, bragged that at Chickamauga the ol' 112th had taken the second heaviest casualties of any volunteer regiment in the Fourteenth Army Corps. Deall had doubted he would ever find summary foes.

Chapter 7

Last Monday, Deall and his men had stood by the roadside all day: a clear, bracing day after the rains, wind-whispery, clearing high clouds, the roads firm now, not dusty. Across embosoming light folds of the ground, he could see the shiny roofs of Davisborough —small town falling from a crossroads to a railroad depot.

The earth was sandy. It seemed high, risen like a loaf of bread from the Ogeechee River bottoms, high as the yeasty winter air. Small cedars stood out across the fields like grenadiers' caps. Deall's muscles had swollen, his hands twitched and clapped together with his energy. He paced among the men impatiently.

(Behind them, in the tawny winter grass, clusters of men had squatted all day over the Second Division's latrines.)

The brigade had stood along the roadsides as far as he could see, awaiting orders to march. To the east, the sunlight gleamed off leather cap brims and rifle barrels. Men rested on their rifles, expectant, blanket rolls over their shoulders, knapsacks bulging with salt pork and cardboard boxes of hardtack, tin cups on their hips. "What's the matter, Sergeant?" Lieutenant Boyer said. "You can't win this war by yourself. Relax."

The captain had come down the ranks. "They say we are to let the Twentieth Corps have the road first." The men settled down, unlooping their blankets and stacking their rifles. The Twentieth

Corps passed for most of the day: men with star badges on their caps and hats. Regimental and state flags were encased. Units were identical except for the badge colors of the different divisions. All morning, men came by with red stars, then about noon—Deall's regiment laconic, dozing, squinting up only as general officers passed—then about noon the badges became the blue stars of the third division, and in the midafternoon the white of the second. Three and four abreast the soldiers passed, strong-calved men like themselves. Eventually Deall matched a type of facial structure with each man in his company, from lantern jaw to bucktooth. Heavy government-issued brogans, light blue trousers, blue coat and black, round-shielded crossbelt, Springfield rifles sloped, trailed, slung, each man encased in his own lean, full-bellied self-confidence. Individuality was only a matter of rolled hat brims. There were even the same pets among the passing regiments: striding bright-eyed mongrel dogs, small arcane raccoons, fighting cocks. Deall saw in the passing column the death of individuality. Each man was of a type: sixteen types of faces (seventeen including harelips) by the midmorning, one of which would surely define any man.

Even the officers eventually looked the same. Their flamboyance took one of seven different forms, from red neckerchief and straw hat to impeccably collared, kepied blue and gold.

Wagons followed each brigade, stenciled massively with stars on the canvas sides. The road filled with mule dung and horse dung.

A regiment passed singing:

"Say, darkies, hab you seen de massa
Wid de muff-stash on his face,
Go long de road some time dis mornin',
Like he gwine to leab de place?"

Deall fidgeted. The soldiers laughed at the minstrel-show Negro dialect.

"De massa run, ha ha!
De darky stay, ho ho!
It mus' be now de kingdom comin'
An' de year ob Jubilo!"

Conversation drifted. "Well sir, then they invited th' boys from this next brigade to take their fill of the syrup . . ." "Molasses, yeh mean." "Yeah, th' m'lasses . . ." "The same they had thrown th' nigger woman into?" "What do yeh think! Of course, th' same!" "Hot damn!" "The very same. And then the big corporal he says to the man, Howd'je like yeh m'lasses?"

The staff of the Third Division passed, and bright-faced Negro women looked out of one of the headquarters wagons. "Look at what they found. By God, them staff officers got all th' luck. Hey, Lieutenant, did you see that?" An officer walked beside his horse upon which a delicately featured young yellow girl was mounted. Her flesh was the same color as the faded double stripe of gold on the saddle blanket. The officer talked with polite deference.

Among the wagons of each brigade Negroes walked. Most of them had coarse cotton shirts and woolen jackets. The women wore head rags. Their eyes shone: all their eyes were liquidly huge, they could not help from laughing out loud, capering backward clapping their hands, the young men whooping. Deall counted fourteen nursing mothers behind the wagons, stumbling over the horse dung. Orderliness was impeded. Despite his sense of personal reduction in the functioning of the army's machinery, he was still irritated at the way the Negroes blocked the march and tracked blindly through the dung. They seemed wiped with hunger; they carried no food, he noted. The thickly painted odor of their sweat offended his sense of precision. "We're gwine where you'se gwine, massa!"

"I expect General Davis'll turn 'em back, soon," Lieutenant Boyer said to Deall.

Deall could tell his soldiers were pleased by the flocking of the Negroes. They affirmed Union rectitude. But by midmorning the men were bored with calling to them.

"I don't see why'n hell th' rebels need dogs to track. I could smell 'em out myself a mile away."

Deall stood all day in his place among his men. The officers were spaced correctly along the length of the regiment. Finally sundrowse and physical contentment had eaten away at his energy. He sat listlessly.

Then the Twentieth had gone, and the road was clear except for trickling stragglers. Deall sat up. Sunlight lay mildly golden over the fields. He could see the far pine horizon and blue ridges beyond that. The road was clear. He stood up, strapping on his equipment. New energy filled him. He told his squad to get ready to march. Keller poured out a freshly brewed pot of coffee. Equipment rattled.

Lieutenant Boyer told him to hold his horses.

The captain came along. "They say we wait for the pontoons."

"What the hell?"

Keller asked him if he was happy—the coffee was all poured out. The men ate slabs of pork on pieces of hardtack.

" 'They say,' " Deall thought savagely. The men adored Uncle Billy Sherman, and the Midwesterners liked Jeff C. Davis, the division commander. But when foolish, frustrating orders came down, the men attributed the order vaguely to "them," suggesting faceless gods.

The pontoons passed for an hour: newly tarred, long-lumbered boats, creaking on their axle beds, swaying and dipping over the ruts. Bestrapped, recalcitrant swarms of mules hauled each. Looking back down the road, Deall could see the whole column swaying, the westering sun gleamed on the blond edges of the dipping, rising parabolas of wood, and the mules' ears were insect thick. Each of the pontoons was stenciled with the acorn of the Fourteenth Corps.

In camp just northwest of Louisville the next night, Keller was eager with news. "Men from the Hunnerd an' something Indiana said the pickin's was prime, yes sir!" Fires glistened all around them through the young pines. The fire-stained sky was murmurous with thousands of men. They cooked fresh pork brought in by the brigade's foragers. Through a thin line of pines the soldiers could see Negro women dancing and clapping—swaying of expensive petticoats, hands flashing orange in the light of a bonfire—with soldiers of the Ninety-eighth. The men around Deall listened to Keller.

"The off'cers? Hell no, their officers don't mind! And Billy Sherman don't mind, neither. It's what he has in mind. Feller from the Army of th' Tennessee told me at the spring. 'S truth. He wants to gut this state." Keller looked challengingly across the fire at Deall. "The only ones that mind are some"—he lowered his voice—"chicken shit officers *and others* in this God-damned brigade." He settled back over an ear of corn. "Only ones."

Two days later, Deall's company was detailed as foragers. On mules and horses and northward away from the line of march, they were as happy as schoolboys on summer vacation. They crossed the path of other foragers from the past two days. A mounted party of stragglers passed them on the road going back south, wearing looted frock coats and clattering with sacked booty, defiantly eyeing Boyer and the captain. The company's delight withered with envy. The captain and Lieutenant Boyer winked at each other and shook their heads disapprovingly.

"Mighty fine, boys," one of the stragglers yelled.

Corncribs were bursting still. They backed the wagon up next to one, and it was filled in an hour of shoveling and hefting. The house nearby looked half-fortified, so spaded and shredded were the grounds and gardens: it was a small log cabin on wooden pillars, unchinked so the brilliant day shone through the other side. " 'S been worked over," Keller said. He had used his ten-minute rest to explore. "Maddest four women I ever seen."

Even Deall smiled.

Plantation houses were disappointing: unpainted big boxlike cabins, more farms than plantations. Slaves tried to join the column, but the captain kept them clear. "Uncle Billy Sherman says for you to stay here. Only the able-bodied should try to join the column at all." An old woman clasped the captain's stirrup, shouting that she had seen the day of jubilee at last. The captain turned from embarrassment to annoyance as she clung to his leg, feet tracing flopping circles.

The afternoon was brilliant with cool light. They paused at a crossroads, laying out a half-dozen slaughtered hogs in the grass and waiting for the wagon to return from delivering the corn. The officers studied their maps.

To the northeast, across white yellow fields and over clear blue ridges, they heard a sudden rattling exchange of gunfire. Smoke rose like fine dusty haze, steam-white against the most distant blue ridge. The road ahead of them led directly that way, red clay and sandy shoulders across open fields. Wheeler had hit the foragers hard the past two days, out this way. "When the hell will they get back with that wagon," the captain said.

Boyer was more confident. He pointed at the hogs. "We have to find Colonel Price some fowls, Captain. Remember he said to find him somethin' beside hog meat."

Another volley rattled distantly, like a spray of pebbles against a board fence. "We ought to be up yonder lendin' a hand."

"Why don't I take half a dozen men and move off down that road to the north," Deall said. The road to their left ran through a pine forest.

"Hear that firing? It's pretty close. You best stay here."

The captain twisted in his saddle. Another burst of fire, sounding like revolvers. "We ought to lend a hand," Boyer said. The officers studied the eruptions of the distant ridge line. The smoke lay in a dim rising curtain. "Let me take twenty men and go lend a hand," Boyer said again.

"Hell," the captain said at last. "We'll all go."

Deall pointed up the road through the slash pine, to the north. "Let me take a half dozen at least and scout up that way. If there are rebel cavalry up there, they can cut you off."

The captain nodded quickly, disentangling his reins so as to free a hand for his revolver.

Lieutenant Boyer had said, "And if there aren't any rebels, find us some chickens."

The captain had said, "Take care of yourself, Johnny. Don't try to fight all of Wheeler's cavalry."

"No sir, don't worry about us. If we are cut off, we can join the column somewhere."

The first house they had come to had been worked over by foragers and stragglers. Someone had tried to build a fire beneath a corner of its ell, but it had burned out. Keller pointed out the roof of another house, in a tree line to the north. Deall could see it clearly.

"About two miles, I make it," Keller said. The seven men paused in the road. The land dropped into a creek basin before them, thicket and pine. The afternoon was darkening, the basin was chill with dusk and blue shadows among the oaks and the cypress trunks. Deall had the powerful sense that crossing that basin to the other gentle slope would be a strong, irreversible commitment.

The sounds of distant fighting were drawing far off to the east.

Gass looked nervously at the basin. "It looks like a good place for an ambush, Johnny. Wheeler an' his men. . . ."

Deall looked closely, steadily, at the fluid shadows. "Ambush, be damned." His horse whickered. Other things than the rebel cavalry were on his mind. "There are six or seven companies of foragers out that road. I expect they are fighting Wheeler's rearguard, if that. More than likely, they have been shooting at each other the whole time."

Keller smiled. "Yeah, Johnny. But it's like th' captain said. Better not try to fight the whole rebel army ourselves. We better not try to rejoin the regiment just yet."

Deall said, "Let us make for that house. Maybe we can find the chickens there." He looked perfectly serious. Sullivan and Keller both grinned widely. Deall looked around. "We can put up there for the night, or nearby." Shadows encroached, bringing deep red to the clay and gold to the grass and blue black to the pines. The country began to echo for him. The northern horizon was clearly undespoiled. Sheltered and confident in its safety. He would spend a day therein. He looked around.

"Want to stay out a day or two on our own, boys?"

Billy Gass started to whoop, but gurgled himself silent for recollection of Wheeler.

Now, on this fresh morning, they left the burning house—the house next over from the one Deall had seen yesterday night across the basin. A Negro had said there were two-three plantations just up the Coffinville road. This was the first.

They angled across the sunken, brush-choked pasture toward the road, away from the column of smoke. Except for Deall, they were in motley now, Sullivan hunch-shouldered in the frock coat, Keller in the beaver hat, Ted Coiner in a cape whose scarlet lining had turned fish purple with age.

"That wasn't much of a plantation."

"Poorest excuse for one I ever seen. John, you reckon that old nigger tole us the truth?"

"There will be a place, boys. We will get some better pickings soon."

Behind them, the rebel soldier's body lay close to the burned house, in the harsh heated sunlight between charred logs. When he had come out of the woods, bursting upon the Yankees and into Deall's trap, in that dew-fresh light he had seemed armored and enormous, his cape slung over his chest into a camail flatness, his hat plumed richly and the brim glistening back against the morning sun like a raised, golden visor. But now he lay exposed, thin lines of blood down a cheek gold-roasted by the fire. His face was pimply beneath the thin beard. The half-inch-wide rifle ball had slammed him on his back and bunched the cloak and jacket and sword belt about his neck. The boy's lean belly was cotton white. His hat was beneath his head, and its crease was rotten with sweat, and the jay's feather in its band was spindly like a fish's skeleton. His eyes were open and filled with dirt and hair.

"Johnny, you think that nigger was tellin' the truth, there's two-three more big places out this way?"

"I trust him, Philip."

"That is good enough for me," Winters said. "If there are any, you'll spot 'em."

Saul Keller, legs drooping down the sides of his mule, held out the beribboned drawers. "Maybe I can get these filled out, hey?"

"Maybe we will get some more silver," Billy Gass said to Coiner.

Ted Coiner, nervous about Wheeler and what they did to bummers, looked around at the smoke columns down the valley behind them. This house, and the one they had burned night before. The smoke from the near farmhouse rose from behind a silver green copse of pine trees at the curve of the road. All was red clay and sand and tawny gold and the heart-bright blue of a Georgia winter morning, except for the smoke.

Chapter 8

WINTER EVENING SQUEEZED THE LIGHT INTO A YELLOW BAND IN THE west. As Thomas Jefferson Malory looked down the eastern lane, the sycamores aisling toward the road resolved themselves into soft grey and scaling white. The fields were masked by dusk.

Malory sighed with comfortable exhaustion. He turned from the front door and walked back into the living room, hands clasped behind the old burgundy frock coat. Celia sat in the rocking chair before the fireplace. Her dress of faded, buff-colored wool was striped as mildly as a fine etching, and fell bell-like from her narrow waist and round high bosom. She frowned down momentarily at a tangle in her crocheting, tugged back one of her pagoda sleeves, freed the knot and settled back into the flickering patterns. Malory stood comfortably upon the hearth, warming himself, reflective.

The living room was not as funereally elegant as the parlor: it was varnish bright, with braided rug and a blue green afghan on the armchair. Heat spread from the curling fire out into the room, against his own favorite chair, a curiously rectangled piece which could recline, and against the old spindle-legged table between the windows, on which Malory's reading—prewar volumes of the *Southern Cultivator*, a deplored edition of Byron—was stacked. Only the oil lamp on the mantel was lit, adding to Malory's rich appreciation for the enclosed civility of the fire and Celia's genteel rocking.

Malory had scrubbed and pomaded himself after a day of harvesting. He had directed and worked beside Shorty and Uncle Mitchell in the morning, opening hills of potatoes while Tobe had worked Jade and Crisp, the three-quarter hand boy, in the cornfield. The day had been mild enough to bring fat perspiration across the muscles of the slaves. In the afternoon they had butchered six hogs which he and Tobe had collected from the pinewoods. Tobe had moved with ritual skill through the butchering, slathered with speckled blood and surrounded by the squeals and snufflings of the hogs. Their bristling brown flesh had burst red and purple beneath his knife, their meat hung like fruit clusters above smoking fires in the smokehouse.

Malory recollected hog-killing days in the past, when the darkies clustered with anticipation and the white folks watched from close-set benches, and the meat was barbecued and the chins of the black children were greasy from the fat-marbled scraps of the meat. Now with so few slaves, he worked from moment to moment, and no chance to lay out such huge and ingathering days. He sorely missed such seasonal rituals, which brought them all together, master an' man, white and nigger. But his delight was undampened: he had worked all day with his own hands and muscles upon his land, harvesting the literal and earned and God-given fruits therefrom. He had had them bow their heads beside the smokehouse at the end, his slaves ringing him in the coming cold, and had offered a brief prayer of thankfulness.

They had been slowed grievously by the lack of the mules and horses. All of the plantation's stock were penned far back in the Brier Creek bottoms, against Yankee raiders (and Wheeler's cavalry, truth be known).

"Well," he said, patting his flat belly in contentment, "may be that we will bring the stock back out tomorrow or the next day."

"Sherman really *is* passed, Mr. Malory?"

He had checked once more with the Home Guard in Coffinville that morning, before ordering hogs butchered. Sherman was not moving upon Augusta after all: "They now believe that he intends upon Savannah, Captain Malory." Any fool, Malory had said, could have seen that. Except Joe Brown and General Hampton (Malory had always known who "they" were, so tightly knit was the world he inhabited: to preserve this, he had supported secession). And I would have to add General Wheeler to that list. I am grievously disappointed by that man. But in any case, Sherman is gone. Frenzied as the Home Guard had been all week, issuing blunderbuss warnings and decrees about crop burning, their relaxation this morning had been enormous. And Malory felt tested and vindicated. He had himself spent three minutes packing corn pone and salt pork into a canvas bag. That would have left him the option, yes sir, of hiding out in the river bottoms. He was certain that the regular Union troops would not bother a paroled man, and the written parole was in his bedside drawer beside his old horse pistol. But he had his mind on the option, and that one packed bag was all the scurrying around he had done. He had seen the elephant, after all.

"He's gone off east and south," he answered definitively. "Ed Guice says the Louisville road is open again, said his cousin made the trip in three hours and did not see hide nor hair of a Yankee. The Augusta road is open, too. I saw the stage arrive myself." He chewed his lower lip thoughtfully, spread his legs, and said, "You know, his cav'ry is out to his left, from what I make of the reports. Had we tried to reach Columbia, I expect we might have crossed them."

The martial speculation touched upon reserves of experience which Celia could not contradict.

"Well . . . ," she said, absently. Malory rocked slightly, hands folded behind himself, waiting for something more. "Thk." She made a slight, bemused sound. He glanced down: she was frowning over another tangle in the knitting. He was surprised at her sudden seeming lack of interest. "Well . . .,"—the yarn cleared—"that is a relief, then."

Her hands were flicking again like soft birds above the nested knitting. She blew softly from her lip up at the loosened strand of hair. It accentuated her silence. Malory noticed it, with sudden puzzlement: beneath her concentration, she was glistening with suppressed emotion. Obscurely, Malory felt he should make some sort of comforting gesture. I . . . reckon she *was* worried. She is wore out.

He leaned down to reach for her hands.

Then he heard horsemen along the county road. Distant consonants of sound, click-clattering, came through the open front door.

Malory's hand was on hers: the flesh of her hand felt marble-sweet.

"Now," she said looking up at the fire, "who do you expect that could be?"

Malory left the living room, pulled the double doors closed

behind him, and went to the front door. His eye had difficulty adjusting to darkness. He stepped out onto the verandah. Dust rose spectrally between the distant tree limbs.

The clattering had paused by the lane.

This time of night, the lane would hardly be promising—a mere country lane dipping down between sycamores and crossing a creek. His heart expanded. For a pending moment, he heard horses snort indecisively. Dust-faint voices of men reached him across the quarter mile. Celia stood beside him, having reopened the doors into the lighted living room.

Malory ran back and jerked them closed again. But then he saw that fires from the kitchen were reflected on the wall of the barn and there were gauzily brilliant cooking fires in the row of quarters. They would silhouette the house, anyhow.

"God damn those niggers!" There was nothing else he could say.

The first sounds of movement seemed directionless. Then Malory heard hoofs rattling down the lane between the sycamores, and through the pebbles where the lane crossed the creekbed.

He stood bolt upright, motionless, hanging before the climax. Violently constricting indecision bewildered him. Deliberate flight was doomed; he could hardly reach the rear of the house before they were here, and Celia's presence entangled his legs and embarrassed him as though he were naked. Revolver and parole were upstairs. His hands closed, opened, thumbs flicked along first fingers. His eye kept pushing through the webbed sycamore branches. He looked the curious host, but this was because his face was frozen in his confusion. The air in his lungs was hard and cold as metal. Mounted men faded and reshaped themselves. Each second (impaled by immobility) inflated in importance: Do! Do something! His heart hammered at wrist and throat. The coming riders floated above a network of clattering sound among the tree trunks.

"Whoever could it be, Mr. Malory?" Celia's voice as brilliant as lamplight. "I must tell Phrony to put out some more places."

He could never get them both away!

Celia's plump hand was posed lovingly around his waist. She was the devoted, welcoming wife.

The horses were rising from the creek bottom, up past the slight bend in the lane (Celia, glimpsing his flaccid smile, not noticing the sheen of sweat, patted his waist with her enlooping hand). The horsemen came now up the left bend, rising chest-high before them—

up the slight left bend where the returning family carriage would take its gentle lurch to the left and he would awaken knowing the carriage ride was over, would raise his head from his mother's moistly pressed lap, would struggle up to see the candles in the windows.

They on my land.

Ferocity battered all other options. His teeth closed lightly, his hands shook twice, freeing themselves of hesitancy.

Celia bobbed on her toes to glimpse their guests.

His mind turned over weapons (They on my land, by God!), not thinking of odds but simply of what was available: shotgun over the mantel? No, it is still unloaded by God so service pistol then. He turned abruptly, so sharply her hand made a stripping noise against his frock coat, and started up for the pistol.

The riders were not more than fifteen yards away (they were something to be erased, expunged). He was already breaking his stride to lunge up the stairs when Celia said delightedly, "Why they are our boys!"

Malory turned back, just upon the stairs.

The riders were as dark and lank as plunging stone. They wore patriarchal long beards to their belt buckles, and their foreheads were clannish, the flesh pale as bone above the hollows of their eyes. Leather crossbelts curled about them like ribs, metal eyelets glinted beneath dank capes, and steel rattled upon them. Haversacks and bags hung over the withers of their lean horses.

"Yessum," one of them said. "Wheeler's cav'ry. Y'all got any food?"

"Why we'd be honored if you all would share our supper with us."

Malory stepped around his wife, back out onto the verandah. He could see that they were indeed Confederates by their lank ferocity. He looked at the looped, twist-necked bags by the men's saddles. One of the soldiers stilled his horse, and a bag scraped against his saber with the chinking sound of small metal.

"Of course, man," Malory looked directly at the one who had spoken, a sergeant by the pale stripes on his stone-dark coat. "You all step down."

The man looked back silently.

"Captain Thomas Jefferson Malory, late of Perry's Georgia Battery. My wife, gentlemen."

Celia nodded politely. Malory stiffened his back, head arched back against the velvet collar of his frock coat. Patrician elegance slowed and iced his speech.

"We are at yo' service."

The horsemen looked among themselves with indefinite meaning. In the blue-dark light of dusk, Malory could see the dry large eyes of the men, like musket balls beneath their foreheads. Ed Guice said his cousin from Sandersville said Wheeler's men were as bad as Sherman's. Recollection of the toddies they had been having at the Coffinville House fused with the memory. The bags on the horses bulged. The spindly, sagging horses dripped dung on the lawn. Malory folded one arm formally behind him, his eye patch as aristocratic as a heraldic bar. Celia's welcoming tinkled brightly.

The sergeant did not identify himself.

"Well, then, *Cap*tain. I expect we need some food. An' we got a shot man here"—one of the soldiers was supported by the one in the black cape—"mought need some rest."

Celia gasped with sympathy.

Malory kept looking directly at the sergeant. "Of course, Sergeant. Sycamore is at your complete disposal."

"Whatchee say?"

Celia clasped her hands endearingly. "Why boys, he means our home . . . our whole plantation!"

A soldier in a faded jacket took off his wide-brimmed planter's hat. "Thankee, ma'am. We don't mean to be no trouble." He held the hat over his chest and looked at the stiff sergeant. "I 'spect I'll dismount, Joe."

Two of them rocked out of their saddles wearily. They helped the wounded man down. He made a grating noise with his teeth as their hands slipped along his sides. Celia stepped down instinctively, small hands rising to help.

The sergeant hunched, shrugged, and got off his horse too.

Then Malory stepped forward another formal stride.

"Tobe! Jade! Come round here! . . . Is it safe to show a light, Sergeant?"

"I reckon." Malory watched him. The sergeant still had his hand on the butt of a revolver thrust in his wide belt.

"Bring a lamp, Tobe, and see to these horses." Tobe returned silently, already blending into the darkness before he turned the corner. "Jade, go tell Phrony to lay out three more places at the table. Tell Zeenie to make up a bed in the corner room upstairs . . . she knows the one."

The three men looked blankly among themselves again: the wounded man hung between the two privates. The four soldiers remained by their horses' heads. They seemed held in the thick odor of sweat and yellow dung and leather. They looked up at the housefront, soaring whitely above, massive in this dark. "We just as soon eat out here," the sergeant said. "And we see to our hosses ourselves." He folded the other hand over the pistol butt.

Celia began with a pleasant, ironic chuckle. "Non-*sense,* Mr.—? . . . nonsense, Sergeant! We would be honored to have some of our gallant boys share our evening meal with us."

Malory could not tell whether she knew the menace confronting Sycamore. The men before them were dry and emaciated and hilltop lank. He could not see their faces clearly in the dusk, and the sergeant's hands were still on his revolver. But Celia's brightly traditional welcome fit smoothly with Malory's own assertion of hostship and tradition.

"No thank you, ma'am," the soldier in the pale jacket said. "We used to eatin' outside so much, I don't b'lieve I'd know how to set down to a meal that was on a. . . ."

"Nome," the sergeant said. "We do just fine out here."

"Mr. Malory, you just make them come inside! An honest soldier never need feel ashamed in *my* house, I hope!"

Tobe had brought the lamp out. Bright yellow light pushed all the shadows behind plastered columns and hanging baskets. Celia looked luminescent as a pearl, beaming at the soldiers. They looked at her with familiar deference. The one in the jacket looked moistly, turning his hat in his hands.

When he saw their faces in the light—beards wispy and long as moss, eyes large and dry, the flesh curling up under their jaws, their necks long and creased—when he saw their faces, Malory was certain of them. They were beat out, desperate, alone, and licensed. They were weighing the plantation, keeping up the forms of politeness to the woman (as they would whatever) but looking for anything loose—horses, silver, food, liquor. Malory recalled he had met Wheeler once, in preparation for the artillery march into Tennessee: a youthful, spare little man. Malory measured the brushed neatness of Wheeler's beard sardonically against the weary dried faces of these men.

"No ma'am," the sergeant began, "we too soiled. I 'spect we might *soil* some of your *things*." He emphasized great ironic discrepancies.

Malory took the lamp from Tobe and held it up so that it did not circle them, so that they could see him the clearer, instead. Gristmill and country store, slave market and political campaign, military service—he had a full education in dealing with Southern yeomen whites. His head tilted back in deliberate, pleased, aquiline frankness.

"Well gentlemen, your modesty does you great credit, yes sir, does you great credit. Spoken like true soldiers, by God. But no Southern soldier will take a meal at Sycamore without sitting as honored guests. And by heaven, if you men eat out here, we will join you!"

"See, boys?" Celia said. "But the places are already prepared at the table, for all of us." And she half-curtsied, turning to gesture the way into the hall.

"Well, boys, if that's the way the little lady will have it," Malory said with masculine chagrin, "I expect that is the way it is goin' to be." And he held his free hand out toward the door, too.

The soldier in the faded coat laughed and came toward the light. The sergeant shifted wearily to his other foot. Codes of traditional respect reassembled themselves.

"Yes ma'am," the sergeant said at last, "thank you kindly."

"Now, I don't believe I caught you boys' names," Malory said, as they came up into the lantern light.

"I'm Sergeant Joe Wolf, cap'n. Of the Ninth Kentucky Cav'ry. This here's Ed Wolf, Tim Riley, and that there's Billy Suggs."

While he spoke, Tobe slipped back down the steps to tend the horses.

In the light, now, they became individuals. The Wolfs had spare tight heads upon gaunt necks. Riley (the man in the faded coat) grinned with pug-nosed, Irish readiness. Suggs was the wounded soldier.

A horse whickered behind them. Tobe's flat soft voice said "Whoa, dah, easy boy." The sergeant's opening face creased again, and he swung about so suddenly his scabbard struck a pillar. "God damn, nigger! Where you goin' with those hosses?"

Tobe's face slid into rigidity.

"Let my man there take the horses, Sergeant. You all come on in for some food and a warm fire. Your man there needs a bed."

The sergeant looked steadily at Tobe, whose eyes were on the ground. Then he turned back. "Well, Cap'n . . . ol' Bill does need some tending. But I'm goin' to leave Eddie with the horses. Not no nigger."

"As you please, Sergeant."

They helped Suggs into the house.

Once at the cherry dining-room table, unbelted from the leather and metal, surrounded by the rich smell of the carpet, warm, eating with chin-bobbing ravenousness balanced by outsized clumsy decorums, Riley and the sergeant became two exhausted boys.

Though it was stiff and uncomfortable and menaced by grease, Malory still wore his frock coat at the table. He made the food circulate with thoughtful concern. He cut his ham minutely and down-speared a small chunk. He poised the fork carefully, while Joe Wolf sucked in a glistening fat-strand.

"'Where did your private get shot, Sergeant?"

Celia looked from her end of the table with bright anticipation.

"Long side the ribs, Captain. Shot like a hog. Bled like one, too."

The sergeant canted the oval dish of beans in his left hand and raked them onto his plate with the spoon. The pole beans fell wetly over the banked corn bread and rice and purple pink ham.

"No, Sergeant. I mean, whereabouts?"

Celia looked up brightly once again, her momentary, decorous frown gone.

"Oh . . ." He chewed ham and bread loudly, paused, pressed the whole napkin over his lower face and sucked back through his teeth, glanced youthfully at Celia, then wiped more gently at the corners of his mouth. Riley never raised his eyes from his eating.

"Back up the road 'bout ten mile."

"Sherman's men? That close?"

"Nome. Wasn't Sherman's army. They pulled off due east two-three days ago. It was a bunch a' bummers, eight I reckon. Lieutenant Dano he took us right down on 'em. Got hisself killed, and near got Bill and me both killed too. I took a ball th'oo my hat."

"How did you come across them, Sergeant?"

"Well seh—" Belly full, he stretched his legs, eyes on the fire and narrowing with youthful shrewdness. "We got run over near

Looeyville. Drove down on the Yankee foragers, and they come back with a whole brigade. We got off th'oo some swampy ground." Beneath the tangled beard, Malory could discern youthful, fluid outlines: good ol' boy, brought up on hard work and the Bible and fierce self-reliance. But the easy line of confidence which should have extended through both of his eyes was fractured. "Killed half Cap'n Barret's company, seemed like. We damn near got caught . . . that right, Timmy?"

"Yep."

He continued in the easy musing recollection. "Just come across five a' these bummers yesterday morning an' shot 'em up, so when we saw these, we come down on them too. Only they saw us first, I reckon."

"Do you think they will come this way, Sergeant?"

"Nossuh, Cap'n. But maybe they might . . ." His eyes were liquidly opaque from staring at the fire. He drifted boyishly, the sharp young line of his chin clearly visible under the roots of his patriarchal beard. "—Maybe they will. Well seh!" He sat upright.

"Well seh! Thankee, ma'am. I best get these boys outchonder and get some rest. We been on the move two-three days now."

"Oh, boys! Won't you stay and have some brandy with us?"

Malory narrowed his eye. Damnation! He felt misgivings. She don't know these men. Then he remembered that the whiskey had been buried in the cellar, along with the silverware.

"Why, men, I am afraid that Mrs. Malory has forgotten that our liquors have been well buried, against Sherman's coming. I am afraid it would . . ."

"Do you know, Mr. Malory," Celia said, smiling in pretty embarrassment. "I believe I forgot to attend to the spirits, 'midst all Sycamore's valuables. . . ."

Tight, tiny lines grew about Malory's compressed lips. He felt like snapping the napkin down across the table edge.

". . . but all the better, for these boys, and for our own reputation in the Bluegrass," Celia was finishing.

"Well ma'am, I reckon not. We been on the move two-three days."

"Oh but you poor boys . . . come now, just a touch!"

Malory watched his wife's fervent hospitality, trapped himself now in the social routines. The planes of his face were stiff. She don't *know* these men!

"Yessum. I'd like somethin' warmin'," Riley said.

"Well, yessum, it would be good."

"Well fine!" She beamed. "Tobe! . . . Tobe!" She struck the tin spoon against the clay pitcher, made only a thunking sound, then struck it against the tin cup which had held the sergeant's acorn coffee. To its faint plinking, she called again. "Tobe . . . Tobe! These servants, I swear, Mr. Malory." Phrony appeared, her face sheened with sweat. "Oh Phrony, do you know where Tobe is?"

"He down to he house."

"Well. . . ." She looked helplessly at Malory.

"Ah, hell!" He slapped his napkin down on the table. "It *is* still in the sideboard, I presume?" Celia smiled demurely. "Listen, Phrony. You know where the bottle of brandy is? In the side cabinet of the sideboard?" Phrony shook her head, good-natured, mystified. "You know where the sideboard is? Beside th'—Good! Well, look in the cabinets of it till you find a bottle of brandy and a bottle of sherry and some glasses, and bring them into the parlor for these men and Mrs. Malory." He closed his lips tautly.

Celia smiled at their guests, her flesh clear and warm in the light of the chandelier, dimples beside her pale lips.

The soldiers were both shoving their blouses back down and stretching after the meal. "This way, gentlemen." They went through the living room and then crossed the hall, ignoring the piled leather and metal of their gunbelts.

The parlor was mauve and purple with close-set elegance. It was always shuttered against light and movement, as sign of established leisure. A marble-topped table stood beside the door, a big family Bible the color of veal resting upon it. A long, striped couch faced the fireplace and two plumply stuffed matching chairs were close against its thighs. The whatnot in the corner bellied into the room, filled with artifacts of old enthusiasms. Bookshelves were lined with dusty, bescaled, bound volumes. The candlelight was absorbed by closely grouped furniture and the hearse textures of velvet and silk and fringe. A settee stood catafalque-grave in the center of the old carpets. The fire loomed. A piano was a long dark box, its teeth as yellow as a slave's.

Phrony brought in a tray with two amber-full, antique decanters and four carved glasses.

"Will the gennelmens . . ." She gestured back through the house.

"What?"

"Will the gennelmens . . . outchonder?"

Malory frowned and shook his head in puzzlement. She wheezed and smiled at her inability to express. The decanters rattled on the tray.

"Will the gennelmens . . . what's back outchonder . . .?"

"You mean the one on watch out back?"

"Tha's the one." She chuckled good-humoredly. "That's the one I mean. Will he take some?" The glass rattled annoyingly.

"He can have my cup," Malory said. "Set it down on the table, Phrony."

"Nawsuh," said Joe Wolf. "He is my brother. I tole Pap when we left, I said I'd keep him out of harm's way."

"What ol' Eddie don't know won't hurt him none."

"No suh, Cap'n, I will take his."

Celia laughed merrily. "Why, Sergeant, that's downright mean! I believe I will just take him a sip of my own."

"Suit yourself, ma'am," Riley said, "but I bet ol' Ed would rather have a full one for hisself."

Pouring a glass of sherry for Celia, Malory laughed quietly at that. Then he poured two fingers of brandy into each of the glasses and they all raised them, the soldiers to look at the liquor with the light behind it. Celia planned a toast.

"To the Bonnie Blue Flag and those that fight beneath her." She shook her head into the last words.

They all drank, the Kentuckians holding their chins up and rolling off all of their drams at once. "Ahhcchh that's good," Riley said. Wolf grimaced, showing his mottled teeth and the lines in the tight flesh of his cheeks.

"Another drop?"

"Why yessum."

Malory, still swirling two thirds of his drink, felt the swallow acidly. There was a growing ease about the two soldiers, who now settled themselves on the couch, Riley with one boot tucked up under his leg. They beamed with pleasure. He looked back and forth from under his eyebrow while he poured the next drams, trying to sense whether they would become mindless or genial.

"Where are you boys from?"

"Kentucky, ma'am."

"Yessum, Barren County."

"Near Glasgow," Riley said.

"Why, Mr. Malory, don't we know someone from Glasgow, Kentucky?"

"No dear, I don't believe we do."

She frowned at his tone. Malory was relieved that they were now sipping the brandy, pursing their lips and swishing it between their jaws. So he said, "Why, weren't the Hunts from around there?"

"Why that's who! Do you boys know the Jerome Hunts? She was a . . ." She held one short finger beside her lips. "Let me see, a Laud, I believe. From Columbia. South Carolina."

"Nome."

"Hunts? Nome. We were from a ways out of town. Cove Hollow?" He looked back and forth.

Malory changed the subject. "How long you boys been in the army?"

"Why Joe and me been in since August and sixty-two, Cap'n. Ed come on down last year. Billy Suggs, he's from Tennessee."

"Sixty-two? How old were you when you joined, then?"

"Both seventeen, Cap'n."

"Oh, you gallant boys!"

"Well, ma'am, you cain't let 'em come down here and tell a man what to do."

Celia straightened on the settee, bosom rising proudly. "Exactly what Mr. Malory always says. Isn't that true, honey? 'States' Rights must be preserved.' "

Malory was embarrassed, seeing the phrase lie in the candlelight across the creased, weary faces of the boys. "We-ell . . ."

But Riley nodded in eager translation. "Yessum. Cain't have them stirrin' up the nigger. They blame well ought to leave us alone. Nome, they cain't tell a man what to do."

"That's right, boys," Malory said.

Joe Wolf repeated it again, all his young exhaustion curling over the words so "they" became palpable—so "a man" became all men seeking honest, decent livings, hard in the best of times. "They ought to leave us alone. You cain't come down and tell a man what to do." In the outspread words, desperately possessed ways of life were menaced by callous foreigners.

"Why, do you know that they makin' *sold*iers out of th' nigger,

Cap'n?" Riley began in sober, incredulous outrage. Old knowledge repeated over and over with the same bewilderment with which it had been first told and first heard. "Why, do you know they givin' the *niggers* guns and tellin' em . . ."

Inevitably Phrony came into the room toward them, indeed already halfway across the room at Riley's explosive *niggers*, wheezing, one more useless glass on the big tray. They were all silent, Malory's one eye looking at her through the bars of his tented fingers, the soldiers watching her steadily, her flesh wobbling beneath the grease-stained dress and apron. Joe Wolf half snickered, snorted; Malory glanced.

Celia was determined to be irrepressible. "Hurrah, hurrah, for Southern rights, hurrah!" She shook her bunched shiny curls and got up lightly, and as Malory shook his head toward the extra glass and Phrony good-naturedly said, "Whatchyou say, Marse Tom?" she crossed the floor and settled dramatically at the keyboard of the piano. The soldiers watched her mistily. Phrony chuckled "Lawdy, Lawdy" at her mistake and shuffled out of the room again. Celia began to play "The Bonnie Blue Flag," first a naked bar, then singing

"We are a band of brothers, and native to the soil,
Fighting for our liberty with treasure, blood and toil . . ."

The soldiers joined in, warmed by the brandy and Celia's brightness.

Malory watched them all, Celia at the center of the boys' attention, her cheeks gleaming in the lamplight, the men in profile singing: Riley nudging Wolf at one verse, Wolf elbowing his hand out of his ribs, both attentive when Celia canted her head at them to start another stanza:

"First gallant South Car'lina nobly made the stand . . ."

But as Malory looked, smiling with a politician's clarity, the room seemed to cluster about them all. Something about the ceilings, the cornices, seemed almost alive, lost in the purple and black. The hangings of the room sealed the singers off in the corner by the piano, in the darkness of high chairbacks and plush brocade and dark wallpaper and tasseled tablecloths. The windows gave back no pure reflection, but distorted and bubbled the light in whorls and loops.

"We gotchee one, ma'am. 'We're Sons of Ol' Aint Dinah.' Do you know it? Let's sing it for her Joe. . . . Naw, not all the verses." Again they fumbled on the couch, Celia beamed, and Malory, detached and trapped in his limited vision, felt the room clustering, all the old heavy wood and close-placed high narrow furniture and dark walls, until he shook his head and rubbed his single eye, and looked again.

The singing carried upstairs, where in an old four-poster bed Bill Suggs—not a relative, a Tennessee boy, forgotten—lay on the quilt and breathed slowly and laboriously. His eyes were brilliant against the one untrimmed lantern, and they watched Zeenie, who sat over against him, implacably bronze, her own eyes bright upon him. His hands lay crossed over his chest, and hers were crossed in a shield of bone and bronze flesh across hers.

Chapter 9

CELIA CAME BACK DOWNSTAIRS AFTER VISITING THE WOUNDED SOLDIER. The gallant boy had been asleep, and Zeenie had been watching him with pleasing intensity. She was carrying a handful of clean rags and an old cotton shift.

At the bottom of the stairs, she could see Malory through the living-room window, just touched with light. He was smoking on the north corner of the verandah, and watching out back toward the barn, where the soldiers had encamped. She could tell from his stance—head thrown back, hands clasped—that he was angry.

She was simmeringly furious in turn. She knew she should have buried the spirits, so there was a biting edge of guilt in her anger. It was poignant to her that the liquor which had given the evening its edge of elegance, which had produced the grouping (as in the old times) around the piano, that this had been available only because of her carelessness.

Well I only have two half-worthless nigger women to help me. I spend *hours* on my knees, burying things in that cellar. . . .

No, she would tell him, I will *not* pour it out. She went into the parlor to collect the two decanters. Heaven knows when we can get more. And though you will not admit it, you know that it was fine that we could offer the boys a drink.

The one time in years, the one time when I can host a group of gentlemen in elegance and sociability, and he will spoil it! (The most lavish entertainment she had ever offered was for their houseguest Colonel Whitgift, as he was recruiting his regiment. All of the men from the county who were going to be officers had gathered, singing these same songs that evening. Her fingers had melded the keys, she had smiled coyly, masking a new song in flourishes while the men—hirsute, sweating, long wrinkled trousers falling from frock coats and roundabouts, hands cradling whiskies—poised themselves to anticipate the opening lines.) The one time in years I can host a group of gentlemen the way *I* was taught, and he will spoil it.

She collected the decanters on a tray, moving with moody silence. She hoped he would come in and accuse her. Hard angles of rebuttal rose in her throat. The one time I can enjoy myself as proper mistress of Sycamore, and you are determined to spoil it. She honed the phrase, moving past the front door. He did not come in. She walked slowly down the hall, holding the tray with the decanters and the rags.

Unused, the phrase was endlessly ramified: her small chin tightened. She put the tray down on a table in the hall, and went into his darkened office to get the trowel. No, I will *not* pour it out. I will bury it myself, I already have the things I need. Your mother (that stony-faced image was useless, so revoked) . . . Sycamore was fabled for its richness of entertainment. Your family used to entertain all the time.

I cannot imagine why you have changed.

She saw her form in the pale reflected light of the south window. She ceased feeling for the trowel and looked at her dim reflection. She knew she had been lovely, gracious, desirable. Dimpling smile, the control of men's attention which spread from her fingers on the piano keyboard, her mischievously arched back—to her these were the ways of making the world into a livable whole. She knew well that otherwise all would be stale pompous talk about slave trading and politics in one corner, and women gossiping in the other. So she had been trained: men, left to their own devices, would stiffen the air with cigar smoke, would inflate moments of social ease into diatribes. Culture, society, the very elevation of man above the brutes would suffer. She fully saw herself as civilizing. Most men eagerly appreciated women's gift of civility. She bridled at Malory's capriciousness. "The house needs a young lady's touch once again, Celia honey." Hogwash.

The boys had certainly enjoyed it—particularly Riley. She had caught Riley's moist eye on her twice during the meal. Malory had glared ferociously at her throughout. (What *is* the matter with him?)

It could not be that Mr. Malory was jealous?—she could not deceive herself with that attractive thought. All she knew was that for some reason, he was determined that she should not enjoy herself this one evening.

Mother, aunts, friends had all trained her to see husbands as merely large-grown, sexually mature boys—still vain, simple, egotistical, and dependent upon a woman's wiles for the simplest management of practical affairs: a precise, if sometimes wearisome equation. But she could not anticipate or categorize her husband's actions, as you could a child's. She struggled fruitlessly against his moodiness or his overmastering sobriety. She blamed the complexity of it all upon the damned War—or, tonight, upon him.

The impact of hundreds of small bruises reappeared. She could not remember all of the specific events, but her sense of injured identity made her see him as a foe. I even did it all for him. He is always concerned about the poor whites, he tossed and turned for hours about whether he should report those Vardaman boys who were hiding in his swamps from the recruiting officers. She had done her very best to inspirit those gallant Kentucky boys—for his Cause (what did *she* care about States' Rights, for heaven's sake?)—and he had sat there scowling the time. If I had not been on the porch, I don't believe he even would have invited them in!

The whole *world* of this place, she suddenly thought, must revolve around him! That is the whole truth. He will be either bored or sullen anytime it don't. With the thought Celia felt a surge of easeful ascendancy: a mature resignation in it. I am afraid that that is just the truth of it.

She was able to put him out of the forefront of her attention at last.

Celia found the trowel in the office and put it on the tray beside the decanters. Through the back door she could see the soldier sitting on the kitchen gallery, outlined by kitchen fires. Malory had even tried to pick a fight over that, for heaven's sake! "Trust as you will, Sergeant, I don't want any of your men prowling around shooting at my cows and my niggers." Cloak and belt over his arm, the sergeant had looked right past Malory. "Eddie, get on back out there like I told you, an' keep an eye open." "You put a man anywhere on this place, Wolf, you put him out at the road, not back at my people's quarters." "You ain't seed what we seed . . ." "And I do not plan to see it, neither." She had intruded effusively. Why, sweetheart, surely he could stay out on the gallery between the kitchen and the house. He could sit right there. There's even ham left over, if he gets hungry.

Celia balanced the tray against her hip, and opened the door to the cellar. She picked up the lamp from the table beside the cellar door. She knew she had glistened before the boys. She recalled Riley's moist long looks at her. (What would it ever be like to be courted by him?) She imagined the friendly, snub Irish face, shaven at her suggestion, bewildered and puppied by her charm. Sex did not suggest itself, but the shapes of power over a man, multiplied by caste difference, did. She imagined springtime situations in which he implored.

Wolf had said it was the best evening that they had had since leaving Dalton. Cold comfort, and his eyes had remained dull. But his brother had been rapt in adoration when she had produced a glass of brandy for his gloomy loneliness: "Nome, I won't tell Joe."

She held the lamp in her right hand and the tray with the decanters and trowel in her left. The tray clinked perilously, and she paused at the top of the cellar stairs until it rested smoothly in her hand. The presence of the gallant boys warmed her. "Nome, I don't, but if you was to sing the first verse, I 'spect I could come in on th' chorus." The sergeant had said it was the best evening they had had since Dalton. Even with the cheap flatware, and the cracked furniture of the dining room . . . perhaps that was quite a compliment indeed.

Her whole world seemed more habitable now. Her mind lingered upon her new self-confidence. The glassful of sherry warmed her thought. With confident swaying steps, she went down into the cellar, which last night she would not have entered alone. Her steps made the lamp throw arabesques over the piled furniture and barrels and across the whitewashed wall.

The door behind her closed suddenly and she gasped. But she arched her back against her own timorousness, and the sharp jut of fear dissolved from beneath her breast.

The smoke-sharp smell of wet stone, and the grainy smell of sunless earth: dirt and old, rich, dust-stiff fabrics leached the freshness out of the cellar.

The north wall, ahead of her, was whitewashed and made of fitted brick. The other three walls were of rough unmortared stone, and old candles, bottles of tonics, waxes, and old rags were stuffed and shelved among the stones like prizes in a spider's web. Barrels of clothing, wooden boxes with remnants of tile, old oil paintings and portions of furniture were stored in choked disregard.

Celia placed the lamp on the ground beside the whitewashed wall. It rose in a tulip-shaped arch of light. She daintily spread the old chemise down and knelt upon it, her hooped skirt ballooning up behind her. Her heels were demurely pressed together. Celia began to dig at the earth with the trowel.

Then the first splurging of enthusiasm began to cost her. The earth yielded only in rabbit pellets of grainy clay. As she scraped, the sherry-warmed confident determination began to cool.

She shrugged her shoulders. A small knot of weariness became wider: became then a hollow sense of exposure to whatever was in the cellar. Conscious of her back, she became dankly conscious of the room behind. One strand of hair loosened and fell before her eyes.

As she dug, she refused to deal with the fear in the small of her back. She knew if she glanced around, the piled old clothes would seem formful, which would give her a needless spasm of fear. The small spade chinked against the brick of the long white wall. The earth floor was unnaturally dull and heavy-textured, corroded by lightless patterns of moisture and burrowing insects.

Celia's spade scraped dry earth off the white brick. This wall was an anomaly, a long, tediously whitewashed section of brick, the dominant, lucent fact of the cellar. It was clearly not part of the foundation walls. Childhood legends about Indian tunnels, ghosts and secret passageways (much cherished in Coffinville—Celia had known of the wall long before her first glimpse of Malory in his corduroy coat) accumulated about the fact that the wall went down only six inches below the level of the cellar floor. The bricks were held in place against frost and water seepage by the wooden pillars of the house frame, their own thick compactness, and the layers of whitewash. But immediately around them the soil was sandy, loose, and came away in easy, rotten trowelfuls, like diseased gum about a tooth. You could dig down beside the wall, slip things beneath it, pack the earth back, and so solid looked the wall that they were safe from discovery. They had already buried their silver dinnerware beneath it (a two-dozen-piece set of London and 1859 manufacture), and the pure silver table bell from Charleston, six old antlered sterling goblets, Malory's christening cup, and Celia's own indifferent personal jewelry. (Malory often insisted, but she was never one for jeweled ostentation.) These things had been waxed, wrapped, and buried narrowly beneath the wall. But the decanters were much larger: the sherry she had had enlarged her confidence, but almost immediately the true *size* of the task became apparent.

The dark elaborate background began to impose more and more nervously. She rocked back, frustrated that the burial was taking so long. She raised her eyebrows, sighed, and began to dig again, nervously exaggerating her gesture. "Well" she said softly, and shook her head.

The wall at each corner was built against one of the supporting columns of the house—immensely solid oak posts, potent with the obvious exertion of their planting. Beside the one now to her right, Celia had fancied the ghost yesterday morning. She considered giving up the chore. Let Zeenie do it. She dabbled the trowel in the earth, ears filled with the buzzing sound of her own intense listening. Her eyes became weakly moistured from staring at the trowel, so as not to look out of the corner toward the post.

The dull fear began to sharpen again. She heard absolutely nothing, but the smell of age seemed to have a sound. The bricks were pasted with all the threat of human antiquity.

Then the smell itself became centered just beyond her vision, off to her right. It pulsed there, slight variations in odor, slight repeated inflections. Something was waiting. Celia tried to smile with bright living courage, and she cocked her head charmingly in an assertion of mindless, heedless self-contentment. The gestures were palpably wooden. *Something* . . . all of her energy went into kneeling up and back upon her heels again, and feigning interest in the small shallow hole. The shape of light on the brick in front of her was comforting, but its edges dissolved into the dark.

All right, look to the right then, silly! She turned her head to the right—blinded by the darkness for a full second—in confident expectation that she would have to smile ruefully at her own childishness. As the eyes found shape in the black, the smile was already growing, a dimpled indrawing of the mouth.

She was looking right at the thighs of a Negro man: cotton cloth, the loose-woven cloth of old slave issue bulging now with leg muscles, legs rising into potent groin, one dark immense hand along the right thigh. All was articulated, all moving toward her, and Celia bounced herself up into the light (and one foot inlaid with yellow twisted nails moved into the ground-cast circle of the lamp, then stalkingly the other). Its head was yet in shadow—while Celia stood tiptoe for the soaring scream lost somewhere in her airless lungs, her heart already a blue sharp weight—its head was yet in shadow but there was a deformity to the trunk, only one arm, one hand, the lamplight still climbing up toward the face of the coming man while Celia's own voice climbed impossibly past her throat. She leaned back, stood trying to catch it with her mind and will, mouth wide open, eyes fixed upon the growing coming figure, back of throat aching from speechlessness, hearing her feeble thin sound a—ahhhhahhh. Celia stumbled backward on tiptoe voicelessly, flesh shaking with the cool helplessness of its exposure, seeming to shrink away indeed from her own corset, all the while watching the light touch the man's fawn-colored coat and open neck, and her own mouth sagged into the very mask of horror.

And then her hoopskirt brushed over the lamp, and it canted the light away from the man, down along the wall, and fluted in its own orange death. In its movement the man himself—Did he OHHH DID HE?—seemed to move with catlike speed into the piled boxes and old possessions so that the darkness away from the wall filled with his menace, and Celia stumbled against the wall holding her hands in front of her face, then plunged to turn toward the steps, only the smell and sound seemed rushing toward the steps too in the darkness and she pivoted blindly toward the steps yet away from the Thing and so pushed herself brutally into the wall and down.

On her back, she could find no air: then she was crawling on her elbows (—nightmare? nightmare?) while her hoopskirts belled up entangling and exposing her, and her hands could not push the petticoats down over her legs and her head arched helplessly and the whole dark room gathered into one coming shape which she saw out of the corner of her eye, then lost it as she looked full at it, but hear it she could, hear it coming up over then coldly down upon her warmth, and finally there in helpless, entangled terror on the floor her voice surged back, coming strangled on the intake of breath but then exploding outward, "AaAAA—HELP! Oh *Help!*"

She floundered away against the wall again, falling once back on her rump, then dragging and elbowing herself back against the white wall until she stood upright, kicking with one soft boot into the darkness while her hands flew about her, uncontrollably, hitting herself with plump frightening batlike violence, while she shrieked and shrieked and the darkness scuttled and whirled at her feet.

Then in front of her the thing rose. She could hear its rise, the push of muscle articulating flesh and the spraying rhythm of its breathing—hearing this beneath the sound of her own screaming. A limp coldness embraced her waist, her hands fluttered outguessed and were entrapped themselves, and then the cold moved up along her back and she felt a long boneless arm climb beneath her ribs then over her breast searching for her mouth.

When the door opened and light burst down the steps and Malory stood there peering into the darkness and casting the lamplight over her—and she could see around herself at last!—she found herself still wrapped in the coldness: but this from the ancient ebony-black curtain which in her thrashing she had pulled from the near barrel and which was now enwrapping her, dank black tassels along her cheek, the cloaking curtain pulled tightly around her and chilling her flesh along side and elbow. And she was in a pool of shattered glass and brandy, still (even with consciousness returning) kicking violently against the splintered decanters and earth. Scattered pellets of glass and earth sprayed against the massed old furniture and clothing.

"Celia!" Then he came down to her, and holding the lamp closely upon her stopped admonishing, and as her huge eyes looked at him with horror Malory—not Celia, but Malory—said with descending exhaustion "Ohhhhhh" and almost slapped the lamp down and caught her against him, holding her until the beating and childlike ferocious terror exhausted itself against his soft encircling.

Celia shrank, in sobbing helplessness, against his shirtfront —even so, dimly aware of Zeenie and Tobe peering down from the stairs into the cellar. And her initial gasping effort to catch her voice was to tell Mr. Malory to make THEM go, make them Go!

He looked around him with sudden fresh pity and then realized it was the two on the steps. "Get out of here, you two."

"What's the matter, Marse Tom?"

"Get out of here, Goddamnit!"

Celia watched the two Negroes reascend the stairs, Tobe ahead, old green coat and gallused work pants and bare feet rising past her vision—until the bare feet stopped and rocked back against a violent impact of sound. Zeenie fell back, arms against the stairway wall, her eyes flaring out of her bronze face. Tobe's bare feet were outsplayed with a cavalryman's boot between them. "All right, nigger . . . this 'en th' one, ma'am?" Celia could see the soldier's calf tighten with exertion, shoving the slave back against the wall.

"No, they didn't do anything," Malory said.

"Naw?" The soldier's leg was still taut, Zeenie still staring up at him. "Naw?" Then the leg straightened back up, but Tobe didn't move. They heard a moment of fiercely significant breathing, then the weight of the soldier creaked back upon his own heels. Tobe stood stiffened for a moment, and then slipped away from the wall and went out. Zeenie still stared up at the man. "You too. Come on up out o' there." She dropped her eyes and slipped on up, and the soldier named Ed Wolf came clattering down, leather gleaming in the narrow light, his hands opening and closing in rhythms along the short barrel of the carbine.

"What's the matter, ma'am?"

Malory was looking down gently at her streaked face, still pressed against his shoulder. "What's the matter, honey? . . . Sweetheart?"

"Ummnnn. . . ." Celia shuddered, catching up her breath. Her face was a wet mask of terror. She seemed trapped in a tight web of chilled flesh, which quivered and shook and burned. But even as she shivered will-lessly, Celia was aware Why, it was *me* that that happened to! And in a lucid, ascending moment she felt vindicated and released, her fears proved true, her self-absorption justified. But then she slipped back helplessly into a visceral moan, and nestled against Malory's shirt.

The men looked quickly around the cellar, Wolf holding the lamp up higher in his right hand and shaking his carbine into a comfortable one-handed hold.

"Who was it, honey? Who was it?" Malory whispered into her ear. "That's all right. We're here now. . . ."

"I . . . I . . ." Her voice soared helplessly again, while Wolf probed into a clump of old curtaining with the barrel of his gun.

Celia took a gasping, collective breath and began again. "I saw it again, M-mr. Malory." She timed the descent, for her voice then collapsed into sobs.

"Saw what, ma'am?"

She shook her head helplessly.

"Look around will you, son? Will you see if there is anyone down here?"

"Yessuh." The lamplight shone down over his beard and cross-belt and butternut jacket as he moved behind the pillars and down the false aisles of boxes and old furniture. Celia thought in another lucid ascent that his home-dyed butternut was the same as the fawn jacket of the ghost. Above her, Malory's one eye glared metal-bright (struggling as ever though to disentangle forms, certain only of the terror of his wife), infinite concern in the very ridges of his face.

Wolf crashed heavily against something in the corner. "God-damn it! Son of a bitch!"

Malory took a step over toward him, but Celia clung to him. "See anything, son?"

"Nawsuh. Ain't nobody here." He reappeared, eyeing the darkness with some caution, but a sly kind of suspicion appearing between his eyes. "Whatchee say it was, ma'am? A nigger?"

Celia shook her head fiercely and wrestled down her breath. "Nnn-no. Um, maybe. A ghost, M-mr. Malory." She breathed measured deep drafts. Her voice glistened with sudden confidential assertion. "It was our ghost, Mr. Malory!"

Wolf rolled his head. "Ghost?" He squinted.

She nodded violently. "In . . . in a brown jacket. Almost like yours."

Wolf thumped down the carbine's butt. Celia was amazed at his disbelief. "I come down here to hunt a ghost! *Hell!* . . . if that don't beat all. I got to get back outchonder on that porch." He stumped noisily toward the stairway.

"The lantern . . . leave me the lantern, son."

"Oh, yeah . . . here ye go. Don't let the buggers getchee."

Wolf clattered back up the stairs. "Thought it was the niggers, but 'y God, a *ghost!*"

Malory's arm still enfolded his wife. He held the lantern up, his back against the white wall. He tried to see patterns in the darkness, which re-formed as he moved the lantern from side to side. The cellar had a stale deadness, an immobility. Now even the shadows which leaped capriciously to the lantern-swing were flat things.

Of the ghost, he could make no sense, could not even envision possibilities. But he knew his wife's terror was genuine, and held her to himself and away from the darkness. And he gave her a comforting squeeze because of the soldier's violent disbelief.

As he stared into the darkness, feeling the whitewashed bricks at his back, Malory again sensed that the darkness increased. As before in the parlor, it began clustering like a tide, like time, around them. But he put this down to yet another trick, an insult of physical science because he had only one eye and it was weak. He took his arm from his wife's side to squeeze proportion back into the eye.

Then he led her up out of the cellar. The air freshened into winter nighttime. Each step was a disburdening of old stained odors of earth and cave and antiquity. When the door to the cellar closed, they stood in warm, dry, light-sheened mildness, and the air was like warm bread.

Zeenie was leaning against the rear door. She straightened.

"What she want?"

"Where's Tobe?"

"He gone . . . what she want?"

"Gone where?"

"Just out back."

"Well, bring Mrs. Malory some vinegar."

Zeenie went out toward the kitchen, moving through patterns of white and black, brown and bronze, and then ghostly dark. Watching her with pale timidity, Celia still clung to her husband, anticipated the touch of the vinegar to her wrists, and framed her first sentences for Mr. Malory. Why, it seemed it tried to . . . force me, Mr. Malory. This with eyes lowered in demure innocent incomprehension.

Chapter 10

JADE WAS ALREADY DOWN THE ROAD, TOWARD FREEDOM.

The southern night was full of dark blue and black lozenges of movement and fear, beneath a deformed big moon. But Jade moved around the bend toward the Louisville road with familiar confidence. To him, the chill mild night was rich. The piney red landscape was now velour soft, the sunlight become aqueously pale moonfall. To his vision, spots of nighttime earth pulsed with significance. Spread of sycamore branch, murmur of creek water down to swamp, slight shiny hump of clay road-shoulder, these stood like paragraphs: sixteen mile to Louisville, th'oo this way to the Husband place, this way past the spot the patroller take his smoke at. Each meaning was rich with physical experience: purchasing journeys to Louisville, lovemaking with Savannah from the Husband plantation (all one long summer, years since—place overgrown now), panting, hammer-hearted respite in the creek, just having beaten the patrol back to Sycamore land. The night was Jade's only Georgia landscape.

The side of his head still throbbed fiercely, the only thing in the world about him which was red and angry instead of cool and soft. His vision improved at night. The sun-squint and shuffling dull truculence became resilience and skill. He could spot-hear the patrols at distances, could detect angle and masking nighttime branch, could delude dogs (though they had used them only right before the war—not any more). He walked with catlike consummate ease, nursing the side of his head.

His anger at Marse Tom had been hammered down by rude, reflexive fear. The whiteness of the world was as implacable as a closely shoved white wall. For Jade as for Tobe, for all the slaves, it was the central fact of life. Powerless, fatherless generations separated him from believing in the necessity of revenge upon a white man.

Jade's individuality lay in small circles between neighboring plantations or post-curfew cabins, petty thievery, stealing chickens, visiting women, evasion a matter of habitual familiarity with overseer and owner. But even in these narrow circles terror loomed, as if embosomed in the mild Georgia sky. He hesitated to steal in sunlight, even if alone in the middle of a humming field. And assertions beyond those narrow realms were breathtakingly doomed. He had heard the story of Nat Turner in Georgia terms: bands of omnipotent unmasked white men lynching niggers for example. (He could dimly recall how his own childish curiosity had been transformed by his mother's slap into terror equal to her own. Torchlight had flared in the cabin rows, Old Master had argued heatedly outside: but had black men really hung from trees like so many dead wasps?) All beneath this mild Georgia sky. His own boldest efforts—one abortive flight, coming at ol' Boozer one time with a hoe—had resulted in lopsided white vengeance.

Flight could change it, flight to a land which he dimly saw as emerald-bright with difference. But white men could change it, too. He had not fled since the War began. Linkum was going to change it. Flight seemed unnecessary. He had waited confidently for the arrival of Linkum's army and freedom. He had planned to be right there on Mist' Malory's place when that day came, for there would surely be revenge. (Jade imagined freedom in terms of reversal, not negation, so constant was white implacability. He—and Phrony and Crisp and Juno and June, his own blood, bound into a loveless family—they would be the ones lounging in the parlor, sleeping upstairs in the big cool bedrooms, sitting by the dazzling light of the chandelier or breaking it, having food prepared with massive exertion for themselves. *Somebody else* doing the planting.)

But he had overheard Marse Tom talking with the soldiers,

and he knew that if the Yankees were going toward Savannah now, they were going the wrong way, the wrong direction. Freedom was descending away from him. It had made the pain in his head flame up, and he had bitterly headed back for his cabin. But when he had turned the corner of his own hut, he had collided with one of the white soldiers, and the white man had rammed him back against the log wall and looked at him out of feverish fierce eyes, looking back and forth from eye to eye for a reason to kill him, and then had turned away.

Implacable, inescapable.

He had stood then in the humming indecisive evening, the night coming with chill, waning light, white as a wall, over the pine ridges. His head had been lamming viciously, his fists closing and unclosing. He had pivoted and trotted down to June's cabin, thrown open the door, and as she rose openmouthed to face him, he had hit her with a blow all the way from his shoulder, feeling for an ample second even his headache fuse into the blow, transmitted into the very back-jerking of June's head. Her impact knocked dirt from the dried chinking as she hit the cabin wall.

Gasping on the floor, she pulled herself back instinctively from his feet. He moved for her again, lips set in a tight line, almost grinning, feeling the anger arch his feet, preparing to stomp on the glistening flesh of her forearm, and feel the pain there too. Marse Tom come in now, we got a dead buckra and a dead nigger, I don' care! . . . "Hear me, woman?" He balanced catlike on the balls of his feet, toward the drag of her body along the flat pine floor. She pulled herself against the wall while he calculated, and managed to push herself halfway up it when his knee caught her midsection and she dropped wetly.

"Hear me, woman?" She crawled again, feebly. "Hear me?"

The door opened behind him. Rage surging through him, Jade pivoted. He was so intensely prepared to meet Marse Tom that he was amazed to see no face, but a green corduroy coat and pale undershirt where Marse Tom's face would have been. But then as he stepped back against his initial impetus, he saw Tobe's yellow eyes, and the outline of his broad head. The expected white face outlined itself against the black, then vanished.

Tobe could whip him, he knew. Had whipped him, five times at least—and once for beating on June in fact. But as Tobe stepped toward him, the stifling sense of the omnipresence of the whiteness choked him.

"Well, driver. What you want? You want some, man?" Jade wished he had a knife. He waited for Tobe's calmly vindictive approach, for the measured stride and easy battering skill. But just let me get his th'oat. I get his th'oat, ain't no . . . He circled, stumbling over chair and bumping against the bed.

"Well driver! Marse Tom send you in here?"

But Tobe looked steadily at him. When Tobe was exercising his driver's authority with force, his face took on a somnolent intensity like Marse Tom's: their eyes took on an identical glaze, while the flesh beneath gleamed. Tobe took on the lineaments as well as the fact of granted white power. He added this to his own intuitive, lynx-quick black strength. Jade was always infuriated by the combination, and always mastered by it. He circled, awaiting his beating, but he grew puzzled.

Tonight Tobe's eyes were blank, wearied, a look which Jade had never seen. He straightened out of his crouch. "Hey, Tobe? Hey? What you want?"

"Don't beat her no more, Jade," Tobe said.

"Who gone stop me?" He crouched again. But Tobe ignored him and walked over to June and knelt beside her.

"Ain't no call to whip her."

"Ain't? And ain't you seen what she done last night, after . . ."

"What she going to do? Hunh? What she going to do?"

"Well, nigger, I'se . . ."

"What any of us going to do?" Tobe's head was turned from him, bending over the whimpering June. Jade tightened his hand on a leg of a stool, to bring it down on Tob'es head. Tobe said, over his shoulder, "Why don't you clear out, man?" Jade released the stool.

Tobe rose and turned back to face him, by the spittling light of the fire and one poorly trimmed lamp.

"Clear out? And you the head nigger, th' damn driver. You got the patrollers outside?"

"Ain't the driver no more."

"Who say?"

Tobe stared at him.

"Who be the new driver?" he asked. "Who the new driver?"

"You want the job, Jade?" For the first time since Tobe had entered the cabin, Jade felt an edge enter his voice.

"Shit no, nigger."

"May be we won't need one. May be the Yankees come."

"What you know? I heard 'em say they was gone off towards Savannah."

"Some of 'em ain't. Some down at Louisville. You heard that, too?"

"It so easy, why don't you clear out, too?"

"They's people hear I got to mind."

"So you *ain't* de driver, *hunh!* Shit you ain't."

"I don't mean them, man."

They both stood in the warm yellow light, Jade slab-skulled, lips loose and puzzled, Tobe looking calmly at him. "What you going to do for 'em, hunh?"

Tobe said nothing. The air around them ached whitely with frustration.

"But you telling me to clear out now?"

"Whut any of us going to do, here? Get out now, while you still got the chance."

Jade had looked down at the ground. His one earlier escape had been a blind emotional reaction to Overseer Springer's demands during the '58 cotton picking: then Trump had cajoled him. It had ended before the whip. Now he looked at it soberly, breathing in against the pounding of his fight-prepared heart. *Flight, freedom*—these appeared to him now in terms of raw chaos, of sunlit white men with ropes and whips and hounds, of mean unknown niggers, of limitless land, flat and strange, but beneath white men. Where I go? Those emerald-chunked images of freedom were insubstantial as heat haze rising across burned fields. Familyless by law, ignorant and dispossessed by law, no human ties kept him here: but familyless, ignorant, it was only at this place that Jade had identity, that he knew the limit and shape of his power—visible in these seconds of slack-jawed contemplation of pine floor simply as his ability *to whip any nigger on the place except Tobe, and have any woman unless Tobe wanted her first* (and Tobe, seemed like, never did). And the *place* itself: the angles behind the board fence from which a man might slip and not be seen from the overseer's quarters, how the work gangs would find the southeastern acres blue with dawn fog when they reached them, which slant of earth a man should save for picking in the afternoon. Even the simple appearances—pattern of pine stump and privy path, cypress swamp, the notch in the distant eastern ridge visible from his cabin window on cold clear Sunday mornings—these references of color and size and smell allowed him to orient himself, the only ones that Jade had ever known.

In flight, Jade saw the echo of chaos. His conception of himself would not measure against that whiteness; it burst like soap bubbles in his imagination.

"Look, man. Yankees down the road at Louisville. Ain't never going to be closer. You know the way down there. Now get."

Mistrust of other blacks was inevitable, and Jade narrowed his eyes. "But *you* ain't coming."

"And I done told you why."

"Who you got to mind about, here?"

Tobe again said nothing, but looked down at the ground. The horror for him was worse than that of a flat unknown land. Equally familyless by law, equally dispossessed, Tobe was not ignorant, but had been educated into responsibility—toward his white masters, but also toward the other slaves. Tobe needed no contemplation of physical distances to feel the horror of losing his identity. He felt it in the slave cabin itself, where June's blood curled across the old pine floor.

They ain't all, good God A'mighty. They ain't all.

They ain't even better.

It was not his brutal reduction from head driver to nigger on the cellar stairwell—though that did tone his thoughts with the bitterness of rebuffed compassion. (Niggers don't ever put themselves where they see a white man's embarrassments, where they see a white man's shame, or a white woman's troubles. I 'spect I should have remembered that. I 'spect I won't forget it again.)

But, it was not that, curiously, that this night so shaped his thoughts. Through the mottled south window into the parlor, Tobe had seen Phrony when she had entered the room with the other cup. Passing by outside, he had seen her shuffling and dull-witted, grinning with kindheartedness, fetching the extra cup. And he had seen the poor whites look at her with bone-hard hostility: heard the fall of voices, the unembarrassed, arrogant sudden silence. He had seen Marse Tom and Mistess with their flat-faced, ill-concealed impatience. He thought of this, principally, on this evening: of Phrony's well-meaning, wheezing, antique simplicity, not of Marse Tom ordering him out of the cellar, or taking June, but of that defiled simplicity.

"Clear out, man."

For Tobe, the implacability of the white man had always assumed evident shapes, enviable, confirming, and beyond the realities of raw power: the clean angles of their houses against the grease and innate heat of black cabins, their clear intricate speech against black successions of vowels, their convoluted generosity, their loyalty even to their slaves, the smell of their stirrup leather on a cold day. Tobe had been educable and bright. He had overheard Marse Tom brag to his father, the old Master, "I swear I believe Tobe has much *white* blood in him. Listen to what he told me yesterday." He had envied and aped clarity, white paint, definition.

Tobe had always been sullen. The inflectionless, meaningless, grease-thick black joy was debasing. Before whites, he was rigidly careful. He grew to be closemouthed. He knew who he was: the best driver, for a black man, in Georgia, his Master said. Maybe, just the best driver.

Tobe's bitterness had always been directed toward the frustrations of his own life. Marse Tom had been his friend and had always treated his blackness as an accident, it seemed to Tobe; as a mere turn of fate which one man would hardly hold against another. To be worthy of such friendship, as an adolescent Tobe had washed himself every evening, scouring at his flesh with a coarse rag, and then scraping the black earth from beneath his fingernails with a pin-sharp knife point. Now, empowered, he took measured vengeance upon black runaways who infected the orderliness of the plantation world: and upon black irresponsibility, amorality, the covert blind hatred of all whites, the vicious beating of their own children, the abandonment of women—things which confirmed the inferiority of his own blood.

But over the last two years, the whiteness of things had begun to fray. They were losing. Had not he seen that himself, twice, on two battlefields? Hadn't he seen them whipped bad? (Bitterness crept in. *Even the high strutters among 'em whipped bad!*) They acting it. On the neighboring plantations and in Coffinville he saw them acting with increasing, selfish frenzy . . . equals in vengeful self-pity to any slave who had lost his garden patch because of a weak fence or an early frost.

They had been rich in arrogance and accidental power, not in any kind of inevitable superiority. An unfamiliar, gleeful, hysterical mood overtook him at moments, Give *us* the damn guns, hunh! Give us the damn guns this long time, see who be the boss and who the slave now! He exulted in the irresponsibility. But he felt as if he were the victim of some gigantic prank, some tomfool trick, whose implacable results were all the more unbearable.

His bitterness turned toward individual whites, first toward Old Master who had bought him, and then toward the old overseer Springer, the only white man who had ever taken a lash to him.

But as yet, the memory of Marse Tom's age-ten smell was still strong on him, when he had shared the same bedroom even if he was on the floor pallet, and they talked about frogs and snakes and pranks of their own. And winter days, like this one, when together they broke up the ice-rime in clay-banked creeks, in the rich colors of a winter morning. And once when Marse Tom had pulled him out of the back branch on a faded November afternoon and wrapped him (shaking bluely) in his own coat. And when Marse Tom bought him Sarah for his wife, from the Husband place.

Sarah had been light-skinned, as light as cream: her forehead had curved so richly, so purely, he had prized her profile as though it were a medallion. Her nose had been almost white in purity of line. Old Marse Husband had raised her as a maid for his twin daughters and she spoke with a refined, clear lightness. Old Husband had kept her in a room in the cavernous old brick plantation house and away from the slave quarters of his plantation (for he encouraged his slaves to breed freely so they would increase his holdings, since he was a poor farmer at best. The Husband women were notorious, their men dull and dispirited, but mean). Buying Sarah had been Marse Tom's first action after the burial of Old Master—"she cost me damned near a half my profits, Tobe ol' fellow. But she looks like she's worth it. At least, she'll keep you straightened up, I expect." Tobe knew she had cost that much, because he had heard the men arguing and dickering for two solid hours over a bottle of rye in Marse Tom's study.

And he could remember how Marse Tom had stayed all night

beside them, the night Sarah had died of the autumnal fevers. He remembered weeping, eight years gone by now, against Malory's old green corduroy jacket, and Marse Tom's iron-rigid arm sustaining him against grief so thick it liked to choke him. He knew that Malory's intensity of concern had invested Dr. Gazzo, who had had tears in his eyes at the end, wiping the blood from his bleeding box and running his shirt cuff over his eyes. The memory was so massive upon Tobe that he saw himself as at a remove—a dark figure shaped by the arm of his master.

And then tonight, he had seen Marse Tom tenting his fingers carefully, pursing his mouth and frowning when Phrony entered the room. One of the poor whites had snickered: Marse Tom's eye had flicked to him in swift acknowledging agreement. One motion of the eye, that single unpatched eye.

Jade left. Tobe stood motionlessly while June reassembled her bedclothing and sniffled against the rim of blood in her nose.

He saw the faces in the parlor, the lean harsh faces of the soldiers, the way Marse Tom's eye rose, and Mistess fidgeting and then walking over to the piano, while Phrony shuffled out. Phrony: splayfooted, panting slightly from her kindly, mistaken gesture (which had taken that old, fat, faithful woman all the way from kitchen to parlor and then back out to the kitchen), but only chuckling to herself at her own slowness, and *not knowing!* Not knowing the motion and the contempt behind her back, only still beaming, still helplessly loyal.

And she don't even *know* it. And me the driver.

And me the driver! His imagination played over a world rich in hidden promise, but with throat-tight anguish in its very brightness. I didn't know, Lord. I didn't know.

But for Jade, it was enough that Tobe had told him to run off. Omenlike, it propelled him through the spaces between the cabins. Even if he was running into a horrifying void, he had been told to flee by the one man who had controlled him night and day, with impassive, brutal certainty. When Marse Tom and Tobe had come back from the War, Jade had grinned up lazily from the barn shadow, still stretched with comfortable ease, sure that Tobe would not drive them like a white man. But Tobe's efficient rage was even more potent, Tobe had kicked him with captured Yankee shoes so hard his ribs stung for a week after, while again his sweat as ever dropped onto the alien Georgia earth. The sting had been less enraging than the exposure of his comradeship, the way his easy conspiratorial grin had been not only ignored but outraged.

And yet here was this man telling him to escape. So rapid and incredible was the shift, the change, that he did not question or even stop to reconsider Tobe's own refusal, but with surging desperation saw the Yankees once more as reachable, not coming but at least available, if not for long.

Born on this plantation, never more than fifteen miles away from it during his life, Jade wrapped spare corn pone in a blanket, sure of no glittering realm immediately beyond, not deluded by thoughts of any, confronted with a wild abyss of possible hope and more likely nightmare, where maybe there were the Yankees and it was man to man but more likely there would be white patrollers and vicious blacks and the small measure of power and control he had here would be voided. But, alone, he prepared himself and then slipped out of his cabin, cautious against that white soldier on the kitchen gallery. He looped the manor, going through the side garden to avoid the barn where the other soldiers were. No need to dodge Tobe this evenin'. In ten minutes he was in the lane, under the shadows of the sycamores.

He settled back contentedly into his familiarity with the fifteen miles between here and Louisville, which he did know. He picked up his pace, once in the road, anxious that the Yankees would not leave before he found them. Mouth slack, eyes seemingly vacant of intelligence or even care, his feet knowingly and surely splayed across, felt, arched from the ribbed dry roadbed and the jutting sandstone rocks and cold night-purple clay.

Set out now, content with activity and the moment, Jade did not reflect or puzzle. But round the third bend and now a good mile and a half from the house, he did wonder with sudden stabbing suspicion if Tobe had been planning something. He going to get it all for hisself, hunh? Then his eyes clouded. But how he going to do it without me? How he going to do it with only Shorty and old Uncle Mitchell?

So he mused, stepping softly through the blue landscape, nursing the side of his head. In another hour he was six miles from the place, beneath the old Husband plantation and keeping softly to the road edge on the other side. For ten minutes the road curved widely around the grounds of the old house, deserted and free of menace to Jade, but he still kept in the half shadow of the roadside. He could see moonshine off one small high windowpane lost among elm branches.

And then, stepping wide and all thought of Tobe forgotten, it hit him, why Tobe had done it, in the second in which from the roadside straight ahead of him the man with the gun appeared.

The man appeared so soundlessly, with the rifle barrel glistening in the moonlight, that Jade's whole body stiffened in his horror, the landscape still familiar but the moon humming, then he dropped on his knees in the clay as the man—coming or forming as much out of his very black imagination, the ghostly brutal white man in the high beaver hat from some realm beneath actual night—as the man approached him, beaver hat sign at once of whiteness and arcane savagery, the gun swinging in openmouthed silver arc upon him. With the vast inbred suspicion formed by his whole time on earth, even in the midst of his terror, he thought Tobe done it for the reward! On his knees, witlessly hearing the moon hum, his lower lip shining like the gun barrel itself, Jade waited, flesh stinging, his blood thickening against the sting of pain.

"Where yeh goin'?"

"Ah—Ah ain' . . ." Jade shook his head, slobbering.

"It's only a nigger. . . . Get up. Come on, Uncle, damn it, get up! . . . You're free at last."

Chapter 11

DEALL HAD HAD THEM BUILD THEIR CAMPFIRE IN THE CORNER BETWEEN the wooden kitchen wing and the brick house, where the firelight would be sheltered from the road. They had raided three farms during the day. Sullen, reticent poor whites had squatted on their galleries while the soldiers prodded among the boots and broken bottles in their garden plots, stole their hams and killed their chickens. All devout Unionists. At the onset of twilight, this tall brick house, dormer windows visible among elm branches, had promised disclosures.

But they had found it deserted. Deall paced the wide, echoing, empty rooms. They smelled of old wood. He heard his men upstairs. Their footsteps clattered and squeaked, the abandoned wooden floors of the house moving in minute striations as they went from room to room. One of them broke a glass pane with a distant clear sound which hung like broken water in the emptiness.

Deall walked into the old drawing room. There were light spots on the peeling wallpaper where pictures had been: rectangle, rectangle, oval. The wallpaper had been yellow gilt and it had faded to buff beyond the vacant rectangles. Two pens and some yellowing, numbered paper slips were banked in an empty bookshelf. When he lifted one of the quills, it left a rusty long rectangle on the old wood. Auctioneer's leavings, he decided. In the corner behind the door, he found an old split-backed copy of *The Dramatical Works of John Dryden,* Vol. II. It had been used as a doorstop when they moved the furniture, and was squeezed into a canted shape.

Pocks on the floor and rubbings along the wall showed where furniture had once stood for a very long time. Against the fireplace was a gilt-painted wooden frame, containing a loose cutting from a printed sheet:

> All of the loyal residents of Coffinville and Coffin County join in lamenting the loss of Colonel Edward Preston Husband, killed while leading his brigade against the enemy at the recent battle at Sharpsburg, in the state of Maryland. Our correspondent reports that the Colonel's furious charges had seriously discomfited the enemy, when he was struck down instantaneously by the Federal Artillery, while rallying his soldiers for yet another assault. His men immediately avenged him upon the battery. *Dulce et decorum est, pro patria mori.* Coffin County's loss is Georgia's, and the South's. Colonel Husband is survived by his grieving widow and his son George Harding Husband, and his daughter, Mrs. Cates Tomlinson of Augusta.

Deall noted that the colonel had been a state legislator and a leader in securing the South its true rights through secession. He snorted at the pomposity. Avenged immediately upon the battery. There must be no one of the family left alive, if they leave such an elegant memento. A black ribbon had once bound the frame and a pasty remnant clung to the glass.

He tossed the frame into the old fireplace and looked around him, absently stroking his thighs to rid his hands of the dust and stain. His scorn dissipated in the quiet, long light of fading day. The uncurtained windows left the rooms strangely illumined. The wooden floors glistened dully, uninterrupted by carpet or furniture.

The house was stained with the antiquity of evaporated pretense, he thought: then, he thought, of evaporated life. Shapes of its inhabitants would not come to his imagination. He made guesses about where the furniture had stood in this room.

Strangers had carved their names into the walls of the dining room:

Ranse Boozer slept her one nite '63	I BEEN HERE TOO C.A. VARDAman Aug1863

A stick figure hung from the gallows:

The chikenshite provomarsHAL.

In the front hall he met Hostetler and Keller, back from their search through the upstairs rooms. Hostetler was wearing an old black riding jacket, which had been wadded away for so long it was harlequined with fading. Keller showed him a drawerful of scrapbook clippings and a small hatbox filled with broken toys: a doll's head rolled back and forth among wheeled metal horses and carved miniature furniture. "This is all we came across, Johnny." Deall took the clippings into the light fading through western windows. More mementoes: the death of George Harding Husband, much lamented by his comrades of Cobb's Georgia Legion: Cates Tomlinson, late surgeon to the Fort McAllister garrison, dead of camp fever.

The grey emptiness dragged at him. His vision was too limited by the scarred, pocked, shining floors and the pictureless walls. He went out back, where Gass and Winters were piling old kindling and boards for the fire. The formal gardens of the house were submerged in winter-dry honeysuckle and reedy brush. In the protected area cold, pale grass stood knee-high. Grey-white boards lay in it, remnants of backhouses and sheds, stamped together with rusted hinges and horseshoes. The slave cabins were lost amid grass and vine.

"Them slave cabins is all empty, Johnny."

"Sold off with the furniture, I expect." In the last of the fading light, John Deall could make out the family burial plot. There were age-encrusted big monuments of splintered marble, and the small elegant plots of small children, and some not yet sunken mounds with pine-board markers.

"We have come far enough, Philip."

"Yep."

"We can catch up with the regiment tomorrow, towards—what's this place?"

He held a map before the crackling new fire.

"Your vision's a sight better'n mine, Johnny."

After they had eaten, Deall left them and walked around to the front of the old house. He looked out across the blue black landscape. There were fires on the southern horizon, small red triangles eerie with their unmoving glow. In the open silence, the chillness, Deall felt his purposefulness and his identity evaporate into blue distance. He shivered slightly. No spectral palmetto, no Spanish moss, no arrogant, dungeoning, swaggering aristocracy. Deserted dog-trot cabins, or dirt-eating poor whites as intimate with their slaves as different breeds of family dogs. And the one huge mansion they find flaccid with emptiness, even working against indignation by its very desertion. Nothing *answered.* The emptiness of the house itself was the War's very hollow grey paradigm.

He leaned against a barrel-huge oak trunk. The moon was brilliantly distant, the arched heavens washed with its clarity. The low flecks of color from his army's distant fires beaded the horizon. Empty chuckling came from his men, he heard a dog barking protectively—no slave dog's baying—out across the fields. Whatever redeeming experience he had thoughtlessly anticipated, whatever action which would shape his world into significance—that action wearingly eluded him still, behind the moled, hairy face of a sandhill woman begging a tobacco plug from Keller while gnome-headed children peered around her, within his own reaction to that nauseous simple defecation of the dying old black, finally in the emptiness of this house.

He sank to balance upon his ankles. The corridors of these piney forests were filled only with distance and loneliness. Down these aisles horsemen burst upon them: one volley: the enemy flees, the clattering of their flight pale in all the space of forest and field. The collision itself was so accidental, so superficial, that it revealed the unblinking hollowness. Star-long distances were open to his sight across the landscape. He shrank, beneath a lonely horror which touched the surfaces of his cheeks. The space between us and the army, the long distances down red clay roads through empty forests, the menaceless, hollow cheeks of the people in their cabins, and now this hollow empty house.

These things are not without additive significance. The only pattern is hollowness. Beneath the surface, however fluid, rich, resilient, there is nothing. Beneath the web of life, bone and flesh—

He drowned in lonely distances.

The people who had lived here came, established themselves for generations, rife with evil and stiff with sin, and now are wiped out, gone. No trace even of their evil remains. All that remains of them are entangled blue black shapes of decay and bone even now mingling with wood, and that with earth. (All that remains of Lucy.) So many millions.

The grass next year will have obscured even their grave mounds.

Not next year, no. The soil is not that fecund.

What does it matter how long it will take? Myriads die each winter and are replaced as ruthlessly as the distance is ruthless between myself and those distant fires—those stars. Mechanical whirlings of earth and sky were vastly speeded in his imagination.

For Deall, since the beginning of the War that last ascending action had tantalized him, by its necessity in his desperate sorrow, and by its seeming war-wombed presence. The flawless purity of the Union cause and then the immensity of the War itself (Our regiment's casualties at Chickamauga, Colonel Price said triumphantly, were proportionately greater than those of the Old Guard at Waterloo, did you men know that?), these things promised that some Presence was among them, that a climactic moment was at hand.

At his most ultimate level of self, fondled but not articulated, Deall had steadily *enjoyed* the War. The world was being purged and prepared, for the sake of his own soul. Higher laws than those of mere human worth quivered on the verge of discovery.

More consciously, he had awaited patiently (for God's sake patiently!) the moment when the shape of reality would disclose itself.

It had to be an action: he had to ascend, climb, bring this physical being into physical action on gold and green-shrouded spires, into action of symbolic worth. His hands curled anticipating the moment. It would confirm his existence as a chosen man in a cataclysmic world.

Now, he doubted.

He saw circles of distance and blind repetitive motion, not spires of ascension.

Ted Coiner paced his sentry, just now circling the far side of the house. It is dark there, and he will shiver because he is away from the firelight. As he watched, Coiner shrugged his shoulders within his greatcoat, then was out of sight around the corner. When he gets to the fire, he will make some jest to the men there. Deall waited, with indifference—and beneath that, an evaluative horror at that indifference. Distant through the wood and brick and emptiness of the house, he could hear the men laugh. He will slip off the rifle and pause by the fire. Deall could hear the down-rattle of wood and metal.

It is human nature. One can predict it with precision. The flesh reacts as it ever did, as it ever will. Time without end.

Deall had never seen *human nature* as something jocularly inevitable, but as something to be overcome. It was foul with animality and decay, and best told by its masked impurities (the stench of the garbage behind the Catholic church in North Liberty, the arrogance of youth which was as rank as human mouth odor, the crawl of sweat beneath thick clothing). In the ceramic pure light of Spiritual potential, Deall saw human nature as no more than bestiality itself. It was man's duty that he transcend his human nature and affirm his Spiritual.

Now, in the hollowness of space and history on this Georgia evening, Deall doubted all that he had tried to believe, and with a bleak, curious indifference.

But as he watched the woods and the road below the house, he saw a man gliding along amid the blue distances which stretched from trees and fields. His long, precise vision picked the man out, though he tried to weave the landscape about himself. Deall's eyes narrowed and focused, so that shadow and distance became significant in assessing the man. He rose from his ankles and backed to the corner of the house, not losing sight of the figure. Once again, Deall put the landscape back under his vision: "Saul, there's a man down in that road. Bring him up here."

Six soldiers, all except Coiner on sentry, sat watching Jade eat bacon and hardtack. He sat with his back to the very corner of the ell, white-painted brick and white board reflecting the roiling light of the fire. Wedged precisely in the angle, Jade's face bubbled sweat, gleamed with rich varnishing from the line of his hair. Periodically his finger moved with quick tracing along the scalp line. Otherwise, he ate with slovenly joy. Crumbs of the hardtack flaked along the coarse blanket rolled over his shoulder. He babbled with expert inarticulateness, sometimes spraying crumbs—"Bress de lawd! Ah's free at las'!" He licked his fingers with wet satisfaction. Only the flicking trace of the finger to the edge of his hairline showed his uneasy fear beneath rolling eyes and jovially swelling cheeks.

He gathered animal joy about him as though it were a blanket. He was framed and trapped by the fire and the walls of the Husband house. He knew well enough to give strange white men exactly the behavior they expected.

The men before him were white.

They were thicker through the middles than the ones he knew, and their hair was close-cropped. Cut clost like the niggers. But they were still white.

Yet he knew they were Yankees, and he was spurred by hope. He thought over and over, Tobe sent me towards a trap, but I found the Yankees. He repeated it, until it achieved a measure of reality—but I found the Yankees. It made sense out of Tobe's generosity (treacherous after all) and his own still-thudding fear, which twitched the hand as he reached for another piece of hardtack.

The sergeant knelt toward him holding out a cup of coffee. The others lay back along the perimeter of the fire, their buttons glinting brightly like pinheads.

"Do not rush him, Saul. The boy will tell us anything we need to know. He eats like he is half-starved. Take your time, son."

"Yas sah." He ask me my name, I say Malory's Tobe. "Yas *sah!* Thankee, sah." He sat on his haunches, squirrellike. His jaws worked over the coffee. He was relieved to see the others whisper and grin among themselves. But the sergeant still knelt right before him, and the closeness was enervating.

"Johnny," the man in the beaver hat said, "I ain't never see a white man trust these niggers the way you do."

Jade could see the sergeant's profile when he turned to stare by way of reply. The sergeant was still wearing his blue uniform: to Jade, it was biblically purple in the firelight. The brass buttons and buckles on his chest and arm glistened like gold, when he turned. The colors were those of righteousness. Jade chewed mouth open so that the bacon-drool gleamed on his chin: when he looked at the sergeant, vengeance coursed through his imagination.

But the other Yankees had removed their belts and had hung them over their stacked rifles. The one that said "nigger" wore that beaver hat cocked over his forehead, reminding Jade of ol' Springer, the overseer. Another had on a moth-tattered black riding coat, and the young one had a woman's shawl over his shoulder. Sullivan wore an old green frock coat. They had the look of poor whites in Coffinville on a Saturday, raffish and spindly. Jade turned his face toward the circle of the white men, grinning widely. He restrained his hand from wiping the sweat off his forehead, and sloshed coffee loudly in his cheeks.

The one called Keller, in the beaver, ignored Deall's stare. "Now boy, you say you run off from the Malory place? Where is that?"

"Fi', six mile up yonder, Cap'n."

"They got any gold up there, boy?"

Of gold, Jade could not be certain, but he was sure that Marse Tom must be of legendary wealth. The soldiers were silent. Give 'em what they wants.

"Lawd, yas sah! Dey bu'ey somethin' in the basements all de time."

"What say?" Saul asked.

"They bury hit. In the base-ment."

"I swear, Phil. You can't tell what the shit they're saying, half the time. What he say, Johnny?"

But the sergeant looked down soberly at Jade. "What happened to the side of your head, son?"

"Marse Tom hit me up side the haid."

"What's that?" The man who asked this time was the bearded one in the green coat. (Jade decided to smooth his accent.)

"He said his master hit him in the head. . . . Why did he do that?"

"I 'spect he wanted my woman."

The man in the beaver hat laughed softly. "Get her?"

Jade, studying his moves carefully, looked around and then started to chuckle himself. Saul and the one in the black velvet jacket were smiling. But the sergeant stood up briskly—he seemed furious. Jade put his hand over his forehead so the sergeant wouldn't see his eyes, while he looked from one to another. Chastened, all except Keller looked up at their sergeant.

"Your wife. He took your wife?"

Jade was confused by his deceptive softness of voice. He didn't know whether to make a joke—lawse dis nigger ain' got de time or de stuff fo' jes' one 'oman!—or not. He risked a glance up at the sergeant, but the man's eyes were looking through him, through the level of his face. "Yas sah."

"And that is why you ran off?"

"Yas sah."

The sergeant's face set quickly, with the same muscular rigidity Marse Tom's face set in before the punishment began, and Jade squirmed with uncertainty. What *do* he want, then?

"Where's your master now?"

"He up at the place."

"Why hasn't he run off?"

"I 'spect he don't believe y'all comin' out to the place."

Jade could not see the man's face clearly, but he could see the big, thick-wristed hands clenching, and the big revolver thrust into his waist belt. Jade sensed the promise of vengeance in the man. But the others were laconic. The man in the black jacket was leaning back against a saddle, hands clasped behind his head, twitching his outstretched ankle from side to side so the bootsole rolled in lazy semicircle.

With brilliant shrewdness, Jade looked innocently around the circle of men and said "Besides, he say he ain't gonna run from *no-o* damyankee. Gin'el Sherman ner none."

Their knees rose into the firelight, they propped themselves up on their elbows, hunching closer.

"Said that, did he?" Sullivan said.

The one in the beaver hat said, "Maybe we should change that tune."

"Your master must be a mean 'un, boy."

As they leaned toward Jade, their uniform blouses appeared beneath the stolen overclothing. Their sudden interest hung in the smoky light-stained air of the fire. Ocher glee filled Jade's thought.

"Yas sah," he answered guilelessly. "He a mean 'un. He whip Shorty an' Jade both, and he kill Trump when he tried to run off to find Gen'el Sherman. Yas suh, he a mean 'un."

"You say your master is still there, son?"

"Yas suh. Say no Yankee gonna run him off. Say he take a whip to any that try. And them soldiers," Jade continued, thinking to swell the pot, "they about as mean as he is. One of 'em lammed me just awhile ago . . ."

But then the intensity dissipated. There was a general "ahh," and the grass rustled as the soldiers leaned back once again.

"Soldiers, hunh?" The man in the black jacket lay back down.

"Well," Keller said, "no wonder he ain't gonna leave. I 'spect I wouldn't, myself."

Jade looked around covertly. They's just two-three, he started to say. But he knew better than to make comparisons of strength between white men. So he grinned again, his gums showing.

The sergeant carefully gave him his chance. "How many soldiers are there, son?"

"Why they's the three of 'em, and one more that's shot up."

The sergeant and Gass were still interested. Carl Winters was noncommittal, head propped from his elbow, looking back and forth.

Deall looked at Sullivan and Hostetler. "That is four, and one of them is wounded. Then they are the ones we cut up this morning."

"Aw Johnny, they were more than five."

"No, there were five. One dead and now we know another one was hit."

"Hell, John!" Keller said. "This ol' nigger says three, there could be *thirty*-three."

"Nawsuh! And didn't I take care of their hosses? And didn't I carry the hurt one upstairs? They's three of 'em and the hurt one, and that's all."

And then he added, again with brilliant insight—looking this time at the big soldier stretched out with his elbow propping up his head—"They said they done busted up a group of damyankee bummers. Said they busted on 'em this morning and tore 'em up."

He rolled his head ingenuously. "Said they never seed men run like that. Oh, they mean. They big talkers."

Billy Gass said, "Why that is a damned rebel lie! The One Hundred an' Twelfth ain't never run from rebels." He looked at his sergeant. "Why we took the second heaviest casualties at Chickamauga of any volunteer regiment in the whole Army of the Cumberland."

"That is what they said, is it?" Hostetler had risen to a squat.

Then the big soldier on the ground said, "We took 'em once, we can take 'em again."

"Well, do you men want to have a go at these rebels who whipped us one time already?" Deall asked.

Phil Sullivan said, "Johnny, we got to get back to the regiment. We been gone a hull day already. Colonel Price ain't a fool, yeh know."

Winters said, "Aw he don't give a damn. Didn't Sherman say to gut the damned state? Didn't he? And didn't ol' Price know Sherman in Lancaster?"

"We *cain't* let 'em say that about the One Hundred an' Twelfth," Billy Gass said.

Keller finally sat up again. He looked into the fire speculatively. "Hell, we took 'em one time, we can do it again. Man stay around, he likely not to bury his gold too far away, hunh?" His eyes shone in the firelight like gilt. "Thing to do," he said, looking up, "is to slip up on 'em at first light."

"Would you lead us back there, son?"

"Yas sah."

"To free the others?"

"Yas sah!" Glistering before Jade now, so that his eyes sparkled, was the very promise of vengeance for twenty years of labor and sweat, a biblical promise of apocalypse. He saw the sparkling white of that housefront, which had loomed over his days, shattering, and from the shattering the splashing outward of prizes, baubles, justice. And himself with the avengers, not waiting passively like the others.

"How soon can we get there, son?"

"Ohhh . . ."

"By sunup?"

"Oh yas suh, Cap'n. At the latest. By dawnin'."

So bright was Jade's sudden vision that he forgot himself for a moment, as the sergeant was turning and the men looking at him. Jade rose slightly, and the forehead lines of quick calculation gathered. "But they be up *afore* sunup, I 'spect . . ."

But the sergeant had his hands clasped behind his back and was saying to the men, "We can get two hours' sleep and be on them at sunrise. You will want to see to your blanket rolls now, and prepare to leave some of the captured provisions here, for we will . . ."

Jade saw that only Keller among the men had seen him. The others looked up obediently at their sergeant, already rolling out blankets and unlacing equipment. Keller leaned out, hands on his knees, so that Jade could see his young, wide-cheeked, cold face.

"What say, nigger?"

"Free at las', law, I'm free at las'!"

He did not meet Keller's eyes. He rocked slightly, grinning to himself.

"You know that th' gold and silver and such is buried in the cellar? That is what you said?"

"Yas suh, Cap'n, I knows." He hummed, eyes looking brightly into the fire.

Deall's voice continued in clarity, above them: "We can stop back by this deserted house tomorrow afternoon. We can rest here, and be back with the regiment—hold up that map, Philip, please—be back by . . ."

Keller came a little closer, bending over now and putting his hands knuckle down on the ground, so that his straight arms took his weight and his face—flat and lank beneath the sun-wash of brown—was right in front of Jade's rhythmic blithe pretense.

"You better be telling the truth, nigger."

"I swears . . ."

"Do you hear me?"

"I swears it's God's truth, Cap'n."

"And about the rebels too. Or we'll string you up for crowbait, nigger."

" 'S truth, Cap'n."

He ceased his rocking glee as he looked, with stricken attention, directly into Keller's bloodshot eyes. Then Keller rocked back away from him.

Deall slapped Sullivan on the shoulder, a quick gesture of earnest friendship, and left to intercept Coiner and take the rest of his watch. The clear moon overhead reflected his soul, encouraged it, keeping steadfast between cloud rack, lighting the distant aisles of the pine forests.

SATURDAY
3
DECEMBER
1864

Chapter 12

In the narrow, wet grey light of predawn, the sergeant awakened his brother and Tim Riley. Hanging dark buttress and rafter loomed above them as they pulled on their boots and rolled their blankets. They walked toward the plantation house through the chill darkness of Celia's garden—spiked clumps of holly and Cherokee rose bushes, now all choked with dank silver-dark grass. Their trouser legs soaked stiffly in the icy cold grass and their footsteps left long gashes in the pale grass between garden and house. Moisture beaded the metal of their guns and sword mountings. Lines of pine trees and far ridges began to appear in flecked details, out of the blanket-heavy silence.

Smells of cooking laced the chill green morning air with odors familiar to the men, the buttery thick smell of grease blossoming from frying meat, and pungent coffee. Fire gleamed through the side shutters.

The three soldiers shivered and hunched against the cold, and stood by the kitchen door on the covered gallery, which ran to the rear door of the big house. Sergeant Wolf pushed the door open, and they looked in. The men's eyes roved with the unexpected disproportions of the kitchen. Against the rear wall a huge metal stove was gassy with fire and lacquered with running grease. Water-rattling big colanders and pans jostled on the two levels. CHEROKEE STOVE

• ATLANTA IRON WKS • 1841. To the peering soldiers, the letters were dimly menacing, the kitchen alien.

Phrony moved between stove and the big cupboards on each of the side walls. " 'Go down Mmmm' "—she broke eggs over a pan— " 'Sezz, Way down in E-egypt lan'.' " The soldiers looked at each other.

But the fire and slick grease invited. Riley's boots were worn through, and he stood on one foot and then the other, trying to keep warmth in his soles. Finally he leaned his carbine deferentially against the wall of the building, then loosened his sword belt and hung scabbard and pistol over the carbine. The others followed.

They squeezed into the room, shoulders touching as though rallying for a charge. Their eyes followed Phrony uneasily.

"You take you all's breakfast here, or in the house?"

"Out here."

"Marse Tom, he say . . ."

"Out here." The three men sat along the benches of the kitchen table, which was behind the inward-opening door.

None of them said anything, watching her movements with hard, round eyes.

"Mistess she say to bring in breakfast for the man what's wounded. I take it up directly. They's some coffee on the stove."

Riley went over to the stove, grabbed the handle of the coffeepot, swore, and shook his hand from the heat, then squeezed it more carefully. He brought it back to the table. Each of the men had a tin cup, slung by a string over his neck; they poured the coffee into their own cups, the edges of their eyes gummed with sleep but still looking darkly at the slave woman. She balanced egg platter and corn bread on one plate with a cup of coffee.

The men huddled over the steam from their coffee cups. The big plantation kitchen had a spicy, fecund smell. In Kentucky their meals had been cooked in the main rooms of their cabins, with iron frogs and primitive grids set about the big family fireplaces. The smell of cooking was dim against their chinked fieldstone, the smells scoured by the bare sufficiency of their economy. Here, there was the slave-kitchen smell of crusted, lavished grease, and the sweetish stench of rotting food scraps. In the cupboards bits and chunks of cooked and half-eaten food, bread crusts and ham butts and gummy milk, were scattered among heavy crocks of potatoes and corn, and jars of preserved meats.

But gradually, the first articulation of flesh over hot morning food eased their sense of difference. They warmed in the heat-soaked kitchen. A hot wood fire pressing back frosty-cold morning mist: they were reminded trenchantly of cove dawns and breakfasts after milking. Though the hundred-fifty-foot kitchen was incredibly more immense, the bricked walls machine-precise compared to their chinked-log and stacked-fieldstone hearths, for them Phrony gradually became an intruder upon homeliness. They now watched her with dark irritation, cradling their coffee cups.

Their young lives had been spent in narrow, febrile assessments of personal worth, made against big mansions and curlicued excesses. They had been baffled by the size and furnishings of the kitchen. Now, watching Phrony, their eyes began to shift—with the hardening of small muscles, the beginning of sarcastic smiles—toward contempt. Unspoken among them with the coming of familiar warmth, was the feeling: for all his niggers, I'm as good a man as he is. We never needed no niggers to fix breakfast for us in the mornings, no suh!

Phrony shuffled out of the door, breakfast tray in one hand with the coffee swirling near the very top of the cups, pitcher of hot water in the other. She crossed the gallery toward the house through green grey light and the drenched, glareless clarity of trees and bushes and buildings. As she went into the hall of the house, she could see the glow of newly furnished fires in the study to the right, and the dining room on the other side. Tobe had built up fires first in the kitchen, and then upstairs in Malory's room and in his mistress' dining room (where the wounded soldier now lay). Now he was downstairs, building the last of the fires in the parlor.

Celia was refreshed by sleeping the night through, with her husband dozing in the big rocking chair by her bedside. She had gone to sleep with her face turned toward him, her hands beneath her cheek on the pillow. She knew her terrifying experience had channeled his sympathy (His compassion was always most intense in response to specific, visible forms of human suffering. In Beaufort on their honeymoon, she had seen him weep at the sight of a mongoloid black child drooling at the rustle of palmetto branches in the ocean breeze).

Her body still trembled with fitful remnants of fear, small pebbling shudders against which she squeezed her fists. But she was quite lucidly in control of herself. She was bathing the face of the poor gallant boy. He was propped upon her daybed, and she knelt before him, her long hair hanging down to the matting in uncombed, dark waves. She wore her old kimono. Celia's hands smoothed the washcloth over his face while her lips pursed with coaxing pity. Then she had to close her eyes and pause through another electric burst of shock.

She squeezed the washcloth into the basin, flopped it open, squeezed it again. She brought the freshened water to his reedy, pimpled face. Celia had the exquisite sense of moral elegance. Public, honest magnanimity fused with dim tableaux in her mind, images out of Scott and expurgated Malory.

Zeenie held the towels and waited for Phrony to fetch up the boy's breakfast and another basin of warm water. She watched the soldier's thin white face impassively. So that Celia would not have to reach across him, the boy turned his trunk so she could cleanse his right cheek. As he shifted on the pillows, his face suddenly drew into blue ridges of pain.

In his own room, Malory was shaving, flicking the straight razor brusquely over the soaped flesh between his spade beard and side-burns. He was bare-chested despite the dawn chill, but he had pulled on plaid-checkered yellow and brown trousers and flexing long riding boots.

Casts of pink and silver appeared in the eastern sky, faint washing pink, and the edge of the sun appeared red over the grey pine forests.

"Shee-it," Ed Wolf said, wrinkling his lips back from the acrid acorn coffee. "Ours is a sight bettern this shit."

Tim Riley blew across his coffee. "Want to get it?"

"Naw. Save it for ourselves."

"We got to be on th' road, soon," Joe Wolf said. They were silent, blowing on and sipping their coffee, relaxing in the liquid heat. There were gradual, rustling, awakening sounds from outside the shuttered kitchen.

"Where we goin', Joe?"

"Up the road a piece. We fetch up with the regiment outside Coffinville, I reckon."

"What about Suggs?"

"We apt to leave him—he's stove up."

Riley held the coffee cup right before his face, studying it. "Why we goin' back, Joe?"

The boys were cousins and oldest friends. Now they were alone, and the close warmth and the tang of coffee against the dawn drew them into honest familiarities and made them loosen. In camp, they affected youthful swaggering and the loose capricious here's-yer-mule cynicism. Now, Ed Wolf stretched out his legs. "Yeah, hell, it's been a rich man's war and a poor man's fight long enough for me, I tell ye that."

"We doin' better on our own." Riley peered out the kitchen door and down the breezeway into the big house. "Three years, and I never had a nigger to my name, nor my old man neither." He leaned forward. "Let's pick up what we can for a week or two, and then cut for *home*."

Joe Wolf sat back, eyes on kitchen ceiling. His face relaxed in the warmth and became soft and young beneath the long beard. His brother was saying, "I'm spent out, fightin' for these high-tone bastards. Let 'em keep they own niggers."

Last evening in the parlor they had responded to the aristocratic, enviable surroundings. Their ferocity and their shyness had been cajoled by the Malorys' traditional decorum and their own pride at being accepted as equals, as Southern white soldiers. Now, alone, homesick with farm-breakfast memories and surrounded by this massive, exorbitant kitchen, they reacted with assertions of defiant independence.

"Cain't you just see your paw settin' up in bed when this ol' yaller-eyed nigger comes in with *wash water* at dawn? Whatchee think he'd say," Riley said, slapping Ed Wolf on the thigh. "Whatchee ol' man say?"

Their memories were furbished by two years of absence. They saw the stilt-raised cabins set in blue clearings amid blackjack forests. Trails to their homes ran over sandstone and limestone and along the sides of mountains, so their calves bulged with steady striding, hills dropped in curving blue curtains ahead. They saw rustling green corn, braided with gold, in coves embosomed in faceted, windblown forests. Meadows flowed smoothly, yellowly along the blue hillsides. Favorite dogs bounced with joy, coons dropped downshearing through tree limbs in moonlight.

Stern loving parents made their concern the more piercing because it was so stoic. Family hopes were invested in frail, proud boys.

"Can you see ol' man Riley—you talk about your paw but ol'

man *Riley*—needin' a nigger to light a fire so he could get out a bed? Hey? Watchee think?"

Sallow mountain girls nevertheless knew the curving patterns of reply, which could inflate a man's esteem. Tim Riley carried a picture of Sarah McElroy, a small plain-faced girl with dark hair, her picture haunting in the courage of the large eyes. He fumbled for it in the inside pocket of his cavalry jacket.

"Seem like a man ought to be able to take care of his own, without no gang of niggers," he said. "What it seem like to me."

Their images of home appeared to them in the favorite colors of memory, azure blue and the bronze and green of springtime. Kentucky villages where huge chestnuts spread green leaves so globosely thick over roofs that livery and smithy doorways appeared like shedded cave entrances: swimming holes with flesh glistening gold and green beneath bubble-flecked black water: all the colors of summer and spring and snowed-in winter.

"Hell," Ed Wolf said, "they never done me no favors."

Joe Wolf and Riley both nodded over their coffee cups. Their voices were still lowered, shielded from the looming of the big house. The soldiers did not notice the irony with which the *they* of the evening before had shifted.

Riley laughed. "I even 'spect I done my duty." He sipped the coffee with a comedian's timing. "I done killed as many of the Yankees, as they have of me."

The other two laughed quietly, though it was an old saw in the company.

"Ain't no rush," Joe Wolf said at last. "Ain't no rush. Let's see what we come across this mornin' on th' Coffinville line." Georgia was a different nation, sand and piney woods. Georgians were strangers suffering familiar disasters with ill grace.

Ed was youthfully truculent against being taken. "It's all a damn dun. They dunnin' on us sure."

"Sure have been, for some time now," Riley said.

"You never see them in the fightin'."

Outside, the sun melted softly from red to orange, and the crisp winter air tingled with level, mist-glancing points of light.

"And all I'm fightin' for is th' right to starve, it seems like."

"It do seem like that," Riley said.

Ed Wolf got up, tugged at his waistband, and paced back and forth. "Where is that nigger woman?"

"What's the matter, Ed?"

"Coffee give me the squitters." His face scowled in suspense. "*Hell.* I got to go." Tim Riley chuckled. Joe looked worried. Ed Wolf lunged to the door, opened it, took a step, and, hidden by the fully opened door from the men in the room, froze.

Back to him, immobile with his own stealth, six liquid feet away, in faded cape and blue cap stood a *Yankee!* by *God!* Ed Wolf stood back, flat in profile against the width of the kitchen wall and the door.

Knowing him to be a Yankee because of the blue cap but (even before this cognition) also because of the width of the man's neck and the close-cut black hair above it, and the thick knees and calves and the cumbersome way he put one heavy shoe down on the brick. A foot-long pistol in his right hand was probing toward the house. The man took another elephantine slow step, his left hand holding a long Springfield rifle as a circus ropewalker a pole for balance.

He stole that cape! He *stole* it! Wolf thought in frenzied silent ferocity. The thought hammered stunningly, disproportionately. Home-vivid memories still glazed his vision, but quick assessments moved his flesh: cain't reach them guns 'thout him hearin' and his own hand was instantaneously pulling the immense palm-bladed bowie knife out of the top of his right boot.

He *stole* it! As he gradually turned out, all the difference—between *that man's* beef-thick healthiness and his own grey thinness, between *that man's* all-over thick clothing and his own chill threadbareness, *that man's* clumsy outsidedness in this suddenly personal brick-stretching gallery—all difference was bursting within him: bright-bursting with anxiety because of his weaponlessness and yet this *chance* to get the Yankee sumbitch, this back-turned *chaince* . . .

And he lunged out in two slapping great strides and his left hand was closed over the warm flesh holding the cavalry pistol while all the dawn rang in Wolf's ears: left arm reaching around across the belly, left hand squeezing the Yankee's entangled fingers against the metal of the pistol, while his right hand with the bowie knife shoveled beneath the faded cape and found the leather crossbelt, the blue thick wool, and the strong healthy back. "Drop it, you son of a *bitch!*" he whispered through clenched rotting teeth into the man's ear: meaninglessly, for this man was struggling to drop the pistol even while Wolf's fingers tangled them into the metal guard, "Drop it you son of a bitch," and then all difference and all anxiety released as Wolf plunged the broad knife into the small of the man's back. Felt the whole frame shake and quiver, plunged the knife hilt deep again thinking how soft it goes in and then turning the Yankee around with a motion as smooth as if he had practiced it all his life, capstanning him with the knife so that he was face to face, the Yankee big but young, his face so suddenly white that the temples bulged, his beardless smooth unchanneled face aghast.

The pistol clattered on the brick, while Ed Wolf exultantly plunged the knife right into the man's belly, right over the belt, and meant to shove him away but lost the blood-slick knife with him, so the Yankee stumbled backward off the brick breezeway and sat down hard on the ground, still holding the Springfield, mouth and eyes still open, his other hand tugging his blouse away from the knife in his stomach, the shirt beneath white but staining red.

And to his left, an openmouthed young Yankee in a woman's shawl was aiming his Springfield at Wolf, who saw him just at the moment Ted Coiner sat back on the ground.

Billy Gass was in crouching shocked amazement: Coiner and he had approached the house from the northern side, the way Deall had said. They had seen the slave woman carry the food into the house and seen the stacked guns, and Coiner said that the rebels were in the house where the woman was serving them, so let's just get between them and their guns. They had waited until they were certain the rebels had to be in the house (nigger woman ain't come back out *yet*). Billy was exultant with the thought of the surprise, like the best kind of schoolhouse jokes, mirth distending and then erasing the rigid lines of his suspense. They gone be surprised, are they gonna be surprised! so ye seen us run tother day did ye? Eh? while he covered the doorway toward which Ted moved. Just thinking Boyohboyohboy and jouncing slightly on the balls of his feet with the delight and then he had seen the wraith (all length and yellow-grey paleness, the knife held high and the eyes rimmed) cross and *merge with Ted* and stick and stick while his own rifle swiveled and bobbed. One moment Ted had been all familiar confidence, creeping up, pistol toying toward the door, and then the spectre had clutched him, long-haired and silent and yellow white like horror itself.

And now that they were free of each other, the wraith balancing itself back from his rifle muzzle, Billy Gass squeezed the trigger in wild terror, aiming too low because of the small red eyes still on him—squeezed the trigger and burst away from scene and concussion, fleeing back for the rail fence beside the barn which he and Ted had crossed in such stealth seconds earlier.

The blue slam of the rifle shot clapped between house and kitchen and across garden and graveyard to the woods on the other side, smoke stinging the air of the dawn. The ounce-heavy soft lead minié ball struck Ed Wolf just above the right knee and pivoted him against the post of the breezeway so hard that it cut the flesh of his jaw. He fell back upon the bricks, leg bones stunned and smashed, cloth and flesh and metal in one burned mass, and when Joe Wolf and Tim Riley lunged out of the door, he was quivering, clawing backward along the bricks, pants-seat stained foully, sobbing with shock and fear.

Through the blue and silver pink dawn, they saw a Yankee racing toward the barn fence. Their possessive familiarity, like Ed Wolf's, instantly enclosed manor house and garden and barn and quarters. Tim Riley and Joe put their hands out for their carbines at the same second, clutching for the barrels while watching the shawl flap about the Yankee's waist as he threw himself for the top rail of the fence. The whitewashed brick exploded beneath Riley's fingers when the second concussion from the other side slapped against the echo of the first, the two men in the doorway jerked back inside as whi-popp! of sound blurred past their faces from another shot from the graveyard side.

Wolf and Tim Riley huddled inside the kitchen, running their tongues over their lips, looking calculatingly at their guns three feet away, and then at Ed, pulling himself agonizingly, whimperingly, toward them. "They loadin'?" But a horse pistol opened from the graveyard side, less loud than the heavy rifle concussions. A lip of earth flipped up near Ed.

"We got to get him in." Joe Wolf breathed through his open mouth, looked out into the new morning now intense with the shapes of menace, and hurled himself at his brother's shoulders. A pistol ball whickered across the brick; another one went right over him. Tim tugged at them both, and they all rolled back onto the floor of the kitchen.

"Gitchee belt around that laig, Joe. I get the guns."

He squatted near the edge of the doorframe, eyes smarting from the danger—just a half-foot outchonder. He pushed his hand for the guns, drew it back with the same motion he had used to squeeze the heat sting from the coffeepot, and wiped his hand on his trouser leg. "Got to get that gun . . . they gone be comin' any minute now." In the corner beside him Ed Wolf rolled his head from side to side, the flesh around his open mouth fish-white.

Riley stabbed his arm out along the wall, squeezing his eyes against the coming shock (more than the pain) and another hot concussive sound burst into his face as his cheek pressed against the kitchen wall: for vastness he felt nothing in his fingers, then found leather and the fingers burrowed into leather strap and metal and he drew back at last, armpit aching from the reach, breath scalding coldly into his lungs. He pulled two carbines—shortened Enfields—into the room, entangled in one crossbelt and pistol holster.

They dived for the rifles, and fumbled in the pouch of the crossbelt for loads. Joe watched the opening of the doorway nervously, the loaded pistol on the floor beside him, while they tore open the cartridges and poured the powder. They worked with smooth and familiar hunters' intensity, not looking at their hands even when they capped the percussion nipples, but watching the doorway edges for outside movement.

Carrying his loaded rifle with open-palmed ease, Riley went over to the north shutter and looked out of the crack between the planks. "Nothin'." At the other shutter, face creased by one slight thread of light, Wolf watched the woods.

"We got to get into the big house."

"It'll be a risk," Riley said, still looking out of the shutter. This was a statement, not an argument.

"We got to get into the house." In their thudding intensity, they had to get into that whitewashed manor of wood and plaster sitting squarely in the center of the wide plantation clearing, in this southern morning. Wolf's only consideration was, Ed'll be all right inside this brick, I reckon. Other than that, the two soldiers did not consider. *They* were out there. The place for us to be, then, is inside that big house. The simplicity of it, the necessity, was like Ed Wolf's blind impelling sense of the Yankee's thick-necked difference.

"Cover me," Riley said. "I'll get the other guns."

Wolf pushed the shutter open six inches, keeping his head back from the window frame. He shifted the pistol to his right hand, cocked it, and scanned the smokehouse, cotton gin, the willows in the graveyard fifty yards off. Long centipede shadows crossed the silver green lawn from the grass itself. The sun looked chill on the boles of the sycamores and willows in the graveyard, and the pinewoods beyond them. He could see no movement. "Go to it."

Wolf heard Riley bluff out of the door on his hands and knees, and smoke batted off the side of the smokehouse and jutted from beneath the willows in the cemetery. He fired the pistol at the Yankee concussions with wrist-stiff deliberations, and Riley lunged out of the door now, while his big revolver by sound alone pressed the Yankees down. Then Riley was back cradling the other crossbelts and guns, and Wolf dropped beneath the window while the smoke drifted in with the morning cold, as blue and acrid.

Ed was ball-eyed with shock, but not with pain. He sat up with feverish alertness, looking at the guns. Pain is gonna set in after a while, Joe thought. "Eddie, we got to get into the big house."

"Leave me with a pitcher a that well water."

Joe cradled his head, and held a tin cup of the water to his lips. Ed drew it in over his stained teeth, with long sucks, and rolled his lips back to keep the water in, squeezing his eyes with the fear and the first pain. "Ohhh . . . it's gonna hurt!"

"We be back for you, boy. Here's a Navy six, and a loaded rifle." Joe pressed the pistol into his hands. The carbine rested across his thighs. His lips drew back from the corner of his mouth.

"Ohhhh . . . Joe, it's gonna hurt!"

Riley tightened the tourniquet on his thigh.

"We be right back, hear? Keep 'em off the back of th' house." Joe Wolf slipped his rifle and Suggs' carbine over his shoulder, along with the inlooped cartridge boxes.

"All right, Joe. Leave me some of that well water."

They left Ed Wolf propped against the wall of the kitchen, white with shock, holding the long pistol in his hands while sucking in against the pain which could come full with any new breath.

Gaunt, homespun against the cold, tight-eyed, the two soldiers broke out and ran in violent strides down the whitewashed brick, firing pistols at the fence and the cemetery and the smokehouse, rifle butts smacking their hips with each stride. Wood splinters skipped from the pillar halfway down, air turned metallic off the brick walkway, revolvers blasted back at them, the smoke from their own pistols spasmed beside and behind them, and then they were flattened, panting, against the back wall of the great house itself, wheezing against the ache in their breasts, unhurt.

In the kitchen behind them, already chill with the open shutter and the smell of gunpowder, Ed Wolf said for the third time "Lea' me some of that well water," his voice suddenly cracking with youth and pain on the last syllable. "Some a' that well wattaAHH!"

Chapter 13

MALORY HAD COMBED HIS SPADE BEARD AND WAS BRUSHING HIS HAIR back over his ears in winglike blades, when Billy Gass shot Ed Wolf.

Malory swung about, the room blurring in his one eye, while the cornices and joints of the house caught and wove the concussion into sharp echoes.

He threw open the door into Celia's dressing room, his scarred chest still bare against the cold. Celia's shoulders were lifted in surprise. Water had spilled down the front of the kimono. Her face was marble white beneath her black hair, and her eyes seemed bruised, her long, undressed hair undefended and unprepared. Malory's sympathy for her expanded into violent rage.

"Sherman?"

The soldier on the bed was painfully swinging his legs to the floor.

The night before, Malory had felt his terrible helplessness, but now rage kindled his confidence. *Shooting,* here, near his house. I don't give a damn *who* it is out there shooting, but I aim to find out! "Stay in your room, honey," he said with rigid ferocity. "I reckon I will find out, by God."

As he turned back into his room he half assumed the damned trash in the barn were letting off their pieces—but he heard the distinct shots from near the graveyard. He could not imagine the

Confederates firing their pistols there. It must be some of Sherman's men. He was methodically pulling on the linen shirt, war-worn into visible rectangles at the elbows. He tucked the shirt in at his waist, forcing down his rage, studying the mottled wall of his bedroom with inattention, breathing in over his teeth, deliberately preparing himself.

Another flurry of shots, and one from the barn side, this time.

He crossed the room with gradually fraying patience: his thigh struck the edge of the bedside table unheedingly. He opened the Chinese box and pitched off the oil-stained parole with the same fluid motion that brought up the Whitney revolver he had carried off to Shiloh. Now he had to make himself pause, blink, and refocus his eye (while fury battered away at his wooden patience, hammered so that his legs quivered) and check the six loaded chambers. All capped *Well byGodI'mset!* and he lunged out of the room and down the hall with rage cold and smoothly coursing down his legs and down to his hands, full violent rage concatenating with his strides. Shaven, armed, dressed, confidence was welling in him as coldly as the rage. He was violently pleased with the weighted battering of his bootsteps down the main staircase.

At the foot of the stairway he swung around the newel-post and, striding toward the rear, his vision skipped for one quick impression through the parlor door: Phrony collapsed in the corner, thick black flesh shaking, cheeks wet *Why she's laughing!* as the wide rectangle of her mouth impressed his single eye, his own driver Tobe standing over her cradling the black pigtailed (*laughing!*) ball of her head against his chest.

The disconnected, soundless vision of rejoicing bewildered him, as it dissolved from eyeball in flashes of light. He shouted "Tobe!" and swung shelter-taking against the wall.

His foot pressed on something flesh-soft on the floor: "Tobe!" His eye batted at the lack of light. A keening sound was as liquid as a current about his thighs. There was a flurry of gunfire, and the deep metal smell of smoke, and smoke drifted in a curtain across what he could see of the backyard, filmy grey through the rectangle of the open door. Stepping away from the floor-flesh, his thigh bruised against a strangely placed chair (chair?). The familiar hallway was suddenly corrupt with menace in the swimming moment since his glimpse into the parlor.

Tobe did not come.

"Tobe, Goddamn it all!" Down the bricks of the gallery he could see a man on hands and knees reach out of the kitchen door.

Why Phrony is crying: he connected the billowing current of sound with the vision: *she crying.* Cautious in his confusion, he now leaned against the wall as another shot came from straight ahead and he saw smoke drifting in the kitchen doorway.

There was a dropped platter on the floor at his feet, meat and eggs which his boot had smeared in tiny lumps on the wood. She is *crying.* His vision was now bruisingly acute upon the details of the hall. She dropped the platter. Things resolved themselves. God damn these stupid niggers, he thought with quick reflex, all in one easy, fluting scale of thought, they more trouble'n they're worth.

Why the hell is Tobe not out here when I call? "Tobe! Get out here!" Wasting his time over a fool nigger cook. Malory pressed himself against the back wall behind the rear door and looked out through the crack of the hinge. He pushed the door closed slightly with the barrel of his pistol to shift the slit of vision. But his eye could make no distinctions in the smoke which hung lightly by the kitchen, and drifted among the outbuildings. He leaned into the door to the office so that he could see the cemetery through its windows. The mottled glass only glazed the smoke among the willows. He peered back through the door hinge toward the barn on the other side of the rear lot.

Then bursting clatter from the kitchen: Malory's head turned to focus. Two of last night's soldiers were sprinting directly toward him. Their faces were bronze, and they fired big cavalry pistols which stuttered their strides, gallery brick and post flicked at them, a minié ball splintered right beside Malory's narrow vision, and then the soldiers tumbled through the door, colliding.

Their heads were right beside Malory's waist as they rose, disentangling their legs, panting so hard their lower lips gleamed in the dim light of the hall. Malory stepped from behind the door and their eyes both climbed blindly over revolver and arm, they fought for stances and swung their hands. He ignored the spidery thrashing of the two men, stepped beyond them, and closed the rear door.

Recognizing Malory, both men got to their feet and brushed at themselves. Malory could smell their new, fear-drawn sweat as sharp as the point of a spear against the old smell of their clothing. He was blind and knowledgeless about the morning. But with the men before him, he moved into the shape of authority, eyes cold and distant, forehead up, hair flared back in disdain, mouth taut and precise.

"Seh . . ." the sergeant panted.

"Sergeant, what the hell happened?"

"Yankees out there. . . ."

Riley said, between panting, "A smart fi-six . . . of 'em, seh."

"Eddie done kilt one . . . he's outchonder in the kitchen. . . ."

"Shot in th' leg. . . ."

"Five or six? He looked cautiously out of the door.

"He don't know," Wolf said. "We saw one for sure. . . . Over by the barn . . . Maybe three-four over t'other way."

"Well, they may be more out front, seh."

"Stay here."

Malory turned decisively and cocked the pistol, striding to the front door. Through the bull's-eye glass lights of the doorframe, he could see only the cream glare of the winter sun shining directly into the house. The front window in the living room, as he looked from behind the draperies, was little better: only dark patterns of brush and sycamore and rail fence against a yellow spreading wall of light.

His fury returned with another gun blast, a circle of sound that seeded whuck! against the back of his house. Riley fired back through the crack of the rear door.

"I can't see a Goddamned thing out front, Sergeant. Come up here and give me some cover."

Riley watched the back from the office. The sergeant stood beside the front window of the living room. "Bust out the damn glass." Wolf shoved his rifle barrel through one of the squares. Both men waited.

By God this is my land. Malory stood bolt upright against the wall by the door. When his teeth clenched beyond waiting, he threw the front door open with his left hand and swung to fill the door, taking the full light of the head-level sun out of the northeastern sky, his vision lost in the blaze of intense light, his flesh rigid against impact, duelist upright. Out of the blaze he heard three interlocked reports while the doorframe jumped and plaster dust and splinters were spurted between the columns in front of him.

Turning in profile to the sounds he raised the pistol and fired deliberately, letting the concussion rock the gun back on his wrist, thumb-cocking it, and drawing another level blind bead at the wall of light. Speckles of pistol fire came back, plucking brickdust out of the verandah. Glass broke at his back.

On his third blind elegant shot the sergeant grabbed him by his left arm and jerked him into the hall against the sheltered south wall. While his fury spasmed against Wolf's hold, in the brilliant northeast light still flooding through the open door one of the polished banister posts broke in half, and then another was pulled magically into the depth of the hall, and then a ridge of wood stood upright on the stairway itself. The sergeant kicked the front door closed.

Malory freed his arm with a tug and an angered pause. Wolf took his temper calmly. "I make out three of 'em out front, seh."

Malory loosened his muscles beneath the white linen shirt. "Ahum . . . well." He looked around tightly.

"You like to getchee self killed out there, seh."

"Goddamn it, they on my land."

"Well, may be they won't be long . . . ye like to getchee self killed. Hey, Tim . . ." he shouted back down the hall. "They's three more of 'em out the front. Maybe another'n in the road."

"The bummers from yesterday, you reckon?"

"May be."

Six, Malory thought, Six or seven. *They* were bespotted dogs of men, coming on *his land, after the night Celia had*. "Tobe, go fetch me my pistol pouch from up side the bed."

Eye accustomed to the darkness, he could make out Tobe, still bent over Phrony, and he could now focus upon the low moaning sound which had been an undertone all morning. "Phrony, you hush that damn moaning. Hear me!" Tobe had gotten Phrony away from the chair in the corner, which was overturned; the small roundabout chair which Malory had had made just for the corner, now its one choice carved leg broken. "Phrony, damn you . . ."

Tobe looked up at him from Phrony's side. She was in the shelter of the parlor fireplace and the settee, head on her bosom, moaning, "Sweet Jesuss . . . oh swee' Jessuss . . ."

"She fell down when the shootin' started, Marse Tom. I believe she hurt *bad*." Malory was only aware that Tobe's normal sullen, eye-narrowed composure was gone. There was a liquid sound in what he said.

"Tobe, I told you to fetch me my pouch. Now I better not have to get it myself!"

"Marse Tom, she . . ."

"Tobe, am I going to have to . . .?" His lips tightened in exertion, he drew the pistol back to swing its barrel against Tobe's head, and took a careful, measured stride at him. Tobe scrambled back up. "Why you fooling with this woman? There are Yankee soldiers out on th' Goddamn front lawn, for God's sake!" Tobe's eyes became semicircles, his head drew back up.

"Yas suh."

"I never see anything like it. Didn't I know better, I'd swear you are nigger-scared. Didn't I know better. Now get that pouch, and keep down when you move." A gunshot threw glass in horizontal glitter from the fanlight above the front door.

Tobe drew his shoulders up and with infinite, blank grace strode —not ran—through the splinters of glass and wood to the stairs, and climbed them two at a time, the plaids of light on his trousers slipping from thigh to calf to heel, and then Malory could hear him upstairs, going into the bedroom.

"Never seen anything like it . . . and you too, woman." Phrony's lips were dull blue. "Quit that moaning." She turned her head massively from side to side, eyes closed, holding her side. Moans bubbled at her lips.

"To hell with it."

In the parlor, Malory hefted the family Bible off of the marble-topped table and then turned the table on its side, blocking the lower half of the big, floor-length window nearest the corner. He stood in the corner, watching the front from behind the dark draperies and the table: he could turn to his left and cover the cemetery to the south through the side window. Sergeant Wolf had pulled stuffed, antimacassared old chairs into both of the front windows of the living room. Over in his corner, he was buried in shadow, watching the north side.

"Cain't see a Goddamn thing now," the sergeant said across the hall. Malory looked from side window to front, the pistol in his hand metal-blue in the level hanging morning sunlight. A single shot came from the office and was answered by two rifle shots from the cemetery side. Tobe came back down the steps, through the lanes of light from the fanlight and the windows of the doorframe, descending with the same sullen blank grace.

Malory took the pouch from him. "Thank you, Tobe. Now keep down and out the way." Tobe sank back behind him into the shadow of the room. Malory loaded the pistol, slipping powder and ball into each of the spent cylinders as he watched the lawn side.

"Show of force like this from th' house," the sergeant was musing, his dry hairy face now in the light of the far front window, "they might leave off. Sherman done gone off towards the east. We got to wait and see." Then his voice came from the shadow near the side window. "Bummers ain't likely to hang around 'thout support right near." Wolf broke a pane of the mottled glass in the north window, and the facets of blue and green in one corner became morning-clear ridge and pine forest. An answering rifle shot slammed away and another windowpane burst into clear shapes of pine trees, and the minié ball splintered the door lintel between the living room and the hall.

"Hup! the little 'un's still there . . . see can I . . . nope, he set down." The sergeant came back to his front window. "No seh, I don't b'lieve they would stay around without some support, and I know for a fact the Yankee army has gone on towards the east.

"Course," he said, suddenly looking at Malory across the hall, "course ol' Ed killed that one out back. We might have to kill 'em all."

Malory looked back at him. "Can your man up there handle a gun?"

"Might can. He had that big ol' Sharps. See didn't I leave it back yonder in the hall."

Malory climbed the stairs with three-stepped long strides, the Sharps and its cartridge box and the leather belts against his chest. The Yankees appeared in speckled shapes of defilement under the pulsing of his ferocity: I hope they *do* fight it out here, by God. Fight it out to the end. As he turned at the top of the stairs, left hand on the banister for his swing, Celia met him in the hall. She was pale and shadowy against the dim blue shine of the wooden floor.

She stepped to him, head turned back toward the dressing room, hands feeling for his chest. Irritation clotted the clean lines of his intensity. Her hands pressed against his chest and touched the metal of the gun.

She is scared pissless, damn it all. I got to tend her, I expect.

She turned her face quickly, hands fumbling now with leather and box and metal. Her face was shadowed by her long undressed hair, her eyes intense upon the big carbine. (Below them another thumping gunshot and breaking glass.) He remembered the blanching of her face beneath the first shots: she seemed trying to stop him. She was trying to throw the gun down so she could press herself within his arms.

She about lost her mind.

He struggled with his own muscles so they would not rip the gun out of her hands too brusquely, his cheeks rising with tight-lipped frustration Well by God all I can do is see to her as soon as I can, let me get this gun to that boy . . .

But Celia's hands were pulling at the gun too. They turned as if in an elegant dance motion above the palely shining wooden floor. Then she raised her head, and he saw no crouching bewildered girl, no fear but a vividness so sharp it was like a slap of color across his eye in the pale light. Her eyes were violent; the arching intense eyebrows and the flaring lashes made them gleam.

The flesh of her face was bright with excitement. For the second time that morning Malory was stunned by the vision of *rejoicing*.

She pulled the gun away from him and the weight of the short ugly barrel tugged her hands downward. She balanced the Sharps under her arm and across her hips, struggling to raise it and at the same time understand the curling breech mechanism.

"Ohhh, Mr. Malory, just show me how to load it, just . . ." She fumbled an adequate grip, and pulled back the hammer with check-dimpling exertion.

Celia had put on a cotton dress with a false brown Zouave's jacket, the only dress he had been able to buy for her since the War began. Over her bosom petite martial braid was crossed in shortened frogging and tabs and brass buttons. She wore no hoops; supple swirling pantalettes and petticoat followed the motions of her legs. "Where do you want me to go, Mr. Malory?" She held the gun at the level of her thighs, in polished hands.

Her eagerness bewildered him.

"What shall be my post, Mr. Malory?"

Trembling, she followed him to the wounded boy, who peered out of the window of her bedroom.

For Celia, the meek decorums of protected elegance were swept away. The hammering of her blood was licensed richly, and the enraged clenching of her teeth. Her legs were warrantably unhooped: she felt released from immobility in the wadded feel of the pantalettes and single petticoat, as they exaggerated her strides.

The Yankees were spaced around the perimeter of the house. The wounded soldier traded shots with those at the front fence. With Celia loading for him, he could keep both the Sharps and an old hunting rifle in play.

Celia carefully shook powder into the pan of the rifle. The fraying of the house, the plaster over woodwork, the persistence of wire grass and weed in her garden, the elegance worn out of rubbed velvet and the stink of the women in their maids' aprons, these things were polished and scrubbed away by the very menace. Her eyes sparkled as a bullet tore the back off her sitting room chair in orange splinters of mahogany.

She knelt behind Suggs, watching the flesh of his neck striate with pain and exertion as he drew a bead with the Sharps. She held the old flintlock, loaded and ready for his next shot. Suggs rocked from the impact of the Sharps against his shoulder, and his head swung with pain. She pressed the hunting rifle against his thigh as he leaned beside the window, long before he could handle it.

Celia worked the breech of the Sharps open and slipped a new cartridge among the hot metal ridges, then put the carbine upright between her thighs and tugged back the heavy spring hammer with both hands. I am here, really, actually *here now*, besieged and heroic. She managed to watch herself with delight, while it seemed as if all her consciousness were focused upon fitting the cap onto the nipple.

Celia held the loaded big gun upright beside her, barrel pressing against her bosom. Suggs looked down at her with pain-shadowed blue eyes, his face wasted and his wound reopened beneath the bandages and the homespun jacket. As he took the gun and handed her the emptied flintlock, she said, "Hit one, Mr. Suggs," with a proud defiant delighted shake of her black hair, "hit one."

The house downstairs was acrid and curtained with gunsmoke, shadow, and shafts of light. Riley and Wolf and Malory bobbed cautiously from window to window, firing pistols back at the smoke of the Yankees' guns. To Malory, cemetery and barnside and front fence were smoke-stained nests, behind which loathesomeness crawled and twined on his land. He fired with jutting steadiness, squeezing all of his outrage upon the damned Yankees squatting out there.

Half-inch soft lead minié balls and forty-four caliber pistol bullets hammered back at him. A vase burst behind Malory in a tulip-shaped splatter, the couch along the south wall puffed dust in a pollen-bright cloud and thumped back into the wall, and the chandelier in the hall—brought laboriously from the railroad station in the month of the beginning of the War—jerked convivially and shed upon the puncheon floor. A plaster dog on the drawing room mantel cracked like a tooth in a wheeing ricochet. The straw-fan souvenir of their honeymoon in Beaufort whirled into darkness, and books grunted and toppled.

Chapter 14

JUST AS RILEY STARTED TO RISE FOR ANOTHER SHOT AT THE CEMETERY, a bottle of ink on the desktop burst and the glass shards flew at him like spider's legs. He knelt back amid the spray of coppery ink.

They planning something. They coming soon, I wager. He had seen a Yankee in the cemetery squirming toward the wrought-iron gate, but had missed him with his shot. He ain't even in the lot no more.

Riley had pushed the office desk flush against the south window. He squatted amid the litter: cotton manifests and ledger sheets stamped concentrically by his own heels, glass fragments, cartridge wrappings. Now all spotted by the copper-colored ink greening into the paper.

To his right, the rear window showed only gallery and kitchen and backhouse and morning sunlight gleaming coolly through the drifting hazy smoke. Well I got to see what they up to, Riley thought. He had located the Yankees in the cemetery despite the flinching rifle duel, and he was reluctant to lose track of the one that moved. He rose cautiously toward the southern window again, holding the Enfield horizontally, his right hand splaying and refitting itself across the neck with tension and calculation. He paused in a half crouch, shielded by the rolltop desk, and looked out into the cemetery lot, thinking himself secure to his right because of the depth of the room and the unmenacing shapes of kitchen wall and backhouse and lawn. The cemetery to his front was misty with gunsmoke. He hung meditatively in the crouch while his vision reoriented itself hedge-gate-then-that-willow through the smoke, then saw a motion, swung his rifle to his shoulder, and in that instant a brilliant white *burst!* concatenated all whiteness through the rear window and the opposite wall slammed viciously against his head.

Malory ran stooping over to the door between the parlor and the office. Riley's toppling had made the print of *Farmer's Life: Harvest Time* slip its nail. Where the left side of his head had hit the wall, a darkened smear laned down to his smashed skull. A half-inch little bluish hole was over his right temple, the flesh curled and lipped within it.

Malory knelt over him quickly, then looked blinking at the rear window. He could not make out shapes in the colors of gentle smoke and sun-shadow. Behind him, a ricocheting bullet hammered into the mantel, burst, and shards of lead rattled down the parlor wall. Malory swung awkwardly about in his crouch, now looking toward the front windows. He could not decide which way to move. The windows on all three sides filled with menace: a fall of broken glass from the front portended a man standing there about to leap in. He slammed his elbow against the doorframe, pivoting to cover it.

He could see Tobe. He was shielding Phrony against the side of the fireplace, cradling her heaving shoulders and looking back over his own shoulder at the dribbling window glass.

"Tobe, get over here." Tobe's eyes and face were sullen-stiff. His eyes did not leave Malory's face, as he shifted slowly away from Phrony, still pressing his long hands across her quivering back, touching her gently, patting the flesh one last time. Then he doubled quickly across the room to Malory's side in the door.

Tobe squatted beside him, amid the sudden shearing fall of the whatnot in the corner. Seashells scattered about them. Malory refocused his flaring gaze upon Tobe.

"Get that piece he dropped," Malory said, putting his hand on the shoulder of Tobe's corduroy jacket. "Keep ye'self low"—his voice was in a steady whisper—"but keep your eyes on the rear side. I can watch the cemetery side of the house from my corner."

Tobe looked down at the dead rebel, not moving, squatting powerfully in the doorway. Now Malory's back began to chill from the unguarded rear window behind him. He squinted back at it. Tobe still stared at the rebel; a pool of blood had gathered beneath Riley's neck. Malory dropped his hand from Tobe's shoulder.

"God damn you," Malory said, "God damn you," drawling out the syllables. "I told you go get that piece and watch the back windows." Tobe now looked at him, still quietly, his eyes lidded again, no muscles twitching or moving.

"I say move, you *move*, nigger! Get that rifle!" Malory twisted from side to side, blinking visionlessly through the office, then flinching against shadows at the parlor windows. Above them—and so that Malory spun around frenziedly again—a row of ledgers shuddered and toppled from desk top to floor, and a minié ball spun up and dropped bee plump on the floor.

Finally Malory dropped from his squatting. He sat down, back against the doorframe, knees raised on both sides. He pointed his revolver at Tobe's two-foot distant chest. Tobe looked soberly at the concentric small rings at its barrel mouth. "One chance, Tobe. That's all I can afford. One chance. Get the rifle."

Tobe balanced both hands along his thighs, wiped them, then stood, rising joint-slow. He looked down at Malory, who scrambled to knee and hand-shove, raising himself. An arrow presENCE drew a line of glass beads from south parlor window into the shaft of morning sunlight. Tobe did not flinch.

"I prefers that shotgun, Marse Tom."

"Well 'y God you shall have it!" Malory leaned the Enfield against the fireplace. The shotgun was pegged over the mantel. To reach it, he had to stretch over Phrony. Lengthily exposed, he bit down against his reflexive fear, and plucked down the silver-mounted gun. Like a nigger, Malory thought, lips flanged tautly, wiping his hands along his thighs. Then he reached for the bag of powder and ball, jerking back from a slamming in the hallway, then grabbing them. Like a nigger, can't shoot worth a damn so he needs a shotgun. By *God* they never learn! "Now watch that back window towards the kitchen. I got the side here."

Tobe walked back into the office and sat in Malory's swivel chair, his back to the desk, turning his head from moment to moment to watch the kitchen while he loaded both barrels.

Malory ducked back to his corner and stood upright to ease the throbbing in his legs. Then he gathered himself and turned to the windows. He forced himself to freeze for a moment at each, looking at sundazzle and smoke. No shapes emerged, no men sprinting for the house. A ball slammed against the wall between the front windows. The lawn was vacuum empty. He heard a shot from upstairs toward the fence.

The sergeant was standing in the living room corner loading his pistol and looking from one window to another, almost lost to Malory's view in his grey and yellow jacket amid the shadow and sunlight. He saw something through the north window and picked up the rifle and drew a lengthy solemn bead, paused, opened his eyes inconclusively over the sights, then put the rifle back down beside him.

Malory knelt to shout across the hall: "Your man's dead. The one back there."

The sergeant's face ridged about his eyes. "Riley? Ol' Riley dead? Well Jesus." He caught another glimpse of motion from the northern window and raised the rifle again. "Just a leetle more, boy, jus' a little . . ." The Enfield slapped back against his shoulder; he opened his face to look back at his target. "Missed him clean. But I got that one of 'em pinned up tight.

"Miz Riley will be a lot poorer for this." He began loading the rifle, "I knowed o' Tim Riley since way back before the War. Way back. We useter"—he fumbled for a cap while looking out of the front window—"hunt together, ye know what I mean? Coon an' quail. Yes suh. Way back, I knew that old boy. . . ." When he got the gun loaded, he ducked casually across the hall.

"I reckon I best take his place back yonder." Wolf was kneeling between the front parlor windows. Malory was separated from him —also on his knees, now—by the marble-webbed shaft of light through the front window between them. Both men spoke hoarsely.

"No need. I put Tobe back there with the shotgun."

Wolf looked sharply back toward the study. Tobe's poll-kinked head was silhouetted against the rear window. A minié ball broke back in the dining room, and something then plated back and forth spirally.

"Ye give the *nigger* the gun?"

"You can trust him, sergeant."

"Naw, I cain't." He spit, his face sharpening out of its laconic battle grace and mildness into outrage. "Shee-it."

Malory's neck stiffened. "Sergeant, I tell. . . ."

"Man, you don't know what *the hell* you're doin'."

"I know. . . ."

"Man don't *give* a nigger a gun to kill a man with."

"It is my nigger and my house, by the Lord, and I do what I need to, I reckon!"

"You don't keep an eye on that nigger, you won't need to do nothin' more."

They both jerked as a ball banked from mantel into bookcase.

"I will take the responsibility for him. You have my word for him."

"It's your *word*, but it's my *back* he's on the other side of, with a shotgun you given him to kill white folks with."

"No man questions my word, on my land."

"And I'm shut up in here with a nigger at my back with a Goddamned shotgun. And I don't question that? Well, Cap'n, when the shit can I start questionin'?"

"I gave you my word you can trust him. I expect that is enough. It is all you will get."

"Well yeh trust him so much, yeh trust him so much, answer me just one question, and you don't mind." His face whitened with straining irony. "Why the hell yeh fightin' to keep him a slave? Eh? Why yeh fightin' if he's man white enough to help ye?"

The shaft of light between the two men was mottled by chewed draperies and dangling window frame and myriad, sparkling specks of lint.

"I *know* this nigger. He is one of my people. And since you ask, yes sir! I trust him better than a damn sight of whites I have known." A low kind of humming had entered Malory's voice, from dwindling restraint. "And I tell you one other thing, sir. As long as you are a guest in this house"—a chair arm splintered behind them unnoticed—"you will take my word, by God Almighty, or you will answer."

Wolf looked back at Tobe in the office. His neck cords stood out above his thin flesh. "Well God damn. Ye take a nigger over your own kind."

"My own people over any kind, by God."

"Well shit." He turned abruptly and doubled back toward the living room, ignoring Malory loudly. "Git the chance, me and

Ed are gettin' out of here. Let him trust whoever th' *shit* he wants. Trust 'em and fight for 'em theyselves. I ain't got none and ain't studyin' to git any more'n that."

Malory pressed his lips together in anger, bones standing out beneath the pale skin. Think I cannot control my own people? Think I don't know them? He glared at Wolf. The sergeant settled again in the far corner and began loading his rifle, lips still moving in his contemptuous soliloquy.

Along the southern wall glass shattered behind a twitching curtain. Malory strode over to the offending window and hammered out a remaining glass pane himself, his vision reddened by the Goddamned hillbilly arrogance, think *he* can come into a man's house, by God, and chivy insults! In the cemetery smoke mounded dirtily among the willow sheaves, sunlight painted one willow bole. Malory emptied the revolver into the shadow and smoke, pumping the pistol balls into the haze, hearing whang and stone-gash off the gravestones. To his right the draperies pumped at him again, but he fired until the pistol was empty, and then bruised his thumb struggling with the lever to open the cylinder. The metal would not yield. Swaying with anger, he tugged at the revolver with both hands and then threw it down on the floor.

Then he noticed that the door to the office was closed.

Irritation flared into concern and, shifting, he almost started toward the door. But the same flash of concern seemed to open a new sense within his mind. He felt weight and motion upon his land, close to his house, as he would have felt an insect crawling upon the flesh of his own back. Instinctively competent, he took two strides to the hallway arch, instead of the office door: he looked down the length of the hall and out the back door.

And the new sense materialized as he watched: a Yankee, flat crest of his cap yellow in the light, drifted (soundlessly amid the sudden volleying clatter from all sides of the house) into his vision, then vanished to the left of the rear door, flat against the back of the house.

And Tobe didn't fire a shot! *Maybe Tobe is dead.*

His lucidity was as clear as water, pouring through the very center of all the heat and anger in his mind. He caught up the loaded Enfield by the fireplace and he plunged down the hallway for the cellar door. He unconsciously counted his footsteps three-four-*five-*

SIX-AH to the cellar door, while his eye watered against the doorway at the end and the muzzle of his rifle covered it *just let him come forward let me see the brim of that cap just let him wait then let him wait!* and he slipped into the dank brown silence of the landing at the top of the cellar stairs, heart slamming, his eye to the crack which gave on the rear door. He held the shortened Enfield along his side, thumbing the hammer. His whole chest surged with the power of potent concealment.

In a monotone he mouthed to himself—still holding his half-vision against the frame of the door waiting for the cap brim and silhouette to appear—That Tobe just like a nigger no gratitude no gratitude shows what I have always said they cannot be trusted not the best of the damned race were Miss Harriet B. Stowe here see what she should say about them then (even while the lucid part of him, above the monotone, was thinking *Maybe Tobe is dead, then. So I got one shot I don't get him with that one then I will club him with the barrel*).

Then he heeded someone beneath him on the steps and he jerked the gun so hard its butt bruised his own thigh. His single eye, blood-dimmed and watered from the staring, made out the nubbed Negroid hair and the brownish coat beneath him. In the sudden, perfect confirmation of his own confidence in his own people, he strained to make out no face, just accepted the brownish African presence. The shining thing beside the man was the shotgun and a fresh comprehension added glittering potency and strength to his trigger hand even as he nodded with blind acknowledging haste at the man two feet below him. The monotone became Ol' Tobe, best nigger I ever *heard of*, even, no suh wouldn't get that one, wouldn't ever get that one there away from me, no suh! And lucidly he thought, *Why that was smart of Tobe. See them coming and know they got to pass here. And I have three shots, now. Kill this first one through and the rest will scatter, or I don't know my Yankees.*

The brown close hush of the cellar made the man beneath him seem to encroach even as Malory huddled against the wall, until the shining weapon he held was beneath his patched eye. *Not so close, Tobe . . .* his left hand making downflicking gestures, then brim edge was there! and the rear door opened all the way and the Yankee slipped through into the hall, through Malory's moving slice of vision, cap-brim-eye-glare-temple and the puncheons were creaking beneath Malory's own feet with the alien weight and *My hall!* he thought against the unendurable anticipation of the next stride, *My hall!* and he spasmed out of all his caution, heaving the door against the man on the other side (unprepared and stunned himself to feel the vicious rebounded blow of the door against solidity) and the Yankee smashed wetly against the wall. Malory's right wrist was jarred by the blind suddenness of the impact, and the Enfield fired off uselessly, and so Malory then turned, through eye-dulling flash and smoke and hand ache from the unpremeditated recoil, for Tobe's shotgun. Echoes flatting in his ears Malory turned with reaching confidence—and saw not Tobe's face but leatherlike notflesh. A face like a leather mask with horizontal slashes along the cheeks, tribal rich but through which bone and blood glistened, slits like razor-made long parodies of the hammered, vicious glare of the eyes themselves: and held up toward him was no shotgun but a separated meat-strung human arm bone.

Chapter 15

AND HE DON'T EVEN KNOW SHE THERE!

He had watched the two white men huddled talking, faces sheened by the eastern light. Hair grew from their faces and hung lank over their collars. Marse Tom was a different man in a different perspective.

Tobe sat in the office holding the shotgun, but he ignored the windows. Phrony was still collapsed beside the fireplace, comfortless now, and forgotten by the white men between the sparkling front windows.

The sergeant left. Marse Tom pivoted between the windows in the yellow and white light. In the shadow of fireplace and settee, Phrony groveled in all the terror of the helpless, the uneducated, the fat and jovial when brought to horror. Small pieces of cloth, which she had tied into her pigtails to keep off the witches, bobbed like flecks of blood against her drooling, hunching cheeks. "Ohhh . . . sweeee—JEEE-susss! . . ." A ball burst through the south window and spanked off the fireplace right above her. She hugged the floor, massive, pathetic, reduced below animality. Marse Tom swung toward the frame.

Tobe witnessed. Marse Tom blasted away through the window, the lines of his face hard-edged in the light, the white lines of ownership.

He don't even know she there. Time was, Phrony's slovenly weight and ignorance had been all Tobe had sought to escape. But now his chest ached in compassion and bitterness. He had a black, deep knowledge of the world she was in—taught only to love heat and food and rewarded only with these base things for all her loyalty; genially encouraged in her superstitions. Now her hulk rumbled with a cautionless fart, she moaned and drooled, glistening with sweat. Her flesh quivered at every impact of sound in the ricocheting room. The way her world looked to her was absolutely present to him: all sudden bewildering menace, without warmth or protection, hostile against old fat flesh, her loyalty no shield now. . . .

Ain't his people, no sir. Talks to a white man instead. All he care about is his pro-perty.

None of mine.

Marse Tom was measuring his shots like a duelist. Tobe shut the door with his elbow, and stared out through the window into the dazzling sunlight and smoke.

All she want is a fireplace corner, and she loves 'em like they wants, and this is what they does.

I done been the driver. He shook his head. I drove for 'em.

But he had been trusted with this shotgun. His hands opened and splayed along the stock of the cleanly oiled weapon.

J. W. Trapp & Sons
PHI$_{L}$A, PENN

1856

Black codes or no, Marse Tom had told Old Man Husband, I need a driver that can read. I got the best driver in the state of Georgia, and son of a bitch I can teach him to read if I want to, I expect.

The weapon had a heft, in the shadowy room. It shone dully. (They left off they shooting. That was the white man upstairs, last time.) The shotgun was oiled, balanced, deadly to the long touch. ('Spect they going to try something.) Tobe rose from the chair and moved over to the rear window.

Hi, Dan'el, fetch! Tobe, that was one hell of a shot. Marse Tom's fruitless concussions hanging in the autumn brilliance, Tobe had picked out the quail as it sank upon darkly fallow fields and had kicked it over and over and now the dog was bobbing toward it and Marse Tom's hand was upon his shoulder. You show me up like that in front of Colonel Husband, I reckon he is going to come up with a price even I cannot resist. Glad he is not here. He laughed: Tobe smiled.

Then a racket of gunfire from the three sides of the house, and Tobe saw a man detach himself from the kitchen wall and sprint down the gallery toward him.

Tobe crouched back from the window and leveled the shotgun and the white man rose over the bead: The framed white face between the rounded grey black shiny barrels raised a sudden, hectic, dark glee in Tobe, a hilarious delight. He looking but he cain't see me in this blackness no suh come ahead come on-n-n. . . .

Save this man was clean-shaven, had not the hairy face of the sergeant or Marse Tom. He ran with a clean-edged stride right for the house, and as his cap—face—chest—breastplate rose over the sight in the second before he passed into shadow and when Tobe should have blown half his chest away, Tobe saw the blue gold gleam of the man, something about him *new!*, distinct, a *new thing* cutting through sun and shadow for this complex confusion of house and room and his own hanging mind. And then in a blind split second Tobe thought He gonna free us (all blue gold striding purpose coming on through the noise and tendrils of smoke and the cascading of splinter and glass around him), he is going to free us all. And did not shoot.

Sweat started from his forehead. He rocked the shotgun back upright.

Not even know she was there, not even know it. . . . Black like me. The man in blue gold was right outside the wall.

Tobe got softly to his feet not thinking, not touching consciously upon anything, treasuring against his chest like the very weight of the shotgun the sense of the Yankee's *difference,* his blue-shearing *difference* cutting into this house and knowing that if he thought at all, he would lose the purity of that instinctive certainty. He paused beside the door to the parlor, cracked it enough to see Phrony's bulk still shadowed on the floor, to see Marse Tom was gone, and then stepped over the dead rebel and the fallen picture and into the room, impelled by just the purity and the newness and the promise of that man in the clean-shaven *difference*, in the gleaming blue gold.

As he moved stealthily toward the hall archway, he paused to pat Phrony in a surge of hope. Then on toward the arch, knowing if the Yankee came through the rear door he would have to expose himself to anyone in the length of the hall, knowing the sergeant was in the front room, uncertain where his master was, uncertain what he would do himself, but possessed now by the cold delight of simple physical assertion. When he come th'oo that door they gonna have a couple of chainces at him I 'spect, creeping closer for the wall beside the archway, watching with patience which continued straining even as the hall exploded in gunburst like the sound of sunlight and in a ratcheted thud! of concussing wood upon flesh, not knowing what he would find, two hostile white men or maybe even three, knowing he would not shoot his master but afoot in the delight of raw assertion, of *earning*, the feeling of stepping into a new world like the feel of an April-cold stream swirling around his thighs as he stepped clear into the hall.

Tobe stepped out with soaring courage, risking everything including life itself, not in old reaction, but upon a new-glimpsed sight, stepped out not for himself but in his pity for Phrony and all the rest of them, stepped out despite his own inmost feeling of gratitude and simple affection, willing suddenly to pay even that price too.

Chapter 16

PAUSING PRESSED AGAINST THE KITCHEN'S BACK WALL, DEALL WONDERED if at last the secret architecture of things was beginning to disclose itself. Smoke hazed across the morning's gold and green like autumn mist on a New England common. Deall held his rifle in his left hand and the revolver across his chest, while the rebel inside the kitchen scrambled to the other wall. "You out there, aintchee, Yankee?" Then his voice turned reedy: "Oh Lawd I ast for a bucket of cold water! An' it hurts, oh Lawd it hurts!"

Deall waited, looking back across the yard-space at the small outbuildings—smokehouse and outhouses and sheds—through which he had dodged. Their board walls were dry and unpainted, and the earth in front of the backhouses glistened with trodden hairlessness. Deall measured recollections of northern farms against this one: In New England, in Ohio, farmhouses were surrounded by well-tiered, tight outbuildings, chinked and painted as thick and new as the main houses themselves. Right has its own dignity. The mansion was in outrageous, blighting disproportion, as if it had sucked dry the outbuildings. Deall noticed, patiently, that its whiteness was marked by calligraphies of rust which stained facade and ledge.

"Hey Yank! . . . Yank?"

Deall cocked his revolver, muffling the sound. He felt stainless and impervious in this mist-diffused morning light. The wet clean smell of the grass offered him purpose. The mansion was light-proud against the morning's clean lines, its caked whiteness pus-ready for the lance. He turned the corner of the kitchen, still pressed against the wall.

"Hell, ain't no Yankee outchonder. Naw . . . I said ain't no Yankee, ohhh God A'mighty it HURTS!"

Deall edged toward the south window, his left hand holding the Springfield tight against his side so it would not scrape on the wall.

"Ohhh—God A'mighty it hurts!" He heard futile thumping sounds. "All I ever wanted was a bucket of cold water! That's all . . . just a bucket of cold water!"

Deall held the revolver along the brick of the kitchen wall right next to the window. "Ahhhh—Joe! . . . Whoo-eee JOE! . . . Joe, it sure'n hell hurts!" Then musingly to himself "Joe, ye oughtn' a' left me. You know what ye said to Mammy . . . said ye'd take care of me." Then Deall could hear him raise himself for another shout. "JOE! Ye hear?"

In one sweep Deall swung away from the wall and followed the long arc of the revolver around so that he faced into the kitchen and the pistol covered the floor: the muzzle found the rebel, against the wall below the opposite window, hugging his shattered knee against his chest with both hands, his eyes squeezed shut with wailing, "Heyyyy JOE! He . . . ," and then his eyes opened and his head puppeted about fully on Deall.

Deall waited, exultant in the cool force of the moment. The rebel's eyes popped with terror and his mouth dropped. Spittle-covered lips and tangled beard, rotten grey blouse, arrogant brass buttons now helplessly pendant, all these things aligned the man before him with his curling hatred of human pride and natural corruption. "Naw," the rebel was saying, shaking his head, "naw." The words upon Deall's ears were distant as the sound of whicking insects in summer fields, strange rasping of ligament and cartilage.

The man was trying to push himself away from the gun muzzle. In Deall's delay, a chagrined, tentative smile formed amid the wet tangles of his beard. "Yank?" Deall stared down the gun barrel. Lines of viciousness and delusion in the rebel's face melted away beneath the purifying fear. In the pleasant heft of the revolver and the moment's long cool weight, Deall felt an overwhelming power: a sense of having been here before in anticipation, that his enemies were being delivered up. (He recalled the slow arrogant rise of the rebel in that lower room, the toying of his hand upon the rifle as he had not known that Deall's vision marked him clearly over the rifle bead.)

Shoveling himself back up the wall, the young rebel came down on his shattered knee, and his face broke, eyes squeezing in agony, mouth opening. Before his cry could reverse the indraw of breath, Deall shot him dead. Light flare and sound were cavernous. Sweat popped from the boy's homespun jacket in a beaded spray.

That is two, Deall thought. He pressed against the wall again, studying the back of the plantation house. The disproportion between trigger's squeeze and vast impact, the lanes of vision upon which it all depended—these shapes of power surrounded him like brilliant lightfall. He felt leanly prepared. He gathered the world about himself, his intense clear vision covering the rear of the house, the pocked walls and splintered shutters. Deall nodded toward Winters behind the smokehouse and with measured head-stroke toward Hostetler at the end of the cemetery. They began to fire.

He ran toward the house. Metal popped about the windows, and gunfire rattled from the opposite sides, drawn out by his signal. Out of the light he ran into the shade of the gallery and in one stride across the brick, and then he paused beside the door of the house.

He could see into the darkly visible hall: bunched rug and entangled, fretted wood and glass. The air was cold in his lungs. He carefully propped the Springfield against the wall. Deall had less than ever any sense of delay, decay, frustration. The two pounds of his New Model Army Revolver elongated—with it he could touch any corner of that hall, even the upper reaches amid the shadows and the reflections off broken glass and the bars of the banister.

So confident was he of the lucid power of his eye and hand that he was amazed, when he took his first step into the hall, that light did not follow. His eyes were suddenly blotted with furious shapes of darkness: shadows and darkness lunged focuslessly. He stepped upon creaking boards which were as resilient as flesh beneath his feet.

Then the whole left wall slammed against him with a shadow-throwing, sulphurous blue burst. Blue, flare-edged pain coursed down skull and jaw and rib in an angular solid sheet. Bone-hammered and stunned by flame and blast and sulphur stink, amid his reeling he knew he saw hell itself. Dark sulphurous Calvinist hell was across his eyes and took the confidence out of his knees.

He swayed against the wall, hearing a dim sound that was his own moaning, feeling his skull weigh down in the cracked shape of an inbeaten helmet. He waited strangling, hand against face.

A man with all satanic lineaments, flashing eyes and darkly swept hair and lean spaded arrogant jaws stepped out in front of him: so close Deall smelled bay rum beneath the sulphur and the edges of sweat beneath that. His will fluttered within him like a moth's wings, enwebbed by concussed bewilderment of bone and sight. Yet the man did not look at Deall, but back and down, gliding even right before him. Delivered.

Deall wearily swung his enmetaled right hand against the man's open collar where his neck cords ran into his shoulder. The metal slammed so hard (even as the man's round eyes were turning darkly and unrecognizingly upon Deall) that his fingers rang with the pain.

He looked at the fallen man, distantly surprised that the sword-swing had not severed his head: that the pain had not left his hand in sword-strike, but remained in his own bleeding fingers: then finding in slow reprise his fingers upon the brass and steel of a pistol.

He was dimly amazed that he had not swung a sword, but a pistol: then, that he had not shot the man, but had swung. Then orange pain absorbed his attention. His chest hurt when he breathed in. He swayed over the fallen man, pistol dangling.

A rebel soldier, no devil this time, a rebel sergeant stepped out of the arch to his left and into a narrow column of light. Deall looked dully at the man, who was lean as a wolf, all beard and crossbelt and dark-shining gun. The rebel came out of his surprised quick crouch and drew himself up and easily into the aim, mouth slightly open, laying his pocked cheek along the stock of the rifle and swinging the gun barrel with delicate delighted ease right upon Deall's chest.

Deall wondered at his own lack of fear.

As he did, he saw the Negro come from his right, sliding into his vision with the shotgun. Balanced by his vision, the men moved obediently—the rebel with another slight shift of shoulder, Negro slipping silently toward him—until each was transfixed, by the ladders of lightfall, down-reaching tubular shafts of light upon lank tangled hair and rope-nubbed skull. The clarity of Deall's vision returned as he watched the emerging pattern: he studied the way the rebel sergeant lingered in aiming his rifle, the way his chevrons rose greasy as silk into the rectangles of light, the way the movement of his arm pushed more tufts of padding out of the ripped-open shoulder of his jacket.

Then the pattern completed as the shotgun blast filled the whole upwelling hall with flaring loud light and struck white glare off the rebel's forehead and flattened him dust-popping into the hall corner. Deall slackened his vision across the chewed belly and chest of the sergeant.

The rebel's eyes hardened like metal, while the flesh around them worked into whorls. "Shee . . . shee. . . ." His eyes were fierce upon the Negro. Blood burst out of his mouth. His back arched.

Deall stepped lightly and easily to the front door, between the light shafts. He threw the front door open until it jammed against the sergeant's leg. He waved the men in from the front fence, and then turned toward the sound from the upper hall.

"Wolf" It drifted down tentatively as first snow. "Wolf? . . . Hey, Joe?"

Deall stepped back quickly. The boards creaked immediately over his head. "Joe?" Holstetler ducked through the door at the rear of the hall, and Deall pointed up toward the footsteps and the voice, his finger as cautionary and urgent in the light as a hand held upwards in a pulpit. Hostetler mimed comprehension, glanced into the rearward rooms, and then stepped slowly along the hall.

The rebel's footsteps creaked with equal caution, a pause spreading his weight across the boards, stepping again. He started to call again, but the name fell off into a spongy cough. He evidently froze against the wall until the coughing ceased, his mouth sounding full: he spat, whispered, " 'Scuse me, Ma'am," and edged along again. Deall glimpsed Sullivan at the front doorway and pointed again.

Then the rebel saw the dead man's figure in the diametric hall corner. "Aww, Joe!" They heard him gather himself, trying to muffle a cough. His steps swung over them indeterminately. Deall held his revolver in his left hand while he wiped his right casually along his trouser leg. Then he fitted the gun into his hand again. Boot-steps thudded against the porch.

"Hey, Yank?"

Deall shook his head at Hostetler and Sullivan.

"Yank?"

Hostetler answered. "Throw down yeh gun, Johnny."

Deall glared at Hostetler, whose young eager throat was lifted up beside a lead-gleaming rifle barrel.

"Don't be a fool, Johnny. Toss down yeh gun."

"Damned if I will, Yank!"

"Don't be a durned fool!"

Deall put his left hand on Hostetler's arm. The rebel's voice became reedy with exertion.

"I come in like I go out, I reckon! . . . Yes suh! come in like I go out!" They could hear him swaying above them, feet shuffling. "Naw suh th'ow down any God-damned gun to ye. . . . Naw suh. Beg your pardon, ma'am." He coughed again, and a faint thin spray dropped through the lead-grey hall. "Here I come, Yank!" his voice wild with hysteria and pain.

Disembodied exertion came toward the sharp rear bend in the upper hall and toward their vision. Deall kept his eyes on the curve, conscious of the hall now filled with his men, blue and sweat and gunmetal, waiting, all pointing toward that spot with him, parts of his own vision. Even then unprepared for the man himself, so vast were their assumptions of size from the foreshadowing noise: suddenly just a pitiable small figure in bandage-white and dull grey black, carbine muzzle spiraling wildly. His gunshot flared down through the slapping echoes and concussions of their own guns. Chips and plaster rained down, the rebel stumbled heavily against the wall at the head of the stairs, his eyes dark as solid balls in his face, still screeching, "Comin'! Yank, comin'!" He fought to brace himself, legs weaving, firing a heavy pistol in lunging arcs, Deall and Sullivan both firing their pistols up at him steadily, and then he pitched back, started to fall forward, pitched back again while his head rocked up like a vomiting man, and then toppled in a long long fall down, through the smoke and air blast and echo and muzzle flash, his rags like wings. He hit with neck-snapping impact. They gathered over him, Hostetler fanning the smoke with his hat. Spreadeagled on the last step and the hall, eyes baleful and dead, the rebel showed his old blue-rotten wound and his new, smearing red wounds. His very youth enraged Deall with cold anger—a vision of natural corruption.

As Deall bent over the dead boy soldier, he felt someone watching up from the top of the stairs, and with the same calm controlled power that had deserted him only once this morning he raised his vision, knowing the pistol and its reach followed the suave leap of his sight. His curling finger reduced the tension of the trigger to a liquid inconsistency as his sight found the heart-throat where the flash and burst would impact—and then he saw the tiny buttons and miniature frogging so erotically prim against the full bosom, and above that the gentle rigid curve of her flesh, and the eyes squeezed shut like fists, all preparation for death, all nobility of suffering womanhood quite consciously displayed in grand anticipation of death's angular strike.

Chapter 17

In the lantern light the floor of the cellar looked as amber-rich as the flesh of some indeterminate race, the white wall like bone. Hostetler and Keller and Billy Gass stuck their bayonets over and over into the flesh-colored floor, step by step, shoving their bayonets in with waning exultation, probing and rotating the metal blades in the earth. Nothing answered.

Hostetler straightened up in the corner, the earth behind him stitched with blade marks. "Not a Goddamned thing, Saul."

"Maybe so, maybe not."

"By God," Billy Gass said, "they're goin' to pay for killing my messmate. Ain't that right? Eh?" He stabbed the bayonet into the ground. "The Goddamned rebels. I want to tell yeh they killed one of the best boys ever born." He plucked at the earth. "I want yeh to know that."

Gass was dramatically grievous at Coiner's death, and in searching he exercised both his grief and an exaltation over the fight—over the four Confederate bodies laid out side by side on the porch, prize and stamp of the squad's power and skill. Keller watched him idly, and then said to Hostetler, "Hey Joe, we are goin' about this all wrong."

"What d'yeh mean?"

"We ought to get us a nigger. They know ever'thing about these places. A nigger'd tell us if there's anything down here."

Gass swiveled his bayonet in the earth near the wall. "Best ol' boy ever lived. . . ."

Joe Hostetler straightened up. "Maybe you're right," he said to Keller. But both men paused for the moment, watching Billy Gass.

After the fight, while smoke still eddied through the chewed halls of the house, they had carried the bodies outside onto the porch, and then put the rebel owner onto a couch in his own parlor. While Deall attended the rebels and the woman chafed the man's wrists, the soldiers had twitched and glared about them with excitement and warrant. "Hell, he be all right" Keller had said to Winters, softly. Then he plucked a miniature off the corner table as if it were a fruit. Deall looked at them momentarily, and then nodded.

They had plunged through the house, Winters and Sullivan beating to the stairway, the other three taking one wild antic circuit of the downstairs rooms, raking plaster dolls off the mantel with their musket barrels, clawing through the books and tossing them onto the floor, pulling corn bread out of the food safe in the pantry, looking for liquor in the cabinets. They assessed a salt cellar from hand to hand, then Keller tossed it over his shoulder against the wall.

They were young men living in the spangled light of righteous and victorious nationalism: they felt flickeringly guilty at their destruction and looting, but these things were justified by the Methodist wrath they were visiting upon traitors. And by their long summers of sacrifice.

It was for a moment like this—their scouring, democratic presence in the nest of traitors—that they had left the pastures and rolling hills of Greene County, Ohio. They recalled the wide-galleried white farmhouses with all the intensity and brilliance of homesickness. Their Ohio countryside was suavely mild and settled, compared to these sour sandy plantations and piney woods, their earth a healthy, rich black. They remembered early autumnal evenings, sitting on their front porches enjoying the muscle-weariness and contentment of an honest full day of work, listening to the train whistle for the Licking Creek crossing across the slopes, the cool sunset spangling the grass-blades orange and rich green between the long shadows of big oaks and sugar maples. Fathers and mothers behind them in the rocking chairs, or young wives wiping floury hands on their aprons.

Autumn recollections came to them most achingly, because the regiment had marched away to Camp Chase in October of '62.

It was for a moment such as this that they had left what they remembered as the practical, soap-fresh women, the clean young farm girls practiced and confident already at homemaking: that the husbands had left the cool dippers of water placed for them by their young wives where they turned the team at the edge of the field.

They had not been among the first drafts of Ohio soldiers, and war had not been a romantic adventure for them. They had responded out of sober patriotism. What sustained them in the personal sacrifice was their honest sense of national necessity, the menace of the rich, arrogant traitors, toad-swollen with pride, flushed in the ease of a balmy land, needing a lesson in whose country this was, by God! Fire on the flag, will they? At Chickamauga and Kenesaw and Jonesboro their regimental flags had gleamed through the powder smoke with religious appeal, the eagle aureoled, the stripes shining.

And here, after all the casualties and the loneliness and fear and thirst, here they were at last. When they had entered the house after the morning-long fight for it, righteousness had been as accessible before them as the polished eagles on the flagpoles ("Gifts-to-our-Valiant-Sons-by-the-Ladies-of-the-Mount-Union-Methodist-Church").

Here, at last, they were.

And this was the real thing, that they had been after, no bare-assed white trash anymore, but sponge-rich, the real thing. You could tell by the rows of nigger cabins and the furniture and the columns out front, and the way they didn't even keep anything up except the big house.

In *this* house they were no longer looking for bonnets and cheap lockets and salt cellars. Their circuit had brought them back to the parlor, breathing hard, empty-handed. The three people at the sofa had not moved. The rebel's wife was looking up at them with beleaguered hate, and Gass and Hostetler drew up: Keller asked if their manners were not up to Southron standards? She raised her chin, and turned her eyes away. Confused, Gass had looked back and forth between Keller's openly contemptuous grin and Deall's silent, assessing stare. Gass hung, blushing: and then out of his nervous energy he had suddenly rammed his bayonet into a small-legged, thickly stuffed chair, so that the padding wadded out like pus. Then, even with the bayonet still in the chairback and his other hand feeling of the cotton, he had heard Winters and Sullivan upstairs and had looked at Keller and Hostetler and simultaneously they had all thought of the cellar.

They had clustered together at the bottom of the cellar stairs, panting against the green smell of antiquity and mildew, while Hostetler fumbled to ignite the lantern. And then, in the sudden spray of light, they had fastened upon the jewellike gleam from tray and trowel and shards of cut glass.

Earth was dug out in a shallow semicircle from the old wall. Stunning fulfillment sang in their ears. They broke out of their frozen, openmouthed exultation and fell to their knees, scraping through the loosened dirt with their bare hands, pawing at it.

"Hot damn, boys! What I tell you? Hey? Stick with ol' Saul. . . ."

"You tell 'em, Saul."

But the sides of their hands chafed across hard-packed earth, away from the wall. The dirt was loose and grain-sifting only flush beside the old brick, from erosion or some seeming logicality of construction. In that narrow space there was no room to bury sacks, or carpetbags of silver. Keller dubiously shoveled his hand into the loose perimeter just as Billy Gass wheeled his bayonet down at it in clumsy enthusiasm.

"Watch your damned bayonet, by God!" Keller jerked his hand away.

"I'm sorry, Saul! . . . Cut yeh? Hunh, Saul?"

"Damn son of a bitch . . . Watch yeh damn bayonet."

"Jesus, Saul. I . . . It cut you?"

Hostetler had already sliced his left palm on a chunk of the decanter. He rocked back on his knees, frowning. The earth away from the wall was indisputably solid.

"You know what," Hostetler said. "They probably were just starting to bury these here bottles when we come. They probably couldn't finish, by the time we broke in."

"Yeah," Keller said, hugging his bruised hand under his armpit. "Yeah. It looks like they smashed up the truck when they couldn't get it hidden."

He felt amid the broken cut glass and smelled his fingers. "Must of been . . . brandy, or corn whiskey." He rubbed his hand across his trouser leg. "Thieving arrogant Goddamned son-of-a-bitching bastards. Busted it up so we could not touch it."

Gass hung back, violently embarrassed by nearly maiming Keller.

"Only place it ar' give at all is right next to the wall," Hostetler had said. "And no room to bury nothing right here. . . . You know, if they come down to bury this when we come on 'em this morning, it don't stand to reason that they would hide it where they had hidden the rest of the stuff, anyhow. Does it? I mean, they must have been too pressed to risk uncovering their jew-lery and such, just for whiskey. . . ."

They had looked around the cellar.

"Yeah," Keller said, rubbing his chin.

"Maybe even they left this here just to lead us *away* from the real spot. I mean . . ."

"Yeah," Keller had said. "Fix your bayonet."

Rubicund with new enthusiasm, they had shoved aside boxes and trunks and old picture frames, to hack at remote corners of the room. When their exuberance had waned, Keller had divided the whole floor among them and they had approached it with more care. Gass had been given the third next to the whitewashed brick wall, and he had started out no more than a deliberate foot from it. Almost immediately he had found another spot of loosened earth up against the wall, and Keller and Hostetler had clambered back across the rubbish to investigate. But again the softness was only inches shallow above hard-packed clay, and it shelved down narrowly toward the base of the brick wall, becoming part of that erosion or fault or looseness they had discovered right off.

"It ain't no room along there. The ground's just looser, is all."

"Shit," Keller said, "it's all a trick. They planned for us to dig over this way, anyhow. There ain't nothing beside that damned wall. Move off from it some."

Now their careful circuits were almost completed, and they had found nothing. Their excitement drained: sweat was cold under their blouses. The grainy smell of the darkness was familiar, the stench of potato cellars and old decay. Keller and Hostetler shivered with drying sweat.

"Yes sir," Keller said, "what we need us is a nigger."

The two men were breathing deeply against their exertion. They leaned on their Springfields and watched Gass. He still probed the floor, wrenching the rifle and mumbling professionally to himself now that their eyes were upon him. Hostetler winked at Keller, sharing superior experience. They were twenty-two. Billy Gass had lied about his age, had joined the regiment only just before Chickamauga, and was only seventeen now. Watching his young efforts, they both remembered Saturday mornings in Mount Union, standing together in the cool blue shadows away from the summer sun, awaiting news from the South. Horses and mules and wagons were hitched out on the square around the county courthouse. Mauve and red brick walls were placarded with fat-serifed signs, including the huge one Mr. Piepho had hung over his new bakery. The air had been rich with patriotic intensity: the government itself (don't care what you say, it's the best ever devised, by God) was menaced. With it was challenged their self-esteem, their lithographed pride in sweeping past heroisms and their sincere estimations of national destinies, things that involved a man's assertions of personal worth, and hopes for personal success: the accessibility of any drawing room in the land for themselves once they had earned it. Don't care how high an' mighty he is, that two-year-old daughter of mine'll be good enough for any man in this republic. They had stood in the cocksure, rawboned confidence of American youth. The younger boys of the village had been playing crack-the-whip on the grass of the courthouse square. The strength of the republic rests on those boys, Lawyer Hayes had said, joining their conversation (Hayes had lost both legs at Peachtree Creek). Billy Gass had been one of the town boys in that summer of 1861.

Keller and Hostetler winked, but they did not want to leave off that righteous hilarity themselves, which still impelled Gass. They watched him. Ripping chairs and breaking bottles were green assertions, while getting a nigger to help required a putting on consciousness. But finding the arrogant bastards' hidden treasure would be like exposing cysts of corruption to air and sunlight. And if they wanted to find anything before Deall dragged them off, they better find it quick. The bastards thought their niggers made them better than other white men, Keller thought. Well, let their own niggers make 'em poorer, anyhow. I might tell that one to Sully.

"Well, I go see . . ."

But Hostetler, thinking again, touched him on the elbow. "Hey, Saul. You know the soil's pretty loose all *along* this wall. . . ."

Billy Gass raised up and looked at the wall too.

"They's that loose spot nearly a foot wide, up against it right there."

"So? What are you thinking?"

"Reckon there's anything on t'other *side* of that wall? I mean . . . reckon it *moves*, or anything?"

"It's the house wall, ain't it?"

The three of them looked speculatively. Gass shivered inside his coat: moving walls suggested macabre, legendary horrors of slavery.

"I suppose it is," Hostetler said. "But it ain't like the others."

"Well shit," Gass said, spasming against his nerves. "I'll see. We cain't let 'em hide their stuff from our squad, hey fellahs?"

He swung his rifle butt against the wall as hard as he could. The clang was ringingly abusive in the stone cellar. Gass slammed at the wall again, the butt descending just past his ear as his forearms drove it down. This time the butt skittered along the wall and he scraped his knuckles against the brick. "Son of a bitch!"

The solidity of the wall jarred sense into Hostetler and Keller. They laughed genially at Gass's shrill, implausible oaths.

"Keep on trying, son. You will have that wall down in another couple years."

"Hit him another lick. Yeh still have one good hand, don't yeh?"

"Well," Billy said, sucking at the raw knuckles, "we *cain't* let the Goddamned rebels get away with hidin' their stuff, can we?"

"Let's get us a nigger," Keller said.

"I will come along too," Hostetler said. "This place is durn close, you know?"

Going up the cellar steps, Keller let his rifle butt batter against the edge of each step.

Gass sat on a box in the cellar, morosely, his hands on the rifle muzzle and his cheek against them. I played the fool *again*. . . . Against his embarrassments, he began to frame statements about Coiner's death. Best messmate, I mean to say . . . and who is going to tell Nancy Summers, hey? They got a lot to answer for . . . He scuffed at the dirt with his brogan toe. His knuckles ached. I bet that there is somethin' behind that wall. Bet there is.

He got off the box and wiped his hands, looking at the wall. There was blood on his knuckles. He looked around for a rag and saw a piece of fluffy cloth by the box. He started to wrap it around his right hand, and then noticed the threaded pink ribbon looped along one edge. His cheeks swelled with blushing and he glanced around quickly. Woman's underthin's, by God. He tightened and had to shuffle his feet. His parents admonished; he wadded and tossed the thing over into the far shadows.

With the toss, he thought he saw someone along that wall. Chillness surged through his chest. He lowered the rifle, peering through the shadows. Ah, nothin'. We been over there. Yes sir, we checked. He moved his lips talking to himself, wishing the big rifle were loaded. Silence hummed. Everybody *knew* these plantation homes were rich with passages and ghosts and crime-too-deep . . . boards creaked behind him and he swung about, the bayonet glittering in an arc through the lantern light. When he swung back again toward the corner where he had seen the movement, the corner of his eye saw dark and light substance in human form. When he peered directly, it resolved itself into nothing—not even the clothes rack or a hanging shirt.

There's nothing, he said, nothing.

He edged back to the wall, washing out his nervousness by remembering the lift of that woman's chin. Well she so Goddamned high and mighty. The Gasses are as good as she is, and a damn sight better. Let 'em tell me Sis' Ellen ain't as good as she is. He fused that memory with recollection of a woman in Nashville pulling her skirts out of his path, right in front of his innocent, smiling politeness. What they all need is a man to teach 'em a thing or two. He saw the elegant softness of both women reduced to animal pleadings by a MAN, the women naked and gleaming-vague, the man a shadow.

Immediately he was chastened with guilt at the very thought. A man or somethin'. . . .

The one upstairs even, why she ain't no decent woman, I warrant you. Naw she . . . she prob'ly . . .

Despite Billy's guilt, the image rearmed him with determination and aim.

There's something behind this wall. He sensed the falseness of it to the housefront. If they're so smart, why'd they paint the wall white like this? Gass ran his palm along the brick face, and chalky whitewash came off on his fingertips. What was behind it must be the things of their arrogance—family treasures and money, cut glass and silver and the things that gave them their airs. He wondered what such things might be, necklaces, jewelry, silver from overseas? Can I find it myself, what'd the lady think of that? One ol' Yankee boy finds what they thought they had hid. And on a girl back home . . . (he envisaged a composite of Winters' young wife Beth with the bright eyes, and Pete Tyler's sister Edith, who was so slim, but round-hipped, going in the church that day. The vision could not involve Nancy Summers anymore).

He pushed his hand along, looking for some secret panel. The bricks were impenetrably mundane and labor-raised. Aw, shit. He began to tap it with his rifle butt, softly, listening for some break or hollowness.

While pressing his ear to the wall, his eyes fell to the floor. His attention went back to the soft earth along its base. Gass hummed tunelessly against the memory of his bayonet blade between Keller's (good old *Saul's!*) fingers, as he began to fret at the edge with it once more. The dirt was indeed much looser there: the blade flicked up sprays of dry, grainy soil. That softened area splayed out just beside one of the white pillars. Wonder if they dug down at an angle *underneath* the wall? But the wall runs too deep, don't it? He tested the dimensions of the semicircle, and started to unfasten his bayonet the better to spade with, his eyes still fixed upon the earth.

A pressure passed across his back as from the fields of opposed magnets—stiff, invisible, rubber-sliding. His hair rose above his collar. Sound howled in his chest.

He swung around wildly, rifle-brass flaring into the light.

A dim human shape—nigger?! nigger?—melted before his full vision. A cry suspended in the back of his own throat, he lunged straight forward in bayonet-drill reflex, the blade slicing through green dark air. His shin slammed against a trunk and he plunged forward and down, wood lathing and chair frames and an artist's easel crashing down around him, an old drapery catching his plunge with ripping striations.

The steps exploded loudly. Men were behind him. They *seen* me! He flooded with embarrassment. Hot flushing humiliation succeeded the cold fear. He had to twist and squat back to escape the curtain and the tangled wood, and then near fell down again plucking his rifle free of dank tasseling and wooden angle.

"You got something cornered, Billy?"

"See a ghost?"

Phil-Saul-Joe-Carl, all watching: and a nigger man, old and shuffling bald.

Billy smoothed at the front of his blouse. He blushed helplessly. "Gh-ghost? Hah. Naw. Naw, I just tripped down. I reckon I just tripped down, that is all. Phil, you and Carl best take care where yeh step. Saul'll tell yeh that. It is as dark down here as a nigger's hide, 's truth. Ain't it, Saul?"

"But you didn't find anything?" He looked from the edge of the white wall, over to the old curtain.

Billy moved a half step so that he stood among the soldiers, and now the Negro was the isolated one. "No, Saul. And I looked right close, too." He paused, deepening his voice into shrewdness. "I tell you, if there's anything behind that wall, I 'spect she grew there. Yessir, it grew . . ."

"Well," Saul said, "this here's the one that will know. What say, Uncle?"

"Yes suh, yes suh, Mist' Yankee." The man was gaunt and vague. He spoke with a hollow, wheezing monotone. "They brought they stuff down here."

"What did he say?"

"Say they brought they stuff down here, seh." He held his mouth open in a friendly half-smile.

"Where'd they put it, Uncle?"

The man looked around wonderingly, as though he had never seen the cellar before. "They . . . they bury it I 'spect." He looked around with the same slow geniality with which he spoke. The soldiers began to fidget.

"Whereabouts, then?"

"Say they bury it, I 'spect."

"I know what you said, Uncle. What I want to know is, *where* did they bury it?"

The Negro looked at Keller slowly, softly, eyes full and moist: Keller was scowling.

"Say you don't *trust* them other two, Saul?" Winters asked lightly. "Say *this* is the one to tell us, eh? Shee—"

"Where did they bury it, nigger?"

"I'spect they bury hit down here. . . ."

Keller hit him with his open palm, the slap cracking off the whitewashed wall. "You said that, nigger. Now tell us where'bouts."

The man held his large bony hand up beside his face, staring wordlessly, witlessly, his eyes still mild. The silence was cold and dark.

"Well," Keller began again, reasonably. "You admit they hid their stuff down cellar, eh? You told us that out back, remember? You do remember, eh? Well now, where'bouts?"

"Why seh I don't recollect that I knows that—I don't . . ." His voice roamed mildly, and Keller with equal facility slapped the other cheek.

"Saul, Saul . . ."

"Well *hell*, Joe. The rebels put th' fear of God into 'em to make 'em work. We got to do the same, don't we?"

The old man's face was wet, still looking wondrously from man to man of them, but the moist eyes staining the face. His mouth was set in a loose line; uncomprehending, no longer smiling.

Saul Keller began again. "Now then, out back you said they buried their stuff down cellar? Good, you remember. Now where? And I don't mean the floor. I know that. They wouldn't bury it in the ceiling, would they . . ."

"No suh Mist' Yankee—they wouldn't hardly bury it in no ceilin'. . . ."

"Well by God you brought me to it. Hand me your Springfield, Billy. . . . I said, hand me th' damn gun!"

Saul leaned on the rifle. "Now, then, Uncle. That is your name, matter of fact? Uncle? . . . All right, Uncle, now where down here is it buried? Now don't lie to me. We done been over ever' foot of this cellar, and some of it twice. Eh Billy? Eh?"

"Damn right, Saul!"

"Now then, do you know exactly where it is buried?"

The black shook his head slightly, face still wet, taking no notice of the bayonet rising between Keller's clasped fingers.

"Yeh don't know? All right. Now tell me this. You been here all your life, haven't yeh."

"I reckon so—I . . ."

"All your life. Now you been here all your life and you," the voice kept on in a steady metallic tonelessness, "you mean to tell me, us, that you don't know where your massa buried his stuff? You mean to tell me that? Hey?" Saul shifted the long rifle so that the bayonet slanted toward the black's neck.

"Now one more time, nigger" he said slowly in the steady voice, drawing the bayonet point up against the man's neck. The black's eyes were still moistly vague and focusless.

"All right, Saul," Hostetler said. "All right, lemme try." He put his hand on the gun barrel. "Uncle, is what you mean to say is, you never saw the stuff, the white folks' stuff, buried? You never saw it actually buried? Is that what you mean to say?"

"Well Mass' Yankee, yes seh—I never seen 'em bury they stuff."

They all breathed deep out. "Well that's what I thought." Hostetler took the Springfield from Saul, and now he stood leaning on it, the bayonet rising beside his fair young face. "Well tell me this, Uncle. Have you ever heard the other darkies tell stories about this place . . . about this cellar?"

"Yes seh, I have heard them tell." The men looked sharply into the black's face once more, raising their eyes from the pocked dirt floor.

Hostetler continued in his steady voice, drawing out the black's story like a fragile thread. "Well now, what did you hear, Uncle? Lots of things?"

"Yes seh, lots of things."

"What kinds of things, Uncle?" It was the minstrel-show rhythm.

"Well, I heard Sukey's son Jewel one time—I heard him tell they was something funny like. Said somethin' movin' round down here all the time, amongst the boxes and the barrels, most *all* the time." The man's voice was wheezingly mild and inflectionless. "Said he was down here one time somethin' moved over in the corner, time he went to look, it gone. Said he said ain't never goin' down in the cellar no more, no suh. The niggers I heard them say that lots of time, there was somethin' down here movin' and Jewel—I 'spect it was Jewel—he say he heard the moaning one time when he was long-side the wall. He heard the moanin' and he went on up, and I heard another nigger Trump—he say they was somethin' *back* of the white wall but Trump he didn't say what, and then just last night"—and again their vision raised to the Negro's face—"why even just last night I heard the shoutin' from the house, clear out to where I stays, and it was Mistess Celia she saw somethin' down here too . . ."

"Why was she down here, Uncle? Did you hear that?"

But his voice kept on, as thin and frayed and soft as worn flannel, unheeding, the big hands hesitant half-raised, ". . . and ol' Aunt Sukey I heard her—I 'spect it was a *long* time ago—I heard her say that they was a *soul* down here huntin' and huntin' for its body, I heard her say that I don't know, but that was a long time ago, she say you look behind this wall you fin' the truth out, but the niggers they never told . . ."

"Now, *Uncle*. . . . Your Mistess. Why did *she* come down here?"

The mouth was loose and open. His eyes settled on Hostetler's face.

"Uncle, why did she come down? To bury . . . bury something?"

"I 'spects so."

"And you don't know whereabouts, or what?"

The Negro shook his head solemnly. "No seh Mist' Yankee, they never lets the nigger down here when they bury they stuff. . . ."

"He's lying," Saul Keller said. "The niggers do all the work for 'em, and he know it. More niggers'n you can shake a stick at around here and you tellin' me that they dirty their own hands?"

The black raised his hands gently, to shield his face.

"They are afraid the niggers'd tell us, I bet."

"Bet, hell. They ain't got no *cause* to be afraid. I ain't never seen anybody more a liar than this ol' darky, I tell you! . . . What are you lyin' for, Uncle?"

The Negro stood with his hands half-raised, watching them.

"Hey? Why are you lying?"

"Maybe he ain't lying, Saul."

"Hell," Carl Winters said, "the rebels have them so scared they about shit when they tell 'em to."

Sullivan changed the subject. "You think there *might* be something behind this wall, though?"

"Well, Phil. . . ." Hostetler started, but Gass's embarrassments overflowed—the bayonet beside Keller's hands and then his own sprawling in the rubbage: why me, all of the time!

"Ain't nothing there, Phil. I can tell you that, and so can Joe and Saul. We looked over it earlier, and I looked over ever' damn *inch* of it again while you fellows was upstairs. Ain't nothing there."

His voice was screeching—high in his ears: so he kept elaborating.

"And those diggings—see 'em there up against it, Phil?—right there, and there?—well that we figure is where they wanted us to look, because they left a spade and some broke glass. That, or that is where they started to bury their whiskey but ran out a' time, so they broke it. Sonsa bitches, they broke it so we could not get it. We come on 'em too fast, you and Joe. . . ."

"Well . . . you all figure there is anything behind this wall, though?"

"Ain't nothing there, Phil," Hostetler said. "Not a thing."

"Yeah, shit. We looked at ever inch of the thing."

Sullivan ran his hand along it. "No, it is old all right. There ain't nothing recent about it. Wherever they hid their silver from Sherman, it ain't behind this here."

"What is above it . . . a room? Maybe there is a door."

"Naw. It is the side yard, I reckon."

"It don't seem like it is the wall of the house, though."

"Well, you get turned around down here," Keller said. "I am telling you, they didn't build this wall to hide their truck in, and that is what I'm after. Buried niggers behind there, they can keep!"

They laughed. The black man stood against the wall, flat, his eyes still moist, his lip loose, hands raised half-protectingly. His flesh was contrasted sharply by the stark bone white of the old wall.

There was a long moment of silence. Hostetler chewed a hang-nail, spit, frowned down at the finger. Then he brightened. "Well hell, a man would let a nigger do his own work, that proves it, eh?" he suddenly asked. Even in the Negro's dull wet eyes, still focusless, senile, the hands still will-lessly, mindlessly raised, they once more saw the gleaming edges of their righteousness. His helplessness was so distant from those Saturday summer mornings in the Ohio town square with bright dust motes in the air and the sharp cleanly cut words of the white children, blond heads bobbing in the shade and sunlight. Like the unpainted outhouses and the rust streaks to the rear of the distant gleaming white house, so this *nigger* was behind all that pride and pretension!

"By God, no white man'd lie like he did."

"Couldn't scare a white man like that."

"Well boys," Keller said, "there's one white man here no rebel son of a bitch is going to lord it over at all. Let's see what the rebels have for lunch, and then have another go at the niggers. What say, boys?"

Billy Gass was the first to follow him up the steps. The cellar seemed old and familiarly dank. They breathed deeply and stretched in the hallway, in the fresh sweet air. They were not bad or evil men, and they were uncomfortable at the lengths to which their righteousness had carried them. They were through in the cellar.

They did not notice the black man in the corner, beside the steps, as they filed back up toward the light. Tobe had slipped down unnoticed during the questioning. He watched them go past, his face in its rigid mask, settled into it after the lip-straining exertion of shooting the rebel. He watched until they were at the top of the stairs, then relaxed the lines of his face and went toward Uncle Mitchell. "They gone, Uncle."

Chapter 18

DEALL SAT IN THE UPHOLSTERED CHAIR, THE MATE TO THE ONE OPENED by Gass's bayonet. The little chair was near the middle of the parlor, scraped there so violently during the house's defense that its brass-mounted feet had scarred the floorboards. He could hear his men eating ham and corn bread outside in the noon sunlight. The man and wife watched him.

Deliberately, Deall put his left shoe upon the plush-caked divan, and tilted his chair back upon its spindly, uncarved rear legs.

The movement, even amid the wadded rugs, the graphite-grey scars along the walls, the overturned table and the glass shards like hailstorm ice, was one of strange presumption for him. He felt it as such. Parlor decorums, those formally drawn forth in the locked-away formal rooms of his lifetime, weighed upon him. He had always sat with hands decorously upon his knees.

But the gesture was compelled: he did it as deliberately as he had moved his soldiers into positions during the fight. Deall felt his weight shift and pivot hollowly, with feathery responsiveness, upon the chair legs and one shoe toe. The slight swaying suggested patterns of lightfall. Cool winter air washed through shattered undraped windows.

The rebels looked at his gesture with silent outrage. He felt strangely and coldly pleased.

Malory was upright upon the long striped sofa (near his side Deall could see the tiny priapic head of a lodged minié ball, just within the striped fabric). He was rubbing the split skin and long bruise of his neck, and spots of his blood were garnet and black about his open collar. He wore the arrogant russet boots and plaid trousers of a plantation owner.

His wife stood beside him, hands clasped, hips at the level of her husband's eye. Her fierce defiant glare was off Deall now, and he looked assessingly at the disordered brown braid and the fastened and the dangling buttons down the jacket of her dress. She was a deliberate study of hostage-tense composure and pride.

Deall had first thought she was the rebel's daughter, she seemed to him so young and full, compared to his dry whiteness. Their features were similar, the precise handsome nose and dark eyes and thick black hair. But between the two of them he had a sense of further familiarity, a resiliency about her waist which seemed to him concupiscent, mature. Her hand now on the man's forehead suggested to Deall the darkest intertwinings of refined lust pursued through sloth and ease. He compared her dress, its disheveled stripes and martial frogging and buttons, to Lucy's demure black and white and light blue.

"You are feeling better now, Mr. Malory?" Deall asked this with cool tightness.

The man nodded thickly, and then raised his face toward Deall, suffering and flushed and trapped, the wings of hair framing his cheekbones. With the man's single eye upon him, Deall unthinkingly raised his other shoe to the divan, so that he did not touch the floor.

"And no thanks," the rebel's wife said, "to you and your men. Do the heroic saviors of the Union customarily disport themselves as unruly boys?" Her last breaking word was as tattered as the room itself. The rebel's single bright eye closed with the pain of trying to speak.

Deall looked with swift, thin-lipped economy at the woman. "You are quite fortunate he is not dead, you know."

"A fair *fight*, sir! Had you an officer about, I would soon tell him about the . . . the unbridled arrogance you permit your men."

Deall placed his brown hand over his lips and chin, watching her, waiting like a teacher attending a tedious and incorrect answer.

"And the destruction, the mess you have permitted, the things you have allowed your men to do before our very *eyes!*" She swept her hand majestically at the ruined chair. Deall smiled tersely at the disemboweled, fat little thing. "Why, these furnishings have been in Mr. Malory's family for a hundred years, and . . ." Her eyes swerved back and forth as she sought for words. ". . . and they are *price*less, irre*place*able, some of them. . . ."

He looked about the room, following the gestures of her polished hand. In the corner there was a roundabout with a crushed front leg, and a thick, dark-plushed chair next to it, the seat too close to the ground, too close to the fireplace. Books were spilled onto the floor from bookshelves within arched niches. The books were subscription issues and mass edition volumes with false, rub-worn gilt arabesques and anchors. A bronze mantel-lamp like some punctured sea plant lay among them. All these things struck him as so different from the New England quadrature of clean line and austere simplicity. He recalled his home: ladder-backed chairs above varnished yellow gold floorboards, books in simplest, age-bronzed bindings, with clearly stamped titles upon black shining squares of leather, the bookshelf edges intensely straight, shelves and walls painted in pure white paint, so white that shadows seemed blue. (He looked about the chipped fireplace at the dull, fleshly buff paint and the peeling, glue-backed wallpaper with its tarnished fleur-de-lys design.)

"And let me assure you, sir, that I am not above sending a letter even to a Yankee officer . . ."

Overswollen furniture, massive empire curves, rich textures, and all the while turkey-feather fans and plaster dogs on the mantelpiece! These tastelessly thick lardings, he thought: efforts to decorate a prison, without taste or the comprehension of simplicity. The sofa the rebel sat upon was rotund with curves of sluggishly blackened wood. Never could the measure of moral truth have been clearer in the very surface of things.

He looked at the rebel in the sweep of this thought, and found the man's eye upon him—hot intense vision, no longer moist with pain, but dry now with hatred.

"And the af*fronts* offered us, sir! Worse even than this mindless destruction, the curses given my husband, a wounded officer, the leers, and all permitted. . . ."

Deall looked coldly and deliberately at her. His vision trapped her eyes and restrained them from sweeping new, orotund outrage from the air.

"You do not understand, ma'am." He found the pure, economically tight phrases, he held his hands clasped before his face. "You are talking about furniture and decorum. But these are hardly the points. Your husband is a traitor, and a *bushwhacker*." Deall had been anticipating the impact of the last, crude word upon the satanic man, but the wife seized upon "traitor" with organized indignation, so it was lost.

"Traitor! Why . . . why he is a patriot, sir!"

Deall dropped his level of high concentration. He would have to deal with the woman's arguments.

"Patriot to what, pray?"

"The South, sir. Georgia, his native land."

Deall felt as though he were leading the lowest classes of the common school through its lessons while the uppers sported with his reputation in the back rows: the rebel continued staring at him. Deall clenched his teeth speculatively, searching the cornices of the room for the most direct approach.

"Whom, ma'am, is this county named for?"

"Colonel Lamar Coffin, who rode at Francis Marion's right hand."

"So he fought in the old Revolutionary War?"

"Of course."

"Of what *nation* was he a patriot? For what country did he fight? The South?"

"Well . . ."

"Georgia, then?"

"I do not see—"

"For what?"

Outside, one of his men broke wind loudly. Suddenly irritated, Deall plunged to the answer himself.

"You know it well enough, madam. For America."

"For our freedom from a *tyrant*, too." She laced into the word, and her eyes sparkled.

"Why . . . who is the tyrant? Who enslaves men nowadays?"

"Abe Lincoln."

Deall had been surprised at her vivacity. Now he was stunned at her willful recalcitrance.

"We are fighting for our liberty as our forefathers did. They fought the Tyrant George, we fight the Tyrant Abraham."

"Why there is no comparison. You have no right to rebel from a representative government."

"States' Rights, sir!" she said. "A compact freely entered into can be withdrawn from as freely."

Deall knew he was trading catchphrases. He looked up at the ceiling again. "No, madam, no. States may have their rights, I will grant. But surely, ma'am, no one has the right to rebel in the name of slavery." He looked down with dismissing finality. "There are higher laws than those of mere States' Rights."

Then the rebel snorted, a flat, contemptuous sound, and turned his gaze from Deall out through the window. Deall dropped his feet from the divan to the floor. He felt growing, glitter-edged rage. "Sir?"

"I never hear of Higher Laws, sir, but what I reach for my wallet. Yes sir." Malory turned and looked at Deall with light sarcasm. Deall had a glimpse of backslapping camaraderie, an odor of a swaggering, high-collared code wherein the impact of humor outreached that of truth. "Yes sir. But what I reach my hand back for my wallet."

Deall began speaking before he realized there was no reply he could make. "What . . . what does that mean, sir?"

"Nonsense, sir. They fought for their own land, by God. Not to replace George the Third with a king in Washington."

"For the God-given rights of all men, I believe, would be more accurate."

"Exactly my point, sir." The rebel's eye was arrow-centered with a shaft of light from the window. "A man's basic right to do as he wishes, on his own land, sir."

Outside, Winters had just plucked out a small rose bush, and the men were bending in the sunlight, spading and probing. Dirt flew in a loose spray from a resilient bayonet.

"Basic right? But what about the Negro, sir?"

"Colonel Lamar Coffin owned hundreds—"(Deall felt an enraged embarrassment at being entangled in the puerile distinctions he had made for the woman. This glittering anger was in his throat.) "—of them. What of 'em?"

"Why, have *they* no rights?"

"Not according to the Constitution, sir. Which all the states ratified."

"And which would have soon been amended, by damn."

"Had it been so amended at the beginning, we would not have joined the Union. We freely and honorably entered, sir. And since you then would change the terms of the covenant, we had every right to withdraw as freely and honorably."

Deall shook his head and again raised his eyes to the ceiling, watching the fluting patterns of light (from the spades and bayonets of his men outside, he dimly recognized). What were such facts, such historical accidents, such inherited past blunderings, to a free, self-reliant man? He had to do not with the past, but with the future.

"Do you know the law, sir?" the rebel was going on. "When a contract is legally—"

"How can *you* talk of rights!" Deall said. He glared down again at the man. "You forfeited your rights the minute, the *second,* you presumed to own another human being.—Ah sir, hear me out! The moment you thought you could do that thing, that you could own a human being, you ceased to *have* rights."

"According to the Consti—"

"God damn the Constitution!" Deall rocked back upon the rear of his chair, then sat forward. "You cannot use a piece of paper to shield you from the truth, man! You have forfeited any human rights when you presumed to violate all human rights . . ."

But the rebel was looking away, shaking his head as if to an audience of chuckling planters. The fold of his mouth inset with resignation and sarcasm.

Deall was swept with a sudden, violent anger. It flared as hot, white ejaculations within his skull, and he found himself on his feet, and his hand opening to slap away the impenetrable, willful blindness.

He steadied himself with a whistling intake of breath, and closed the hand to his side.

"Do you hear me, sir? Do you?" He breathed shakily while the rebel's eye came back to face him, shadowed slightly by its dark brow. "Are you really going to say, that it is a *right* to own people? To own slaves? You have a *right* to own the sweat of another's brow?" He could not limit his voice to the swing of the questions. It flared. "Is it a *right* to be able to sell men as if they were draft animals? Is it a *right* to be able to buy women as if—"

"You want to talk about a man's rights, sir? By God, then, you want to talk about a man's rights?"

"—they were brood mares? Is it a *right* to sell childr—"

"Rights, you were saying, sir! *Rights*." The rebel stood up in front of him abruptly, in one lean movement which jerked Deall's head up and back. The man spoke right into his face, and Deall, even in his intensity, was startled by the brass odor of cold outrage.

"What in the *hell*, sir, do you Yankees know about rights? For I will tell you one thing only. When a man no longer has the right to take care of his own family and his own people, there is no other right left worth the Goddamned name. There are no other 'rights' left."

"Well, but you must have slaves, in order to take care, as you put it, of y—"

"*Must* have slaves? *Must* have 'em? Son of a bitch, what the hell do *you* know about it? Let me tell you this. I wish the first nigger had never come over. I wish it every day and every night of my life, sir. You cain't train 'em to take care of themselves, they are dirty and ignorant and wors'n a mule for the stubborn meanness. No sir, I never wanted the *first* slave."

"But you seem quite desperate to keep them. Three years of war have proven the lie to your words."

"No sir, they prove the truth of my words. As long as the nigger is over here, the only way I aim to live side by side with him is as his master, by the Good Lord. You, none of *you*, live down here, and you all plan on stealin' us blind and going away. But I can't leave. I got to stay here, and the only way I aim to stay is as master."

The violent absoluteness of his speech was damning. We will never change these people, Deall thought. Destruction, a hammering reduction of them, is all. But, looking once more up toward the cream-white ceiling, he still sought for an argument, some pattern of proof. He still felt lineaments of power about himself, the same down-reaching power that had balanced Negro and rebel sergeant. The recalcitrance of people entangled and frustrated him.

Malory was looking through the window across his land, and saying more mildly, "And did you know them as I do, you would . . ."

"So," Deall said, "they will never be ready for freedom?"

"I misdoubt it, sir. When they take care of their own children. When they marry their women," the rebel said with the ease of imparting empirical, conclusive evidence, "then perhaps. But that day will never come—or not soon, sir."

"Then you cannot—you cannot conceive of the black man as a human being?"

"Oh I reckon he is that, but a human of a certain kind."

"But, you cannot conceive him as being as good as you and I, as capable of being as good as a white man, with a chance, with training?"

"Some, I expect. Perhaps—from my experience, sir—one in ten. Perhaps one in ten could change."

"Only one in ten? But we were led here, do you know, by one of your blacks—Jade, I believe . . ."

"A worthless nigger, and always has been. And it remains, sir to see whether—"

"But—ah wait, wait and hear me—did you know that another of your unchangeable 'niggers' saved my life? In your hall?"

The rebel stared at Deall.

"Yes, sir. Another one of your 'niggers' killed a rebel soldier who was on the very instant of killing me. And he did it with no training, I expect, without even the benefit of . . ."

"Who? Which one was it?"

". . . even the benefit of preparation. With a single chance, a shotgun and a moment, he proved himself to be capable of change, and thus potential, and is not that the meaning of man? Potential?"

The rebel's eye glared with a violence Deall had not seen before —not a cold outrage but a malevolence, and Deall knew he had touched him then.

"Tobe," the rebel said, "it must have been Tobe."

"Yes. But did you think he was one, ah, of your tenth capable of . . ."

"No, by God, no!"

"But I assure you it happened. You may see the man's body."

Then Deall recognized the direction of the rebel's answer. "*No*, by God. All it proves is that they *are* worthless. If after all these years, and all we have done for him and his people, if after all these years, he is still thus capable, do you know what that does prove, sir? It proves there is not a *single Goddamned one* of the race capable of improving or even saving." The rebel's long face was bronze with rage, which he was mastering by force of will.

"No sir, I deny your argument. It don't prove change at all. It does prove we can never live with them in any other way. Change—to violate all trust, to violate all affection, to violate years of kindness? Do you call that change? Well at the North, perhaps. Here, sir, we call it something quite different, let me assure you.

"And what has gone on, then, between you and him? What trust, what affection . . ."

The rebel turned away beneath Deall's high clear stare, but turned away Deall saw not with understanding—too sudden was his turning for that—but with his recomposed sullen contempt.

"Yes sir, here we call it something quite different."

"*We* would call it what it is, by heaven. A downtrodden human being, asserting himself for his freedom! And in the very face of generations of—"

"For freedom! You think *that* is what Tobe wanted! He don't know the word, I wager." The rebel's stare was distant and flat, out across the land. "He don't know a Goddamned thing about freedom, and I—but sir, let me tell you this. You don't know us and our ways, and you don't know the nigger."

Tobe was too much an individual case. Deall saw he could offer no superior proof, nor disentangle whatever relationship the rebel had deluded himself into believing existed. "I do know," he said, "that there are slave cabins out back with locks on the doors, don't I?"

"You just confirmed the truth of my words, sir."

Indeed, that had been guesswork. Deall felt momentarily along the wall of his experience, recollecting what he could from his dodging sprint to the kitchen that morning. He could not remember bloodhounds. Locks on the doors? He tried to remember the two cabins at the corner of the first row, whitewashed, a splintered doorsill, one door closed, faces in the door of the other—and then he remembered one mild young boyish face and again the pattern of his argument was before him, and he said suddenly (all this happening in two seconds' delay), "Well, sir, this I do know . . . there is a little, half-black boy out there who looks much like you, sir. With your eyes and brow. Eh?"

And now the rebel stared with rage again, this time fury directed, Deall realized, toward him: the face not bronze with control, but livid white.

And Deall turned, for the first time since the rebel's argument, toward his wife, a deliberate almost formal turn, a slight almost mocking inclination of the head, a bow of recognition (why he did these things was not rationally clear, but he felt the power of them). Before she had moved with her husband's comments, glancing back and forth. Now she was motionless, her thigh pressed against the arm of the sofa, and she stared at Deall with wet, deep eyes.

Facing Malory again, Deall leaned comfortably into the moment. " 'Know the nigger,' you say? Well I question whether you know them now, because one of yours led us here, and another took a gallant and conclusive part in the fight. But you've known *one* of them, I will wager. Yes, you've *known* a single Negro, I'll bet."

The felicitous irony of the word appeared to Deall a very part of the whole moment, the crowning sign of his resumption of power and potency, lost earlier against the rebel's obtuseness. Not the triumph of reason he had sought, but even better. They had followed that, and no mistake! Untouched by logic, they could be moved by rhetoric. The language itself was a sign of rectitude.

"You blue belly son of a bitch," the rebel began, slowly and softly, talking so low that Deall almost had to lean to catch the words. "You talk about 'Higher Laws'—"

"I talk," Deall said, "about what I see."

"And let me tell you what I see. I see a Goddamned hypocrite. I see a nigger lover."

"You see nothing. You are blind to light itself."

"I live here," the rebel said. "I live here."

Deall looked at him a long moment, his hands circling for the power to hammer the man down. Hopeless then, hopeless at the last. The man was beyond even the reach of shame, not merely the reach of logic or rhetoric.

Deall drew his shoulders back up from stooping to hear the rebel's words, and he drew in his breath. The past minutes were futile and wasted, but outside was the brilliant sunshine of early afternoon, and the purity—not infected, beyond their power to infect—the purity of nature itself, in clean long shapes, tawny with winter and blue with distance and green with the pines. That purity touched Deall's heart.

"No," he said. "You have lived here, but soon you will die here. You were taken as an armed civilian. As a common bushwhacker," he said out of a distant argument. "I am very much afraid I will have to have my men hang"—*Hang* seemed to glitter—"have my men hang you."

"I never expected nothing else from a bunch of bummers."

"I beg your pardon, madam." Deall stepped past her to the side window. Sullivan and Keller were leaning on their rifles, watching Billy Gass dig in the garden. His spade brought up a mound of sandy earth entwined with rose bush roots, hesitated, and then turned so that the bruised, green-split roots fell into the tangle of leaf and wood and dirt beside the hole.

Deall called Keller and Sullivan to come in and take the prisoner and lock him in the cellar. Then he thought better of it. Keep him in the very symbol of slavery, one of the Negro cabins.

He sat back in the chair, and put his feet upon the divan, as the four left the room. The winter air hung about him in clustering bright shapes.

Chapter 19

THE OLD CABIN HAD BEEN DESERTED FOR TWO YEARS, AND IT WAS DANK with the smoky stench of deserted wet wood and lifeless hearthstone. "Well, Celia," Malory said, using the last half hour of the time that the Yankee sergeant had given them, "you will find the family papers in the office desk. They are wrapped in an oilskin, with a piece of red tape binding. Now I expect they will burn the house, so you are going to have to take the papers before they fire it." He lectured her slowly and formally, with exaggerated detail, lips pursing over the sentences.

Celia stood in hand-clasped dignity, listening to him. When he had been led off, she had immediately gone upstairs, put on the metal hoops beneath the striped brown skirt of her dress, and hastily plucked her hair into thick ringlets and a bun. Then she had had one of the soldiers take her to her husband.

"The house and the land will belong to you, by my testament. But this is my latest will, the one I drew up after Francis' death. Now this is why you must take the papers before you remove anything else from the house."

Outside the hut, Jade and the Yankee sentry were talking much louder than Malory:

". . . That's the truth, Cap'n?"

"I mean to say. See that five there. Well that little figger, it's a five. You flick the sights this way—there now—you can lay out a man at damn near half a mile."

"Say can?"

"Now, take the road down there. I 'spect I would put it on three—this'n, here. . . ."

Malory's instructions continued formally and precisely: "Now take the papers and deliver them to Mr. Hoyt, at his office. If there is any problem, you know that Mr. Sanders—Mr. Sanders—was the witness. But I am certain there will be no problems. Now the estate will belong to you. You may do with it as you wish, my dear, but I am sure you know that my fondest desire would be that it stay in the Malory family, and I suggest you work something equable with Agnes and her children, and with Cousin Andrew in Effingham County. But I leave all of that to you, of course."

He spoke so deliberately and formally as much for his own sake, as hers. He was holding himself rigidly above considering *his own death*. The deliberateness of the lecture aided in concentrating his attention and his breathing.

Malory believed casually in an afterlife, largely in dim images of family reunion. But more strongly upon him were images of his burial in that graveyard which had always been an integral part of the family's grounds. If death was terrible, it had nonetheless been faced daily, it was familiar and constant. He and Francis had played among all the tombstones, ambuscaded behind the ashy-stained shaft of his great-grandfather's stone, or huddled beside the boot-high lamb over his infant sister—and now there was the temporary board above Frank's own body. So he was soothed with images of death wherein future Malory boys, boys looking like himself and Francis, would play in the eternal afternoon sunlight and would exert their resilient young limbs amid the cedars and willows and tombstones (one of the stones sentiently his own), and the sky would be the same mild Georgia sky.

But there was still the loathesomeness and the terror. He recalled how thrown stones had clanked against the doors of the family crypt, and he and Frank had thrilled to the echo. *Death* was dark visions of corruption, of rot and jawless skulls and hair growing after death, those images he had exercised in lugubrious, sentimental poems all his adolescence.

And if he considered *death* directly that Gothic horror might lunge spiderlike at him, and raw terror might overmaster. His flesh ached. As he spoke, there was a slight panting in his breath.

"Now among those papers, you will find some deeds to the two hundred acres in Lafayette County. Those acres are not worth a great deal, but they do complete our property to the northwest, and adjoin your family's Ogeechee lands. So you would be well advised to hold them, in my opinion."

He held both her hands in his own dry white hands, looking with elaborate patience at her demure, downcast eyes. "Do not worry about trying to remove anything from the house besides those papers. The Yankees will not let you. But I doubt they will find any of our buried silver. After the danger is past, return with Mr. Hoyt or perhaps Dr. Stephens and look through the ruins where it is buried. In addition to the family attachments, those settings should carry you over well. Do not hesitate to use any of it to purchase your way. Do not hesitate."

Outside, Crisp and Covey had joined Jade, talking to the sentry.

"Say he can? All the way to the road?"

"Hush up, you."

"Now then, you just take your bay'net and give it a quarter turn—*ah!*—there goes. Now you're ready."

"Man, ye ever *kill* a man with that long sticker?"

"What he say?"

"Now then, about the people. Take those that you will need with you to Coffinville. I expect Phrony and Zeenie and Uncle Mitchell. And perhaps Shorty. After the Yankees have left, call in all the ones that remain and tell them they are free—tell them all. But caution them that there are bad times ahead, and they can follow these Yankees if they wish, but unless they stay on the land, you cannot tend their needs. Any that do stay here, you will return and protect, once these days are past."

His voice became measured with righteousness. "All, of course, except Tobe. I personally would not have you nor any of my own have anything to do with Tobe. He has proven himself dangerous in the worst extreme. If he stays, he may make trouble, so stay clear of him until you are ready to go to Coffinville. These Yankees will not bother you but I confess you must watch Tobe, and to that end you might ask help from the sergeant."

She glared at him.

"Well he is a white man, do not forget. In any case, take your leave for Coffinville soon upon the Yankees' departure. Return only when the patrols are out again and there is regular commerce on the roads. That is the best sign, regular commerce on the roads. But if you return and Tobe is still about the place, have Mr. Hoyt or the patrol or the sheriff handle him. He has grievously betrayed me."

Then his voice became calm and deliberate again. "Jade, for all his weakness, is a well-meaning nigger. You might—yes, you might suggest he be made driver. But find yourself a good white overseer before you return to reside here. I expect the war to be over soon, and there will be many looking for that employment. Never trust a slack-jawed man, and look a man in the eye and shake his hand. That is the best way to tell."

Through the small side window, Malory could see the pines. Wind shivered them, silvered them, they roiled in his weak vision against the cool blue sky. As he continued talking ("Now Tobe helped me hide the stock, so of course you cannot expect any of that to remain, but you should be able to find hogs in the pinewoods back of the old Husband place. . . ."), his vision rose gradually and mistily, from her face to those distant woods.

For Malory was discovering rapture and even delight. Controlling himself had its own special elegance. He discovered that his most deep-seated fear had been the fear of blind terror—the kind he had once seen on the face of a slave in Savannah on his way to public execution, the eye rolling, the thrashing head, sweat flying from its impact against the bars.

The flicker of terror, the spark of the flesh's fear of extinction, made his lungs ache. But even so, this was immured, walled about, in the simple steadiness of his self-control. He was reminded of himself on the parapet that day.

And: death was more appropriate, more controllable by far, too, than the blind terror of those cellar steps. It was a modest fear compared to that horror, the memory of that face and presence which had even had the magnetic pull of solidity, which had occupied space, and which the burning of the house would purge beyond need for encounter or explanation. The warm earth was refuge indeed, his place by the miter-shaped northside cedar, between Francis Marion (Frank) and their sister Caroline dead at sixteen, just above the small rectangle over his own day-old son, and beneath those boyish generations to come who would plan their games in the same mild cemetery, in knee britches and curly hair against the shadowy brilliant light of sunny afternoons a century distant.

The Yankee sentry outside was alone now, and humming to himself, "out of the wilderness, out ahh the wilderness . . ."

"Lastly, you will find some small sum of cash in the Georgia and Atlantic Rail Road Bank, at Augusta, some two hundred dollars in gold. I suggest you employ someone such as Mr. Hoyt to secure that for you, and that you live out the rest of the war in Coffinville, or perhaps Columbia, does Mr. Hoyt advise you to try to reach it."

What he had seen on those steps had withered him with fear, the very cumulative horror of all his sleepless nights worrying about the rasp, the chuckle, the scraping noise *out back*. But it had nothing to do with cedar trees and children's footsteps in the calm shady soil of a cemetery plot, or the shapes of the rustling pines in his now moist, soft vision.

"What did yeh find!" The Yankee sentry bellowed, and his tanned, gleaming face appeared through the half-shuttered window, his breastplate glittering. Someone yelled back something about hams.

There was a cream-easefulness upon him, where he expected torment, and what seemed painful now were the details that held him to life. *Hams*. The Yankees' banality, the concern about heirlooms, the securing of wills and deeds and patents, and the entangling responsibilities toward a wife he still did not quite assume could fend for herself.

". . . depending upon the condition of travel, but I know how stubborn you are . . ."

Malory glanced down at her. He expected to see self-pitying helplessness and the olive-ivory lids of her eyes. His voice faltered: her gaze was intense and vivid. The bright hunger of her vision struck his eye like sudden light. He remembered the upstairs hallway that morning.

"Well," he said, fumbling. Her eyes dropped. He had to clear his throat before the final rehearsal of his instructions:

"Two things you must remember. You must not let them burn down the house before you secure the family papers—and you know where they are?" Eyes lowered now, she nodded softly. "Well, the second thing is, take those papers to Mr. Hoyt as soon as possible, and then rely upon Henry Hoyt for everything." He prided himself upon so arranging the coincident conclusion of the two points. He repeated it.

Then he put his hand upon the nape of her neck, beneath the pendant black bun, and began to pull her formally toward his shoulder for his farewell. But one other thing insisted itself. "No, three things," Malory said, regretting that the neatness of the first instructions had to be violated, "three things. One, get the papers, two, get them to Mr. Hoyt, and three—three, trust even these Yankees beyond Tobe. If you need protection, go to the Yankees. Even to the sergeant." His voice rose for emphasis: "I would even say any of the Yankees, over any of the niggers, not just Tobe. After what we have seen."

"Now," he said at last, and he pulled her against his shoulder. Malory tried to abandon himself to the olive and sea-green of the pines and the blue sky and the smell of her thick hair. But the spark was jagged in his lungs, and so he then stiffened himself, for now he had a firm sense of family witnesses, of the publicity of every gesture.

While Malory's one eye strained toward the shifting distant pines, Celia was looking over his shoulder, her eyes tracing a whittled pattern in the frame of the door. The pattern, blonder wood beneath the worn surface, was almost that of a formal urn, but asymmetrical, lopsided, incomplete:

Within his formal embrace, Celia remained quite still and pressed her cheek into the thin fabric of his shirt. But she was not so decorous. She was bewildered by her own emotions and almost exultant in them.

While her heart burned with loss and love and sorrow, and while she felt her very breath constricted with helpless hatred, she was aware that she had occasion and license for vast passion. Exigencies had undercut to their very threads and pasted backings all the finery of the plantation world. Celia's own life had been circumscribed rigidly with decorum and helplessness. Now she sorrowed with checked sobs, hands upon her soon-to-be-taken husband's shirtfront (this cloth needs mending, but 'twill never be mended now), but she was almost joyfully *aware* of the sorrow itself, delightedly conscious of the great soaring and warranted emotion within her. Her eyes gleamed as they had when she was loading the rifles during the fight (I shall lay him out in broadcloth and gold!).

In the trembling of her luminous left eye and in the play of her hands which brushed and plucked tiny splinters off her husband's shirt, she showed him plainly (and, yet, consciously) the depth of grieving. "But . . . is there no hope?" Her eyes flicked across his face. "None, sir? None, M-mr. Malory?"

"Malory women, my dear . . ." She did not listen, but shivered and allowed (and measured) one gasp which almost broke into the sobbing spasm that comes before wailing.

When she was aware he had finished, she clung to him more tightly, clutching his length with new possession, thrilling with the awful white presence of his coming death, which made him (this man that *she*, that *she*, Celia Coates was holding, clinging to, feeling the hardness and the muscle and spine of) lustrous with strange attraction.

Oh, how can I lose this man, she thought, and then instantly whispered, "Oh, how can I lose you?" Yet while he held her in mournful silent response, her eyes against his chest sparkled with the very certain knowledge that this loss, this sacrifice, was that moment toward which all of her life had been doomed and patterned (as the sorrowing heroine on the frontispiece of a book, in whorls of engraving, is doomed to loss before the first page is even read). The years which she would have had with him—which she would have with him now!—were gleaming before her.

She smoothly envisioned herself surrounded by the five or six children they would have had, poised posed elegantly on the side lawn of the house, and Malory riding toward them at the end of the day, all of them bathed in sunsetting colors of emerald and orange gold. He would dismount, beaming with pride and love, would catch the children and dandle the youngest. Her gloved hands would be clasped at her waist, her head tilted with warmth and love. Her loveliness was mirrored in his face, across their infant daughter's bonnet. And after dinner she would crochet as he sat in red leather and asked her opinion, across rustling newspapers, about the plantation.

All this she would have had, and been, save for this—tragedy. Her arms and hands tingled upon his physical presence. Celia's eyes swept, unseeing, up the left side of the whittled trench in the door-frame, filled in the missing top, then traced down the too-long right curve.

In that bereft future, she would remember this mansion, all the elegance, all the irreplaceable uniqueness: the pink-hearted plantation-baked brick of the walkways, the curve at the top of the stairs, the square sense of its front, the way its angularity inside surprised after its seeming width, the way it had beckoned across the quarter mile once you made your turn through the gate (The Sycamore mansion had been famous throughout the state, had stood with the Harris plantation at Eatonton and Refuge at Waynes-borough).

She anticipated her aching future recollections: the fall of the springtime light on waxy mahogany and on the Philadelphia-made chairs, the elegant buffet made in Athens, the plush empire divan ordered for the very middle of the parlor (which had never arrived because of the War). How could she stand to be bereft of the very fabric of her life?

Stand it she would. Her future life would be shadow of a better one. Cold city drawing rooms would be her mite, but in their midst she would see another, a distant, a lost drawing room, wherein a scroll-armed backless empire divan stood, fine mahogany and darkest purple plush and brass-clawed feet.

A whole way of life, indeed: husband and home and the darkies, this rich, quiet and peaceful life, shared on the land between master and slave. Phrony's shuffling lovableness, Shorty's wide carefree smile—the way they had adored their young "Mistess" and the way she had managed them, wise beyond her years and loving in return, nursing their children through disease. She and her light-haired sons and bonneted daughters and her husband, on the verandah, watching the happy slaves coming past through amber and pink sunsets, all that would be lost forever to her: accessible only in memory. And thus she would retire to them in moments of recollection.

She felt sadly superior to the girl-wife of the evening before, kicking and moaning in childish terror at ghost or man or whatever. The vexing complexities, the inability to make her husband believe her about that cellar, her own shifting and reshifting of certainty, of half-terrified puzzling not only at what the thing was but if it had been at all, that belonged with the fear of old houses and hollow trees, she told herself. With the weak, eye-batting fears of childhood. Black and faceless, the thing had been an omen, of her husband's death and her own blank doom. She had culled it forth from some dimension of herself that had foreseen all this (such second sight ran in the Coates family). Celia was awed and thrilled at her prescience, so real had the vision seemed.

Pressed against him, Celia felt her husband absent already, in the dry resilience of his flesh. Already he is being taken from me.

This, at least, they shall not take away—my memories of what our life was, my ability to conceive what our lives would have been.

Death would at least leave with her the ability to conceive, to visit through faith and love and imagination, to linger at her own choice, magnificently untouched by events, unconcerned with superficial realities. With the unterrified and unterrifiable elegance of a lady, she would be able to visit and to dwell in that lost realm.

"My dearest," Malory said, with absent formality.

"Oh, Mr. Malory," she said, wailing softly, taking his vagueness as the measure of death's shadow and anxious to show how willingly she could respond, "Oh Mr. Malory, you will never be absent from me, dearest. Not you nor Sycamore nor all that should have been." She almost let too much emotion slip, and had to gasp to keep from bursting with tears. The vast lump of loss in her throat loomed brilliantly.

"You, dear Mr. Malory, and Sycamore, and our lives," she said into his shoulder, gulping to deflect the pain and contain her emotion, "those shall always be with me. We will live together in them, beyond any corruption, and beyond . . . beyond any regret, any loss. No one, no thing, can touch us or our love . . . or our life, evermore!"

Saul Keller and Sullivan and Hostetler opened the door brusquely. They found the two statuesque and formally elegant in the soft yellow light. She was still and silent in her husband's arms, face against his chest: his single-eyed vision was dim upon the future. The three soldiers clattered to silence and half-consciously assumed the round-eyed, transfixed, open-lipped silence of the minor figures in a painting.

Chapter 20

Malory and the three soldiers crossed the rear lot and turned the corner of the house, following the path that ran southeastward toward the Brier Creek bottoms. Malory walked in front of the others, holding himself stiffly, the sun gleaming off his bloodstained white shirt and his boots.

Hostetler held his loaded rifle across his chest and walked immediately behind him. Saul Keller and Sullivan were a few paces farther back, both trailing their Springfields. Sullivan had the coil of rope over his arm.

The soldiers had removed their stolen clothing, though Keller still wore his beaver hat. They were uncomfortable and the government blue and brass and light blue trousers made them feel more official.

The old path, sandy and clay orange and worn by slaves' bare feet, ran from the quarters through the side garden, angling for the piney woods and ignoring brick walk and boxwood plot. To their right, the soldiers could see Gass and Winters spading in the little plantation cemetery, digging at the newest of the graves. Winters leaned on his spade, while Gass's shovel hefted and turned shining amid the cedars and the willows. The rebel did not notice.

"Heh, look at that." Saul Keller whispered to Sullivan. "Winters found somebody to do his work again. You know, Gass's better'n a detail of niggers."

"Well," Sullivan said, "it don't seem right to dig like that, digging in a graveyard."

"Do you think it's any better to bury money in a graveyard in the first place, hey?"

"Well, no."

"Well then."

As they followed Hostetler and the rebel over the stile in the rail fence, Sullivan kept looking back at the little fence-enclosed cemetery. Gass had taken off his blue jacket and had draped it over a thin white slab.

The path skirted the edge of the woods. The field was fallow, with reedy brush and pale sedge grass. The rebel ahead of them moved with a stiffness so massive that he seemed to be struggling to keep his very flesh from quivering.

"But I wager he ain't going to find anything in that grave," Keller was saying, "no they ain't the type. Me, I would like to have a crack at those nigger cabins. Yes sir. The way these niggers act, you know they got somethin' hid in those cabins."

"Why so?"

"They all say the same thing—'lawsy me hit's down in de cellah'. I bet the silver and such truck is in those cabins right now. Where else could they be? And why else would the niggers be so all-fired sure it is in the cellar, unless that is what they were told to say?"

"Well, maybe that's where something is."

"Damn if that is so. I been over every inch of that floor, from wall to wall. There ain't a Goddamn thing hidden nor buried."

"Maybe that's where the niggers *think* something is."

"Naw. The only time a bunch of niggers all get together on the truth, you know it's a lie."

"Why would they be lying?" Sullivan asked mechanically. He was preoccupied with their immediate task—hanging a man.

"Beats hell out of me. A white man wouldn't lie to help the man who owned him. But then a white man wouldn't be owned in the first place, would he? These slave owners have 'em so scared they about do anything they told, I guess. But I'd give a damn sight for a look at those cabins, I tell yeh."

They entered the woods and Keller and Sullivan crowded together between the macelike boughs of the pines.

"Well Saul, I reckon you will get your chance to take that look."

The path slanted in ribbed clay. Keller held his hand to his beaver so branches would not sweep it off. "Eh? How is that?"

"Johnny said he thought we would stay at the plantation for the night, and set out again at first light."

"Well now . . . does he reckon that is safe, with reb cavalry all over the place?"

"I asked him that . . . whups! watch the branch. I asked him that, and he said he thought the rebels were about played out. They have gone on east."

"Well hell's bells. It only takes a dozen of them and they been thick as flies the last two days."

"Yeah, well, Johnny says he thinks this is the same bunch that we ran into yesterday. And anyhow, he says he figures we will be as safe where we *know* there wasn't any rebels, as out on the road where we might run up against some."

"Well it suits me. But I thought Johnny was so all-fired set on getting back to the regiment tomorrow."

"I did too," Sullivan said, holding back a pine branch so Keller could duck under it, "but after the talk he had with the rebel and his wife, he changed his mind. He must have found something out from 'em."

"Maybe he found something out about th' money," Saul Keller said, musingly.

The early afternoon light was mellow in the pine woods. They came to a place bare of undergrowth. The path curved between tall scaly columns of pine trees, and the ground was coated with brown and grey pine needles and yellowish grass. Wind turned the high pine boughs in sparkling rustles. The light was warm upon their shoulders and necks. Sullivan and Keller had to jog a few strides, canteens rising and flapping, to overtake Hostetler and the rebel.

The ground was dropping away beneath them, sloping down toward the bottoms. The slope, the fall of light, the tall pine trees, the few metallic jogging strides, all forcibly reminded Sullivan of Chickamauga: but with vast differences. Then the woods had been September hot and flush. Then they had smelled of thick, close-trapped heat, the sap baking within tree trunks. Now the smell was of piney cool distance and quiet. Chickamauga, to Sullivan and to most of the men in the 112th, stood for sacrifice and highest patriotic endeavor. He ruminatively shifted his rifle across his chest, remembering when the Reserve Division had gone down beneath the pines, the red clay in the paths and all the blue uniforms and his own jolting strides going down.

But toward something far, far different, that time! He remembered the weary self-satisfaction they had all felt afterward, even though the army had taken a licking: the pleasant, earned way the sweat had dried on their arms, and how sweet the water, the hardtack even, had tasted on the road back to Chattanooga. The rebel's head bobbed before him, his white back spindled with the afternoon light.

"Say, Phil," Keller suddenly said to him, "say do you think Johnny really meant to string him up for real?"

The question so clearly suggested Sullivan's own thoughts that he stopped and looked at Keller, who squinted back at him.

"What do you mean, Saul?"

"Well are you sure he meant to kill him? Or just run him up a little, till he spills about the money?"

"What money?" Sullivan said, sagging into his bemusement again.

"Whatever they was talking about when he was with th' . . ."

"Hey, we got to catch up." Again they clattered down through the pine trees, equipment flapping, rifle barrels glittering.

"You know . . . if he found out the reb and his wife would not tell. Maybe he just wants us to run him up a little, put the fear of God into him just a little." He cleared his throat behind his wrist, catching his breath, while Sullivan kept looking sadly ahead, after the rebel. Overhead a large hawk swung above the tree limbs. Below the pines, they saw flickering shadow-fall, and had intermittent vision of flashing, muscular grey brown. The motion was spectrally discordant amid the ease and calmness of the cool light beneath the pines.

"I been thinking, Phil. You know it's not like Johnny, to string up a man. For no reason. Now . . . I wager he wants us to find out from this feller where his silver is hid."

"But you know it's not like Johnny to want to find out that kind of thing, anyhow."

The pinewoods were choked again with fallen trees and the ash-splotched trunks of blackjack and a few distant sycamores. Fifty yards beyond, water gleamed and tangling, thick, bushel-full moss hung over trees and stumps. A squirrel scampered in a coalescing grey moment of leaf and needle and vine. Both men flinched and swung their rifles up to cover the tangled alleys of the woods. Even more, Sullivan was reminded that this wasn't a white man's job. This was a bunch of chicken shit, running a man up.

" 'S just a squirrel . . . what did he say, Phil? Did he say hang him? Did he say hang him when the reb *wasn't* there?"

"No . . . but he didn't say not to hang him. . . ."

"Of course not! And spoil th' game? Johnny's no fool."

Sullivan stopped.

"But, damn it all to hell, what *is* Johnny's game? He don't give a damn about silver or buried spoons or any of that crap. You *know* he don't."

"Maybe I do, and then maybe I don't. But I bet he is after something and wants us to find out where it is, or what the reb knows."

Phil Sullivan stood thinking.

He roused himself to shout down to Hostetler that that was far enough. A live oak, thickened with Spanish moss, overhung the path twenty yards below them.

"Look, Phil. You know Johnny is a soldier, and this ain't a soldier's way. You do admit that?"

"He did shoot at us."

"Well, hell! It is his land, ain't it? And Billy Gass says he didn't start the shooting, anyhow. Billy fired the first shot, he says, after one of the rebels knifed Ted Coiner."

Sullivan was as impressed by Keller's sudden earnestness as he was by the argument. "Look Phil, I ain't up to it, and I bet Johnny ain't either. Let's run the man up, find out what he knows, get him good and scared, and then fetch him back. If Johnny wants him dead . . . which I doubt . . . he can still kill him. But if we kill him and that's *not* what Johnny wanted . . . !"

Sullivan started down toward the two men ahead of him on the path, eyes still opaque with concern, not believing Keller but moved by his fervency, bewildered by Deall's actions, and above all possessed of the image of himself as a soldier in the 112th Oh Vee Eye, as a soldier of the Republic, a soldier by God of th' Republic, and aching against having to perform this brutal and unmanly thing. Well, he said weakly to himself, well we see, I reckon.

"At least," Keller was saying, "at least, give it a try. Run him up a little and see what he has to say for himself. See if he offers to talk."

(For Malory, the world hummed and dazzled with insistent life and motion. The myriad surfaces of the living world fretted at his vision, the way sun-drenched, insect-ripe summer creekbeds hum and buzz with life. His own physical quivering excitement angered and frustrated him, his hypnotized staring at the large branch of the live oak, the clamoring voice in him yelling *this is it so this is it*. He ached for the damnyankees to finish him.)

The path splayed out where the feet of slaves and patrollers had swung wide of the tree trunk. Fallen logs stretched away from it, long wales of white and flecked grey amid trunks and dry saplings and wreathed dry vines. Sunlight was partly shielded from the ground by the slant of the hillside, and the sun touched the men about their thighs as they stood beneath the tree, while Sullivan tossed the knotted rope. It tumbled back and Sullivan drew the rope through his hands for a second toss.

Fifteen feet beyond and below them, the path ended at the leaf-slick edge of the water, and became worn smooth skipping places between the tree roots. Cypress stumps looked like melted castles. There were vertical masses of beard-grey moss, and the gleaming false depth of watery reflections.

The rope swung back and forth over the branch, and Sullivan swung his whole weight upon the two strands. Rope and wood creaked. Looking up to test the swing, his eyes carried up and up to wax-thick clumps of mistletoe, shining in the high sunlight against the echoing blue sky.

Hostetler had finished binding the rebel's arms behind him with canteen cord. The man stepped forward toward the rope, his one eye as black and brilliant as the glimpsed water below them. From back and above, wind tussled in the pine boughs. Sullivan had to slip the noose over his head, and he checked himself as his arm started up to smooth back one wing of the man's hair.

Sullivan stepped back, a little bewildered, feeling his limbs move at an unaccustomed distance from his will. The yellow-new rope sphered the rebel's head with dramatic distinctness against the woods. "Well now. . . ."

Keller stepped past him. "Well now, ain't that pretty? Good old yellow rope like that. But we need us a blindfold, don't we reb? Don't we, old fellow?" Keller held up his checked handkerchief. The rebel shook his head, looked at the handkerchief, then shook his head again.

"Well, you're all set then, I reckon. Yes seh! All set."

To Sullivan, Keller's brusque humor was an aching surprise. His face was still set in gentle puzzlement, while Keller bustled around and the rebel's one eye followed him. He bent to check the man's hands, he brushed away a spiral of grass from the toe of one of the boots.

"Well then. Any last words, old fellow? Anything you want to say before you go to meet your maker?"

The rebel obviously had to struggle to meet the tone, shaken out of whatever reverie had carried him so stiffly. He lowered his head. "Tell my wife . . . tell my . . ." His eye caught Keller, who was smiling at Hostetler and Sullivan. The head came back up. "You bluebelly sonsofbitches will not get a last word from me, for your sport." He snorted, and raised his eye instead to heaven. Sullivan appreciated the gesture.

"We will not, eh?" Keller said brightly. "Suit yehself, you rebel bastard." He snapped the knot to the man's neck. "Lend a hand, fellows."

Sullivan still stood in bewilderment as tone and event wildly diverged. Keller swung himself down suddenly on the rope so that the strands welded and creaked and the man's head rose at a bewildering angle, eye starting with puffing quickness like a part of some trick doll. Sullivan was both hypnotized and repulsed—he glimpsed the swinging hawk above them, and the darkness of the moment began to regather.

But then Keller stood up from his swinging crouch, and as he did, still toylike, the rebel's weight sank again to his feet, and his one eye closed and his flesh mottled as the bronze color faded back to lead white.

"Why, I be damn. You know what I forget, Phil? Joe? Why

didn't you tell me to let the man say a few prayers. . . . A few prayers, Mister Rebel? A moment alone with your maker?"

The rebel sank to his knees, stunned, face mottled.

"Stand back, fellows. Stand back. We don't want to come between a man and his God at a moment like this, do we?"

Back up the trail, the three turned to look down on the rebel. He swayed on his knees, twisting his neck against the tightness of the noose.

"Well boys, I believe we got him now," Keller said. He was studying the rebel, his eyes bright with pursuit beneath the rim of the beaver hat. Sullivan roused himself to look at Hostetler: he was boyishly alert, looking back and forth between Sullivan and Keller and anxious to be in on the fun.

"What do you think he knows?"

"I don't know for sure, but Johnny figured he knew something. He came close to saying, didn't he? Didn't he come close, back there? All we got to do is loosen the bastard up a little more, a couple more swings . . ."

The three studied the rebel carefully again. Sullivan didn't know what he could say. But as they started back toward the man —the rebel's eye was on them now, black again with ferocity—Sullivan accepted the delight of the new arrangement himself. Outsmart the bastard. Show him he can't hide nothing from boys of the 112th Ohio, by God.

The rebel's arrogance had returned, not removed now, but violently intense. No drawing back of the nostrils, but a quivering white anger. Hostetler helped him up.

"Are you all set, old fellow," Keller said brightly. He put his hands on the rope and tugged experimentally while the other two made great shows of slipping their rifles over their shoulders and taking purchase on the rope. "Okay now, fellows . . ." Keller sucked his breath in and made as if to pull. The others followed his guide.

"Naw, naw, wait another minute." Hostetler and Sullivan kept their hands on the yellow rope, keeping the slightest tug against the rebel's neck so that he had to strain tiptoed against the rope pull.

Keller stood right in front of the rebel, who could look at him only from the side-twisted corner of his eye, like a dog trapped by the neck. His eye rolled down at Keller.

"Now then, Mister, I tell you what. You sure, are you, that you haven't got any last words for *us?*"

The eye stared at him, uncomprehending.

"Tell you what," Keller said, leaning even closer. "Now, suppose we work out something. Now we don't want to have to string you up. And I don't think Sergeant Deall wants us to have to, neither. If you was to tell us what we want to know . . ." He looked up attentively.

The two men on the rope let it loosen slightly. Sullivan knew that everything had slipped from his hands. He watched Keller.

The rebel twisted his neck from side to side again, licking his lips and coming to speak. The rope had chafed the skin of his neck into reptilian diamonds.

"I . . . I told you I have not got a thing to say for your sport."

Sullivan and Hostetler hauled sharply on the rope, and the rebel's feet cleared the ground, his tongue bright-swollen in the corner of his mouth. His voice gargled out in hoarse vowels.

They lowered him.

"Well, then," Keller said, "well perhaps not for our *sport*. But maybe you could tell us somethin' for your *life*. Eh old fellow? For your life."

The rebel drooled bloodily from the corner of his mouth. His one eye was squeezed shut now, and his whole head rose and fell with each violent, rasping breath. Stubborn son of a bitch, Sullivan thought. He distantly remembered his own terror when Cleburne's men had come at them over the limestone at Tunnel Hill. Got more pride than sense. Whyn't he talk?

The rebel finally raised his head, painfully. His eye opened, dull this time, all its moisture spilled in tears down his cheek. He flushed his nostrils and cheeks, catching his breath. His eye fell on Keller. He shook his head shortly, setting the lines of his jaw.

This time Keller helped, and even when they would have lowered the rebel—his dangling toes lifting up tiny scurfs, curtains of dust from the path—he kept his weight against the man's neck. The rebel's face turned bronze and then dark: the gurgling "AAaaccchhhh . . ." became a windlike hum, then stopped, then Keller let him back down and with one motion was even beside him, looping his arm about the man's waist to keep him from falling. The plantation owner's face was upturned, his mouth fish-open.

"Now then," Keller said, coaxing-cold, "now then, old fellow. Is that better? Your tongue loosened now, eh?"

The rebel's head slumped then on his chest, face wet and shining with tears and spittle. He nodded, short jerks expressed in the flexing of the gathered ruche of flesh above the tight noose.

"You know what we want to know, I 'spect."

The rebel shook his head jerkily.

"Well the gold, Goddamn it! Goddamn it, where you hid the gold! Your silver. Your truck. Where you hid it! . . . Son of a bitch, but the man is stubborn," he said back over his shoulder, easing his voice. Sullivan started at the rebel. "It won't do you no good if you're swinging here rotting in the wind, man. You know that. It won't do you nor your family any good if you're swinging here in this holler. And we will not tell your wife where you are. Your corpse will rot at the end of this rope, unless you tell another story."

"The . . . hi . . ." The rebel rocked on his feet, dazedly, turning his neck. "It is in the cellar, what we got . . . we bu'ied what we got in the cellar."

"Ah son of a BITCH. You know it ain't! We been over ever' Goddamn inch of that cellar." He sighed with resignation. "Well, old fellah, I guess you don't ever learn." He reached back for the rope with his left hand, gradually slipping the right from beneath the man's arm. The rebel jerked his head again, quickly.

"The cellar is where . . ." They paused. The rebel again began to swallow and suck his mouth for moisture, the beard jerking. "I tell you . . . we buried what we got in the cellar."

"All right. Where'bouts in the cellar, then? Eh? Tell me that?"

"Ag . . . against the wall. There is a whitewashed wall."

"Now I know you are lying, by sweet Jesus. Now I know it. At *that* place, I know there ain't a thing. You are trying to make fools of us, but we'll make you tell another story before we are done with you. Swing him up again, boys."

"But we did bury it there. You do not know . . ."

"Swing him up." The three men heaved once more, their brass buttons glinting in the winter sunlight, shadows purple over their blue jackets. The rebel's legs dangled clear of the ground and his last the long "o" sound exploded in agonizing slow fragments and his tongue bulged, at the last, black against the beaten bronze of his strangling head. The rakishly checked cloth wrinkled with the frenzied thrashing of his legs. Then his legs twitched only, and then they swung inertly against the shuffling pull of the soldiers.

"Son of a bitch he will not crack," Keller said.

Sullivan released the rope, and Hostetler did the same. "Son of a bitch."

"That is enough, Saul."

"Might as well let the bastard swing, like Johnny said." But Keller let the rope go slack. "Tough old bastard, I will have to give him that."

They gathered around the prostrate body of the man, his hands still bound behind him, his legs oddly twisted beneath. His eye was closed in a net of taut tiny muscles.

"I believe he is dead."

"Stretch him out."

Bending over him, they were out of the sunlight altogether. Hostetler jerked his head up, eyes starting, at another thrashing sound from the swamp.

They cut the cord from his wrists and began chafing them, Sullivan's fingers working nervously along the deep red marks. Hostetler poured some water into his handkerchief and began to rub it over the man's face. Then he noticed the tight noose, and began to jerk at it to loosen it, plucking at it as though it were hot. Keller reached past him and pulled the noose open firmly.

"We liked to carry that game too far," Hostetler said.

Sullivan felt cold and chill in the little ravine. He felt monstrously exposed to the swamp: his vision was lost among the ancient, vertical forms of stump and root and vine and distant grey hummock, while his fingers rubbed over the metal-feeling flesh.

"Liked to have killed him."

Keller stood up. "I believe we did kill him, damn it."

Sullivan sat back on his haunches, looking down at the rebel's face. The man's body had a violent presence. He felt tremendously abused by it—the sweat stains beneath the arms of the shirt, the moles at the base of the neck, the dark tiny spots where his beard had that morning been shaved. He wished the man's body was in leather and braid, instead of the planter's collarless shirt and the yellow brown trousers. Oh, to have the last half hour to live over, oh. The finality of the man, the body stretched on the sandy, pebbly earth, was all so enormous compared to the trivial fraction of time they had suspended him.

"Well shit. We did not find out one Goddamned thing," Keller said. But he was looking down darkly, too. None of the three men ventured to open the rebel's eye, or feel for the pump of his heart. They all stood back distantly, remotely, from the presence of the body.

"Well hell. Johnny told us to kill him. He said to hang him."

Sullivan agreed. "That is what Johnny told us to do."

But climbing back up through the pines in silence, Sullivan kept thinking, but not that way. Not that way! He remembered the jesting, the brutality, the swift heave up and the sarcasm when they let the startled strangling man back down. Was a yellow action. It was not a white way for a man to have to die.

The earth was still springy beneath his feet with the accumulation of pine straw and the wire grass. But the sun was in his eyes, and the whole landscape was the metallic color of sun glare. His lungs worked, going back up through the pines. Now we even goin' to eat his food. He slung his rifle, letting the dead weight sink onto his shoulders.

"Say what," Keller said suddenly, "perhaps we ought to bring up the body."

The three men paused. Revulsion against seeing the body again lay across their faces. Sullivan swung his hands slightly with indecision. Then when he glanced back down the trail, the revulsion, the very sacrifice of going back, appealed enormously to him. He turned without answering and went back down through the pines. The path veered down darkly into the thick-packed oak and vine. Sullivan walked down toward the spot with earned purchase of each step, struggling against his revulsion.

His eyesight was tense, dreading the first sight of the corpse. I will see his boots first, they kind of stick out. But he did not see the boots. He is back up under the bluff more.

But there was no body there.

They all gazed around swiftly, into the swamp, down over the fallen logs, back through the tangled brush.

"He was not dead after all," Hostetler said.

Sullivan felt no relief. The swamp was now myriad with ancient eyes, with ancient vision. He winced. "We got to look for him, I reckon. Look down along the path. Saul and I'll see if he's off in these woods."

Their steps crashed on leaves and dry stalks. Within ten paces,

Sullivan was blocked by a rope-thick, flaking mass of vines. As he pushed into it, a dead branch plucked his cap box off his belt, and another gouged at his eyes. Hung in the vines and tree branches, he could see cold distances of the swamp through the tangle.

Keller gave up too, eight feet below the clearing. He drove his musket butt down on a log and leaned upon his knee, tilting the beaver hat back off his forehead. Sullivan backed out of the vines and got down on his hands and knees to recover the cap box. He stood up halfheartedly.

"He sure did not come this way," Keller said. He squinted sourly through the thick woods.

Hostetler came back up the path from swamp edge. "Ain't no sign of a new track, Phil. He must have followed this here path right into the swamp."

"Hell, we never *will* find that son of a bitch in that swamp. He must know it like the back of his hand."

They looked at cold water-glisten.

"Leave him go? Leave him out there?"

"Why not? What is one more live rebel. We know he ain't in any shape to go far, between now and sunrise."

Sullivan stood indecisively.

"Come on, Phil. Let's get back up yonder to the house and see what the boys have found. Son of a bitch, they might have found everything by the time we get back. Let the reb go."

Sullivan's hands rubbed along the stock of the Springfield.

"What do you want to do, Phil? . . . Find him so's you can hang him again?"

All three turned back to face the late afternoon sunlight, shrugging their shoulders into their jackets to get more warmth.

Chapter 21

DEALL STOOD IN THE AFTERNOON SUNLIGHT BEHIND THE HOUSE, with the six Negro men and boys before him. Five of them had been digging graves for the dead rebel soldiers, and they leaned on their shovels, their collarless, cotton-drilling shirts slick with sweat and the ocher stains of clay. They were slack-jawed and scowling, still blank to Deall's meaning and sincerity.

The sixth, the one who had saved his life, stood a little apart from the rest. He was wearing a green corduroy jacket.

"Ummm . . . where was I?"

Behind him the fat black woman was toiling up the stairs again, breath coming in soft "ohh lawsy" grunts, while the wood creaked receptively. Going back upstairs to her mistress, bottles and remoistened towels on the tray. She had distracted Deall again.

The big black in the frayed green jacket said, " 'Bout the guns."

"Oh. Yes. The rebels' guns. We will leave you with the rebels' firearms, then."

There was a long silence.

"With their guns, you should be able to hold this place for yourselves, eh?"

He looked from face to face. They remained immovable: mottled teeth as yellow as their eyes. No flicker of responsibility or empowered identity.

The slain rebels had been buried, the recalcitrant owner had been executed. Coiner was dead, not wounded, so their return march would not be slowed by that complexity. But now these men: the tight flesh of Deall's face was seamed.

He finally looked at the black man in the jacket (what was his name? Tom?). "*You* do know how to use firearms. I know you do."

"Yes suh. I reckon I does."

"Well then!" He pulled the revolver from his own belt, and jerked it over so that its smooth handle was toward Tobe. "You take this revolver . . . here now." He slapped the man on the shoulder. "I will make you sergeant. You can train the others in the use of these weapons."

Deall smiled at the other slaves, though he felt oppressed by the clustering presence of them all.

"As a soldier in the Army of the Republic of the United States, I invest this man with authority. He has already shown his courage and his desire for freedom at any price. Let him instruct you in the use of your weapons." He could not quite be certain of the man's name. Tom? Tobe? Tug? He could not afford to be mistaken in this, so he resolved it by gesture. He put his hand upon the man's shoulder and tightened his grip with masculine friendship and all confidence. The man hefted the pistol without commitment, and with no sign of gratitude.

The gesture seemed to fall endlessly between misjudged heights. The one called Jade licked his lips, furtively. The other slaves were hollow-faced.

The black man finally unbuttoned his green jacket and thrust the pistol into his belt, and Deall squeezed his shoulder. But then the man (Tobe?) said, "What we gonna do when you all be gone?"

Deall's arm felt heavy with theatrical camaraderie. Behind and above him he could hear the heavy slow tread of the woman's feet on the second floor. Damn it all. If he could just think for a moment. The clear shapes, the arranging patterns of thought eluded him.

"We've broken them, don't you see? We've broken their backs." Deall patted his shoulder with forced assurance, the gesture allowing him to withdraw his hand. He tucked it into his belt. "We will take Savannah by Christmas and Charleston by springtime, and the War will be over."

"But what we going to do when the Yankees leaves?"

Muscles stood out in Deall's face in strong columns of frustration. The cloying obtuseness of all flesh!

"I tell you, they will be beaten by springtime. Fend for yourselves until then, at the least!"

The black men themselves, stolid and irreducible, blocked Deall from the light. He stepped back from them, up onto the brick gallery. The sunlight glistened in the sweat of their polled heads. He stepped back another half stride, his vision compacting them into a group. Deall looked assessingly at them, relieved by the distance.

"Are you not free? Are you not as good as any man, black or white?"

They looked at him with blank caution. He squinted: their calves were thick and their wrists massive with sinew, but despite their strength, they were all round-shouldered and slouched—their hands seemed to weigh too much for their shoulders. His first sight of a slave, in Kentucky, had made him want to seize the man's shoulders from behind and pull him upright. Stand up straight, he wanted to tell them. He looked from one to the other, tight-lipped.

Then he said, almost softly, "If a rebel comes up to you with a whip, you let him whip you? You have no choice . . . you must?"

Their vision seemed to tighten a little.

"If a rebel rides up that road with a whip, and wants to whip your wi—woman, you let him? Is that right? Do I have it right? You let that man whip her, because you have no choice?"

Deall's free right hand closed with the cool wood and metal of the Enfield: this was shielded behind him from the black men.

"*Now,*" he said, swinging the gun up into the afternoon clarity, "*now* if that rebel comes and you have *this*"—and their eyes went up upon the upthrust rifle—"then what does that man do? Does he wait and get whipped? What does he do?"

He twisted the rifle in the brilliant light. They swallowed and blinked.

"Does he wait for that lash, then? Wait and get whipped? What that man going to do?"

"What he gonna do," the one called Jade said, softly, wiping his hand along his trouser leg, eyes on the gun. "Yeh, what he gone *do?*"

The sixth slave—Tobe? Tom?—studied his face slowly. It irritated

Deall, but the others were looking at the upraised, bead-glistening oil-bright rifle.

"But only a *free* man would use a rifle, to keep from taking the lash. Only a free man would do that . . . are you going to be free men, or are you going to take that whipping?"

"Free," the old man said softly—almost irrelevantly.

Then Jade said, "Free at las'."

"This land is *yours*, if you are free men. All this." Deall leaned forward toward them, aware of the gleaming of his brass, and of the gold and green lanes of afternoon light. His voice surged with his confidence. Words came to him like stones fitted for arches. "*You* have the guns, this time. You will have the guns, to hold land for yourselves. Your master will not be back, ever again. I have told you that. You have my word. What was his, is yours now, if you are free men instead of slaves. That shovel, *that* is for a slave. Who is *this* for?" The weapon rocked in his hand, upraised in the light.

"Free man."

"Free at last."

The black man (Tobe, yes) was still studying him. Deall ignored him.

"You are free now. No man can give another anything more than his freedom." The last word floated.

"Listen to me. We have brought the freedom, and we have brought the power." The rifle rattled as he shook it. The slaves began to shift with a torpid rhythm beneath his voice, and Deall easily matched his words to it. "You have got the freedom and the power. Know it. All it takes, to be free at last, is to use that power. Know it!"

He looked from face to face.

"Listen to me. You are as good as any white man. You have been lied to! You are as good as any white man. And with this" —swinging the Enfield in the fine Georgia sunlight—"with this no man is your better. No man be the master, no man be the slave.

"No man be the master, no man will be the slave."

He brought the rifle down across his breast. "*Know* you are free, then!" Deall slapped the rifle into the hands of the black man right in front of him. The Negro held the gun clumsily, like an axe.

"Where any one of you stands, there stands a single man. And there is no thing greater. With only one loaded musket, already you show it. You can hold your shoulders back. No man be the master, no man be the slave."

The five black men were looking down at the gun, their hands curling vicariously. Their eyes were alight, and one said softly—as softly as Deall himself—"Yeah, Lawd. Freedom."

"Yeah, Lawd, free at *last*."

Deall stood back watching them through the pure winter light.

"Free!" the old man said, dreamily.

"Show that man."

"Yes suh, show that man!" said one of the boys. Their eyes were fastened upon the gun.

Oh Lucy, could you have seen! The gold and silver colors of the grass, and the myriad green shades of the pine trees glowed at the perimeters of his attention. He stood bare-handed and emptied. He was dimly impatient and realized his impatience was at this prison of bone, lineament, flesh. The granted joy was infinitely clear and uncloyed at the last.

And then Tobe grabbed the musket by the middle of its barrel, his green jacket between the blacks and Deall. He tugged at the gun once, while the black holding it tightened his grip instinctively. "You, Jade!" Jade loosened the gun and Tobe pulled it away from them and let it swing by his leg.

"One gun, what good that do?" He gestured contemptuously with his chin at the other guns along the wall. "Five guns, what good they do? What good, when the Yankees go and the white folks come back?"

The five blacks looked at Tobe, their faces lapsing again from their fascination. Deall could see the impact of these sodden, mean fears among them. Tobe's eyes came back to rest upon Deall's face.

"One man, well armed, is the equal of any other man that walks. . . ."

"What good that do, when they all comes together? Fifteen or more come, what good five men gonna do?"

Deall looked around for enthusiasm, but the shadows of the woods were complex and cold, now, against the winter light. The slaves' work shirts hung wetly, entanglingly, upon their shoulders. A breeze shivered through the pines so that the needles of the uppermost branches rustled above the blue shadows of the lower.

"All we can give you is your freedom. It is up to each man to retain it for himself."

"What I wants to know is, what good five guns here gone do against a county of white folks?"

"You have a cause. They do not." Deall's voice took on a straining urgency. "You have a taste of freedom. No man can find anything finer to inspire him to fight. They will fight only to enslave you again. No cause could be worse. You must whip."

"I don't 'spect they gonna give up that easy," Tobe said.

"Well, you must fight your own battles, in the end. We cannot do that for you. We leave you the choice of fighting and dying for freedom, or reentering slavery of your own free will."

"Ain't studying dying nor being a slave, neither."

"Well?"

"I reckon we come along with you folks."

"*No.*" Deall said this with reflexive speed, but already the single phrase had tapped a unanimous hope, an expectancy among the blacks.

"Yes suh!" Jade said, "find Unc' Billy and the day of jubilo!"

"Yes suh! Leave this place . . . one more river to cross, I reckon."

"One more river," the young one said. "Oh Lawd, one more river!"

"I 'spect we better come along with you folks," Tobe said, still quietly.

"Wa-ay over Jordan," the old one said. "I see it all."

"No!" Deall said again, surprised at the finality of his own voice.

I did not mention this, for fear of just such a . . . a mindless reaction. Now look at them.

Tobe drew his head back slightly, dark eyes still intent on Deall's face. Deall looked back calmly at him. They cannot come with us, and that is all. A sense of his own white integrity, the sheen of his flesh amid the gathering shadows of late afternoon, helped him maintain his poised even look.

"I 'spect it'd be better for us to come with you Yankees."

"We must move at dawn, and we must move rapidly. There are too many rebels along the way. Some of your innocent people might be killed."

Tobe watched him. "Be so many of 'em on the way, why is it better for five of *us* to stay here til they *come?*"

"You will not be free unless you prove it here, and now. You will not be free, ever, by running away." If, Deall thought, my intuition is so strong against their coming away, it *must* be for this reason. I know this is right. (He ignored a spattering quick doubt: the very quickness and felicity of his response was proof enough!) "If you do not win your freedom here, you will never win it."

"Up north, from what I hears. . ." Jade began.

"No. Here only," Deall said, and as he talked, the words still coming to him with ease (". . . you see, the issue is not, nor has it ever been, one of *place* . . ."), he suddenly and intensely envisioned the slaves with Sherman's columns: the deluded old man who climbed on a box to preach a sermon, but who ended dancing juba, witlessly grinning back at all the distended, laughing white faces around the campfire; the cavalry's wagonloads of Negro women, hairy beneath their chemises, crossing in front of the infantry outside Sandersville, drunk, satiate, beckoning lewdly to the soldiers. No, surely they do not want that! Here, the women still wore their clean headrags. ". . . and you see then that no *person* . . ."

Tobe interrupted.

"You mean to say you won't let us come with you?"

Deall sighed. "No, no. It is that I am certain you cannot . . ."

"But we cain't come, then. You won't wait f' us?"

"I have seen what you do to . . ." Confused, he began again. "I mean, what has happened to the Negroes who have run to the army." He cocked his head with patronizing weariness. "I have seen. I am certain that you should not leave this place. The War is nearly over. They will be broken in the spring. You have my word."

"What do that mean to *us*?"

My word? Is this black questioning it? Deall's patience broke, justifiably.

". . . What do the War mean to us, we still be here? Where you all gonna be?"

"We will be back."

"Hoss shit."

Tobe turned and walked away, around the corner of the house. Deall stared after him, with a rage so sudden and intense that it was actually cold upon his flesh.

The five stood looking after Tobe. They had never seen a black man walk off from a white one.

Deall seized their attention with callous ease. "Look here, son," he said to the young one who looked like the dead rebel owner. "Look at how this one works." He looked at the boy with a cold, distant smile and easily reached the Sharps and passed it down to him. "You should see the *hole* this one leaves." The other young black sidled over and looked down at the big carbine. "And see here. You open it this way, from the rear. That way, no rebel will be able to get a shot at you while you are loading." The two boys were enraptured with the sliding metal mechanism.

Deall now was squatting before them like a man selling patent medicines after his show. "By the time that shot comes out, son, there is a hole so big you could put a canteen half over it."

"They is!"

"God's truth, son."

The other boy looked up eagerly at Deall. "That one other soldier he say he could kill a man at *th'ee hund'd yard!* . . . Is that right, Cap'm?"

The blacks were now hefting and examining the rebel guns, fondling curved wood and metal under that spell or aura of personal power that balanced weapons convey through the very palm and muscle. Deall looked benignly at them. He stood up and folded his arms.

Well, he thought, these are the good ones. But now he felt a yellow disappointment. The *way* he had had to win them over was mangled. He looked out wearily over the afternoon landscape seeking a natural restorative.

What he saw stunned him: his naked, unprepared glance collided with the land—no October maples which he had half expected, but distant, metal-colored pine flats. The strangeness of this land, its brutal actuality: those sycamores, across that flat horizon another rebel town (we shall never see it), Louisville that way . . . hollow distances. The blacks before him shrank to a handful of untutored men and boys in dun-colored clothes, lost in an alien sour landscape. Lurching, he saw them as rebel horsemen would see them from the woods. Those black people whom we will never see again.

His bruised vision recoiled.

They do not have a chance!

But . . . at least they will *taste* freedom. We will have given them their one taste of immortality.

He breathed deeply, re-creating his spiritual man.

And when the spirit clothes the flesh, wonders can indeed be accomplished. And have been accomplished, ha!, in *deeds.* (Winkelried's body absorbed all those lances . . . he recalled primer's engravings of the Swiss hero: the stunned foemen in them became rebel cavalrymen, in stiff *Harper's* poses, aghast at suicidal black heroism.)

He blamed his dis-ease upon Tobe. His questionings and his expletive had momentarily dislocated Deall's guiding, intuited certainty.

"Yes suh, nigger," Jade was saying, snapping the hammer on the Enfield, "that ol' overseer Boozer come back, I 'spect I can set *him* free, with this here."

"An' what if Marse come back? Him too?"

Jade raised the gun to his shoulder and squinted along the barrel. "Ain't *coming* back, time he find out ol' Jade got him this here gun."

Threading the words together into meaning, Deall laughed, too, a split second after the blacks. He dismissed Tobe. These men—bent with slavery and exhaustion and centuries of humiliation—yet, here making light of their own new power and freedom, holding it with certainty, these men are the very symbols of all human potential. It is Tobe that is the nigger among them; as much a nigger as the fat one who is still tending to her mistress.

He heard someone calling him from the other side of the porch, and he turned and saw Sullivan and Hostetler and Keller crossing the formal garden toward him. Then an exploding "ooo—JEESUSS!" behind him, and he spun back around and saw the thumb of the black boy caught in the Sharps, the boy's eyes wide with the first blast of shock. Red blood curled over the metal. Ahh*Damn*it won't I *ever* rid myself of them? He hung: the three white men came toward him. Then he gestured once, quickly, toward Jade—downswing of his hand, down-stabbing, and when Jade had moved with caution toward the boy ("open hit ooh opennn hit!"), Deall turned back toward the three men.

They were clustered together, looking back and forth among themselves. In the familiarity of these men, in the way they held their Springfields and in what he knew of their dependability, Deall felt a clean relief. He prepared himself for the report that the rebel was dead.

"Johnny," Sullivan said, grounding the musket butt, "Johnny, he got away."

Deall's amazement fluttered against his prepared sad rectitude. His face shook slightly.

"What?"

" 'S truth," Keller said. "He slipped off. We strung him up and thought he was dead. But he must a' been alive, because when we went back, he was gone off."

Deall looked back and forth, facing the three white soldiers on the other side of the porch, while behind him the boy was shuddering "oo-ooo-oo" and Jade was whispering, "Hush up, he gone take that gun away. Hush up."

"Now tell me exactly what happened . . . he got away?"

"Yeh, he did. Slipped off after we thought he was dead."

"*Thought* he was dead?"

Keller and Sullivan looked at each other. Keller said, "We thought our game had gone too far, Johnny. We thought we'd killed the son of a bitch."

"Game?"

"You know, Johnny," Sullivan said, doubtfully.

"String him up, and make him talk. We thought that was what you wanted, Johnny."

"Not only did he slip off," Hostetler said, "but I be damned if he told us ar' a thing." The three grinned ruefully among themselves, and looked back at Deall.

Behind him, the boy got his first glimpse of his thumb and screamed. The sound entangled Deall's attention. "That nail gone come on off," the old one was saying. Deall turned his head furiously, and glared at the blacks: cannot they keep quiet! He saw bright red down the front of a cotton shirt. *Damn* them! "Hush up. You, Covey, hush up! Less you wants him to take these guns back . . ." Flat pop of palm against flesh. Game?

"Game," he said to the three soldiers. "What game, for sweet reason's sake? Who—"

"Why Johnny," Sullivan said, "you didn't mean for us to *kill* him, did you?"

"Why no, Johnny. I said to Phil and Joe, I says 'I know John Deall better than that.' I says, 'You can depend on it, he don't mean for us to kill the rebel bastard.' Ain't that what I said?" The other two nodded. Keller looked up at Deall. "But if I was wrong," he said, looking accusingly, closely, at Deall's face, "if I was *wrong*, why by damn I don't know if I ain't glad of it."

The others studied Deall.

Keller put his foot on the gallery walk, and leaned on his raised knee. "Well anyhow, Johnny, we run him up two-three times. Even if he did get away, he is one scared rebel. You can depend on that. Yes seh, you can depend on that."

Hostetler shifted himself, relaxing beneath Deall's vacant silence. "I bet that rebel son of a bitch is halfway across that swamp by now. That is one scared son of a bitch. He won't be back, no sir." He smiled, crow's-feet white against the red sunburned temples below his cap.

Sullivan hadn't shifted his stance. He still watched Deall's face. "Did you *mean* for us to string him up, Johnny? I thought you did at first. Did you?"

Deall focused on Sullivan. "*Game*, Phil? What did you do to him?"

"We run him up two times, like Saul just said. Lowered him each time, and give him a chance to talk. Then the third time, we thought we helt him up there too long. Thought he was dead as a doornail. But when we went back down to fetch up . . ."

Deall shook his head violently. Nature, he was thinking disjointedly, human nature comes clawing and fornicating and devouring. You cannot deny it. "You thought I would order that," he said. "You thought I would order you to torture a helpless man?"

"Well, hell!" Keller said, jerking himself upright. "Well if you . . ."

"No Johnny," Sullivan said. "I wasn't sure. But it didn't seem right to take him off and hang him, neither."

"So you did this . . . you did this game to find out what?"

"Why, we figured to find out where he had buried his gold. We thought that was what you wanted."

The sunlight was fading, trapped in pines and sedge grass and the piles of refuse and skeletons of old cooking fires. "Torture a man for that? Just to find out where his gold—his material possessions—are *buried?*"

"Well . . ."

"Well God damn it all," Keller said. "So you did want him just strung up, hey? Just kill him out of hand? And you call that better? You call that better, Deall? Sheeee . . ."

Keller swung his head in a short arc of contempt.

We had every right, Deall started to say. He fired on soldiers. But he found himself saying instead, "They must learn."

"Learn? Learn? Even could we teach 'em anything, how he

going to *learn*, swinging from a tree branch down yonder? Answer me that!"

"Who gave *you* the right to reinterpret my orders?"

Keller snorted. "Jesus Christ." He pivoted and walked away, making tossing motions with his right hand and looping his rifle to his shoulder. "Shit!"

Deall watched him blankly.

"He is right, Johnny," Sullivan said, hoisting his own rifle. "But had I known you wanted him dead for sure, I'd have done it, I guess."

"I don't know as I would of," Hostetler said. "Aw hell, Johnny. Hanging is nigger work. It ain't work for a white man."

"We must find him," Deall said. But even as he began to work his hands over his equipment, settling cartridge box and scabbard, the tangled dark image of *swamp* consumed all zeal. His eyes were vacant. His hand felt absently in his belt, where he no longer carried the revolver (I gave it to— to? —Ah, the one named Toby).

"I reckon there is little use to that," Sullivan said. "He is probably away off in that swamp, and it would take the whole regiment to get him out of there."

"The three of us looked pretty good, anyhow. Ain't that so, Phil?"

It would take all of us, at the least, Deall was thinking. And if I order Keller to come along, he will not do it. Even if I ordered him outright. And Hostetler might not. And then what? He paused. The afternoon light decayed around him. And then what?

Sullivan had not answered Hostetler. He sighed, and then said, "Tell you what, Johnny. Suppose I take Billy Gass and we make one quick sweep down through there, in about a half hour. Maybe we will spot him if he is still on this side of the swamp."

And Deall, his eyes clouded, his hands still upon his equipment, nodded his head.

The voice of the Negro woman came down to him from the upstairs hall, falling through the shadows in meaningless soft consonants. Deall's head suddenly came up, and his eyes flared upward toward the sound. Damn it all to hell, he thought. Damn it all to hell! He turned and slammed open the rear door, the Negroes watching him, Hostetler and Sullivan shrugging at each other on the other side of the gallery.

Deall strode through the hall, through the clustering grey shadows still smelling of gunpowder and loosened dust. He swung at the banister and hurtled up the steps, hitting every third one, boot nails clattering. With the violent ascension, his purpose and rage reassembled. Those Goddamned idiots. Nature will come, with appetite and defecation. He had a violent sense of pushing and molding recalcitrant clay, of shoving and shaping irresolute human forms—black and white—into patterns only to have the patterns (like faces dissolving in water reflection) distort and gape and laugh and fragment. He took the last steps four at once.

The door to her room slammed against the closet door, rebounded beneath his hand on the brass knob: he was aware of woman's garments tumbling down softly behind it.

She was propped in front of him, half-raised, eyes smudged blackly with weeping, face shiny. "He got away," Deall was saying, coldly. "He got away. I would have hanged him, in his stubborn pride. But he got away."

She was fumbling behind herself, pushing herself upright from the pillows. Her dressing gown was open widely at the throat (against the hour of lamentation?) and with her sudden, startled upraising, he could see deeply between her breasts. Deall's urgency lost itself as a blunted shaft: her flesh was framed by the whiteness of the lace-topped chemise and dressing gown and sheet, her breasts shadowed and white, too, but with a soft lucency. They moved richly with her intake of breath and shifting of position.

And—still in the door, his hands still on the knob while his vision lingered in the light-rich difference between her bosom and the lace barely encircling—Deall was aware of her stunned reaction. At the door's opening, her face had been proudly tense: now lips and cheeks were openly exposed, unshielded. Her eyes broke back and forth upon his own.

The girl fumbingly found hauteur: no gladness or visible relief, but a superior pride.

He smiled beneath it.

"Well sir! . . . I am sorry he has been inconsiderate enough to . . . to *ruin* your sport."

Deall was not listening. He watched the girl now assuming arrogance, as before—upon pillows—she had been prepared for noble bereavement. Her hands closed the top of the dressing gown firmly, chin upthrust.

He was almost delighted, after all his disappointment.

Her contempt flicked off his attention. His abrupt sudden announcement had dislocated her posing: had disrobed her. He had a fresh consciousness of power. He had stripped her open, for a moment, with his prompt instinctive response. It reminded of the morning, when he had stung them with mention of the Negro child.

With bleeding nailless thumb.

But he still felt a coursing pleasure. They live so by form. Their whole life is one of self-deceived, self-deceiving artifice. And when the world does not move as they have deceived themselves that it will, they are naked, exposed, helpless.

Chapter 22

THOMAS JEFFERSON MALORY LAY FACE DOWN IN THE CHILL SWAMP water. The grey viscous mud beneath it was as resilient as boneless human flesh to his squeezing fingers. His eye, pillowed above the water by his forearm, could see the very surface of the swamp water itself, scummed with currentless accumulation—the myriads, the maculae of insects, the minuscule fragments of rotting leaves, all sinking, sunk, flecking away across a blue brown, shadowed darkness. The mud was cold and, stirred, it stank of rotting. Insects' tiny bodies, like spermy flecks, touched his flesh at the surface of the water. He accepted it all.

Despite the wash of swamp water, he still tasted the salty red cream of blood. Curds of blood and phlegm corded in his throat. In a moment, he would have to spit again. His shirt was already streaked with his scabbing blood. Malory was long certain the Yankees were gone. He was waiting for sure self-control—no longer menaced by white spasms of shock—to return to him.

In such white spasms of will-less horror had he dragged himself off the path after the Yankees had left, sucks of air as tactile as rough flannel coursing down his throat. He had flopped onto his front and then his back and so over a log, away from the light which had lain over the path like acid. He had been wedged beneath a log, aware of the scampering ants and the unbraiding of a black centipede next to his flesh, while one of them had grounded his rifle on the very wood above him and they had called to each other through the cold.

All his life Malory had shunned the unnecessary spoilure of the swamp, with the disdain of a man marked out by having other men to do the most roiling kinds of labor for him. But after they had gone he had scrambled for the swamp on all fours, sobbing, squeezing his blood between his teeth so there would be no trail, floundering into the water and the scum and the stumps and dank liquid earth like a reduced, spike-furred animal.

And here he still lay. And the major pattern of his thought—above the choking need to spit again—was one of blind, triumphant rage. Focusless, voiceless, it pressed against the inside of his forehead like a golden spike.

Then shock and nausea washed whitely over his consciousness again. He groveled, squeezing at the mud. The waves of raw, blinding, physical helplessness surged; passed; and once again he could drink that steady, furious exultation. The swamp stank in an undertone of gathering twilight and the brown smell of fallen leaves. The stench reminded him strangely of the vision on the cellar steps, with the Yankee sergeant before him. But bathed in the swamp stink, the memory of the apparition carried no fear at all.

No, that was not true. (Soon he would spit, and rise.) That was not true. The apparition still terrified. But he put the terror before the cold deep rage in his mind, and it was flattened.

He did all this in a second of reflection.

Malory raised his head and spat, sucked and spat again. The clots of blood and creamy mucus lay in the water before his face, swirling gently in minute archipelagoes. He began rising, one knee upright, the cloth of his shirt already grey green with the mud now receiving a thin quick thread of blood from his mouth. His shirt and trousers ballooned with the transferring, falling waters, and the swamp water burst whitely about his thighs and calves as he struggled erect.

He took two lunging, monstrous strides, heaving one side of his body ahead of the other. Then he collapsed to his knees again, water swirling about crotch and thighs, and then rose upright at last.

Malory felt a hot ratchet of pain in the left side of his neck. The suddenness of the pain made him gag. He coughed bloodily. He tried rolling his head on his neck, but the pain grated again and spots of color stung his eye.

Holding his head cocked to the right, away from the throbbing pain, he made for the bank. He stumbled and nearly fell over an old log. He tugged and struggled against waist-high vines, trying to thread his way through them. At last, with the vines webbing across both shoulders and a log forking ahead of his legs, he gave up his efforts at clumsy silence and thrashed blindly. The vines held and he gratefully lunged: they broke and his body hung with crashing freedom over the log, he put one boot upon it and when it rolled slammed his other heel down upon it and was free, with the fork of wood sunk and splintered into the mud behind him. The sound of his thrashing collapsed through the dim lengths of the swamp, and a yellowhammer burst in low flight, white tail weaving between the cypresses.

"By God almighty, this is my land." He looked up through the branches toward the late afternoon sky. But his exultation and his rage were checked by an oncoming new burst of shock: his ribs hurt, his eye dazzled and the sunlight wavered in the high tree limbs. "Acchh . . ."

Malory floundered, drooling, to the bank. He sank amid the leaf ruck, and again waited helplessly to endure the thing. His neck was chafed and stinging, his head burning to the touch. He shivered violently in his soaked, iron-cold clothing, panting, awaiting the blast. It came: his heart lunged again and he rocked backward, shuddering from the vivid white shapes of nausea. Stop it, ohh stop it. The branches over him swam in the helpless race of his pulse. He squeezed his side viciously.

It passed. Man, I got to stop this! He hated his body in its weakness. I got things to do, I got to stop this. He swayed upon his haunches, feeding his frustration to his fury, digging his nails into his palms against the very helplessness of his body.

I will bathe my face, at the least . . . maybe it will help. He balanced himself on one hand while he paddled at the bitter-cold water with the other. His hand aroused the stench of the swamp bottom, black beneath old green and brown. The water burned against his neck. He bathed his forehead in mechanical handfuls, laces of water trickling silvery.

The next burst of shock began in his ribs, rising vomitlike toward his brain, and his blind fury surged up against it, raised up wavelike against it and he surged out of all caution, hating his body, and hunched forward onto his hands and pushed his whole head—blood-filled mouth and nose, then swollen beating brain—beneath the dark level of the water, eye closed, the shock of the cold water driving everything from him in its single sepulchral burst of white COLD. He held his head under until his brain, beating against the cold and the stinging pain, lost all sense of past-present-now, and then he raised up, his long lank hair throwing water back from him in a spray. Malory's hair crested upright, water streamed down his face, and recovering from the agony his mouth shaped itself like a suppli-cant's.

He rose stiffly. The scouring coldness of the water had washed away the neck pain and the bursts of headache and the nerve-end recollections of shock. He smelled the odor of the swamp, the thick dark stench, upon himself.

He had lost the eye patch.

Malory looked down at the pooled edge of the swamp. A cloudy pattern hung suspended like grey paint upon the black water, mud which his face and hair had raised from the suppurating bottom. His wrist twisted, anticipating the reach and probe for the eye patch. But he did not kneel. Hell no. I got more at my house.

Thus the rage within him overcame the beat and pump of his own instincts for survival and the simple weakness of his nerves. The rage dominated his consciousness. He chaliced it in repeated specific thoughts. By God, he better not be on my land come sunup. He expects that I am gone. But now *I* got the darkness. By God he bet' be gone before sunup!

Thomas Jefferson Malory turned and began to climb back up the slope. Physical exhaustion weighed upon his calves and legs as if in betrayal of his exultant new rage. He fought back at it with long strides, cherishing each length traversed in his teeth. Head cocked to the right, he surged, taut-lipped, past the pebbly round place where they had strung him up: the rope dangled whitely.

And as he climbed, his body responded to the transcendent vio-lence of his spirit. Potency flooded through his weary legs, pulsing from his fury. He stalked above himself, moving soon with a hunter's swift lightness. And everywhere his vision carried he saw alleyways and pathways and radial lanes of dark light. His stained trousers and mud-grey shirt blended into the shadows of the woods, his open-collared shirt hung from him in the cloudy shapes of a swordsman's blouse.

Ahead of him, as he climbed through the oaks, he could see the late afternoon light glowing through the frieze of the woods: the light lay buttery on the sedge and glistened in the olive and blue pine branches.

Suddenly, Malory *knew*—just as a hunter *knows* that the next field will blossom with quail—Malory *knew* that even as he was climbing, Yankees were coming down toward him. His head twisted up, and his eye flared upward toward his instinct.

He paused then, just beneath the level of the sun's rays coming through the pine trunks. His body was stained like the sycamores, and it sank back into the shapes of vine and trenched trunk.

He thought of his blacks, lurking in their darkness. I beat 'em out here, this evening. My turn!

Before he saw the two Yankee soldiers, Malory was aware of them as an irritable flickering upon the periphery of his senses. Then they came into sight, coming down through the pines, metal clattering upon them, buttons winking in the cathedral-shafts of leveling sunlight. He stood in the woods edge, motionless, exultant at his cold invisibility. The one with the beard, and the young one—it seemed to him that he could smell them, an oily, metallic smell. He howled with a silent joy. They passed fifty yards off, and he could hear them following the path down toward the swamp.

A half-assed effort. And unwillingly done. They will not be out after me again. No sir, not in this chill twilight. They at the house, taking their ease.

And I reckon he is still there, too. He squeezed his thighs and moved his head slightly to the left, partaking of the spurt of pain in his throat, letting the spurt send the landscape toward his eye in sprays of more vivid shape and color.

He followed the flight of a red-winged blackbird, its red patch as bright as though the wing had been ripped away freshly from the shoulder. The woods were filled with decaying shapes—the smell of coming cold, of sunlight in pine needles, of thin dust, and beneath it all the stench of the swamp, a mouth-stench still on him.

Ten minutes, and the two soldiers came back, rifles slung over their shoulders, talking about railroad rights-of-way.

He waited long after they were vanished from him—indeed, long after he knew they must be back upon the family's grounds. He delighted in the way in which his fury was shaped and molded by his cold patience. And, in the flowing, fondled surges of the rage, he ignored the Yankees. He felt no way to strike at them, he would not expend his rage against them foolishly, like infantry against cannon, like solid shot bouncing off the sides of ironclads. I fought 'em three times, and lost ever' time. I reckon even a Malory has to learn sooner or later. The ones who had swung him up were as impersonal to him now as the Yankee artillerymen at Shiloh. The sergeant was as inaccessible to his revenge, behind the men with him, as the Yankees had been behind the shield of their gunboat at Swift's Bend, where they had blinded him.

Anyhow, Malory thought, I reckon I'll quit while I'm still ahead. Yes sir, even a Malory will learn sooner or later. Malory repeated this to himself, chuckling inwardly. Yes sir. He still watched the waning light in the pines ahead.

He did not need the Yankees—inaccessible behind hanging iron—for his rage. They will be gone soon, I expect. By sunup. And I know a nigger better be gone with 'em. Tobe's face, rich for the stroke, cherished Judas-like in niggerhood, stood before him; and underlying it, superimposed upon Tobe's face, was the apparition. Living, dead, I reckon I'll have me a go at all of 'em. Shoot a white man in my house with my own gun, by damn. By damn. We just see.

A nigger Judas.

He started forward, into the long sedge and the pine needles, just beneath the fall of the light. His head was cocked consciously to the right, his left eye a lidded wound against the white untanned circle of flesh, following his right eye visionlessly.

Late that evening, the risen moon was ghastly bright, a white so pure that it seemed as though the night itself was pierced by a true look into the very creative locus of the world. And as he watched, shivering in the cold but warmed by his rage, he could see the spider shape embossed within the circle: in palest gray, the long spider's multiple arms reaching down the sides toward the right lower rim, the faceted eyes in the center, the hunching back.

Chapter 23

The Negro woman backed through the door from the hall into the dining room. She turned with elephantine care, her face shining above the steam. On the tray were the second portions of roast chicken, bronze skin dimpled with juices.

"He-ey-ey, now, Auntie!" Keller said.

Deall sat at the head of the table, still wearing his blue uniform blouse, wool as thick as armor in the heated room. The other four were sprawled backward, chairs back-tilted, blouses off in the heat from the fireplace and the lamplight. Their shirts were stained and foul from the tense morning skirmish and then the digging and butchering. Keller took the platter proprietarily and gestured it toward Deall, who shook his head. Saul Keller forked one of the chickens onto his own plate, amid the sweet-potato skins and the grey brown chicken bones.

Keller had arranged it all, giving a quarter to the woman when she passed him the last time from her mistress' room ("Aunty, I bet you the cook on this place"), and a quarter to Jade to set the fire and light the lamps. They had shared the food with the slaves—hams from the floor of the smokehouse and chickens that Gass and Winters had killed—laying the meat on the gallery and letting them carry it away. "But I believe we've earned us a sit-down meal," Keller had said. "I've ate enough hardtack and bacon over campfires to stuff a mule—don't point that there ham at me, Winters—I bet ol' Aunty here would not mind cooking one time for us."

Taking the platter, Winters settled back into his chair, and then hurled himself upright. One of the grease-speckled chickens rolled off onto the table.

"Son of a bitch! Look at that splinter!" He rubbed himself.

Gass whooped, and Sullivan said, "Serves you right, Carl. You shouldn't have worked over the dining room so." All of the furniture was marred: the chairs cracked by minié balls, the top of the table sprouted with splinters and scarred in orange curlicues from the collapse of the cut-glass chandelier.

"Now a bottle of whiskey," Keller was saying, angling a bite toward a piece of corn bread, "would make this perfect."

"Well, I don't like it a damned bit after they killed Ted, we can't find their gold," Billy Gass said.

" 'S the niggers," Keller said. "Damned closemouth bunch. At most places they tell right off where they buried the gold. That is what them Indiana boys said, didn't they, Carl? It is what them Indiana boys said. I never seen anything like this."

Sullivan glanced at Deall. His vision was distant, through the broken window at the rear of the room. He broke off a fragment of the corn bread and took it in finger and thumb to his mouth. He had eaten the white meat from one breast of chicken.

"What's the matter, Johnny? Sorry that the rebel got away?"

Deall looked at him. Sullivan noticed in the angled lamplight how tightly his flesh wrapped the bones of his face.

"Do you not think the blacks should be in here, eating in here at last? Cooking for themselves?"

"Aw *hell* no!" Keller said, peppering his chicken without looking up. "They got they own cookfires out back. I expect they prefer a barbecue."

Bright orange light from the quarters painted the trees and the fences near the house. In it they could see Hostetler leaning against the barn fence, on sentry. The bright, false wash of light turned his blouse brown and the buttons orange. Sullivan and Winters, facing the side windows, were reminded of the burning of Atlanta, with the regiments passing through swirls of sparks and band music. Deall was looking out of the shattered rear window: the big cooking fires flared spectrally.

"He don't know niggers," Keller said, now buttering a slab

of corn bread. "They having a high old time. Ain't nothing like a nigger"—he sucked at a chicken wing and followed with a bite of the bread—"for knowing how to enjoy himself."

"Except," she said from the doorway behind Deall, voice shivering shrill, "exce-*ept* for Yankee soldiers out on a spree, I observe."

Deall looked back at her over his shoulder.

Celia was wearing the brown dress with the martial trim—buttoned to her throat this time, wide-skirted, small-waisted. Her white flesh was glistening; her chin trembled, and her bosom rose and fell, molded above the waist.

There was a quivering nervousness upon her like moisture, but she had measured her glance into amused, half-veiled disdain. A corner of her mouth was indrawn in amusement while the clear cast of her features was scornful.

Keller continued, ruminatively, through a mouthful of buttermilk, "Why no, ma'am, I expect you are right. Especially when the feed is on the house."

But the others had risen politely. Deall, tugging at his blouse and bowing with exaggerated courtesy, was suddenly articulate: "I beg your forgiveness, madam, that we did not await your arrival before beginning our repast . . ."

"Why I would hardly consent to dine. . . ."

"I am sure," Deall said, "I am sure you would not. You would not deign to take a meal with common soldiers. But you see, that is why we went ahead without you."

"Abuse me all you wish. I am in your power. But many is the meal I have taken with our own gallant soldiers, of any rank." She raised her chin slightly. The risen soldiers gazed.

"And of any birth?"

Sullivan looked at Deall, puzzled by his quick volubility, who had sat still and silent all evening while Keller had held the floor.

". . . and our cause depends upon Southern men of every class, sir. Many is the humble grey jacket that has sat right where your men are sitting. We are a people united."

"Which people? Surely not your Negroes!"

"The best of them, sir!"

"Well," Deall said, moving from behind his chair and standing deferentially close, bowing at the end of his phrases. "Who is to say that? It depends, one might say, on whose ox is being gored."

"We know our own people, sir . . ." But then she blushed intensely.

"We have been through that, have we not? Well, I forget myself. Won't you please join us, even at this late moment?"

She looked at him deliberately, eyes round and bright. "No."

"Well, may my men then be seated?"

She said nothing, chin upraised again, turning half in profile. Deall gestured with his hands and the three men sat down, Sullivan watching Deall and the woman, the others falling to their chicken again, their fingers tearing white flesh from the light bones.

Keller said, "Hey, Johnny, maybe she will sing something for us. I expect I would take a rebel song, even."

The girl in the door held herself rigidly. She looked at the wall above them, eyes sparkling with public scorn, mouth half-smiling. Sullivan squinted uncomfortably.

But then Deall suddenly changed, shifting from the bitterly ironic politenesses. He held his own chair away from the table for her, stroking the smooth wood of its shoulders. "Sit down, please . . . please. You have nothing to fear."

His mild gentility was like a sudden splash of pale pink upon a canvas: daring, reshifting all of the values. Celia turned her head away farther, her face frowning in confusion, polished small fingers plucking at her skirt. Deall motioned softly toward the chair with one open, light palm. Sullivan realized she had been made helpless by the gesture.

Billy Gass picked up the chicken to free a last piece of the flesh with his teeth, and then, with his mouth pressed close to it, he remembered the woman and dropped the chicken back into his plate. Still an' all, Sis is as good as she is. Gass glanced over to see how Sullivan was eating his chicken, but he wasn't touching it.

"Well. . . . my men, have some coffee. I imagine it has been a long time since you have had real coffee. Would you care for some?"

Sullivan knew the woman was entrapped in her own anger—as in amber. Deall's curving gestures had surrounded her. She can't leave right *now*. And she can't hardly cut loose, neither. Fascinated, he watched Deall with a farmer's humble shrewdness. Gass thought, she sure is g-good looking. But stuck-up. I bet Johnny could make her say *uncle*. The suggestion tightened in his groin.

"Got some sugar, too," Keller said. The other men looked at

him. The cant of his head and the buttermilk stain over his stubble made the words palpably obscene. Winters and Gass quit eating and wiped their hands, looking at the woman.

Her face burned. Deall looked down at Keller and then quietly at the girl. "I assure you, madam, you have nothing to fear in your person or in your possessions, from my men." The big fire in the fireplace suddenly shuddered against a draft through broken windows. "If it will reassure you, I will post myself in the hall of this house all night. But these are Union soldiers, and it is hardly necessary for you to concern yourself about their conduct."

Deall said this with a quietness that surprised—inflectioned mild words. But then the girl shook her head so intensely they thought that she was refusing assurance.

"—sss" she drew breath over her teeth, flesh beneath her eyes welling with irrelevant fury. "Ohh— you men are *so* brave, alone . . . tormenting a helpless, lone female! But where was your courage on the field of battle, sir!" Her black tresses shook. She twitched her shoulders upright, nervously, defiantly, her bosom rising. The girl looked at each of them as though she expected some violent rebuttal. "Where was your courage at Manassas!"

Keller said, "I don't reckon I was ever *at* Man-ass-ass, ma'am."

Gass began, "The One Hundred and Twelfth Ohiah took the highest casualties of any volunteer regiment in th' ar—"

"The One Hundred and *Twelfth!*" she said, sarcastic smile flickering desperately. "One Hundred *and Twelfth!* Why, with so many men, I am surprised you weren't inside the gates of Richmond within a week! The Hundred and Twelfth! Why sir, why aren't your columns in Richmond right now? Weren't they supposed to have *crushed* the poor little South within a week, sir? On to Richmond? Are they there yet?"

Gass shut his eyes as if this would make him deaf and began again, "*The One Hun'erd an . . .*" but this time Sullivan interrupted: he was amused and pleased by her resilient spirit.

"Well by all! This is about the fiercest rebel I have met yet. If the Confederates ever draft the women, heaven help us all!"

"Damned right," Winters said. "Ma'am, it takes as much courage for me to stand your fire as it does to stand up to the fire of Hood's army."

"*. . . heaviest of any regiment in the Army of the Cumberland at the battle of Chickamauga,*" Gass completed, sightlessly.

Deall said, "No, no, it is not a question of any of this. We will not harm . . ."

"What *of* Chickamauga, sir!" She was looking fiercely at Keller: the challengingly addressed question made the others pause. "I expect you were *there?*"

And then Keller suddenly smiled, with the most innocent pleasure any of them had seen him take. His face was easy with humor, the hands wiping his lips as he framed an answer.

"Did we not whip you there? Did we not whip?"

She was still quiveringly nervous, but her head was prettily cocked now and flushed with their rueful admiration. "Did we not whip you there, sir?" Keller delighted in the focused attention. "*Somebody* must have run off, then."

"It is not fair to ask Saul that, ma'am," Winters said. "Ol' Saul didn't stay around long enough to get a real close hand look, did you, Saul?"

Keller laid his napkin down. "Time I see men who want a piece of property I don't even have a stake in that bad, I reckon I let 'em have it, as a rule."

Except for Deall, they laughed.

"Well, long as we're on the subject, ma'am, what about Atlanta, then? I seen a lot of rebel rear*views*, thereabouts."

Her eyes were alive and roaming among them, full lips preparing a reply.

"And I heard they run pretty good at Chattanooga, too," Winters said. "You heard of those battles, did you, ma'am?"

"You best be quiet about Chattanooga, Carl," Keller said. "Maybe she heard tell a' Tunnel Hill, too."

As the men laughed, she looked from side to side with prim confidence. "All through the fault of that fool Braxton Bragg an' that"—her lips made the shape of *damned*—"hothead Texan John Bell Hood." She put her small fists on her hips, and leaned slightly toward them. "But with Joe Johnston it is a different thing, and you all know it."

"Well we beat him all th' way back to Atlanta, didn't we?" Gass said.

"But by heaven, miss," Sullivan said, "that is the dern truth. Truer words were never spoke, I reckon."

She tossed her head. "On a fair field, Mr. Yankee, a Southern is as good as ten Yankees."

"Say you've had a hard time comin' by fair fields, ma'am?" Keller asked.

Sullivan found himself hoping—with urging silent lips—that the girl would reply.

"There will be enough of them, I expect, before we let Mr. Sherman's army go home."

Her eyes were sparkling, her small, rounded body was coy with debate and defiance. The soldiers had anticipated legendarily hot-spirited Southern belles, and now they hunched and moved in the chairs with delight. The girl's bright defiance was gleefully received: the harsh realities of invasion softened. They warmed to her. Sullivan, married and immersed in rural proprieties and Bible-heavy family traditions, was nonetheless vastly charmed. He noticed that Deall was tense and impatient. Sullivan was not surprised. He figured Deall most often to himself in terms of clear, unalloyed intensity, and assumed it was good to be so upright.

Sullivan said, "You mean between here and Savannah?"

She nodded determinedly at him. "Hardee is at Savannah. You will find that a tough nut to crack. And the Georgians are rallying from all sides." Gass was openmouthed. Her pertness, the lift of her pearl-bright flesh and the soft jut of her bosom made his member stiffen against his thigh. He had dim glimpses of her thrashing amid sheets, but he could not focus them.

The other three privates looked at her easily, genially without calculation. Her political ferocity made her inaccessible physically, so they were lapsing into that easy, prizeless freedom of pleasant talk with an unattainable but attractive young woman. Keller's face was settled into warm easy creases, free from the sheen of self-aggrandizement, the man Sullivan had known back near Mount Union of an afternoon's plowing in adjoining fields. He and Keller forgot that they had nearly hanged her husband.

"Rallying, ma'am. What are they rallying *to?*"

"Seems to me they are rallying wherever Uncle Billy *ain't.*"

Gass laughed loudly, and Winters smiled at his own joke.

"Could be, Mr. Yankee," the girl said, "but could be we have a surprise for you all."

"Will you come visit us in jail, ma'am?"

"Once you are *there*, then I will sing some good Confederate songs for you."

Pleased, the four privates all laughed. Sullivan was forming a rejoinder—chickens before they hatch, these chickens we are eating, our chickens are tougher than yours—when Deall said, curtly, "It is not a question of that. The South is beaten to its knees, and you must come to see that, if you are to live at all." Now he stood up again, stiffly, beside his chair.

"The good, that which must be, will drive out the evil. This is no game, madam, no town ball between neighboring villages. It is far more serious than that."

He had caught her distant from her earlier, sheltering disdain. She was flirtatiously exposed. She pulled her shoulders back and her chin up, breathing deeply, staring at Deall.

Sullivan regretted losing this clean pleasure. But he was not surprised. Deall was this way.

"But it will not do to debate this with you, ma'am. You will not heed the truth, and so it will only be a waste of all our times. But again, I assure you personally that no harm will come to your possessions or your person."

At the word "person," Keller went back loudly to a leg of the roast chicken. Sullivan noted that the girl's stung eyes had fallen just then upon Keller, searching for support. She looked back hollowly at Deall.

"Well sir . . . I . . . I must ask then that question for wh-which I first came down."

She stiffened herself with a deep breath.

"When, sir, may we expect you and your men to be gone from my husband's premises?"

Husband momentarily surprised Sullivan.

"A fair question, ma'am. With the dawn."

"Well, I shall remain in my room until then."

"At your pleasure."

"Perhaps you will send for one of my maids to attend me during the night?"

"I shall ask if she wishes to accompany you. She is your maid no longer. Which one will you wish me to beg for you?"

The tears made her eyes glisten in lamplight. "You wou—," she swallowed against the sob, "you would none of you treat your own wives and sisters this way!"

"We have no wives or sisters, ma'am," Keller said, rummaging in his blouse pocket for pipe tobacco. "We are picked for that purpose."

Winters and Gass chuckled. Deall smiled tightly. He stood in the hall doorway, watching the girl ascend the stairs. His strongly defined, tough, clear features and his thick jacket were outlined against the cream paint and the ripped pastels of the wallpaper. He was rough on the girl, Sullivan thought. But he did offer her the coffee. He looked admiringly, vaguely, at Deall's rectitude: not distracted even by such a sweet little thing as that.

Men like that are winning the war for us, I s'pose.

Gass's thinking swiveled about his erect flesh. He recalled, in loose mindless rambling, the yellow girl he had seen in the cabin (rich flesh beneath thin chemise). "Say, Carl, you ought to have seen the nigger l-lady I saw this afternoon." Winters looked at him with interest, and he went on.

Chapter 24

THE COOKING FIRES WERE ROARING WITH FRESH PINE BOUGHS AND CORD after cord of cured wood. Orange rushing walls of heat beat all whiteness out of the slave cabin rows, squeezed back the night, and gathered the slaves in a yellow brown ambience in which they rocked and laughed and reached for the food. The light and heat alone were violently intoxicating: across the fire from Jade, even old Uncle Mitchell was reached in his cellular trap of habit and ancient memory. He laughed to himself droolingly, out of some 1820s recollection, holding a whole chicken in one gentle hand.

And Jade was drunk on the heat and the food. His vision was absorbed in the swaggering fires, his flesh squeezed between the heat of the fires and the warm distended repletion of his belly. He swayed slightly, moaning to himself.

Christmas come early this year. Christmas gift, Massa!

Roasting chickens and barbecuing pig hung on spits, fondled by the fires, popping and faceted in their own juices. Sweet potatoes and Irish potatoes were tossed among the coals, a whole demijohn of molasses was there for lacing the meat, and the flesh of the potatoes.

No slow moonrise this evening, no cold blue nightfall between the bone-white huts.

Plantation nightfall always came with small, blue-ringed cooking fires which never held back the chill, and with single measures of cornmeal and bacon. Occasionally Jade could steal a chicken. Now, Juno's little boy Jackson passed through Jade's vision as if seen through honey, carrying clusters of chickens to the fires like clusters of grapes. It reminded of the holidays, the old Fourth of July and especially Christmas, with the permitted drams of rum and the dancing. On the last Christmas before the War, the Husbands had come over to Sycamore, and the slaves had gathered for the Husband children, shouting "Christmas gif', sah," while the white children shrieked to watch them prance and caper over the bright cloth and coins and sweetmeats. There had been bright frost on the ground.

Jade got to his feet slowly, his shirt greasy from the feasting. He was dazed by the warmth upon his eyes, the bathing heat, the taste of chicken and potatoes and molasses behind his teeth. He wiped his hands on his trousers, staring at the coals of the fire, the rectangles eaten and reappearing between the surging silky curtains of flame. Christmas come early this year, yes suh! He gathered himself.

Now I 'spect I got a gift for Marse Tom myself. Jade reached behind him, still not completely convinced by the weight of the Sharps carbine. He patted its breech. The gun's weight stiffened his back with pride.

He walked uncertainly between the fires, heat laving his face and plucking at his eyebrows. The carbine thumped his back, its brass buckle gleaming on his chest.

"How long 'fore that barbecue be done, Shorty?"

Shorty turned the spit slowly, basting the hot flesh.

"Ain't too long. 'Bout a quarter of en hour."

"I 'spect I be back by that time."

Jade went off toward June's cabin. The wash of light reached up the row. At the first light touch of the winter night, away from the fires, his flesh was swollen with desire. He was paradefully certain with the carbine strapped across his chest.

See what that woman think now. See what she think bout ol' Master. And who done brought the Yankees back here? Answer me that. Who you think?

He noticed the man standing beside the hut when he was almost past him. The green jacket was clouded by the firelight into grey brown, but he could tell it was Tobe by the furrows of the corduroy, and then by the straight wide nose. Jade went toward him with lurching, pompous geniality. Tobe turned his head slightly to face him.

"Who you telling to clear out now? Eh?"

Tobe looked steadily at him.

"Ain't you gonna tell me to clear out, one more time?"

"I 'spect it might be the best thing for all of us." Then Tobe looked back toward the blacks around the fire.

"And why you say that? Ain't I done brought the Yankees here?"

"And how long they gone stay?"

Jade slapped the butt of the Sharps. "Ain't we got the guns, for when they be gone?"

Tobe looked at him fully once more. The yellow-ringed eyes were plain in the light. "Them old guns ain't gonna do you any good. What you got, anyhow? Five, six? What you gonna do when the whites come with twenty or thirty of 'em?"

"Hunh! What you know, nigger? You just the damn driver, but I 'spect your driving days are th'oo."

"I told you I ain't the driver no more."

The calm, lifted ease with which Tobe wielded the power, the way he stood against the whitewashed wall so poised and black, had always stung Jade. Sometimes to action: the first strides toward the inevitable whipping were always golden bright.

"And you ain't planning to kiss they ass when they come back? That ain't what you planning?"

He had made the challenge so abruptly he was chilled, himself, by the audacity. He felt the bright thump of his heartbeat against a bellying fear. By this time, Tobe's jaw should have come up with sudden power.

But it went unanswered. Tobe reacted with a pale personal indifference.

"No man, no. I tell you what I'm figuring." Tobe even turned his face away from Jade and toward the fires again. Just like las' night. "They ain't gonna be nothing here. Not *nothing*. Not even wood for the winter. No meat, no corn, no molasses. . . ."

To Jade, the speculative, careful words were quicksilver cold above the warmth he felt. The words were alien. "Hunh! What you know?"

". . . and what they is left, the white folks will get the most of. We won't have nothing."

" 'Cept our freedom. And this here gun."

"And what good freedom be?" Phrony, released from the house, crossed shuffling against the fires. Tobe's vision was fixed upon her and the fires. "The Yankees ain't planning to stay. Way they tear up and burn up, you can see that. And when they gone, things are gonna be the same as before, but the white folks are gonna be meaner. You can see *that*, too."

Jade measured the vacant, contemplative stare in Tobe's eyes. Then, leering, he said, "Say they will, eh?"

"You can see that, too."

"Say you can? Why, how you come to see that?"

"The Yankees are leaving. But they done embarrassed these whites. They whipped 'em. And we took up with the Yankees. You can see what these white folks are gonna do, time the Yankees be gone."

Listen at you, nigger! Jade nearly said. Sarcasm quivered at his lips, but he put it off. "Well, what do you *ex*-spect we ought to do?"

Tobe began to trace his toe, looking at the ground.

"Well, I figure we ought to get us all out of here. Right fast, by clear light tomorrow. We ought to get us some hosses, and the wagon or the carriage or both, for Phrony and Juno and the ones cain't walk, and be on the road by day clear. I figure"—here he looked speculatively up at the treetops, webbed orange against the night—"we can be on the other side of Millen by nightfall, following the Yankees towards the sea."

"That far? Towards the sea, you say?"

"We get that far, maybe we can find some shippin' for the north. It's the onliest chance we got."

"Shippin' for the north, you say?"

"Yeh, so I want you and Shorty to go down to Marse Tom's stock pen in the bottoms pretty soon, an—" But Jade's voice was interrupting him softly and triumphantly.

" 'Shipping for the north,' he say. Heh heh heh heh. 'Shippin' for the north.' Listen at the nigger. Hee hee hee . . . And leave all this? Our day has come and you gonna *leave* it? Who gone get Shorty away from that fire tonight? . . . *You?* The *driver?*"

He pulled himself upright, not needing to test Tobe's strength or the shape of his power now, afoot with confidence. The firelight, the thick weight of the gun on his back, were sign and seal. For the *black* man, Jubilee was here and he had brought it. " 'Shippin' for the north,' " he said, "that's *white* folks' talk."

Tobe stared at him. I'se free at last, even of ol' Tobe. He smiled back with the arrogance of a man secure in his own race, fixed into his racial identity at its most certain. Jade knew Tobe was cast loose: and Tobe knew it, too. "From a white folks' nigger."

When a man talked the way Tobe did, it was white, daylight talk, of calculation and discipline. It was alien above the heat-soaked amber of the slaves' world. "Yes suh, that's white folks' talk, from a white folks' nigger."

He had brought the Yankees, and they had brought fire and food and warmth, and it was the niggers' time then. Out of the white man's time and season, here it was the night full of fire and warmth, with food and the promise of fornication (he was already on his way, leaving Tobe staring, stung, and he was chuckling "heh heh heh heh"). Curfew gone, rigid white discipline gone, it was the black man's time now!

I 'spect ol' Tobe forgot who he is.

Free from Tobe at last. Tobe had always been doubly blessed with power, with the black strength and insight, and with white trust. Yes suh, they *always* liked ol' Tobe. But now Tobe ain't got his white folks. It's the day of Jubilo, and I brought it. Now let's see what good his white folks do him.

" 'Shippin' for the north!' Heh heh heh heh. . . ." Still chuckling so Tobe could hear him, Jade fondled the butt of his carbine, thinking of June's pliant buttock, thinking with each rhythmical stride Now let's see what good his white friends do him.

Head down and swinging with confidence, his caution diffused with lust, he did not notice the noise from June's cabin until his hand was on the door—woman's laughter and the creaking of floor-boards beneath feet.

Shorty, he thought in hammering rage, *Shorty!* Flesh broke open over bone in his pounding vision: he gone *pay!* He drew his hand into a fist (as it closed regretted he had no knife) and kicked open the door, lips smiling over clenching teeth.

Light warmer, smokier, yellower than that by the open fires: he went into it with mating impatience to feel the bone break and then enter her flesh. She was kneeling upright on the bed, her thighs as yellow as the light itself, her skirt raised above her hips so that the man could test her buttocks, her lips and teeth shining in a flattered arrogance that did not break when her eyes met Jade's.

Jade went blindly for the man, distorting cones of anticipation keeping him plunging even while he was realizing they's white, they's WHITE (white shirts, flesh, soaked green gold in the light), they's the *Yankees!* even while he lunged, all reckless power still sheathing the backswung fist.

The man's eyes were hardening upon Jade while his mouth was still poised caressingly above June's golden shoulder. Then a rifle barrel was yoked viciously across Jade's chest and he was snapped back so hard his legs splayed out and thin porky juice filled his throat. The hammer of his own carbine dug into his back with a sharp yellow pain and he twisted with frenzied strength and more hands were on him and he squirmed until the pain went blue and his eyes closed, and then he was being held loosely and the two white men were looking at him and the man behind him was breathing into his ear, "Easy, nigger, easy ol' buck."

The man who had been squeezing her ass still had on a beaver hat, at a wild toppling angle. The man was the one who had caught him the night before. Caressed by the white man, June smiled down contemptuously at Jade, who gurgled with pain.

As his muscles loosened, the man behind him relaxed his grip until the pain in his back subsided into a dull ache and the gun barrel across his chest slipped down. The Yankees were in their shirt sleeves, smoking cigars, the room had a yellow, intimate familiarity. Jade did not know what to do, or how to feel. He tried to calculate his place, blinking, mouth hanging.

The one with the rifle now patted his shoulder.

Rumors of *completest* equality at the North were reflected in the cigar smoke and the white man's hands upon June's Negro flesh. They had shared the guns and the food. Maybe the women too. Maybe that, too! It seemed a part of the way the old days of labor and helplessness were shifting into rich fullfillment.

He was still stabbed by the pain in his back and confused by new uncertainty and the spasming of his old instinctive anger.

But he was standing alone and the white men were looking at him. So he dropped into the drawling, whining, slack-jawed pose of the night before. "Well law me, boss. I 'spect I thought you was that worthless Shorty, in here wid my woman." He had to force the grin, against the throbbing pain in his back. "But time I sees it's *you,* boss . . ."

"What the shit is he saying?" the one with the beaver hat asked.

The man behind Jade laughed.

"He said he thought it was a nigger named Shorty, with his woman."

"His woman?"

Jade grinned widely, though his lips were rigid because of the pain. "Why . . . just from time to time, boss. When I wants it."

"I reckon I know what that means," the man on the bed said. He stuck his cigar back in his mouth, smiling. "Man after my own heart." The other two white men laughed, too, and picked up their cigars from the floor. The man on the bed gave a cigar to June. She took it in her strong even white teeth and beamed at Jade with inaccessible seductivity and contempt. She squeezed the white man's arms tighter to her.

"Same idea we had," the man with the beaver hat said. "Same idea, old buck. We be through with her fore too long, eh honey?" The cigar went up sharply in his mouth, he slapped her bottom with a shaking resonance. She smiled at him.

One of the Yankees had put his coat over the window, and the buttons were pale against the green-looking cloth. The fire in the fireplace was sweating hot. "We be through, old fellow, don't you worry."

The man with blond hair said, "You don't mind, do you, old sport?"

Jade looked from man to man, assessing them beneath the veil of shuffling witlessness. His back still stung from the cutting carbine hammer and, despite the fact that they were the Yankees, the old assertive fury began to touch his wrists and the line of his jaw with shrill silvery itching. They sat with disarming ease. But you cain't never tell with white men. Recollection of Marse Tom's bludgeoning in the same light, in this same room, confused him. And there were three of them this time.

They's the Yankees, he told himself. They's the *Yankees.* He shook his wrists free of the tension, smiling wetly.

The one in the beaver hat said, "Hell no, they don't give a damn." He stood behind June, his hands now moving over her waist to her breasts, resting lightly beside them. June had on her best chemise—hand-down from Miss Celia, with ribbons faded from pink to yellow along the bodice. The Yankee in the beaver talked around the angled cigar. "You don't mind, do you, old sport?"

Jade laughed ingratiatingly. "Naw suh, boss. Naw suh. I can wait my turn." The Yankee in the beaver hat fished in his pocket and brought out some money—Jade saw some greenbacks. "Naw suh, I don' 'spect I minds at all." He dropped to squat upon his hams, grinning.

"That's the tune, old sport."

Jade thought the money was for him. He was disappointed when the white man tucked the greenback down in June's bosom. Then the hands cupped her breasts and squeezed so the flesh stood above the top of the bodice.

"Okay, boys, we all get a turn, don't we?"

His erection visible beneath his blue trousers, he still kept one hand on her bosom, but slipped the other down to her buttock, guiding her into the back room. But as she went, June kept looking back at Jade, her eyes vivid with arrogance, her tongue pressing to her teeth and popping softly against them. Even as the door closed she was looking with infinite contempt at him.

One of the white men offered him a cigar. The other was shout out the door, "Billy, hey Billy!"

While Jade thanked him and beamed convivially, the man at the door began yelling at the boyish soldier, who put his face in the light. "God damn you, Billy! When I tell you to keep a watch on things, keep a watch! This ol' buck might have taken Saul's head off, way he busted in here."

"I was just taking a piss out back, Joe. I just left for a minute to take a piss out back."

A bearded soldier pressed up beside the boy. "What's goin' on, Joe?"

"Come on in here, Phil. Come on in an' close the door."

As he came into the room, loosening his rifle, the man at the door was saying, "Jesus, Phil, wait till you see what we found! About the juiciest piece of calico I ever see."

The other soldier, stretched on the bed, grinned. "Aw, Hoss. He's a married man. He ain't interested in this kind of stuff, are you, Phil?"

"Well, now, boys . . ."

"She's yaller, Phil. A yaller wench as pretty as you've ever seen."

"Aw, let him be."

"But nigger, Phil! It ain't the same thing."

The heat and smoky light worked on the bearded soldier's face. "Well now, boys, you know no man ever tried to be a better husband."

" 'Strewth, Phil."

"But it don't seem like the same thing, with a nigger," the blond soldier said again.

"Well, boys, I don't see how it can be but one thing, anyhow."

The other two laughed, and Jade joined in. From the back room, they heard the bed's legs scrape across the floor in dry dots of sound, and a sudden moaning "unnnhh . . ." The bearded soldier licked his lips, while all three men stared at the door.

The bearded soldier cleared his throat. "Well, boys, I suppose I try to be a good God-fearing man, and when the good Lord in all his wisdom makes an offer, it don't seem quite right, you know, to say . . ." The others laughed and the blond soldier slapped the bearded man on the shoulder. ". . . to say No, does it boys?" He took off his jacket, and as he turned he saw Jade, and his eyes squinted.

"But Phil, you got to take your turn, you know."

"But"—the soldier on the bed looked at Jade—"do you mind if Phil goes ahead of you, old sport? We got us a busy day, tomorra', Do you mind?"

Jade laughed wheezingly. "Naw suh. I 'spect I don't mind atall. Just step right up and take yo' turn."

They offered him another cigar. The white soldier inside the room whooped, and the yell broke silvery upon the yellow light in the room. The soldiers all grinned broadly and, when Jade laughed, they laughed too, rich masculine laughter. The three soldiers talked and whispered, while Jade grinned foolishly in his squat on the floor, his back aching.

Chapter 25

In the darkness beyond the cabin, Tobe watched. He had heard the thrashing when Jade had gone in. Now the little Yankee soldier had come around to the rear of the cabin again, trailing his rifle. The soldier was peering through the unchinked spaces between the logs at the rear. In faint red-orange light he could see the soldier's face, squeezed in pleasure as he masturbated, his body tense against the spasms.

Tobe had followed Jade through the row, away from the fires. He now stood on the edge of the quarters, in the first fringe of the pines, buried in the clear black night beyond the fires. The moon fell in cool bellshapes of pure white.

White folks' talk from a white folks' nigger.

The words stung, because he recognized the half-truth of them. But his lucid, desperate imagination still worked despite the sting: he could not shed the knowledge of what dawn and the oncoming time would bring. White inevitability had been the truth of his thirty-odd years of existence. He saw it an opaque bar between himself (which now meant all these blacks he had once driven) and free distant green and gold beneath blue skies. Now that white inevitability was gone, pried loose for a few moments. And he could go. And take them.

We got to get away now—this morning at first clear light. This is the onliest day there will *ever* be. He knew this with a cold intuition. Ain't I lived long enough among white folks, ain't I had to guess what they wants before they asks, all my life? They be some through here right soon, to see what the Yankees left. To see how we be carrying on. White men sooner or later would reclaim the landscape. But he had come to know, after seeing his master wounded on two battlefields and then beaten in his own home—and by a nigger, in part—he had come to know it was not the way it had to be, just the way it was.

So he thought of flight with aching earnestness. Despite the sting of Tobe's words, he still formed the details and planned, moving his lips silently. The Yankees prob'ly burn the barn, so I best stay here and save one or the other, the carriage or the wagon. But I send Shorty and Jade down to the stock pens and pick us out two good horses. Queen and Select, I 'spect, because Shorty knows Select and Queen is calm enough. Meantime this evening the women fix up some meal and salt pork—smoked ham, they be any left—and then I got to get them shut of their truck, else they be taking ever worthless thing they got. . . . Until for Tobe, the whole vision was complete before him: the horses' breath steaming in the dawn light, the women on the wagon with the half-awake children on their arms, black flesh touched pinkly by the first of the dawn light, the Yankee column just vanishing up the road toward Louisville and them almost underway, while he took one last look around. . . . What about Miss Celia? What of her? Leave her be. He thought of Celia's petulant, then desperate, loneliness in the deserted house. She seemed contemptible, when he thought of how poised and strong Zeenie and Phrony would be, sitting on the wagon. Ain't studying her. He would take that one last look around. (Little columns of white ice would be pressed from the flesh-colored clay, down in the ditches beside the road.) Then they would be off, into a dawn of pink and coming blue and green, against the golden sedge of the winter fields, and the distance stretched into silence. Silence.

And then what? Well, he had been at Savannah—cobbled streets and awnings over the riverfront—and he had seen the thickets of masts and steam funnels, holding the parcels while old Mistess shopped and Marse Tom's father was at his factor's. He figured he could find the waterfront again. And then we see. But we be there with the Yankees, when they captures. And we be warm and fed and together, and I 'spect I can do *something*.

When he thought of Yankee faces—faces as hairy as the faces of the white folks around here, hair cut shorter but as straight and tangled—a watery sense of uncertainty dissolved some of his vision of hope. But can I run a plantation of twenty-some slaves way I did, for near 'bouts a year, I 'spect this nigger can do anything a white man can.

He pulled himself up again, dazzled with the image of escape. Then he heard a gust of laughter from the big bonfires. Looking over at them, he could see cheeks risen roundly in laughter even at this distance.

He sighed. Who you fooling, nigger, he thought. Who you fooling? He leaned against a pine tree in the weariness. Why they gonna follow you? He remembered Jade's insolent laughter, and the way the sides of his skull had reflected the light as he had walked away.

He looked again at the flaring orange light from the fires. Why they gonna leave this, anyways? Why they gonna follow anybody, but specially you? You been the white man's driver.

The fragile colors of his vision—the cool pink of dawn, the blue of the sky and the simple cool yellow of the sedge fields—he could not enforce against the roaring heat and the bright orange. No man could. Especially not him. His desperation to escape and his sure sense of his helplessness left him with a weak feeling along his bones, a watery feeling in his wrists.

The flare of morning light and gun-burst off the rebel's forehead splayed before him again like flung milk; the ripping *thuck!* of the buckshot. He had been confused this morning, but when he had crossed the parlor, Master's shotgun in his hands, it had been with the chill simplicity of physical assertion. *Earned* freedom: that time, his responsibility for the other blacks had enabled him. He had turned amid the back-concussion of the shotgun, while the lifelong familiar hall—spindles, shafted wallpaper, bare floors—had glistened with outrage and menace, and his flesh had been as cold as ice over his bones and his spirit had soared.

And Marse Tom there stretched out on the floor, outflung arm and pooling blood and he never even saw it, even! Never saw it.

And the Yankee soldier had walked right past him, ignoring him, blind to his presence.

Like all the white men, Coffinville, Savannah, or Boozer in the quarters, coming right past the slave without even noticing, fitting a slave man into place like mule or fence post. The chill had gathered then in his belly and was still there. The quick assertiveness had left Tobe's limbs then, the chill had gathered in the pit of his belly.

Tobe could see the little Yankee soldier behind June's cabin, spent now, still peering through the chink.

So later, Tobe had not been surprised at the cold, white, unanswering refusal of the Yankee sergeant. We must move at dawn and move rapidly. He be white, *too.* I reckon he be white hisself. So he was trapped after all. All afternoon and evening, he had struggled against a growing sense of doom, inventing plans for elaborate flight in the remote colors of fantasy. Now he was weary of all that tracery, the struggle against the bellying black feeling. The frenzied courage of the morning's single, heroic gesture had become a cold feeling of personal exposure.

But Lord, I cain't run away and *leave* 'em all. He thought of the other slaves with long aching pity—pity verging upon feverish, downplunging guilt.

They going to stay here and eat and sleep and fuck till the day is past, in spite all I can do. He sank into the smell of the barbecuing pig, and images of the sensual sliding of dark flesh landmarked with tufts of pungent curling hair. And I can get *me* all of that I wants, he thought suddenly.

The sky was high and clear, but wind shifted the thick pine boughs over his head, and the fall of moonlight was interrupted into blackness. Yes suh, I can get me all of that I wants. The revolver suddenly weighed and bulged in the center of his trouser waist. Standing in this sudden blackness, his despair turned into a ferocious delight.

'Spect we gonna have to *fight* ol' buckra, then. Tobe's consciousness descended completely into the weight of the gun and his hiddenness in the night. Cain't see me—I can get me all of that I wants. He reveled. White faces burst open before the blast of the revolver. The long, hairy white faces (Boozer, Ol' Marse, patrollers, Marse Tom) lurched through fields of hectic brilliance, exploded in bright fountains. Yes suh, I 'spect we gonna *fight,* this time. Let 'em come down on the niggers and see what they finds this time!

I can get me all of that I wants.

Irrelevantly, he thought how easy it would be to kill the little soldier. But what good that do? He is on our side. What good? But still he thought of slipping along up to the little soldier, who now leaned, fingering himself again, staring through the chink while he heard faint whooping within. He thought of taking the small white neck in his hands and wringing out the life, squeezing it out. The feeling was so vivid his hands formed a circle in the darkness, and his blood hummed.

Jade stood beside him, Unc' Mitchell, Shorty, shadowy fleet ambushing others equally masked, dark nighttime shadow upon black flesh. . . .

Who *that* nigger? He jerked, startled by the realization that there *was* another black man there beside him—polled head, and fawn-colored coat and eye-gleam like silver. He peered amid the pools of darkness, pool upon pool. Who was that one?

But the light was upon him again, suddenly, with the shifting of the boughs in the mild wind, and the form resolved itself into pine trunks and low branches and the clear depths of night. The moonlight showed him the wales of corduroy upon his sleeve, even as his hand ceased pressing the butt of the pistol.

But the whites won't come in the night. They will come tomorrow in the morning light.

Tobe sighed. Moonlight gleamed upon his cheekbones, making the shapes of the darkness confused. The moon above him was so brilliantly white that the sky about it was not black, but pollened into faint green and yellow.

He shook his head. Tobe abandoned the visceral contemplation of fighting as a man abandons warm blankets on a cold plantation morning. I cain't help it, what I knows. They would cut us up. They got all the stren'th. His consciousness returned to the level of his eyes, now staring sightlessly into the arches of moonlight. And what would they do to that boy Crisp? He is hardly twe've. Covey? Ol' Uncle Mitchell? Helpless Negroes were ridden down like animals, against dim horizons.

Hunh! Ain't no white talk. It's the truth.

But it was both. Daylight truths were white.

Marse Tom, he always been good to us all, anyhow. Tobe turned to this with confused desperation. It had the silvery feel of truth to him. He straightened his shoulders in characteristic imitation of the old Master when he savaged a slave. Ain't I been the driver for a *good* man? I wouldna been the driver for him lessen he had been. A good man made me the driver. (He don't even know it. Tobe could remember the stiff pulse of Malory's breathing, as he bent over him, and the thin rim of white beneath the closed lid, while the new gunfire filled the hall . . . Tobe's breathing became sharper, his nostrils flared minutely. He don't know it.)

They say, if you get a good master, stick with him. The images of his plantation power were upon him, as familiarly comfortable as the green coat. He made me his driver, instead of a white man.

Maybe I can help, when Marse Tom comes back in the morning. He is going to be mad when he sees all the wastage. I got to tell him the way it was, with the Yankees, less he near *kill* Shorty and Jade and the others. He won't listen to Jade, that is for sure.

I 'spect he'll listen to me. To Tobe, Malory's sympathy was almost palpable. He remembered the way his master's forehead creased in pity, his eye clouding, when he had seen Juno just two nights back.

They his people. He recalled Marse Tom's feigned anger with Shorty: Say you did? and what then, you black horse thief? Lord, Marse Tom, I ain't studyin' no hoss. By God I know that is the truth, because you can't eat a horse. But a chicken? Eh? You never just *came across* one of Mr. Husband's chickens, did you? He loves that man, Tobe thought. Shorty, he is one of Marse Tom's, he belong on this place. Ain't any worthless white trash. Marse Tom, he taken care of his own ever since old Master died. (He don't know it . . . why, sure, that man wasn't one of ours.) The glare off of the rebel's forehead was as white in his recollection as the moonfall. (He ain't none of ours, though.)

Silver moonlight made diamonds and pools amid the dark black shadows. The pine boughs, like insect claws, shifted in short wind-tangled tangents.

Inconsistent, badgered by recollections which cast Marse Tom as the implacable white man, and the Master, and then as a familiar, individual, known and liked human being, Tobe hung amid his shadows, as confused and helpless before the future as Jade was before the Northern soldiers. He was not certain *what* he would do, come morning. The expiring seconds dazzled with their brilliance. The inaccessible cool images of dawn flight were clearly before him because of the force of his desire (the wagon dark against pink silver dawn, and the black women wrapped in their kerchiefs and blankets in the wagon bed—cain't run away alone and I been the driver!). And the pistol still dragged potently at his trouser front, at surges of black despair. But he kept saying to himself, Sho now, he been a good master. Made this 'en the driver . . . stick with him.

Tobe started back toward the bonfires. As he got closer to them, the black figures in front of them became people he had known all his life. When he loomed up behind them, they all turned—Shorty and Unc' Mitchell and Zeenie's Crisp and the others—and looked up at him guardedly. Well, he thought, while Shorty sliced off a strip of the pork from the turning, sizzling, blind carcass, black above the orange fire, well, maybe me and Marse Tom can work something out to last us all th'oo the winter.

He stood upon the fringes of the fire. Its heat pressed upon his face and chest and he sweated into the worn thick corduroy. All day he had thought of taking off the old green jacket, and he unbuttoned it now.

But then Tobe remembered that he had only the slave-issue cotton shirt underneath it, as shapeless and fouled as the others'. So finally, despite the heat, he kept it on.

Chapter 26

Deall sat in the front room, where he had argued with the rebel and his wife in the afternoon. The room was dimly candlelit, and cold. Through the shattered windows, he could hear wind in the pines and see a faint orange wash of light in the limbs of the sycamores. The plotless interlacings of the tree branches invaded the room through the wreckage of the windows. Shadows moved all around him, as though he were in a cold forest himself.

Deall's mind was hectic and despairing. He was unable to remove from the forefront of his attention the image of her rich breasts, moving within the soft tangle of chemise and bedsheet. He propped his feet carefully on the chair before him, forcing himself to conceive of other things. But when he did so, his mind turned with an odd, clicking helplessness, to reflect upon his own savage frustrations.

Eating, drinking, fornicating, does nature come.

This morning it had seemed that the Symbol itself, haunted, stung with pride and decay, had hung before his vision. Calligraphies of rust and dirt behind proud facade, Coiner's treacherous assassination—the Symbol of all that maddened and tormented in human nature and natural corruption. *One swift, clear action* . . . he recalled, in mocking bitterness, the fluting sense of his rush into the hall, the stunned satanic rebel helpless before him, the black man counterbalancing the sergeant. That one intuited, inspired action which was somehow to have lifted his burdened self-consciousness above all his loss. . . . (The cloudy mild vision of the Great Idealists, Emerson, Parker, the achieved imperishable calmness about the eyes, the landscape above the flesh. . . .) He sighed, slumping and shifting his feet upon the chair, gazing sightlessly into the wine-dark shadows.

That one action, that first stride into the hallway. . . . When he shrugged his shoulders, they seemed (mockingly) to touch again the furls of his gold green purpose.

Nothing manifested. All was hollow, at the end. Nature's irredeemable patterns coursed, undermined, water beneath sand castles. He winced, thinking of the rebel's torture and escape. The very shapelessness of his power pressed acidly upon him. The blacks whom he had made free men in the afternoon by early evening were bathing in heat and the juices of butchered animal flesh, guns abandoned. Saul Keller with the buttermilk webbing over his chin. Philip Sullivan, decently married man, entering that cabin with the light the color of yellow flesh itself.

Her small waist flared out beneath the skirt: did the flesh? His own flesh pounded. Deall put his feet back down on the floor and got up nervously and swept his hair back off his forehead. Lips open, he moved from window to window. The glass was shattered, the wood dangling and splintered. He could see himself in broken panes: fragmented, all forehead in one, all jaw then in another, framed by the last pale light from the guttering candles upon the mantel. On the lawn in front of him, he saw the yellow light from her room, strained by jalousies.

He went to the next window. Tension rested like sweat upon Deall's forearms. He looked out of the window until his vision could distinguish the edge of the fields. No one was about.

I go up one time, and slip up, and see what she does. I go up, and see if she needs anything, but just one time. After all, it is only fair. I have sent her servant away. Her servantless upstairs. Perhaps she needs something. He raised a cheerful sneer: are we such parlor soldiers that decorum keeps us from the simplest acts of humanity? But he was wondering if he might not catch her in her chemise. I will walk loudly—no, that would frighten her the more. All the while, his legs were carving wide arcs through the rooms of the house, he was peering through the windows, standing behind curtains to see if anyone was about. The lanterns and candles seemed dying throughout the house, ruddy warm light decaying into olive and debased gold.

Where the dining room door entered the front room, he paused, and leaned against one wall. Thank all of the gods of consistency and decency, thank my Inspiration itself, that I have done nothing yet. There is time yet to do nothing. But that time before him was squeezed dry, was dusty.

The pattern of the scars in the dining room tabletop reminded him of the skeletons of prehistoric creatures, trilobites preserved in whorled stone, in delicate networks of bone and shell. In which—his mind moving into habits of speculation, away from the images of her curved cunning flesh—in which the naturalist philosophers had detected certain symbols of coming human perfections. The upraising of all forms through guided purposeful chains, finally yielding man. Deall had believed that science was on the immediate verge of discovering the final full secrets of creation: and that these final secrets would reveal a cosmic Order and Intention. Leaving—after man had seen how the molecules and atoms and husks and failures had fallen away over the centuries—leaving man to make the final step for himself, that final intuitive, inspired stride from his bestially human to his spiritual nature. (Man is a king in chains: his liberation will come when he recognizes his royalty and discovers his ancient anointing.) With Lucy's death, he had lost that optimism: had tried to reconstruct it during the War. But now . . .

All of his conscious actions during the day had been mockingly debased, into the torturing of an unarmed man and the butchering of chickens. On this evening, washed by the southern winter winds through the shattered windows of the house, Deall once more glimpsed other things. That man's bestial nature was eternal. He brooded against a doorframe, head down. Despair rose in him, hysterically, obscenely.

Is it so monstrous, to see if she needs anything? Why she will hardly be in her bed yet. And if she is: the memory of her surprise, her inability to clothe herself in poses, came back. A good lesson. He was at the foot of the stairs now, looking upward. He put his hand on the newel post and shifted his weight, the slight movement of his right foot easing the peaked rubbing exacerbation of his flesh within the coarseness of his trouser fly. The right foot was spongy with weightlessness, poised above the first step.

When he realized there was someone in the hall by the cellar door, he was at first relieved. Well of course. As he stood right before the steps, he glimpsed someone around in the hallway, bullet-headed and framed by the bright orange light from the Negroes' cooking fires. The light over his shoulder seemed to reveal an old fawn coat, with long skirts. The figure moved toward the staircase wall at an odd angle. Well of course.

Deall coolly busied himself with hefting and adjusting the lantern on the hall table—ample reason for hesitating in front of the stairs. Then he turned with elaborate preoccupation into the length of the hall, ready to feign comfortable surprise at seeing the black. The raised lantern in his hand spread hollow light upon the green wallpaper of the hall. The door to the cellar was open. There was no one, he realized, in the hall.

The papers from the desk, spilling over the chair and the bench in the office, made him think a man's body was sprawled out therein. But he waved the light into the room and it pitched the shadows back into the corners. There was only the smear of blood down the wall flowing as if from an oval tear in the wallpaper itself.

Well then.

Certainly, he kept thinking to himself, we are not such parlor soldiers that mere form, mere ceremony deters us from a humanitarian act. After all, I do bear the responsibility. Parlor soldiers. The jarring of his flesh-daring made his mind cling to words. Mere ceremony. His heart was part of the metallic surge, he could not feel his feet, his legs were paper-light with anxiety. He looked up the stairs from the rear, but could not see past the stiff angle of the upstairs hall.

Then Deall realized the man in the hall was watching him from the cellar door. Of course. He swung around, arranging his face in a careful, weary smile, mouth pursing to speak You gave me quite a start What is your name. But the doorway was empty in the light from the raised lantern.

Light fell partly into the cellar, and Deall walked, still with stiff-legged caution, to the top of the cellar stairs. The clay floor was as pale as flesh. Deall went down a few steps and peered. The sense of a presence was strongest here. But by this time, Deall could not pretend relief. He was furtive, quick, searching, and he could not focus quickly because of the blood-pound in his skull. When folded draperies were just that, and not a crouching man's shirt, he was taut-lipped in gratitude.

Deall left the cellar, putting the lamp down carefully at the head of the stairs.

Turning in the hall and moving for the bottom of the main staircase, his face was upraised to the dim, green gold gleam of light in the upstairs hall. His strong young jaw muscles worked beneath the heft of his face, swallowing secretively, mechanically, as the back edges of his mouth filled with watery saliva.

Parlor soldiers. Parlor soldiers. Mere ceremony. He imagined the amazed exposure of her breasts as the door opened. His legs, rubbery with frenzied stealth, slipped up each step. How is this different from what they all do? But of course not that. He squeezed a lime yellow pattern of thought above the raucous confusion of his blood. Perhaps this will shock her out of her complacency. If I just enter. Perhaps it will penetrate beneath that arrogance of demeanor. That blind pridefulness. It will help her to see herself as she truly is. But beneath this scurrying reflection, there were images of her white-dark body rising unshielded before him.

Deall ascended the stairs with prodigious, painful steps, hand over hand along the banister, head back, upward watching the acute bend in the upstairs hall. The weakly patterned thought subsided into weak jeering: she will be surprised she has never been so treated they do not treat them so. He wanted to giggle wetly at the image of her surprise. Shields dropped: why not? who will tell on us? To what teacher? He felt a giggle tickle his throat, he toyed with relaxing into it. Why not?

He climbed upward, avid as a saint, straining.

One of the old boards sank and creaked in a line of noise against the darkness. His throat clotted and a conscious act of his will quieted the hammering of the blood in his ears. Whispered long noises came to him: but nothing from above, or the hall beneath.

Ahh—well.

John Deall looked about himself.

He was poised midway up the stairs, amazed. Brown faint shadows of light ascended about him, and the air had a funereal stench of age and violated dust, green from the wallpaper, green and cold as stained brass. Rigidly immobile against the banister, foot held upright over the board, he thought What in the name of God am I doing here? What madness? Thank God I was not seen. Bright resolution filled him. But he did not turn.

Consciousness poured in upon his vision like quicksilver. As he organized and gathered his thoughts, breathing to discipline himself, he recognized how quick and acute they had become. Return now, before you are seen. Or formulate an excuse: I was on my way to seek bedding . . . *no!* I was on my way. . . . But then who *will* know? She will. Perhaps she does indeed need something. Perhaps she has heard and is waiting, paralyzed with fear. Perhaps I will call out. Miss! No. Madam! He knew he could not trust his voice. Decorum shut him off from calling out her name. Well then, return now.

But his vision was still locked, his face still yearning upward.

How timid! He was aware of the spectacle he would make, one leg poised stiffly above the board, hanging onto the banister. How apologetic! Is this the way for a man to behave? He scoffed at himself, filled with sudden growing insight into his own intuitive virtue. Impelled here by my higher self, by my Intuition, impelled to be of service, I thus cringe and hide! I reflect upon parlor decorums, upon conventions and consistencies.

Do you know yourself so little, Deall? Do you really believe that you cannot trust yourself to offer this woman help? Do you not know that you can never violate your own nature? (*Your own nature* he took familiarly for granted: rectangular honesty and trustworthiness aligned with his best perceptions of the world.) Brought here so spontaneously—indeed he saw himself as having been deposited on the steps as if by a golden wave—why do you try to interpose conventions, conformity, between yourself and your Inspiration?

Curiously, he could only dimly perceive the purposes of his ascent: to teach her humanity? to shock? to soothe? The vast, complex-seeming passion which had puppeted him through the house and deposited him here suggested Intuition, though—and, despite all of his introspection, true to his ancestry and the romantic age and the clinging optimisms of his faith, he had ever trusted Intuition beyond all mere reason.

Deall took the rest of the stairs with surging confidence, in two long reaches of his legs. His stride down the varnish-pale wood and green gold hall was elated. What he would do, he did not know, as he knocked at her door and then opened it, but he was in the grasp of his best nature, of bold, golden certainties.

Chapter 27

Deall had a quick glimpse of the bedroom: buff and pink wallpaper, heavy black furniture, warmth and camphor-rich closeness. The girl was still fully clothed, in the cumbersome white and brown hoopskirt with the Zouave's jacket.

Then his look was fastened by her own desperate intensity. She stood with her back to the wall, struggling to maintain a haughty, impenetrable poise. Her voice was whisper-hoarse: "Why, sir, how dare, how *dare*, as a man, not merely a gentleman but a *man* . . ."

Deall heard the words only as a tone. The hoarse indignation was masking quavering, helpless fear, as the feverish firing right before a line of battle breaks in panic. Her eyes were dilated into deep black, and they were moving helplessly over his face. Deall noted, distractedly, beneath the hoarse fluttering of her words, that the dress was stained about the forearms—from building her own fire, he assumed—but he knew she would not change from it into a looser nightdress the whole of the night. She had pulled an unwieldy old rocking chair in front of the fireplace and thrown a blue green afghan over it. It reminded of a child arranging her dolls for the night.

Beneath the febrile role, the outrage, the posture of lifted chin and arched back, the pale, charcoal-smudged fingers holding the sewing scissors defensively—beneath this Deall gazed at a single, small, terrified young girl. All that golden certainty which had risen about him vanished. He was embarrassed at his own power. He smiled easily, holding both hands open and out. "Now, now then."

". . . so we have no choice but accept your own *word* for it that you are a gentleman, yet you come here, you come here, sir. . . ." Her eyes searched walls and floor and his own uniform in a desperate sweep for words.

"I came to see if. . . ."

"Does your invasion not stop at our kitchens and our dining room and our pro-property? Does it also continue into a lady's boudoir. . . ."

"Why, I came to see if you were in need of anything."

". . . and . . . and n-not content with pillage and s-slaughter . . ." Her face burned.

Deall continued speaking steadily so that the girl would not have to finish the sentence. "To see if you need anything for the evening." He closed his eyes and swallowed lightly, as a sign of his own weariness. "Before I retire myself."

"All I need, sir, is for you and your men to leave this property as soon as possible. That is a-all any of us need, sir, let me assure you."

"But do you need anything for the evening? I came up to be of whatever small assistance—"

"Is that why . . ." Her voice fluttered with its dread. ". . . is that why you paused on the stairs? you crept about, sir? Is that why you sneak about . . ."

Deall was pleasantly surprised at the silver ease of his response. "Why, do you mean the reason I paused on the stairs . . . ? Why, I merely waited to see if you were asleep, madam. I did not wish to disturb your repose, in that instance. Had I known it would give you anxiety . . ." He spread his hands in sign of his apologetic regret.

"Did you *really* believe we could sleep, sir, with your men letting the people loose? With strange men all over the place?" Deall was happy to note that her shaking nervousness was stopping. "Well sir, let that pass."

"Yes, madam. Well, my apologies for giving you such unease. Now. Is there anything I can do for you?"

"Again, sir—" Her voice shivered, but now she looked at him directly, pausing for effect. "I see I must repeat myself." This was rife with implications of decorum. "Well. All we need, any of us, is for you and your men to leave this plantation as soon as possible."

"At your pleasure, madam." He gave an ironic short bow. "And, of course, as soon as my men are rested." Deall was instantly sorry for his sarcasm. "By first light, still. I promise you." And then he added, with a lightness that surprised him, with a small self-exposing gesture, a light smile, "I wish that all of my promises to ladies were so easy to keep."

Celia looked completely certain of herself, when he looked at her face after his short deferential bow at "ladies." He could see that she was trying to return the scissors to the table without his noticing. She brushed her smooth, silver-pale forehead with the back of her hand in a distracting gesture, and then the scissors were slipped onto the little table.

She looked at Deall more steadily, clasping her hands demurely in front. He was aware of the thin pungent odor of her perspiration and noticed the beads of sweat upon her upper lip. He was thoughtlessly smiling in easy condescension.

She noticed the smile: her eyes flared. "Gallantly spoken, sir. But tell me this: Are those ladies you speak of, those to whom you promise things, are they used to receiving you alone in their rooms, at this time of night?"

A menaced composite—dressed simply, slim, blondly pure and sincere—gathered before his vision. "I came up," he said stiffly, "to see if you needed anything. I realize that it was through my agency that you have no private servant for the evening. Not that I regret this, but I would not personally"—she attended this closely, almost smiling—"have you inconvenienced while it is yet within my power to aid you. Now, I see that you have built your own fire. Do you need water, or perhaps linen?"

"A gentleman would hardly use his own *barbaric* actions to justify finding his way to a lady's room at this time of night, Sergeant," she said, with a superior smile. "Now, would you please find your own way downstairs?"

But what she said was not in dismissal, Deall knew. *Barbaric* was to fix him there. Self-confidence returned, she inevitably assumed the pattern of feminine power familiar to her: an ironic coquetry. She turned away from Deall slightly, glancing at him with half-veiled superior coolness, but her eyes were sparkling and almost coy beneath the long lashes. He felt a stale, frustrated anger.

"Barbaric, madam? What action of *ours* has been barbaric?"

"Why depriving me of my personal servant for the evening! Leaving a lady unattended at such a time!"

His first thought was Why *you* call *that* barbaric? But, gazing at the girl, he did not say it. She equates decorum and this . . . this patter with moral superiority! His gaze began to crystallize her into a type.

"But I do not, as I said, regret that. I do not regret that, for surely nothing as little becomes a lady as the use of enforced personal servitude."

"Why, do not those *ladies* that you spoke of at the North have personal servants?"

"And pay them a fair wage, if they do."

"Is not their servitude enforced, then, by their poverty?"

"It is not the same thing, though . . ."

"Why, Sergeant, I should *say* it is not. Our servants are bound to us by deeper ties of loyalty than those purchased by money, I assure you." She smiled in inaccessible, deliberate charm.

"Worst sign of slavery of all," Deall said, no longer able to refrain from lashing out. He now no longer saw a lone woman, but a symbol of entrenched depraved human arrogance. His single desire was to shake her out of her demurely smiling superiority, as one chastens a child. "Worst sign of all, worse than working the fields, when you can force another woman to minister to your needs, to carry up your food, to button and unbutton your clothing, to carry out your chamberpot and your night water!"

"So you stand here, refusing to take your leave of my chambers, and offering these obscenities to a helpless woman? A gentleman at the North, indeed. Why, I can just *imagine* the quality of Northern womanhood, if this passes for polite intercourse."

He continued with his peroration, but oh! he preserved, savored this effort to defile blond Northern womanhood! "But worse even than that—than carrying out another's waste. Worse sign, madam, than that. Your slave girls serve more than the mistress of the house, do they not . . . ? The comely yellow girl, is *she* not your husband's servant, as well as yours?"

But this time Celia smiled with dimpling, calm self-control, cool above Deall's sudden awareness of his own uncontrolled invective.

"More insinuations, Sergeant?" she said with lilting light friendliness. Deall felt trapped in his own rage. He breathed slowly over his slightly opened teeth, his lips rigid.

She clasped her hands behind her back. "Why, I don't even have a husband here to protect me now, do I?"

He watched her with stiff silence.

She turned slightly from side to side as she spoke, all innocent decorum: feignedly ignorant of the import of what she was saying, innocent of the rich full-bosomed appeal of her stance—shoulders back, breasts risen above tiny waist—the inevitable effect of her very physical presence in a warm, perfume-enriched bedroom as she teasingly asked, "Well, Sergeant? Well? Well then may I ask *you* one question? What are your men doing right now to the nigra women?" Hands demurely behind her, eyes dropping sweetly from his face. "Is it because you are gallant protectors and benefactors of the niggers? But of course it is, Sergeant! You and your men only have their *best interest at heart,* I wager.

"And yourself, Sergeant? I dare say? Did you do your service to *black* womankind before you so generously came up here in the middle of the night, to offer them to white. . . ."

The question, still forthcoming from the girl, was as irrelevant as the just-missing cast of a spear. The defiance drew him striding across the room. Her eyes were downcast, pretending to search innocently for words, and she did not see him come.

In his outraged determination to *shake* the woman out of her arrogance, Deall caught her hands as they were still clasped behind her. And then even as the words formed whitely within his mind (*protectors and benefactors we are and will be, fleshly actions still leave sacrifice . . .*), he was violently aware of the flesh of the girl, firm cool hands, encased breasts softly resilient against his chest, the smell of her perfume-enwebbed hair.

She was whispering amazedly, "Sergeant! Sergeant!": it stirred the hair at the side of his neck.

Then she was starting to scream, and even while his mind fumbled at apologies (and still formed for his lips the words *benefactors, protectors*) his left hand gathered both her wrists, and his freed right hand rose mechanically, unwilled, to block her mouth.

And then the words dropped completely away. *Now, Now* hammered in the full presence of her flesh, his hands and forearms tingling in a consciousness as golden as his righteousness had been.

Then with her stiff jerking four of the gilt buttons pulled open down the jacket, and there before him was the dark light from her bosom, exposed pressed roundly against him. She, the *thing*, the symbol darkly frustrating for so long, but *now* accessible, *now there*, helplessly exposed! So dim shapes surged into their fulfillment across Deall's straining attention.

Her voice murmured like pressured water behind his palm. Deall was caught up in the practical difficulties, but step by step they resolved themselves, tumblers falling into place, as they did when they had taken the house in the morning.

He thrashed with her to the bed, her hoopskirt ballooning up about them. From the look in her eyes, he could tell she was inbreathing, an unheard scream completed. He drew his hand swiftly away from her mouth, and snapped the button at her throat, so that the false brown jacket fell away from her shoulders, exposing the breasts behind the old white of the chemise and corset. The martial little jacket, worn velvet and frogging and buttons, was tangled behind her.

His boot kicked over a table, and then he was kneeling on the bed with one thigh between her legs, feeling the snap and spring of the hoops. Pressing her back against the pillows by the hand against her mouth, he started to loosen his belt to bind her with it and then realized that her arms were trapped in the webbing and buttons of the brown jacket.

She plunged up at him behind his hand. His left hand tore at material, came away with semicircles of crinoline and cotton, and then he pulled free an adequate long rectangle, and with both hands looped it over her head and bound it across her mouth. Her thighs thrashed softly, entrapped in the steel and cloth of her hoopskirts. She was tangled in her own clothing.

He stepped back to one leg, keeping the other knee between her legs. He began unfastening the front of his pants with mechanical urgency: then he paused, both hands upon his trouser front, and looked about, breathing deeply.

Her eyes surged about the room desperately. They flew from his opening light like frightened quail. He intuited the dark deep wood of the massive furniture, the old armoire looming in the corner, the rich black wood of the bedstead, the chest of drawers with the old mirror. Before he thought clearly he had taken the pitcher from the stand beside her bed and thrown it against the mirror. Only a fragment of glass, reflecting the distant corner of the room, still hung in the mirror. The mirror else was eyeless deep lead. The only reflections were now those in the old furniture (pre-Revolution massive, with pegged joinings rising in minute rectangles beneath the liquid dark of the finish), focusings of warm colors dim as gold in the old polished dark wood, waxed and polished and rewaxed by generations of slaves.

Attention reassembled: Deall left his trousers half-unbuttoned so that he could strip off the thick woolen uniform blouse instead. Beneath it his shirt was brown and transparent with his sweat. He tossed the blouse across the old rocking chair. Its faded blue merged with the colors of the afghan, except for the wrinkled light blue stripes. His vision caught on the chevrons: then he looked at the headboard of the bed (pressing upon her more firmly when her one last effort surged against her own clothing) and he could see all his movements—his torso itself, chest and shoulders and long arms—as a golden dim mosaic in the old wood. Beneath him, the woman looked dark as ivory in the headboard.

He was quivering-stiff, and even the final dragging open of his pants wetted it. Sceptre-swollen, it stood away and clear into the room. He looked at the woman's face, but her eyes were squeezed from his light. The coolness upon his flesh was soothing, enrichening.

Deall bent over the woman. He was unified in shafthead completeness.

He reached beneath her to tug the sides of the corset open, and it came away like an opening shell. She screamed again behind the gag, and looked at him from eyes so dark the sockets were like enameled rectangles. Her bosom mounded softly before him under the chemise—white old cotton with a small olive ribbon inlooped upon it. The chemise had tiny buttons. His hands pulled it softly open, the buttons delaying then opening in smooth sequence.

Celia's freed, softly smooth breasts moved in light-rich mounds as her back twisted. Deall placed both palms upon their dark centers, buried his face between them in flesh that smelled of lilac and sweat, then knelt back upright again, looked down at her, and began to tear at the mesh of steel and cloth.

Petticoat and edged drawers came down silkily over her thighs and legs, Deall panting slightly, looking down at the three dark references of her body, mind awash with uncaring fullness. Her flesh was as pale as alabaster—protected from sun and wind, lotioned and rubbed. Images of opulent ease, exquisite perfumings and long stroking massages—cultivation as of a garden—inflamed his golden strength. Again, words formed tentatively, broke, re-formed in his mind: *protectors, benefactors,* opened for me, *protectors,* opened, garmented and anointed, anointed for other purposes than these. Other purposes, yes!

He forced her thighs apart (barely muscled beneath the olive-pale richness). Deall knelt carefully between her opened, soft-spasming legs. Guiding himself—*protectors, anointed*—he only half noticed and that through squeezing eyes that her eyes which had been thrashing from side to side for aid, looking with insane minuteness for coming protection, were now shutting too. Blood was upon one of her thighs like rich enamel upon marble.

Deall sighed as he rocked his hips forward, gently butting against furry irritation, then finding easeful close-fitting. Slipping sceptrelike, he was covered with perfect warm odor-rich tightness, liquescent promise dribbling like light.

He was dazzled by the surging thrill of pleasure. He held himself above her on straining forearms and his two eyes squeezed shut in imagining: he saw himself as in a race, slanting up into the golden light, one member touching the earth in rigid, shivering touch, integrated, isolated. Then one pumping and, feeling all light, all goldenness, all merging of himself and the overarching patterns of life and light, he burst within Celia Malory in three long, shuddering golden departing coils.

At that moment her eyes exploded open, sightlessly.

He raised himself back from her, wiped himself openly upon one of the torn pieces of her petticoat, and saw the pink stain of her blood upon his thigh. A brown pink watery stain, lost amid the hairs and shadows of his thigh.

He backed off from her, looking down.

He swayed, mechanically raising his trousers about his hips and beginning to button them, both hands moving in slow dull speculation. Then Deall stopped his hands.

He leaned over her, and looked at her open, visionless eyes. He started to put his hand upon her head as one does a sick child. He shook the hand back and wiped it upon his hip. He saw no more golden patterns. He looked over his shoulder nervously. Then he tugged her linen drawers back out of the tangled cloth and steel around her ankles. He buttoned the chemise again, fingers plucking the cloth away from her flesh to fasten it. He wadded and tossed the corset beneath the bed, and tugged at the steel hoops and the cloth, pulling the steel free at last as her body rocked with mild instinctive exertion to free one hip and then the leg. The steel was like a curious crushed gate, a wire-webbed pattern of wide rectangles. Deall looked at it with drunken, musing curiosity, and then turned his attention back to the woman. He arranged the skirt protectively, and struggled intently with the jacket—fingers thrusting through the tangles, jerking off the entrapping buttons—and freed it and tried to refasten it upon her chest, tentatively slipping the button-torn nubs through the braided holes.

He looked at her once again. She lay unhooped, unshielded upon the bed, eyes still wide open. He did not loosen the gag. Her hands were free. She might do that as she would.

He gathered his jacket from the afghan and looked once more, one last time, at the woman. He would not put on his jacket in front of her. His hands now finished buttoning his fly. Deall could think of nothing to say. He was drained, his mind a series of dry webs. He was vastly thirsty. He had a dim belief the woman was pretending insanity. The moment I am gone, she will rise up and scream.

In the upstairs hall, he was stunned at the dark cold the moment her door closed to his pull. Winter air came through the shattered windows of the house in liquid currents. Faint light gleamed along the green wallpaper of the hallway, shadowed by the banisters into long upreaching fingers. He walked through a cold dark cage, with the light visible through bars. The lamp he remembered leaving on the cellar stairs.

A yellow taste of triumph lay like spittle on his tongue. He smelled upon himself the acrid stink of her fear and the smell of her flesh—green-inlaid smell of flesh and hair. That will show her not to fuck with a soldier of the Union.

But Deall was instantly ashamed. He saw the girl's young face, beaded with the light moisture of fear when he had first entered the room. He thought of her drawing the chair up to the fireplace earlier in the evening, bending over it, tugging it across the floor in truculent semicircles. Shame made him wince. Descending the steps, he thought he saw a face in the hall, around the edge of the light, beyond the barlike shadows. Only the same genius, he thought, the same ghost that led me upward.

I gratified my lust like an animal.

But when he reached the bottom of the stairs, he paused, glancing back upward while he slipped into his uniform blouse, surprised by the cold feel of the old gathered sweat in his armpits. As he straightened and buttoned the blouse, his mind began to work in familiar, interpretive, transcending ways. What I did, he thought as he buttoned the last button at his throat, I was led to do by this place.

What he had done was a dark emblem of the evil which is in each man, which can be released by the influence of a fallen world. Proof, he thought, that nature is hard to overcome. I had forgotten that, and accused my men too hastily. I have been fairly chastened. He envisioned his own pale forehead and flesh struggling to rise above the spectral ribs and massive dark colors of the house, entangled by them, the house itself alive.

The appeal is always overwhelming, he thought, the walls themselves are instinct with the endemic old evil passions and lures. Pausing in the hallways at the foot of the stairs, he looked all over the fabric of the house as it met his vision: carved lintels and cornices, shattered fanlights, painted pillars, serpentine hatrack and dim-striped wallpaper. Purify: the word came quite inevitably to him. Nature is hard to overcome, but she must be overcome.

Admit your part in the human web of evil—and again he saw his pale clean flesh entangled by the ribs of the house—but be willing to purify always.

Thus resolved to burn the house, Deall swung around the end of the banister toward the cellar door, and saw the bullethead again in the light. His heart rose sharply within his chest, bursting into his rhythm of breathing, and even as he thought it is only another trick of the light, my evil genius, it was Tobe.

Deall paused, looking at the yellow eyes against the black flesh. He breathed deeply.

"Your mistress seems ill. We are going to have to burn the house." He struggled against a panting in his voice. "Of course, we shall have to burn it. So find one of the women and move her out."

Chapter 28

BUILDING THE FIRE WHERE IT WOULD DRAW THE BEST, AGAINST THE white wall and almost at the bottom of the cellar stairs, Deall could hear black voices falling in gentle, compassionate vowels down through the halls. Footsteps thumped and cocked through the old plantation house.

He would have taken off his jacket, but his back felt unprotected. Deall moved with exertion, plucking shards of old curtains and bolts of wallpaper from the barrels and adding them to his mound beside the wall. The buttons on his cuffs glittered in long arcs. His mind lapsed from its tenseness of speculation into easy physical promotion. When he ceased the accumulation of paper and cloth, he tugged some of the large barrels closer so that he could feed the fire from them.

Dimly, Deall felt the presence of a witness, a watcher in the shadows, a brief void in the inanimate surfaces of the lantern light. He turned, looking acutely into the corners. But his vision could not develop anything beyond the litter of plantation gentry: barrels of old clothing, truncated sections of furniture with exposed blond pegs, gilded frames, a barrel indomitable with dusty grey tile.

After three sudden pivotings, Deall knew the "witness" was merely a trick of his mind—childish nervousness awakened by the grey green light of the single lantern, and the gloomy ancientness of the cellar. He anticipated the next and dismissed it, not pausing this time from spreading a thickly woven curtain where it would catch most readily from the litter beneath.

The main stairway creaked with the careful weight of a cluster of people. Servants were removing their mistress. He was set to light the fire.

Deall took one last look around. The cellar was strangely innocent. There was no hint that this material accumulation reflected slaveholding, or especially concentrated human evil. Merely, he thought, cupping the lucifer in his hand like golden gleaming liquid, merely man's eternal zest for the gaining and keeping of things. He associated this with the dry rot, the flaking brown odor of old wood and dust-stiff cloth.

But as he stood holding the match, eyes transfixed by the flame in his hands, he felt the chill of a breathing *presence* upon the very back of his neck, not mere unease, but a click of motion, of passage, and the dry grey outflow of breath. Sense of his exposure exploded upward within: his flesh tingled and then grained in freezing stiffness. His hair rose.

Someone there!

He swung around. From the corner of his vision he saw the similitude of a man moving through the shadows, a black man in a light-colored coat, but without the symmetry of a man: with a mangled stump-shape where there should be an arm, with scars like silver in the flesh. His mind whistled in fulfilled horror. But when his full vision was upon the man, the wraith, the genius, he could see only a grey arabesque, shaped like the fire in his palms, which blotted out his vision; eyes squeezed shut and the shape went yellow; open, again his vision was blotted. He twisted his head from side to side.

Nothing came. In the final unfulfillment—the sense that space and darkness were doom-potent, but that now nothing was moving through them—his breath shuddered.

The match gnawed at his fingers. He looked at it dazedly, and then threw it onto the piled debris.

There was nothing there. Mere composite? of broken chair arm and spooled bedstead, old bed slats, old mattress ticking? The fire began to smolder behind him, while he still struggled to clear his vision of the flame's print. He could not make out the precise configurations in the shadows which had so shocked, and this was frustrating.

But there was no one there.

The curtain became beaded with orange and black dots, and acrid smoke rose from it. Deall added another match, this time to the edge of velvet and paper wallpaper scraps.

He was impatient in his ebbing fear, and he began looking for lighter material. Old clothing, women's clothing, would be ideal. Beneath the cellar steps he found two trunks with broad curving sides. Clearly, one had contained women's clothing—an old linen zone with whalebone ribs was in it which reminded him of depictions of the French Revolution, two high combs, and a bonnet beclouded with stiff black crepe. But there were no other things except scraps and fragments: part of an undersleeve, an old bandalette without the elastic, a chemise from which the decorated hem and top had been cut away. Where, he wondered, was the rest of it? Women never throw clothing away. Perhaps they gave it to the slaves? After cutting off the frills and embroidery and ribbons?

But when he thought of ribbons, he remembered the olive-green ribbon upon Celia's chemise, and he suddenly thought Ah they are blockaded. They must have been forced to use their old clothes as remnants. At first, realizing this, he held the cloth in wadded triumph. Symbol of the death of this rebellion. He recalled a cartoon —was it in *Harper's?* the *Herald?* well, no matter—depicting the blockade crushing the rebellion as an anaconda crushing a plaster-bearded Jeff Davis. His strong fist wadded the chemise into a knot. And thus the course of evil. Recall, they claimed cotton was king, yet here they cannibalize their own fabrics as their delusion bears its fruit.

"They" manifested the rebel and his wife. He remembered Celia's small hands holding the sewing scissors when he had first entered the room. In a pale ivory green image the girl was bending those hands over the old chemise she had been wearing this evening (the cotton had been yellowed), sewing the olive ribbon onto it.

Stung, Deall tossed the ball of cloth into the fire, where the flames immediately traced the minute network of the weaving.

The other trunk was packed with children's clothing, old-fashioned, but folded for saving: pantalettes and opera drawers and a muslin frock with undisturbed pink embroidery. Deall kept himself from collecting sentimental images and reproved himself for having done so over the scavenged women's clothing. Again, the clothes were better as symbol of the sterility of this rebellion.

He pitched the children's clothing onto the fire, the buttoned pantalettes, the draw-stringed sleeping gowns, the muslin dress whose ribbons burst in coils of smoke in the flames.

Then he stood back and gazed as the fire grew from bulldog's teeth to fluting joined columns, and then to a tuliping hot roar. Glowing flakes of it lurched upward upon the fire, his flesh bathed in the liquid rich heat.

And as he stood there, the accumulated exertions of the day came upon him with sudden, withering exhaustion. Weariness soaked his mind. From our predawn ride all of the way down to this—I *am* nearly spent, he thought, with self-satisfaction. Perhaps there were things he should contemplate: *protector, benefactor*. The rich suggestions of this root-blasting fire, which now began to bubble smokily against the wooden pillar.

But his exhausted eyesight was consumed by the fire. The muslin child's dress warped and curled like a leaf, then became a powdery dim skeleton, then melted into liquid invisibility between the columns of flame. Symbol or not, he thought with unaccustomed, weary jocularity, it all burns the same. I be damned if it don't.

Deall turned and began to pitch wood upon the fire. His mind descended again into physical actions, selecting and freeing the old chair limbs and table legs and tossing them into the flames, ripping the staves from the most blossomed of the old barrels and adding them judiciously. He lost his burdensome, omnipresent mental intensity. He sweated, measuring strength of muscular endurance against the needs of the fire and the adhesion of the wood. If it does not come free with one wrench, unh!, so forget it. Use this barrel lid instead. Arms and shoulders ached. He measured his energy in jiggers of remaining power, at the end of each swing and toss. He was free, at last, from measuring anything else.

Symbol or not, it all burns the same. I be damned if it don't.

His scalelike brass buttons glinted in the flames as he worked. He was enshrouded in the orange glow from the wall and the dusk-orange of the shadows. The ceiling over his head was like a barred sky, with the smoke.

Raised at last by his final exhaustion, Deall stared vacantly at the fire, panting in the smoke. His eyes rimmed with stinging tears. The column braced against the whitewashed wall was coiled with flame like a moorish pillar, and the beam above it poured steam across the ceiling toward the open cellar door.

The last thing he did was drag a burning barrel stave from the fire and toss it amid the old trunks and remaining barrels beneath the steps. When they were scummed with smoke, he moved wearily for the stairs.

Deall's knees were spongy. The bottom steps were already lost in steaming white. He stepped on the first, felt the heat through his boot soles, and jerked back. He had to brace himself against the banister and then stride over the bottom two stairs. His knees plunged unresponsively, and he fell stiffly across the fourth and fifth steps. He had to climb with his arms, floundering, vision blinded by the smoke and the hollow roar.

Deall hauled himself up the last steps by the banister and the doorframe, and then sprawled panting, head and shoulders in the hall, body still upon the landing. He rolled over and looked back down into the seething steam and smoke. The fire garishly illumined the old darknesses of the cellar, the floor and wall along the far side were lighted as a stage by gaslight, and stonework and knots in the wooden beams stood out minutely.

On all sides of him steam was rising through gaps between the boards of the landing. The smoke that came up through the cellar door was yellow with the age of the burning things, furniture and barrels and clothing. Entranced and exhausted, Deall was aware of people in the hall, people by the cellar door, but his vision hung in the smoke and rubbery light below him.

The pillar against which he had built the fire turned ashy white and black: it cracked a third of the way up in a vicious hornet's nest of splinters and burning dust, and swung spearing down. Crashing down above it came the weight of the smoke-infested beam, dropping in pure lines of mathematical sequence amid the clouds of dust and burning flakes.

The whole fabric of the stairs and house creaked and swayed in curves of sound above him.

But when the column and beam fell, the white wall cracked open, the old bricks spilling outward as the crack splintered the wall, their black sides toppling behind the thick facade of whitewash like fecal mud beneath snow.

The gap was yards wide. And through the aching hot smell of the fire Deall was stiffened by an ancient stench, a green black odor almost cool with the stink of decay.

And so through that flatulent outrush of decayed air, Deall saw the human skeletons. One sightless skull was looking at him from amid the bars of its own rib cage. The other faced away from him, against the back of the now-fallen white wall. Its own bones were still held together in parody of living sequence by a coat (now faded a pink green) once fawn colored: and in the waves of light the skulls and bones waved and moved, and the coat itself seemed as articulate as flesh.

From the opposing dark wall, a tube of the flesh-colored cloth dangled down from a manacle. Ripped off within it, downswung for this century, was a fawn-encased armbone. Fingers of bone splayed out above the manacle and sleeve like some preserved sea specimen, long lost beneath waving green depths.

The wall within was as rudely unfinished as the surrounding three cellar walls, but it was preserved in green antiquity. Within that chamber all was green rot and the single upraised warning white splay of the skeletal fingers, still maintained above the manacle and the leafily laced, pink-rotted sleeve, and on the floor the sightless skeletons. Above the violently warning hand—warning of what, to whom? in that lightless chamber?—the explanatory paper sucked flame upon itself: nailed to the wall and brownly stained, the paper striped and curled and upon it the words

Acteon Acteon's Arc—us
Trai— —

were lost even as he read them, beneath mottling, spreading slow discs of flame.

Deall's mind struggled to appraise but he could not—he was too weary, too stunned with the sum of the day and the night, too blind from the heat.

But he was aware that he was moaning at the sight. He was aware it would be gone in a moment, that the flames had fed for an instant brightly upon the rotten old air and now the rest of the whitewashed wall was collapsing inward upon the remnants, that the house itself was settling down upon it: dining room and chandelier, parlor and punctured chair and marble fireplace and copies of Byron and Dryden, office records and ancestral oils and daguerreotypes, the banistered stairs of the main hall, the pre-Revolution armoire and chest and broken mirror, the dark bedstead and rocking chair and afghan and bloodstained bedclothes, all sinking down upon this cellar and this hidden deep chamber. He moaned warningly as in a nightmare.

A man was behind him in the hall. Deall rolled his head back to see. In the light bouncing from the fire, the black man in the green coat was bending down to help him up. The moan ached in his throat, and his hand fumbled in a boneless gesture toward the sight behind the white wall. But even as he struggled, he saw the black's face: no toothy grin of assurance and aid, not even furrows of concern. No whispered Lemme he'p yeh, suh. Cold, distant contempt.

And the yellow eyes were narrow with knowledge of *what he had done*. Deall drew his hand back in quick spurting self-justification. Of course the black does not understand. How can you well expect them to?

He shrank from the flame-reflecting hands. He shook his head in pretended self-reliance and drew himself upward. The Negro straightened in front of him. Deall's watery knees made him lurch against the black man as he rose, and the man pressed him back off his chest with cool force. *He knows*. The hall about them swayed and creaked like a ship's passageway.

Deall smiled, his face as stiff as a crepe mask, and gestured courteously toward the rear door. He began smoothing his blouse beneath the Negro's gaze. His blue coat had been darkly stained by the smoke, and one cuff was burning in a thin weaving line of orange. His eyes were running in greasy, lugubrious clown-triangles. But he still tried to affect dignity. Then his wrist touched the burning cuff and he jumped, swearing sharply.

After Deall's gesture toward the door had emptied itself, Tobe turned and slipped out of the hall, which was moving like a box above the fire.

Deall came out deliberately. Thin smoke was licking along the wallpaper like decorative striping. Deall told himself not to hurry. Tell whom? Tell what? What does it matter? As his mind had relaxed from the stress of thought and moral appraisal, now it retreated from communication. His own men were as unmalleable as stone. Disclosure of the chamber would be received with shivers of delight and school yard speculations about the minutiae of the horror. He could not find the rebel to accuse him, he thought easily. Columns, swarming columns of soldiers and refugees and contraband slaves obscured his vision of the man. It would not be gallant to trouble the woman: he thought this quickly, repressing —skimming just above—sudden agonies of recollection. Those same agonies underlay the thought of telling the blacks. There is no reason to stir them up. (*They know.*)

Amid the circle of witnessing faces, the blacks of the plantation swaggering or silent, his own men whistling low in amazement at the technical progress of the fire, Deall avoided the faces of the Negroes.

Turning among his own men, he felt satisfaction at their appreciation of his fire. Soon he watched with a connoisseur's detachment himself. My actions have spoken enough. We know a man by his actions, surer than by his words or his reflections. Words are wind: spirit comes from the word for wind. But actions are testimonies.

He thought this pridefully, as the power of his fire now touched the corners of upstairs bedrooms, made their ceilings glow with light.

ACTEON
A Southern Biography

Born Arabella's Acteon, on Congaree plantations about 1740; sold to Charles Malory (172?–1769) in one of the first drafts of Negro slaves permitted into the Georgia Colony, 1752.

Referred to in records of the Malory plantation, St. Matthew Parish, as "sturdy promising Man," 1759; as "best of field Hands and blacks," 1760; and in several places as "my son's man, Act." Personal servant to second son Alexander Coffin Malory (1741–1803), and made over as his property, upon son's request on his twenty-first birthday, 1762; departs with master, as body servant and "leader of Slaves," for the newly purchased Malory lands in St. George Parish, 1763. Referred to often thereafter, in records of the St. George Parish plantation (called Sycamore after ca. 1815), and occasionally in private correspondence of Alexander Coffin Malory: once mentioned as "worth more than any other Servant of mine or slave & would Wagar in the Colony, more than a Slave to us a friend," 1765; given "slave woman Sally Ann" as his wife the same year, "with much Celebration & Merrymaking Christmas." Rewarded with master's cast-off frock coat "which he has ever Admired" 1768: was leading the crews digging the foundations for the manor house "with his usual Capacaty," 1775.

The last reference to Acteon in the Malory family records was in an entry for June 17, 1776: "Acteon has fled with wife three sons & John /,/ Quamino, Manuel & Duncan. Reported to Patrol & Council on Safety, & am sorely Aggreaved at this unsuspected Treachery. All were stirred up by Ld. Dunmore & Rumored Ministerial fleet off Charleston we must suppose. It is a Miracle we were not all slain in our sleep, they took my Guns & Musket, most of my Ammunition furniture & all Powder and ball. After Dunmore & these Florida troubles, all the People have been restless, but I looked for Acteon to calm them, I must regard this Misplaced Trust in a Niggar as an *erratum* of my Life & its Sorest. Creeks and Tories upon our Borders, & these blacks & Traitors within."

There are no further references to Acteon in Malory plantation records, and none in personal correspondence. But the slave was captured and was returned to his owner for punishment. On July 2, Captain Peter Houston of the Savannah Militia reported to his Council of Safety that "Corporal William Wirt and seven Private men intercepted eight negro slaves & one slave woman stealing a Skow upon the Savannah & evidently intent upon reaching the English Vessles at Tybee Island. Wirt was slain by the slave Man in stolen Coat, called Axe: woman & four blacks killed, and our men hardly restrained from killing Axe cut him severly about face & Neck with Bayonets. Returned to owner all four men, since it is known Alexander Malory their owner is one of Staunchest Patriots, and had promised to make example of them."

These slaves were seeking the British lines and the freedom promised the Virginia slaves by Lord Dunmore, in that Colony.

Upon the return of these four men to the Malory plantation, the owner decided at first upon making of them all an example. But the peril of the times dissuaded him from public execution, which is why Quamino and Duncan were whipped severely and then sold off to Jamaican slave traders, but Acteon and his remaining son were secretly executed.

The two were stripped naked, except for the frock coat which Malory said was now only good enough for a nigger to die in, he reckoned. Then they were manacled side by side against the north wall, in the cellar of the yet unfinished plantation house. About nine o'clock in the evening, the two white men who were overseeing the construction began completing the wall of the chamber therein, once intended to serve as a shelter against the raids of the Creeks. Malory watched their work with patriotic dutifulness, and the ferocity of rage's gratification, rigid in the torchlight, making casual suggestions to the bricklayers in a cool voice beneath the screaming of the twelve-year-old boy, Arcturus. Acteon called Act had ceased at last his desperate pleas: that he had never harmed any of the Malory family despite occasion and that he had restrained the others (particularly Quamino) from doing so, that he had ever been loyal save when finally offered a chance to achieve freedom for his sons, and that at least the boy might be spared. They left no door or opening in the wall despite the original plans. As the boy's screams ascended into insanity, so horrible that it made the two bricklayers pause and fumble in their work, Acteon began a mindless wild heaving at the single manacle. Finally as but two layers of bricks remained to be placed, he had torn himself loose by tearing off the arm, and with blood spurting from the shoulder had lunged for the opening. The white men drew back in understandable terror, from the blood-sprayed black head and the face still tiger-streaked with the unhealed bayonet cuts: so that Malory himself stepped forward and fitted the last line of bricks, despite the slave's desperate fingers. Both of the slaves were howling as the last of the bricks were set into place. Of Acteon, his master's final comment was "just like any other niggar. Savages all."

It is possible the unusual severity of this punishment was occasioned by the times, with British and Loyalist armies upon the coasts, and Indians upon the frontier. And as well, perhaps, by Alexander Malory's abiding concern with the wild quality of the blacks he had had to purchase for the new estate, slaves less expensive because recently landed from Africa and so unconditioned by servitude in Virginia or the Carolinas.

And all of this happened in August of 1776. The fall of Savannah and Augusta subsequently forced Alexander Malory to withdraw his slaves into Carolina, and financial straits forced him to interrupt completion of the house until 1790. The house was thereafter twice remodeled, once after an upstairs fire and again when the columns and piazza were added, but the cellar remained untouched. Alexander Coffin Malory and then his son Charles Lyman Malory (who planted the sycamores) were influential in persuading the state of Georgia to establish its first capital nearby at Louisville, in 1795: father, son, and grandson (Thomas Jefferson Malory's own father) all served in the legislature of the state.

And it happened at that place chosen for the Malory plantation house and estate: chosen because of the salubrious clime and the promising soil and the fresh, clear, darkly pure water.

SUNDAY 4 DECEMBER 1864

Chapter 29

The Yankee soldiers moved among the horses, their jackets purple beneath the columns of watery blue dawn light. Beyond the lawns and fields the pine forests were black walls.

Jade sat upon the brick of the gallery, holding the carbine, studying the Yankees mutely. Their breath and the breath of their animals came in short frayed bursts upon the cold air.

The burned plantation house was a stinking fountain of carbon-grey odor against the high dim morning, cradled by the four gaunt chimneys. The kitchen had not burned, and in it Jade heard Phrony, whistling and moaning between butcher block and oven and fireplace. One last meal for the Yankee gentlemens.

The Yankees moved with short-tempered, despairing energy. Jade knew it was the white man's response to exhaustion. They were facing the dawn sleepless from the night before, and they worked jerkily among the horses, tying bundles over the saddles and swearing *shit!* when they had to bend for loose rope ends. Their sergeant squeezed his hand open and closed in impatience, waiting for one of the soldiers to hand him a knapsack.

Jade sat with jointless stupor-ease beneath his own weariness, only his eyes moving.

They were spotted and rimmed with blood from the night before. He had squatted on his hams, cat-quick to grin or to drawl earthy phrases that the white men chortled over and repeated. He had been both violently alert at their physical proximity and bewildered by the combination of their joviality and easy superiority. When they had all rushed out to see the big fire, Jade had had to stand up against the invisible patterns his limbs had settled into for the two hours.

Now, Jade watched coldly as they shuffled among the mounts, hung blood-soaked batches of chickens over the saddlebows, and blew steam from their cups of coffee and pursed their lips above the metal.

Come and gone. It has come and gone.

He mused easily.

He had seen the big Yankee with the beard come out into the yellow light and smell his two long fingers appreciatively, and say "Yes sir!"; he had seen the other slap each other on the back. "You say you don't b'lieve in turning your back on the Lord's gifts? Hey, Phil? That what you say, hunh?" Jade had seen the big man button his pants, his member flaccid and small, vanishing behind the flap. When they had risen to the yells about the fire, he had seen the one in the beaver hat slip June's biscuit box into his trouser pocket, the biscuit box filled with a mosaic of handed-down jewelry and polished stones and Liberty head coins, and Confederate script from Mistess for gathering a basketful of cones to decorate one Christmas. The Yankee had toyed with the box waiting a second "turn." Then when they rose for the fire, he had slipped it easily into his pocket.

It had left him with no sense of outrage. Serve her right. He knew he would have to beat some sense back into that woman's skull, time the Yankees were through with her.

Jade's mind moved easily over the discoveries he had made about the Yankees. He was used to occasional, disproportionate harvestings. The night before had been one of these. The Yankees had promised more, the way the whiskey at Christmas promised a sure plateau of future-reaching golden joys. But as deceptive, not more delusive.

They just white mens.

He looked upon them with vague envy for their ability to ride away from sure retribution. The way they's eating, they ain't studying staying past sunup.

And sunup was almost upon them, a pink ribbon of light all over the clear eastern horizon, settling the soldiers and horses into lighter air and more clarity as he watched. The soldiers chewed at ham and biscuits with their gloves on and with the reins of their mounts already looped over their fists. The little pink-headed boy burned his lip on his coffee cup and swore pipingly.

'Spect old buckra—composite of porcine-faced patrollers and the florid man who had first owned him and then that man's son, Marse Tom—'spect old buckra be coming back pretty soon.

Then Jade noticed Tobe, paused on the path from the quarters to the kitchen, studying the Yankees too. Tobe hesitated, then angled off the path toward the sergeant. The Yankee was bent over his horse, capless, adjusting a swollen bundle of rations to one flank. Tobe stopped behind him and spoke, and Jade could see the Yankee's head come up, stiffly, and then the man turn to reply.

Jade sat in his own cloak of exhaustion, motionless. He studied Tobe's quick gesticulation. He could hear the driver's voice. "And what then? You can spare us a hour, at the least, cain't you?"

Jade could not hear what the Yankee said, but he shook his head. Another Yankee, tossing a rope over the back of his mule to tighten a smoked ham, hit Tobe in the shoulder with the rope end. Tobe brushed at it with a distracted, mosquito motion.

"What is another *hour* gonna make? What difference?"

The Yankee sergeant reached down past Tobe's leg and caught his bridle, and put his boot in his stirrup. He rose, bareheaded, into scattered watery light. When he settled his seat, his horse made a lunging stride. It caught Tobe full in the chest as he reached forward toward the sergeant's leg. Tobe stumbled backward and sat down. Jade chuckled softly, chest rising beneath his slave's shirt. The Yankee patted his horse with calming soft strokes.

Tobe scrambled up. The man pivoted the horse away from him, its hoofs cutting semicircles out of the lawn.

Tobe came over and stood beside Jade, facing back toward the Yankees. The pistol was still thrust into his belt, seemingly forgotten. He was breathing deeply. Jade could smell a brass bitterness about him.

"They got to get off 'with the dawn.' That's what they say. What a hour difference gonna make, that's what I want to know."

"Is that right?" Jade asked with sarcastic lightness.

Tobe looked down at him. "You planning to follow 'em?"

"Maybe I is, maybe I ain't."

"Another hour," Tobe said, looking back at the Yankees, "I 'spect I could get us all outn here. Get the wagon and the stock . . ."

Jade chuckled again, with whistling little sounds from his nostrils. "And where we goin'?"

Tobe studied the Yankees. "We foller them," he said vaguely.

"Why we do that?"

Tobe said nothing, and Jade looked up at his face, hawk-sharp against the milky morning sky. "Answer me that. And ain't they all of 'em white folks too?"

Tobe continued looking at the Yankees.

"Ain't they all of 'em jest the same?"

Random words of the Yankee soldiers came to them harshly, like tin. Their own low voices were as fluid as the shadows above the winter dew.

"No," Tobe said at last. "I don't 'spect they is."

"You don't *'spect* they is? And why not? Which one of 'em ain't?"

Tobe looked at the white soldiers, mounting now with cautious heftings and muffled thuds of bundles and flesh. Their animals curvetted. Keller swore bluely at his mule as he leaned far over the animal's neck for balance. The boy soldier dropped his rifle.

With the dawn above and ahead of them, red like the blood of gods, the column trotted down the lane, Hun-burdened with loot and butchered meat. The boy toppled off in his eagerness, picked up the rifle, danced in blue and purple heavings around the horse, rose stiffly into the saddle, and pattered away over the water-rich winter grass. The hoofs of his horse made a scurf of dust when he crossed the road. Otherwise, the departing soldiers sank in shades of black and dark blue.

"Which one of 'em, nigger?" Jade asked for the third time.

"That ain't all the Yankees. Don't be a fool."

"Maybe that ain't all of em, but that's enough for this nigger."

"Don't be a fool."

Jade grinned widely. His flesh was all shades of black: chocolate, deep blue in the dawn. "That's white folks' talk," he said.

"You keep a eye out for Marse Tom. You hear me, man? You keep a eye out, you with the gun. That's all I wants from you."

Jade was laughing softly, in tiny siftings. Tobe laid his hands on Jade's shoulders and tugged him back and forth. "Hear me!"

"I hears you, nigger."

"Keep a eye out for Marse Tom, coming from the swamp."

"And what I do when I sees him?"

Tobe looked down darkly, hopelessly, at him, his palms still on the shoulders of Jade's slave shirt. Jade grinned, settled in his physical indomitability, watching Tobe struggling with his own confusion.

"Say: What I do when I sees him?"

"See you can keep him off, for a time."

"And what for I do that?"

Now Tobe straightened and looked back toward the quarters. Shorty and Crisp were talking together in the thin morning light. Phrony was coming back down the path from the kitchen, through the dim-painted grass. They were featurelessly black in the azure, loosening light.

"Gimme time."

"Time for what?"

"Gimme time to see can I set some of them free." Tobe said this in a soft whisper. The last word hung helplessly.

"And what does you mean by that?"

"I'm gonna see can I clear 'em off this place, 'fore it's too late."

"They don't need you for that. If they's gonna leave, they do that without you, I 'spect." And even as they watched, Shorty and Crisp were lifting bundles to their shoulders, Shorty with a rebel's gun over his chest.

"He ain't gone leave Juno, is he?"

"I 'spect he is."

Tobe looked quickly down at Jade. "Keep a eye out for Marse Tom. See can you keep him off."

"Why . . ."

"Do it, God damn it, man! He be coming from the swamp side."

And Tobe was then off across the yard toward the two Negroes, who paused watching him come.

Jade propped himself upon the barrel of the Sharps and stood up stiffly, unhurriedly, then wiped his hands. He watched Tobe. The sun was a disc above the horizon, laying long soft patterns of pink over the clay and the white sedge grass. The pine forests were dark, but the trunks of the trees were emerging duskily beneath the boughs.

Tobe was talking to Shorty and Crisp. He could see him shout toward Phrony, who paused heavily in the doorway of her hut, and then began to walk toward him. June came from the privy, paused, and then came toward Tobe. Unc Mitchell too. What he gone say? Jade thought.

The readiness with which they had come—June had broken off her lazy walk back to her bed—made Jade angry. He hefted the carbine and turned down the path through the old garden.

Keep a eye on the swamp. And then what I gonna do? He was aware the Sharps had a charge in it. He had not capped it yet. He settled the cartridge box and the cap box about his waist, walking slowly through pink and silver colors of the dawn. The leafless little redbuds were weak as ink against blue silver mist.

Hunh. He don't know *what* he wants. Do I come across Marse Tom *alone*, I 'spect I know how to keep him off, all right. With this here.

Irritation with Tobe's power shifted into vengeful pleasure at the heavy gun in his hands. He put his foot on the stile to lift himself over, and Marse Tom arose in front of him: red where the morning was pink, hard white where it was silver, plastered with blue grey mud. The blank red eye in a white circle of flesh bludgeoned Jade's breath back into his throat. He stumbled backward in the mist of the garden, colliding in minute scrapings against a boxwood, jaw fumbling toward speech.

Marse Tom rose and rose above the fence, the one red eye vicious. His hand was outstretched as he came above mist and slash pine and the high sedge.

Jade proffered the gun, half-pointed, hand fumbling for the trigger, sounds wailing in his ears from the silence. Marse Tom kept on coming over the stile, down but looming closer, head at the striking angle of a snake, reaching for the gun.

"Yo . . . Yo don't come . . ."

Marse Tom stopped, still holding out his hand. Jade was lost in the cold red eye.

"Give me the damn gun, Jade."

Weight of metal and wood was between Jade and the figure. His nerves squeezed against the wood. The barrel wove helpless gestures toward Marse Tom.

"Do you want to be the driver, Jade?" The hand still reached for him.

Jade rose out of the crouch. What Marse Tom said refocused Jade's blind terror, upon the familiar emotional objects of all his life: plantation power and prestige, to be the driver. Now his hands opened and closed upon the gun barrel.

"Soon as I tend to a little weedin' out, I expect I will need a new driver." The hand still reached for the gun.

Jade now slid his own hand off the trigger guard and onto the barrel.

"I don't have the whole day, God damn your hide! Give me the gun!"

Familiar promise, familiar threat: and still Jade's hands opened and closed on the rifle barrel. Tobe's power over him had hung like an iron box. Now he would be the driver.

He handed the carbine over to Marse Tom. Jade's landscape rearranged itself. Marse Tom turned away from him, checking the load in the chamber, his back and neck exposed to Jade. Jade wiped his hands on his trouser seat and peered with involvement as Marse Tom angled the gun to check its cap. He looked at Jade out of the red eye, it seemed, over which the lashes bristled with cold wetness.

"Caps." His hand flicked closed and open. Jade looked at it. "Give me the Goddamned cap box."

Jade jerked his head with comprehension, loosed the cap box from his waist, and handed the little leather pouch to Marse Tom.

Malory put the gun under his left armpit and started toward the burned plantation, striding evenly, coming into view of the assembled slaves even now as he emerged from the boxwood and miter-shaped cedars. He was not even looking at the slaves. He was plucking in the little cap box for a percussion cap, head cocked, black hair tormented into splayed sharp points, lips drawn back with intensity. One cap slipped out of the box and fell from his fingers and he did not pause, he felt for another, walking steadily toward the slaves.

Jade walked carefully and deferentially to his right rear, dull eyes studying the other blacks with assessments of new personal power.

In the middle of the other Negroes, Tobe was saying ". . . so if you wants to get free at all, you best leave this place this morning . . ." when June giggled, a drunken single hiccup. Tobe looked sharply at her, saying, "An' take what vittles you ca'culate you need 'tween here and Savannah . . ." and then from her face to what she was looking at, finishing his last sentence "and travel light, an' don't mess with no whites, and take care of the women, and I be along soon as. . . ." and then he saw Marse Tom, crossing the gallery beneath the charred shingleless network of the gallery roof.

Marse Tom came toward them steadily, walking with stiff jolting deliberate strides, eye piteously uncovered. Tobe frowned sorrowfully, involuntarily, at the vision of the exposed maimed eye, thinking And I 'spect his other eye patch be burnt up, too. Tobe forgot the gun at his waistband. He turned toward his master, noting with swift pity the hands fumbling at the hammer of the gun, dropping the flakelike percussion caps as he could not fit them over the nipple.

He knows it, Tobe thought.

He knows what they done to Miss Celia, *and* to his place.

Lord, Lord, he been a *good* master, and now look what they done to him, look at what he be. He knows about her, too. He even knows that.

Tobe left the group, shaking his head softly, walking toward his good white master. He completed thus the many ringed but steadily concentering path he had begun the night before: starting back to the black bonfires in his corduroy coat, then noticing the splattering of the lamplight in his Mistess' bedroom, and circling those fires to go into the house, just to check, just to see. (The arcs of his path were like the lateral threads of a spider web, slung between three radial lines: him as black man, him as driver and friend of a white master, and that central, ill-defined, suspended line between, of human compassion and accumulated, irredeemable human responsibility.)

Pausing the first time, when he had heard the thrashing from her room, muffled but familiar downthrashings of fabric and wood. Yellow eyes upraised, Tobe had stood trapped in the depth of the main hall, amid the dark, cream-shafted wallpaper and spindling shadows from the lamp, recollective of Marse Tom's shoulder in this very jacket comforting him while his own wife was laid out, and now unable even to conceive of looking into his white mistress' bedchamber. He had paused thus, trapped by his black identity from all aid, from all simple compassionate help, as time hummed, paused with his foot still half-raised for the next step. He had not moved: and at last he heard the man coming down the steps with spidery softness (glimpse of lamplight upon edge of his eye socket coming down) and even then he had had to wait, with deference ready to clothe his expression like a dark mask, as the Yankee turned the corner at the foot of the steps. From the unlaced look on the man's face, Tobe saw it had been rape. Then his foot had descended completely as rage flooded, while the Yankee brushed past with his white commands.

Then his path had continued in its arcs—a dozen—first shepherding the black women as they brought the dazed girl downstairs, then returning to upper and lower floors, bringing out her clothes (Marse Tom he don't care nothing for clothes, he can make do with mine—and so forgetting the eye patches), and an oil painting of the old Colonel Alexander Malory and modest remaining heirlooms like those turkey-feather fans, and necessities like a shaving kit, passing and repassing the cellar door, while inside it the Yankee in far shorter, spinning motions was tossing similar things into the fire.

The path then interrupted only the second and last time over the lank body of the Yankee, flecked by his own fire as he sprawled in the cellar door watching it. Then Tobe's hand had gone to the remembered pistol. He had thought not to shoot the man but to mash it down so hard that the bead at the barrel end would find his brain, to bring it down in one violently simple black reflex, his jaw muscles gathering as he yielded to the impulse. And then as the impulse hung in his brain, his mistress and Marse Tom were forgotten except as white integers in a completing pattern of hilarious revengeful destruction, penetration of her flesh like burning of the house like the barrel sunk into the Yankee's white head (I done killed one of 'em already today. What more they gonna do to me for another one?). He restrained himself by a conscious tightening of his limbs. Ain't no sense in that. Just cause he *white*. . . . It had been a blind, field-nigger reaction, of a piece with their gouge-and-homemade knife. Tobe's whole life, whole identity, had been to confirm something in himself superior to that animal-like blindness, that black slavehood of simpleminded racial gut-violence. No suh, it ain't no sense in that. Won't help no one that way, them or Miss Celia or me even.

Then the path had resumed, weaving its arcs this time out amid the black quarters: collecting food and provision, trying to jostle-persuade the blacks watching the house burn down, trying helplessly to force them away, into motion, action, preparation for the (doomed) flight. Until he had actually packed for most of them, in fact, had even selected by instinct and guess their most prized portable possessions—bright stones, a handful of polished flint arrowheads hidden by Covey, headrags with polka dots and chevrons, Unc Mitchell's daguerre picture given him by Mister Charles Lyman a long time past. Then he had spent the dawn moving between huts, trying to rouse them with impatient exertion, trying to stir them.

Now the path completed its doomed, concentering web shape, midway between the burned house and the slave quarters, as Tobe walked toward his master, forgotten pistol in his waistband beneath the green corduroy coat, his face loosened in commiseration at the sight of his exposed, spirit-maimed master dropping the percussion caps.

And he stopped immediately before the man, looking intently into his face, while Malory glanced at him, then back down at the Sharps, fumbling with the percussion caps.

"They's too many of 'em," he said softly. He moved his hands to press down the short barrel of the carbine, but Malory twisted his torso away so he could not reach it, and Tobe shook his head and wiped his hands against his sides. "They's too many of 'em, sah. Let 'em *go*."

Malory swore over the gun barrel, his mouth making a characteristic tightening of concentration, familiar to Tobe from quail-hunting days in the early fifties, from crossing fresh, bright winter mornings as this was turning out to be, looking for the quail to rise above the sedge and the pines.

"Marse Tom. Let 'em go. She's restin' easy now, Marse Tom."

At this, Malory glanced at Tobe again, lips clenched. Tobe could see the red, visionless eye flare upon him, then back down upon the gun. Tobe looked briefly to Jade, for help. Jade was bewildered, eyes clouded by doubt, vertical thick lines above the nose, lower lip pendulous.

"She couldn't help it, Marse Tom. I swears to it, she couldn't. And she resting easy, now. . . ." Tobe's eyes were trying to discern some flicker of hesitation or comprehension.

"I 'spect you ought to go to *her*, instead, Marse Tom. Maybe some cav'ry run 'em down. But she resting easy." He wheedled. Jade had never seen this. "She resting quiet."

Thomas Jefferson Malory got one of the caps fitted at last,

and said with a bronze dark flush, "There, by God. Now hold one time."

"Marse Tom?" Tobe was still looking into his face, his earnest yellow eyes softened, flesh of the cheeks drawn up minutely below the yellow. "Marse?" His vision was confused, because he kept looking back and forth between the eyes, from one eye to the other, as you would in questioning—with pity, with sorrow—a two-eyed man. So his vision stumbled, flicked, from the eyeball back to the clotted lash-spiked red. "Marse?"

Then in one long motion, butt of the carbine upon his hip, other hand sweeping its wide muzzle toward Tobe, Malory turned on him, his face still intense with that long familiar purse-lipped expression of concentration.

Tobe's hands came up, under and over the gun so Marse Tom would not accidentally hit him with the barrel, while his eyes still searched, placating.

And with gun aimed and cocked and capped, Marse Tom looked at last fully at Tobe, and the eye was liquidless, Tobe realized, cold as stone, and his vision once again went to the vacant red other eye, and *found* confirmation this time, mouth still forming "Marse?" but the flaying *wrong* of the thing pouring down upon his nerves and muscles. Then he saw the gun barrel upon his face: ring of steel scuff-sharpened.

"You worthless nigger."

Gun vision forehead exploded in a metal-bright blank, like the blank center of the web. So Tobe went down in the same long earth-ending, earth-cushioned dive that the four young rebel soldiers had taken the morning before (indeed his body was buried close to theirs: they lay near the family cemetery, and Tobe was buried quickly—his body from his jaw down—the rest of his flesh gathered by Lu-Belle in an old cigar box once filled with cigars that Marse Tom had given him in the Christmas of '58—in the woods nearby, beneath layers of sheltering pine needles, and beneath the soft soughing of the pine branches).

He lay in the rotting fabric of his corduroy coat for shroud, free at last, in the end: free as the four young rebels themselves, from the nets of memory and identity; freer, no brass buttons of national loyalty to spot his body, no family-tended pine headboards of belated appreciation for him, no Memorial Day flowers.

Chapter 30

THE SHOT BURST WITH AMAZING CONCUSSION AGAINST THE STILL morning. Three men in clear vision of the other blacks, then one man blast-erased from mouth upward so that pieces of his green jacket fluttered like falling ashes and the body was hook-jerked up and back and lay broken across the path. Clots and tendrils of blood seeped pinkishly amid the dew. Strips of blood by strange rebound crisscrossed Malory's thighs and waist. The blacks in the group scattered. Shorty and Crisp were floundering through dew-rich high grass to the west of the lane, making for the road, twisting from their hips to free themselves from the blue-shadowed long grass and leaving green wakes behind them. No one followed. Jade stood shivering, arms shaking from elbows, flesh of his lips pale.

"Now then," Malory said to him, "let us find Miz Malory."

The Yankees heard the shot. They were free of the lane and the netted shadows of sycamores, and had turned onto the road to the east. The sun was brilliant before them, red turned to purest orange and gold. The beams of light leafed fence rails in gold and absorbed the chill from the fallow fields on either side of the road. Thicketed young loblolly and laurel and the fringing cedars were minutely, beadedly clear in the morning light. A fresh wind came from the east, cold and golden with sunlight and morning.

The shot echoed and telescoped in flattening concentric waves.

"What was that?"

"Rebels, maybe?"

Keller shrugged out of his rifle belt and placed it across his thighs. Billy Gass had just been arranging Coiner's fish-faded cape across his shoulders. He began to tug it clear.

"What do you think it was, Johnny?" Sullivan asked, squinting because Deall was facing the full, golden light of the risen sun.

The men forced their mounts. Coiner's body bobbed within its blue government blanket. Hostetler had been taking up the scout; they could see him halted up ahead, and looking back.

"Did you hear that shot, Johnny? What do you reckon?"

Deall had buried his vision behind his eyelids. Black, then the grey milk of blindness, then full marbled red, the sun had worked upon his eyes until they were lost, warm, and comfortable in the deep red. He had heard the shot and had reduced it to a small flicker of emotional response. With reluctance, he turned and squinted.

The impress of the sun masked his vision with veils of light: through them he could make out only doubly focused pines and cedars and the high buff and yellow grass of the winter fields. Back toward the house, he could see the grey white tangle of sycamores, four blackened white-tipped chimneys, and thin columns of smoke rising from the ruins into grey films in the high air. No sign of immediate foes, no dim flickering movement of rebel cavalry. The chimneys pulsed in his blinking vision, and he could discern no human motion near them.

"One of the blacks letting off his piece, I expect."

He let his vision slip into the warm contentment of the blood once more. His consciousness slid, all aware, into the simple driftings of weary, physical contentment, wherein the insistent present—in the midst of enemy country—was blanketed by sunlight, warmth, and simple motion.

He fell into a real dream: he and blanketing warm thousands of soldiers about him were halted, while a long column of pontoons passed, snakelike, limber, tarred gleamingly. All was dictated by distant unerrored prevision, and finally transmitted to them by the slightest of commands, We wait here, from colonel to captain and then they all could just sit—just sit, at responsibility's end, at reflection's end. If he thought, he knew he could disentangle the reasons why that corps' pontoon trains were passing ahead, but there was no need to think. Bright warm spring sunlight bathed everything, sank all reflection into easy swaying motion, grass-chewing mindlessness, drowsiness. Into this recollection-dream Deall slipped fully; at first with conscious pleasant anticipation and then simple yellowish relaxation of mind, identity, and conscience.

"It is this kind of thing"—he awoke, eyelids gummed together from the sun's heat and his own exhausted drowse—"that is winning the war for us, you know." He recognized Sullivan's voice. He half knew that Sullivan was talking of their raid upon that plantation, but what he said sleeved his dreaming so smoothly.

He slipped back easily into those shapes of victory. A nation energized: by its organization down to the most minute making the Spirit's will its own, and men free. He sleepily anticipated the return to the regiment, and so to the lifting of woven, individual responsibility.

Thomas Jefferson Malory followed the path down toward the black quarters, searching for his wife. He walked with a consciously weighted authority, planting his feet squarely and solidly, twisting off the ball of his foot for the next step, negligently letting his boots stray into the grass on each side of the path.

Head canted, hair in mud-plastered spikes, he nonetheless bore himself with vivid arrogance. The flesh beneath his eyes was bronze and full, his neck was stiff, his mouth bitter tight. Jade heeled behind him in the path, bare feet skipping to close the distance when Malory's steady strides lengthened it.

It was day clear in the opening the plantation made in the pine forests. The sky was high and pure, stained by a thin dark scurf of smoke from the house, and above that the gauzy scarves of high white clouds.

As they turned the corner into the street, they passed June's cabin. She stood in the doorway, languorous, hip against frame. She smiled at Malory and licked her lips. She wore the chemise she had worn the night before, and her yellow bosom moved behind the bodice as she shifted to the other foot.

Her eyes were smokily dull from sleeplessness and casual, acquired arrogance: the smile was palpably intended for both Malory and Jade. There were faint purple blue bruises on her shoulders and neck, and blue shadows beneath her eyes.

Malory stopped. He put one booted foot onto the step into her cabin, and crossed his arms over the knee. He studied her. She shifted her stance again, her tongue pressed wetly against the front teeth. She was looking at Jade instead of Malory, moving her body for Malory, but her high humorous eyes were on Jade, splayfooted in the dust.

But when she looked at Malory, glancing demonstratively, humorously, her smile broke. She straightened in the doorway.

Malory was untouched by lust. He nodded to himself, a hard cold confirming smile.

He turned and looked at Jade, taking his boot from the step. "'Y God, she's like all nigger women. I expect she got laid by the Yankees. That right? Well then, there's only one cure for her." He was walking past the cabin as he said it. "Take her back and give her twenty lashes."

Turning the corner, Jade grinned back at the woman victoriously.

"Only one thing for 'em, when they get that look in their eyes. Ain't that right, Jade?"

"Yes suh, Marse Tom!"

"How about Lu-Belle, she behave herself?"

"Yes suh—I 'spect so, Marse Tom."

"Where is that worthless Shorty?"

"I don't know, Marse Tom. I 'spect he run off." Jade skipped again.

"He be back. Soon as he gets hungry enough, he be back. When he comes back, I want to know it, you hear?"

"Yes suh, Marse Tom."

He paused suddenly, close to the cabin Celia was in, and turned back to face Jade. The one eye was tight. Jade shifted beneath it, grinning loosely. "I want to *know it*. Now I expect I know you niggers, by this time." Jade kept smiling with mindless submission: Marse Tom had always been approachable, even by a bad nigger like him, a generous man moved by what he saw right before him. "You are giving me that Goddamned darky grin, but I expect I know you by this time, damn it all. Grin all you want, but I want to *hear it* when Shorty gets back."

Jade had begun the shuffling, beaming pose. He could not abandon it now. "Sho I knows what you wants, Marse Tom. Ain't I been on this place. . . ."

The flesh on Malory's face moved in normal patterns: grim

dubious smile, eye ranged back speculatively—but beneath the flesh itself, there was a permanent hard cylinder of preconception. He turned away abruptly from Jade's wheezing, rising catechism. "By damn, you niggers are all alike. But I know you and I won't put up with any of your tricks any longer, by God."

Even as he knocked on the door of the cabin, he was still saying in a hard tonal weave, "By God, they are all alike. But they better not cross me this time."

Zeenie opened the door. She had heard the shot but did not know Tobe had been killed. Her eyes were laced with sorrow: she was trying to warn Malory with her eyes and the slight indrawing of her lip.

Malory looked at her closely and Zeenie shook her head and nodded over her shoulder at the rear room of the cabin. But as she looked again at her master's face, she realized his eye was still coldly on her. The eye seemed to her like the eye of a doll: black centered, clear, glassily relentless.

"Well, woman. Is she here or not?"

Zeenie stepped aside, and Malory went in to his wife.

Celia met him at the door of the back room, in a white dress with blue vertical stripes which Tobe had rescued on a fourth trip back into the burning house.

"Oh, Mr. Malory. I was *so* worried, and then so *relieved* to hear of your escape!" She put her arms decorously under his, curling over his shoulders. She laid her head with soft precision against the front of his blouse.

"Well, Mrs. Malory. I am relieved to find you untouched." He reached to stroke her hair in formal reassurance, but she had jerked her cheek back from the front of his shirt, repelled by the dried mud.

"Ough!" She wrinkled her nose prettily. "Zeenie, quick now! Go and fetch Mr. Malory another one of his shirts. You may just put it on here, Mr. Malory," she beamed up at him, not mentioning, perhaps not noticing, the missing eye patch. "You may just slip on a fresh shirt right here!" By this she intimated a sweet relaxation of proprieties.

"It is a pity they have burned the house, my dear. But I expected it of those vandals. But you are unhurt, which was my chief concern." He patted the nape of her neck.

"Oh, there were some anxious moments, Mr. Malory. They behaved very badly with the nigra women."

"You are all right, my dear?" He held her at arm's length, studying her formally.

"Why of course, Mr. Malory. Now that you are back, and safe . . . ough! Where is Zeenie with that clean shirt?"

Celia's vivid brightness was characteristic, but with an edge of frenzy, a dandelion-bursting focuslessness.

"All morning the niggers have been mumbling and mouthing something at me. What it is all about, I cannot tell." His gaze came to rest upon the crown of her head, the pure white, freshly combed line between the dark masses of her hair. "A man cannot waste his time with niggers' hints. It don't mean a thing about you, I see that clearly." In his assessment he did not look at her eyes closely.

Zeenie came in with a slave's shirt. "This is the onliest one I could . . ."

Celia intercepted the ragged, clean shirt. "Why, Zeenie! What ever has come over you? You know there are *five* clean shirts in Mr. Malory's closet this very instant!"

Malory took the shirt from her, and laid it on the slave bed before stripping off his clotted one.

"But lost to us forever, my dear."

"Well, it is still such a shame that you must go about in rags."

"My main fear, Mrs. Malory, was that I might return too late. After the Yankees . . ." Here he had to pause while he tugged the entangled cloth over his head.

"Why, Mr. Malory, Zeenie and I would have been quite safe. Zeenie has stood by the whole evenin' haven't you?" She smiled in gratitude. Zeenie looked from Malory to his wife. "They did offer me some effrontery of language, Mr. Malory." As his head came free of the shirt, blinking, she shook her small fine head earnestly. "Brave indeed, to use vile language to a lone lady and her maid."

Malory was buttoning on the slave-issue shirt. "Well I was certain that a woman could hardly expect gentility from such gutter sweepings as those. The way a soldier bears himself will always tell. Those men were hardly under command at all, drafted men and bounty jumpers. You can always tell, from the way a soldier bears himself."

"Indeed so, Mr. Malory. Just as I told Zeenie—"

"But," and here he interrupted as he tucked in his shirttails, "my main fear was for what might happen *after* they had gone. These black bucks gave me cause for concern. So I slipped in as close after the Yankees had gone as I could risk."

"Why, Mr. Malory, I am sure none of our boys would have offered me any reason for alarm."

"Well, you do not know what I do, and I am relieved at your confidence. Best women should be untouched by the kind of knowledge men must have."

She nodded and lowered her eyes. Then she said brightly, "In any case, Zeenie has been *faithful* as a watchdog this whole night! Despite that s-sergeant, she insisted on staying with me."

Malory raised his forehead back to look assessingly at Zeenie again. "Of course. I know Zeenie, and that is what I would have expected. But I am quite gratified to hear it."

"I 'spect I better go and see about a eye patch," Zeenie said, confused, but accepting the praise with her usual mask of humble capability.

"You can always tell, my dear," Malory went on, turning back the cuffs of the shirt. "It is the white blood." And indeed Zeenie's flesh was light brown, and her bearing always poised, and the architecture of her flesh Scottish tight.

"Why, Mr. Malory, I am sure I wouldn't *know* . . ." She began smoothing the front of the shirt with her hands, running her hands down the length of his chest, collar to waist, smoothing at the cloth.

"I had to kill Tobe, though," Malory said. She felt the rise of his chest into a traditional, definitive judgment. "It is what they have always said. Give a nigger an inch and he will take an ell."

"You know, Mr. Malory, I never *did* see what you admired so in that nigra!" She looked up at his face. "Why, I remember clearly, one morning I asked him for a little help in my garden—just moving some rose bushes into the sun, just from one side to the other—and he said he had more important things to do! Why, you understand, Mr. Malory, he may *have* had. The little south garden is unimportant, I would be the first to acknowledge. But to put it in that tone of voice! . . . The other Sycamore darkies were always so helpful and devoted."

"Well. Fool that I was, I never believed it before. But it is true. Give a nigger an inch and he'll take an ell. Yes sir. But I have been chastised for my blindness, I expect. For believing otherwise about 'em."

Through the shutterless front window of the cabin, he could see the ruins of the plantation house. Celia was stroking his shirtfront with smoothing, ineffectual motions—the faceted wrinkles kept reappearing in white triangular motley.

"Chastised enough for my foolishness."

The four blackened chimneys with the white, untouched tops rose into cobalt day, and tendrils of smoke ascended about them.

"It is gone," Malory said, "ghosts and all. We will have to rebuild."

It was an impossible, distant statement—conflicting all probabilities of the hardening winter and the end of the War and the collapse of the nation. But the willfulness and endurance and manic attachment to place was promising of reestablishment in their very white, hard, pure blindness.

It was as if the indomitable, blind new certainty of his maimed sight made him stronger, less exposed. As if the hard white outlines of the house were embedded beneath his flesh, in the hard impenetrability of his will and vision. So that when the black laborers of five years hence returned to a land washed by terror and nighttime, insouciant, secret control, and they scavenged among the ruins for brick and foundation stone and found the tossed obscured fire-blackened skeletons from the old cellar (not far from the silver which they found too, those heavy goblets and spoons exposed by the wall's collapse and so blackened and baked too, but now heirloomed with scratches and scars from the time the Yankees burned the old house), when they found those bones, Malory would have the stiff recollection and precision to say Shorty and the other one, his son, I expect. Drunk, probably. Takes a nigger to get drunk in the cellar and have a house fall on him.

On this wartime winter morning, Celia nodded absently. She was already inhabiting a dream of the past which was as tangible as she had yesterday prophesied to herself that it would be. Therein she rearranged and remolded until the world was shaped with white smoothness to her touch and her enhancement. Sightlessly, her fingers continued smoothing the smoothless front of Malory's shirt.

Within that dream, she would be cheerfully untouchable. She would be sheltered, by curtain walls of lightly iconoclastic wit, and behind that by a formal moat of decorum, and behind that a citadel of familial arrogance founded upon all the lost glories, and within it all—unrecognized—a final keep of honest, protective, entrapping insanity.

So she need never again yield herself to the assaults of humanity, with its pitiable, shapeless, love-seeking, love-potent reality.

Never again would Celia lament the screams of a black human being, or smile genuinely as her husband gave the coin to a Negro woman (in the new Atlanta) for the lamed child, or feel, ever again, a spur of selfless affection. She was closed, as if within a white cell. Her hands smoothed at the shirt.

Malory formal with reserve, and with the assurance of a man whose world now always answers (no matter what his vision yields), in affirmation of his own will: Celia vivacious with ceramic-smooth references to a mythic past, and with the hollowness of cold insanity beneath her vision: these were the parents for the child with which Celia was now pregnant.